Sniper Shots

by

Kathy Lane

Sniper Shots

Cover Art by *Kim Mendoza*

The Wild Rose Press, Inc.
PO Box 708
Adams Basin, NY 14410-0708
Visit us at www.thewildrosepress.com

Publishing History
First Crimson Rose Edition, 2012
Print ISBN 978-1-61217-441-9
Digital ISBN 978-1-61217-442-6

Published in the United States of America

He stepped up onto the porch, using his size shamelessly to herd her back, right up against the wall beside the door. He leaned in close, watching her eyes, always watching her eyes. Not a trace of fear darkened the blue. No shadows at all except for the ones created by the chilly night surrounding them. If anything, she looked curious, expectant, with a little touch of amusement thrown in for good measure. A damn potent combination.

"I can't tell you how glad I am that you see the difference between me and Chet Wassile. Don't, however, make the mistake of believing just because I'm not a Neanderthal that you're safe."

Her eyes widened innocently. "Are you saying I can't trust you to be a gentleman, Uncle Josh?"

He chuckled and shook his head at her little girl impression. "Dirty pool, Ms. Sheridan."

"Of course. What else do you expect from a woman when you back her into a corner?"

"This." He took his time getting there, giving her a chance to say no. She didn't make a sound as he slowly settled his lips on hers. Somehow, even with the need to rush in and devour threatening to swamp him, he kept the kiss light, a meeting of lips only. Not until he felt her pouty lips quiver and part did he bring his tongue into play. Then he tasted her.

God love her, she tasted like a rushing mountain stream swollen with spring rain, pure, fresh, bubbling with life. He delved deeper, grinning inside and mentally licking his lips at the hint of hot chocolate teasing his taste buds. A small moan vibrated into his mouth, sending a fresh rush of blood to his groin, making his already hard shaft ache. Hell, he'd never been so ready to be inside a woman.

Praise for Author Kathy Lane

"*SNIPER SHOTS* is a "sit-on-the-edge-of-your-seat plot with unexpected twists and turns. There's enough action and sex to keep you turning the pages straight to the end."
~Lorelei Confer, Romantic Suspense Author
~*~

BLOODSWORN: BOUND BY MAGIC
Best Fantasy 2011 Prism ~ FF&P
Best First Book 2011 Prism ~ FF&P
"I like nothing better than to get my teeth into a nice juicy romance and this had all of my favorite elements, fantasy, adventure, action, and real depth to the plot. I was truly transported. I can't wait for my next chance to return to the planet Avalyr."
~Cyd, Night Owl Reviews (Top Pick)
"One book I wouldn't mind reading again. This is a great story about what happens when magic meets science...solid romance with a lot of action."
~Romfan Reviews (5 Stars)
"It had everything you want in a book—action, sexy men, romance, adventure to other worlds and also a great plot..."
~Rights of Romance Reviews (5 Stars)
~*~

BLOODSWORN 2: LINKED BY BLOOD
"This book has everything. I can't wait to read more from Kathy Lane. I'm definitely calling both Bloodsworn books the kind you keep and reread."
~Kathy F., The Romance Studio (5 Hearts)
"Ms. Lane's solidly brilliant storytelling skills had me captivated and entertained."
~Cyd, Night Owl Reviews (Top Pick)

Dedication

This book is dedicated to my daddy, Oscar Lee. No, he wasn't a sniper. As far as I know, he spent his military time as a sailor on board a ship. He was, however, a man who knew and loved the woods. He took great pleasure in the outdoors, making sure to teach his children the fine art of fishing along with the stealthy craft of hunting.

From the time I could hold a cane pole, I remember sitting with him on the bank of a good fishing hole, avidly watching our corks for the next nibble. Well, at least I was watching avidly. Dad always seemed to have patience to spare, spending the minutes between bites watching the clouds pass by while softly whistling "You Must Have Been a Beautiful Baby." As for hunting, I never went as often as my brothers, but I attribute my skill with a rifle to my dad's instruction—concentrate, breathe shallow, and don't jerk the trigger.

I lost my dad in 1979 to cancer. He knew from my high school days that I liked to write, but I doubt even he ever thought that I'd one day be a published author. He did, however, always encourage me to follow my dreams. So, in honor of his skill as an outdoorsman as well as a father, I dedicate this one to my dad, cross-hairs and all.

Chapter One

Some assholes never change. They just get more stupid with age.

Joshua Colby frowned at the assholes in question. The three Wassile brothers didn't even glance his way as he eased his Jeep onto the gravel parking area outside Fagan's Auto Shop. They were too busy harassing some teenage girl on the other side of the river running nearby.

A fast mover, the narrow river funneled water noisily down the mountain through a deep cut in the rocky terrain. Someone, probably the county, had installed a metal safety rail along the far bank since he'd been home last. There were signs of sawed-off limbs, stumps, and worn down grass where the thick forest used to meet the steep bank. Joshua tracked the shiny rail to the new pedestrian bridge suspended over the water about thirty yards down river. The brass plate of a trail marker winked in the late afternoon sun, pointing would-be hikers to the next leg of their journey.

Joshua snorted softly. Every time he came home, he found things changed. Not always for the better. People who needed trails and markers had no business in these woods. The North Carolina mountain forest around the little town of Clear Springs was still remote enough to be wild, untamed, and damned unforgiving when it came to fools.

Hooting laughter drew his gaze back to the drama unfolding across the rushing water. Too bad some things didn't change, he reflected, eyeing the three idiots who never seemed to grow up no matter how much time passed. They were still just as annoyingly obnoxious as they'd been in high school. He had to hand it to the girl, though, she had spunk. Didn't seem the least bit intimidated as she patiently tried to talk her way past them. Unfortunately, she wasn't having much luck.

Joshua heaved a sigh and shoved open his door. Schooling the Wassiles hadn't been on his agenda for the next couple of weeks, but no way would he stand by and let them get away with their bullying tactics. Since they weren't showing signs of leaving the girl alone, he'd have to step in.

"Back off, Chet!"

Then again, considering Kyle Fagan's opinion of bullies, maybe he wouldn't.

He leaned against the Jeep, thinking it was good to hear his best friend's voice, even if the absence of an expletive every other word still sounded a bit strange. A wife and kids had really done a number on Kyle's more colorful vocabulary.

The three Wassile brothers, the youngest of which was pushing thirty, looked toward the garage. One of them flipped Kyle off, all three laughed, and they quickly returned their attention to the girl without glancing once in Joshua's direction. Yeah, the assholes were definitely getting more stupid.

"Damn it, Chet, I'm not kidding, leave her the hell alone!"

Joshua grinned. Apparently, not all of Kyle's expletives had been deleted. He shook his head as another blue-tinged sentence followed. From the sound of things, Kyle just might need a little help after all.

Keeping one eye on the Wassiles, Joshua eased around to the back of the Jeep. He took out his compound bow and quiver of arrows just as Kyle appeared from around the side of the building. His back was to Joshua, his attention focused on the brothers and their prey.

Chet, the oldest, took another step closer to the girl and reached for her dark brown hair. She knocked his hand aside. Joshua thought he saw her roll her eyes and heave a sigh.

Kyle delved into his retired vocabulary again and started limping faster toward the pedestrian bridge. He'd almost reached the stone steps leading down from the garage to the worn path along the bank when Joshua spoke.

"Hold up," he said, stepping quietly into the shadows next to garage. "Let me get their attention for you."

Kyle spun around, catching himself against the rail. His surprised gaze bounced from Joshua to the Jeep and back again, a wide smile spreading across his face. "Damn, Joshua, I thought that was Carl Fells pulling in with his Cherokee. Hell, but it's damn good to see you."

"I'm telling Farrah you're cussing again."

Kyle's eyes brimmed with humor mixed with good, old-fashioned possessiveness. "Yeah, you do that. Make trouble between me and my wife and I'll bury your sorry ass under that ratty cabin of yours."

A round of rough, male laughter drifted from across the stream.

"Shit," Kyle muttered, the curve of his smile sinking into a dark frown. He glanced back at the three bullies and their victim. "Give me a minute, Josh. Chet and his brothers need a—"

He broke off as Joshua leaned the quiver of long, black arrows against the side of the garage and began checking the string on the matching black bow.

Kyle's frown slid into a nasty grin. "Oh, hell yeah."

Joshua smiled back, feeling the old camaraderie

between them snap into place. They'd spent so many years running around together they were more like brothers than friends.

He slipped an arrow out of the quiver and notched the shaft as he appraised the area on the other side of the river. Distance wouldn't be a problem. The wind might, considering the influence of the fast moving water. He gauged the swirls and eddies by the movement of leaves and grass, while part of him assessed his targets.

Arney and Franklin Wassile stood a bit behind their older brother, letting him take the lead as usual. Chet appeared to be trying to see just how close he could get to the girl without touching her. Seeing the bastard lean over her so aggressively kicked Joshua's irritation into anger. Time to put the idiot back in his place.

Sunlight winked wickedly off shiny dark wood as Joshua raised the compound bow and pulled back string and arrow. Maybe a foot of space separated the girl and Chet now, less between their faces. Not much room for error.

He sighted down the straight length of polished wood, past the razor sharp point, and selected his target. He took a shallow breath, held it, and then released his attention-getter. The arrow zinged straight across the water, slipped between the girl and Chet, and sank into a skinny tree. The feathered fletching quivered close enough to tickle Chet's nose.

Chet stumbled back, rubbing his face. "What the—"

Joshua aimed a second arrow at the tree next to the skinny sapling, noting the girl seemed frozen in place. Was she in shock? Damn, maybe he should have pinned Chet's boots to the ground instead. Too late now.

He set the second arrow free. All three brothers stumbled back into each other, arms flailing like a trio of drunks. By the time they untangled and turned to look across the river, Joshua had a third arrow *nocked* and aimed in their direction. Chet shoved away from his brothers and stomped to the rail. "Fagan! Are you crazy?"

Kyle leaned casually against a matching rail, ostensibly taking the weight off his leg, and crossed his arms. "You and your brothers leave Amy alone, Chet." He nodded in Joshua's direction. "Or Josh here is going to stop aiming at trees."

Chet squinted against the late afternoon sun. "Josh Colby, is that you? Damn it, man, this ain't right! We're just trying to be friendly here!"

"Go be friendly somewhere else," Joshua advised, raising his voice over the noisy flow of water.

Kyle yelled again when the brothers didn't show any immediate signs of backing off. "Look, Chet, you've been warned to stay away from Amy. Now back off or I'll call Penwell and have him arrest your asses for harassment."

Joshua stared at Chet over the point of the arrow. The younger man's face flushed so dark with anger he looked like he was going to explode. The possibility made Joshua curse silently. He didn't need this kind of shit. His orders were to lay low and keep his eyes and ears open, not get arrested his first day home for putting an arrow in the local bully.

Then Chet's expression changed, smoothing out into a smile. He held up both hands. "All right, all right, have it your way." He propped a booted foot against the guard rail and pointed a thumb in the girl's direction. "Though with this kind of temptation running through the woods, I don't see how you can blame me." He leaned over and brushed his hand against his leg as if dusting off his jeans. He was so damn easy to read it was pathetic.

Focused on his target, Joshua's peripheral vision still took in every movement the others made—Arney's hand rubbing against the bulge of a knife in his jeans pocket, Franklin restlessly shifting his weight from one foot to the other. Only the girl stayed still, for which Joshua was extremely grateful. She could cause problems if she took two steps in the wrong direction.

Then she moved.

Joshua tensed, his brain automatically registering the little twist of her hand and flick of her fingers. He was still telling himself the move was just a nervous gesture when Kyle murmured, "Watch it, Josh, fool's got a gun."

Chet's fingers slipped into the top of his boot, making the question of whether or not the girl had used the Special Ops sign for "concealed weapon" moot. Joshua turned the third arrow loose. The lethal shaft zoomed across the stream and nicked the baseball cap off Chet's head, pinning it to another tree. Chet yelped and ducked. Joshua had arrow number four in place and ready to go by the time Chet straightened.

The little bastard swung his hard, angry gaze back to Joshua. "Damn you, Colby. I'll get you for this."

"Maybe later, Chet. I don't have time for you today."

Chet's hands curled into fists. He shot a glance toward the foot bridge. Arney stepped close to his brother, talking fast and low.

"That's right," Kyle said under his breath. "Listen to your brother for once, you sorry sack of shit."

As if on cue, Chet nodded sharply. He met Joshua's gaze and spat on the ground before looking away. Then he backed toward the tree line, motioning his brothers to do likewise. Arney and

Franklin kept their nervous gazes on Joshua and his bow. Chet's eyes moved to the girl and stayed there. His lips moved as she walked past, and she gave a small start.

"Easy, Josh." Kyle said.

A hard smile tugged on Joshua's lips as his hand tightened on the bow, making the wood creak. Kyle knew him so well. He knew if Chet made a grab for the girl, Joshua wouldn't hesitate to put an arrow into the arrogant bastard. Three warnings were enough for anyone.

He kept the arrow pulled back until the little brunette was on the footbridge and the Wassiles had disappeared back into the trees. Their place was just a mile or so through the woods. Or at least, one of their places. Rumor was they had another cabin somewhere up the mountain.

Joshua waited while Kyle limped down the last steps to the road to meet the girl. He wanted to make sure the Wassiles didn't decide to be totally stupid and take pot shots at anyone. A few seconds later, he relaxed the bow, but kept the arrow nocked. Thankful they didn't appear to be quite *that* stupid today, he followed after Kyle.

"You okay?" Kyle asked, his hands going to the girl's shoulders.

She smiled, a brilliant flash of teeth that lit up her face. "Of course I am."

Joshua watched in surprise as she rose up on her toes and gave Kyle a quick kiss on the cheek. Just how well did Kyle know this girl?

Still smiling, her dark blue eyes slid to Joshua.

For about two seconds every instinct he had screamed danger. His heart rate jumped up, the hair on the back of his neck rose, and his internal alarms rang off the scales. Then she blinked, and the moment was gone, leaving behind only a faint sense of recognition and a faster than normal heart beat.

7

Joshua did a quick dredge through his memory, but came up empty. She wasn't someone he'd met before. He would definitely have remembered. Hell, he had a feeling he wouldn't be able to forget her even if he tried, and he didn't even know her full name yet.

Still, he'd swear something about her eyes seemed familiar.

He kept walking toward her and Kyle as if nothing had happened, meeting her politely interested gaze with one of his own. At the same time, he wondered what the hell had set off his internal alarms. She didn't look the least bit dangerous. Not physically, anyway. She appeared completely normal, a softly feminine figure in blue, cropped-off exercise pants and a white tank top. Standing next to Kyle's taller, wider frame, she appeared just a little slip of nothing.

A cute nothing, a part of him registered, making him blink in surprise. It wasn't like him to focus on whether a woman was attractive or not. He was more used to gauging a person by how much of a threat they were, be they male or female. Usually he was spot on, but this time, he wasn't sure what to think. Not even his first assessment of her age was correct. She wasn't a young teenager. Young, yes, but her short height and slight frame were misleading. Whoever this Amy was, she was definitely a woman.

He'd depended on his sixth sense for too long, however, to dismiss his first reaction, even if his neck hair had settled down. He'd definitely watch her, find out what Kyle knew about her, maybe do some digging on his own. Damn if she didn't put him on edge, and he didn't like it one bit.

Finally, after what seemed like forever, her blue eyes returned to Kyle. "You do realize that your friend here didn't need to do his Robin Hood impression. I was handling Chet."

Kyle shrugged and started to speak, but Joshua beat him to it. "The point being you shouldn't have to. Chet and his brothers are old enough to know better."

"See," Kyle said to Amy, "I'm not the only one who thinks those three need a permanent time out." He waved a hand in Joshua's direction. "Amy, this strict disciplinarian and expert bowman is my best friend, Joshua Colby. Josh, Amy Sheridan. Amy bought Sarah and Buck Weston's place about a year ago."

"Mr. Colby." She held out her hand.

"Miss Sheridan." He wrapped his fingers around hers, almost grinning at her firm, confidant grip. No wimpy, hesitant handshake for this little lady. "Sarah and Buck sold out?" he asked Kyle.

"Yeah. Buck said driving the mountain road was getting too nerve racking. They bought a place further down the valley. Somewhere close to where their kids built their places."

Joshua nodded, not taking his eyes off of Amy Sheridan. Shorter than him by a good foot, she had the toned body of a runner. Sleek muscles flexed beneath tanned skin when she moved to prop her foot on the handrail to re-tie her shoe lace. Even the skin he couldn't exactly see. Sweat had her white tank top clinging to her torso, showing off a wide array of interesting curves.

Curves that would take a long, leisurely night to explore.

He felt his body stir and gave himself a mental slap. *Down boy*. He knew absolutely nothing about this woman other than she and Kyle appeared to be friends. That didn't make her safe for him to get involved with. In fact, if she were friends with Farrah and Kyle that pretty much put her off limits as far as he was concerned. Getting involved in a quickie affair with one of Farrah's friends was only asking for trouble. And a quickie was all it would be. He'd learned his first year in the military that long-distance relationships lead to nothing but heartache.

Of course, there was no reason he couldn't enjoy the view he told himself. The blue material of her jogging pants stretched tight over her backside as she bent to give the lace a final tug was a sight well worth a second glance. Though even looking had its price.

Joshua shifted his stance a little, easing the sudden tightness of his jeans. He hadn't been this affected by a woman in, well, he couldn't remember when.

Maybe never.

And on that note, it was time to think of something else. "So, how do you like living here in Clear Springs?" he asked when she stood up.

"To tell you the truth, I wasn't sure I liked it to begin with."

"Don't tell me, you're a city girl."

She smiled. "Something like that. But I have to admit the place has grown on me. The mountains and woods are beautiful, and everyone's been very friendly."

"Some more friendly than others, I take it."

Her cute nose wrinkled a little and she waved a hand in dismissal. "The Wassiles are no more than a nuisance. Kyle knows I can handle them."

"Chet been bothering you long?"

"He started a couple months ago," Kyle supplied. "The bastard hasn't given her a moment's peace since. Penwell gave him a formal warning about ten days ago. Said he'd file a restraining order if Chet gave Amy any more trouble."

Joshua held back a derisive snort. Sheriff Dan Penwell was a law officer, not God. Nothing short of a heavenly commandment would keep the Wassiles in line. Maybe not even then. "Penwell might as well save his ink."

"That's what I told him," Amy said. "Something like that's only good if the police catch him at it. And except for today, Chet's been very good at not getting caught."

"Shit," muttered Kyle. He immediately ran a hand over his face, skin flushing, while his eyes slipped Joshua a "shut up" glare. "Excuse the cussing, Amy. But are you saying this isn't the first time Chet and his brothers have bothered you since Penwell warned them off? If so, you need to tell Pen. And you've got to stop running these trails by yourself. Where the heck is Bors, anyway?"

Who was Bors? Joshua wondered. Her sheepish answer didn't tell him much.

"Home. We were out running yesterday and he stepped on a big thorn. I pulled it out clean, but his foot's still sore. I figured it would heal faster if he's not putting stress on it running, so I snuck out while he was taking a nap."

Kyle snorted. "And you think he's just lying around taking it easy while you're gone? You know better. He's probably pacing back and forth in front of those big windows in your living room right now."

She winced guiltily. "Yeah, you're probably right."

"No probably about it. You need to stop jogging until he can join you again."

"I'll think about it."

Kyle huffed and ran a hand over his neck, amazing Joshua with his persistence. Just how serious was Chet's obsession with the little brunette?

"I'm telling you, Amy," Kyle said, "I've got a funny feeling Chet's up to something. I don't want to hear from Dan Penwell you've gone missing."

The last few words sent a shiver through

Joshua. He tried telling himself it was because he didn't like the idea of any woman being at Chet Wassile's mercy. The man had a nasty reputation for hurting women, having served more than one short jail stint after beating on old girlfriends. The thought of Amy on the receiving end of Chet's fist actually made Joshua's stomach churn.

Amy patted Kyle's arm and smiled. "All right. If it'll make you feel better, I'll stick close to home until my sweetie is well. We'll both just veg in front of the TV for a couple of days." She pulled Kyle into a quick hug, a completely innocent hug, nothing but a friendly embrace.

No reason at all for Joshua's blood to suddenly start pumping harder or for his breath to quicken. Kyle's fault, he reasoned. *The man is married. He shouldn't be hugging any woman but Farrah.*

A handy excuse. Much safer than the alternative. The flare of irritation igniting his temper couldn't possibly be because Kyle's hands, not his, were brushing Amy's bare shoulders and skimming down her arms.

The sudden urge to correct the situation made Joshua take a couple of steps back. The added distance didn't really help all that much. He still wanted to touch her.

"Thanks for humoring me, sweetheart," Kyle said. "You still coming to dinner?"

"Wouldn't miss it. You know how much I love seeing the kids." She turned to Joshua and held out her slim hand. "That's a really beautiful bow. Thanks for the help, Robin. Or should I call you William?" The teasing light in her eyes told him she hadn't really forgotten his name.

"William?" He reached out to take her hand, enjoying the feel of her soft, warm skin more than he should.

"William Tell. You know, the guy who shot the

apple off his son's head. Snatching Chet's cap was priceless. You have to be pretty good to take a shot like that."

Considering the number of men he'd killed with a bow and the difficulty of those shots, he was better than pretty good. Not that she needed to know that.

He returned her smile, shrugging and trying to look harmless. "What can I say? I like bows." He let her hand go, acutely aware of her fingers sliding along his palm. "Do you shoot?"

He didn't know why he even asked the question except he wasn't quite ready for her to leave. Unfortunately, he didn't get the response he was looking for. The teasing look in her eyes vanished, like sunlight behind a cloud, setting off more alarms in his already confused brain.

"Can't say I've ever shot a bow before." Her voice held a distance that hadn't been there a moment ago. She turned away from him, clearly in dismissal. "Tell Farrah I'll be there around five-thirty to help with the kids." Without looking at Joshua again she headed toward the trail leading off into the woods north of Kyle's garage.

Joshua found himself focusing on her tight backside again as she broke into a slow jog and disappeared behind the foliage.

"You and your natural charm, Josh."

He blinked and looked at Kyle in surprise. "What do you mean *my* charm? What the hell did I say that was un-charming?"

"Don't know," Kyle said, turning back to the garage. "But whatever it was, don't say it again."

"You're being awfully overprotective, aren't you, bro? Who appointed you her guardian anyway and does Farrah know you're hovering over another woman?"

"I'm not hovering, and if you hurt that woman Farrah will be the first person to kick your ass."

Kyle limped back up the stone steps. His lean body lacked the smooth, fluid movement that had once been his trademark. The man had been a hell of a hunter, stealthy, all but invisible to his prey. Now, he limped along in stiff, jerky movements, clearly favoring his right leg—the leg he'd come very close to losing along with his life.

The memory of Kyle on a makeshift stretcher soaked in blood flashed through Joshua's mind. Other images followed, flowing in reverse to the precise moment Joshua realized everything was going south and there wasn't a damn thing he could do about it.

Fresh guilt hit him hard, turning his stomach sour as he watched Kyle lean heavily on the railing. Joshua didn't offer to help him. If Kyle needed help, he'd ask for it.

"You didn't see Amy when she first came here," Kyle continued. "She looked about as whipped as we used to coming off a hard mission. Took Farrah and me a good two months to get her to smile and another month after that to get her to start coming over for supper."

Joshua frowned, not liking the implications. He didn't want to think of that dark look in Amy's eyes being there all the time. "She ever talk about whatever it was that happened to her?"

"Nope."

Joshua narrowed his eyes at the clipped tone, his sixth sense kicking up a fuss again. Kyle was hiding something. He followed his friend inside the garage to a pickup truck with its hood up. Most of the truck's engine was scattered in pieces across a heavy duty workbench. Kyle started putting away tools.

"So," Joshua said, careful to keep his voice even, "I take it you don't know very much about her."

Kyle shrugged without looking up. "Amy's the

quiet type. Likes her privacy. Farrah and I decided early on not to pester her with questions."

Which was a nice sidestep to Joshua's question. Kyle definitely knew more about Amy Sheridan. He just wasn't sharing.

His buddy slammed the truck's hood before meeting Joshua's gaze with a smile that looked forced. He'd always had a lousy poker face. "I advise you not to ask her anything either, bro. At least not where Farrah can hear you."

"Taken Amy under her wing, has she?" He'd let the subject drop for now, maybe do some digging on his own. Plenty of time to confront his stubborn friend later if necessary.

Kyle snorted. "Like a mother hen with only one chick. Which is pretty strange considering we already have three of our own."

"That's right. I heard Farrah blessed you with another bundle of trouble back in December. Congratulations."

A proud grin split Kyle's face from ear to ear as he limped to a desk in a corner of the garage. "Thanks. Another daughter this time. We named her Amber Lee, after Farrah's grandparents. You have to come see her, and you won't believe how much Katrina and Trevor have grown. Hey, you will have time to come over for dinner, right? I've got a new western on DVD I bet you haven't seen yet."

"Damn, Kyle, you'd think we were back in elementary school planning a sleep-over," he teased.

A greasy wipe rag came sailing through the air toward his face. He caught it and laughed. Kyle laughed with him.

"Screw you, Josh. I just don't want Farrah boxing my ears for not bringing you around before you leave again. She about barbecued my balls last time you slipped off without saying goodbye." His expression turned serious. "She misses you, bro.

15

Hell, we both do."

Joshua heard the touch of bitterness in Kyle's voice. Someone else might have interpreted it as jealousy. Someone who recalled that Joshua and Farrah had been an item for a time back in high school.

His gaze shifted to the picture sitting on Kyle's desk of a beautiful blonde woman. Sweet, sweet Farrah Hastings. Two years younger than he and Kyle and as innocent as a spotted fawn her first day at high school. Joshua had taken one look and tossed himself head first into adolescent love. She'd represented everything he'd craved—warmth, softness, family, a place to belong. He'd placed her on a bloody pedestal and tried to keep her there. Only Farrah had a mind of her own. She quickly recognized the impracticality of an eighteen-year-old marine-mad male staying true to a sixteen-year-old he wouldn't see for months at a time. Not to mention her dislike of the military in general.

Then Kyle had come back home six years ago with his busted leg. Funny how life had a way of working things out. Or maybe it was God. Whatever the case, Kyle and Farrah had bonded almost immediately and the rest, as they say, was history.

No, Kyle's bitterness had nothing to do with Farrah and everything to do with his injured leg. For the men Joshua worked with, forced retirement was a hated phrase that ran a close second to killed-in-action.

"Don't worry, I promise I won't put your ass in the fire this time," Joshua assured him. "I'll be around for two or three weeks at least. You two will probably be glad to have your privacy back by the time I'm gone."

Two or three weeks. A long time between missions if somebody wasn't half dead. Joshua could almost see the wheel of questions turning in Kyle's head. Instead of asking them, Kyle laughed and said, "What do you mean privacy? We got three kids."

"That's what I mean," Joshua said with a smirk. "You guys have to have some privacy tucked around your house somewhere, unless you expect me to believe those three rug rats are adopted."

"Yeah, well, just remember, you were at the hospital when Kat was born.

Joshua shuddered dramatically, not all of it feigned. "Don't remind me. I don't see how you and she got through two more."

"Epidurals," Kyle said, grinning.

"Whatever. Just let me know when number four is scheduled to arrive and I'll arrange to be out of town then, too."

"Deal. But only if you come to dinner tonight."

"I think I can manage that." The fact that Amy was going to be there made the decision easy. He wanted to see her again. "Just make sure you warn Farrah."

Kyle gave him a dirty look. "Do I look dumb to you?"

"Not lately. Though flirting with another woman when you've got Farrah at home is probably on the stupid side."

Kyle shoved a stack of papers into his desk drawer and locked it. "You're not fooling me, you know. I saw the way you looked at Amy."

"I don't know what you're talking about." Damn it. You'd think Kyle's attention to detail would have waned a bit in six years. "Besides, sounded like she's married."

"Not that I know of."

"So who's this Bors? Her boyfriend?"

Kyle let out a loud laugh. "Oh I'm sure he thinks he is. He hates letting her out of his sight and literally growls when any other male comes near her. That's why Chet stays away from her when Bors is around."

Despite what Kyle said about Chet staying away, Joshua couldn't keep from frowning as he left to retrieve his arrows while Kyle buttoned up the garage. He didn't like the sound of Amy's live-in boyfriend. He'd seen firsthand what too much possessiveness could do to a man. His father had almost smothered the life out of his mother with his obsessive jealousy before he died. Joshua swore long ago he'd never be like that and so far, he'd kept his vow. Of the few women in his life, none had ever stirred the least bit of possessiveness in him. Not even Farrah. He'd let her go, hadn't he?

Joshua returned to find Kyle leaning over the hood of his Jeep, waiting for him. He stowed the bow and arrows in the back before leaning on the other side of the hood across from his friend. "So, this Bors, he's in love with Amy?"

"Damn right he is. Wouldn't you be, if you were drowning in that blasted river and she pulled your butt out and nursed you back to health?"

"She saved his life?"

"Better believe it. Saw the little guy floundering in the water and jumped right in after him. 'Bout gave me a heart attack."

And while nursing him back to health, they'd fallen in love. He'd seen it happen before, the dedicated nurse, or in Farrah's case, doctor, falling for the wounded soldier.

Jealousy snaked its way though his gut. Not jealousy because Kyle had Farrah—he didn't begrudge their relationship for one second. But jealousy over what his two closest friends had together. Love, a family. Things that, considering his job, he couldn't afford to think about right now. Maybe not ever. She'd have to be pretty special to accept the danger involved with his choice of career.

A woman of strength and courage, loyalty and honor. A woman of heart.

Unexpectedly, the image of Amy standing up to Chet's bullying flashed into his head. He snorted the image away. He wasn't going to find what he was looking for in his own back yard. The women of Clear Springs had heart, but not the kind Joshua needed. He only had to think of Farrah to realize the truth of that.

Something Kyle said finally registered. "Wait a minute, just how little is this Bors?" He couldn't see Chet and his brothers backing off because of some runt.

"Oh, bigger than average, I'd say. We figured his age at about nine or ten when she fished him out, but Doc said he was closer to six."

Joshua straightened, incredulous. "He's a kid?"

"Nope." Kyle's grin spread from ear to ear and Joshua knew he'd been had before his friend even opened his mouth. "Not six *years*, you fool, six *months*. Bors is her dog."

Chapter Two

Amy ran along the familiar forest trail, part of her mind on her surroundings, the other on the man she'd just met.

Joshua Colby.

Something told her he wasn't just a man with a better than average aim with a bow. He was something else. Something dangerous.

Dangerous to her? Well, that was the question, wasn't it? It would be just her luck. She'd spent twelve months making a place for herself, was finally feeling safe enough to let her guard down, and along comes a man who pinged her radar like a live grenade. God, she hoped it was only a coincidence. It had to be.

She'd heard Kyle and Farrah mention the name Joshua Colby before. Not often, and not in detail, but passionately—though they probably hadn't realized it. The small town bad boy who'd put his woodsman skills to work for his country. The best friend. The former boyfriend. The current godfather and surrogate uncle. Joshua was part of the Fagan family in everything but name.

Stupid of her not to realize she'd have to meet the man at some point. Now she'd have to dig fast and deep to find out what she could about him. Find out if he was a threat to something more than just her peace of mind. Damn, the man was sexy as sin. Broad shoulders, muscular arms and chest, flat stomach, lean thighs. Oh, yeah, she'd noticed every detail about Joshua Colby. Right down to his attractive, dark brown eyes that didn't miss a detail, and his disarmingly pleasant smile that didn't do a thing to hide the fact he was a predator.

Lucky for her she'd sworn off predators a year ago.

A mile from home, Amy took to the trees. She forced her meeting with Joshua to the back of her mind as she climbed one of the more difficult trunks. She couldn't afford the added distraction. Lips pressed into a tight smile, she quick-stepped along one limb after another. Bors hated this part of her exercise regime. He usually ran beneath her, whining the whole time. Poor baby. Kyle was right. Her little black knight probably *was* pacing up a storm. Still, pacing on polished wood had to be better on his paw than running a rocky trail.

She swung up to a higher limb, balanced for an instant, then jumped to an overlapping limb of a different tree. Her right sneaker slipped on a patch of moss as she landed.

"Crap," she muttered, as her shin scraped against rough bark. Pain bloomed and quickly settled down to a burning sting. She didn't pause to examine the damage too closely. Time outs weren't allowed in the real world, and she didn't want to get into the habit. Her only concession was to snatch off the stretchy headband holding back her hair and tie it quickly around the abused skin. Blood trails weren't allowed in the real world either.

She slowed her pace as she neared her house, sticking to trees with thicker foliage, choosing positions giving her line-of-sight while keeping most of her body hidden. Some habits you just couldn't shake, even after a year. Besides, Bors would be watching for her. She wanted to see how close she could get before he spotted her.

The house, a two story split level cabin made of stone and logs, sat in a small clearing surrounded by thick woods. Too big for just one person really, but she'd fallen in love with the beautiful home the moment the realtor had shown it to her. That it was located near the river had made the property even more attractive. The faint sound of rushing water sometimes helped to put her to sleep at night. At least those nights the nightmares chose to stay away.

Innocent, terrified eyes, spattering blood. Would those images ever go away for good?

Amy circled round the small clearing until she reached a tree with a nice broad limb growing near the river. Stretching out on her stomach, she eased along until she found a spot where the leaves were thin enough to see through. The tiered garden of her back yard lay fifty feet ahead. Water gurgled, birds sang. A tiny chipmunk scampered in the dead leaves below her. Everything looked peaceful and quiet, the back windows empty. Bors was probably right where Kyle said he'd be, wearing a path the length of the front windows.

Amy rolled off the limb and dropped lightly to the ground. She grinned as the chipmunk dove for cover, scolding angrily. Ten seconds later she silently mounted the stone steps of her back porch. Almost there, she thought, reaching for the door knob.

"Woof!"

She started as a large canine head suddenly filled the back door's window.

Amy blew out a defeated breath. "It was the chipmunk, wasn't it?"

Another deep woof. Dark brown eyes gazed at her in adoration and, she imagined, admonition. Amy grinned back.

"All right, you win this one." She raised her hand and gestured. Obediently, Bors backed away from the door and sat. His head tipped to one side, keen eyes watching expectantly as Amy entered the kitchen. She shut the door and crossed to the sink without a word, filling a glass with water. She turned and leaned against the counter while she drank it down. Three feet away, the large dog waited, still sitting in the same position, his head turned ninety degrees to keep her in sight.

Amy finished drinking, rinsed the glass, and set it in the drainer. When her hand fell to her side she twisted her fingers together. A low whine, quickly cut off, answered her. Another practiced motion. The dog stood, whipping around to face her, but held his place on the kitchen floor. His whole body quivered, nose to tail, ears forward, eyes locked on her hand.

Amy gave the release sign and Bors bounded forward with a happy bark. She sank to her knees, laughing, and accepted his homecoming lick.

"Good boy, Bors, good boy. You are such a sweet, crazy mutt, you know that, right?" She dodged a lick to her mouth. "Yeah, yeah, I missed you, too, buddy. No more solo runs, I promise. Come on, I need to get cleaned up." She rose and headed for the master bedroom, Bors following her like a dark shadow while the shadow of a man with dark hair and darker eyes seemed to follow her thoughts in her mind. One way or another, Joshua Colby was going to be a problem. She needed to find out just how big a problem.

She dialed a number on her satellite phone while gathering up fresh clothes. A number she hadn't called in months.

"Amy, sweetness, it's been ages, girl! How you doin'?"

The deep Brooklyn accent drew a smile from Amy as she hesitated. She hadn't really expected to get Monty Cristofaro in person. The communications and information expert rarely answered his own phone. She'd intended to leave a message for him and wait for a call back. Now she had to scramble to get her thoughts in order while his voice brought back memories; good ones, bad ones, and, unfortunately, worse ones.

"I'm doing pretty good, Mont-man. How's everything over your way?" She winced as soon as the words were out of her mouth. Stupid question. He couldn't actually tell her anything.

"Oh, doing about as well as can be expected." His predictably vague answer held the slightest hesitation, the tiniest hint of suspicion. A surge of anger and regret welled up inside her. She hadn't expected being on the outside to hurt so much.

"Look, Monty, the reason I'm calling is because I need some information." If anyone could help her get info on Joshua in a hurry, it would be Monty. The question was, would he?

"Of course you do. You know everything and everyone eventually comes to the Mountain," he said, using the code name he'd claimed for himself. "Name your pain, sweetness." The sudden interest in Monty's voice was encouraging.

"I need whatever you can get me on a guy who's supposedly in the military."

"What branch?"

Good question. Even after a year she wasn't exactly sure what branch Kyle Fagan had served in. He and Farrah always seemed to side-step the question. She'd put it down to bad memories concerning his leg injury and left it alone. Upon reflection, she realized she should have dug into his background a lot sooner, too. "If I had to guess I'd say Marines or Special Forces. Or maybe Seals. I don't have a birth date or social, but place of birth is probably listed as Clear Springs or maybe Asheville. Check anywhere from twenty-five to thirty-five years ago." Holding the phone to her ear with her shoulder, she peeled down panties and pants together and kicked them toward the clothes hamper. "I'm not asking for a lot of details. If he is in something like Special Forces you won't find much anyway." Mainly, she just needed to know his security clearance. That would tell her how lightly she needed to tread.

"You got a spook haunting you, sweetness?"

"Not haunting. I think I just happened to land in his back yard. Think you can help me out? Make sure I'm not dealing with a psycho here?"

"You bet, love. Do you at least have a name for Mr. Psycho?"

"Oh, sorry. His name is Joshua Colby."

A long silence followed.

"Monty, you there?"

"Yeah. Uh, Amy?"

"Hold on a sec." She took the phone and switched it to speaker. Setting it down, she said, "Can you still hear me okay?"

"Yeah—"

"Good. How long do you think it'll take?" She whipped her shirt and sports bra off waiting for Monty's answer.

"Oh, not long at all." Despite his assurance, there was a lot of hesitation in his voice. Amy was about to ask if there was something wrong when he cleared his throat. "Is your Joshua Colby about six three, two hundred pounds, dark brown hair and eyes?"

Even knowing how good Monty was, she felt her eyes widen in surprise. "Yeah, that sounds like him. And he's not *my* Joshua Colby." Not now, not ever. Her lifestyle didn't allow for attachments. She'd learned that the hard way.

"Un-huh. Amy, honey, do I even want to know why you're asking about a Special Ops unit leader? And not just any old unit leader, but the Harrier himself?"

The name froze Amy in the act of reaching for a

clean towel. There weren't many people in the world of covert missions who didn't know that code name. The Harrier headed up the NightHawks, the elite Special Ops unit all the other units were patterned after.

The identities of the Hawks weren't common knowledge. Like everyone else in Special Ops, they went by their code names. That's why she hadn't known who Joshua was right away. It also explained why her senses had told her he was dangerous before they'd even shaken hands. Joshua wasn't just a nameless cog in some military machine. He was the whole damn engine.

The Harrier home on leave. Damn her bad luck!

Chapter Three

His cabin looked the same as always. Nice to know some things didn't change while he was away.

Joshua parked the Jeep under the pole barn and got out. Grabbing his bag, he made a circuit of the old cabin before mounting the steps to the porch. Even after over a year the key turned the lock without so much as a hint of hesitation, thanks to Kyle and Farrah. They took care of the place for him, cleaning, repairs, whatever was needed. Kyle even had a security hook-up that fed alerts to his satellite phone. One reason Joshua had stopped at the garage before coming home.

Home. Joshua smiled as he entered the small, one-room cabin. Done in dark, warm colors, the place was the epitome of a masculine rustic retreat with its heavy furniture and well worn rugs. Exactly what someone might expect the home of a bachelor with roaming tendencies to look like. Except he hadn't called the cabin home for a long time now.

Ignoring the inviting furniture, he crossed the room and used a hidden thumb pad to open a panel in the wall. A series of lights flashed on starting at knee level, revealing a staircase leading down and to the west, toward the cliff face and Joshua's real living space.

As soon as he stepped out of the stairwell, Joshua paused. The view through the tinted, two-story tall, bullet-proof glass wall hit him like it always did, taking his breath. Built into the side of the mountain, his hidden home had the best view in the world. The whole valley spread out below, a wild, untamed stretch of thick forest and rolling hills. When the sun was low, like it was now, the tops of the trees were lined in silver. Civilization in the form of the town of Clear Springs lay far in the distance, hidden by a thickly forested hill. If he wanted to, he could imagine himself the only person on the mountain. For this view alone, he'd fight hell and high water to get home.

He finally turned away, walking to the end of the third floor balcony where his bedroom was located. He used the brass palm pad to open the door and tossed his bag inside. Backtracking to the sweeping staircase, he made his way down to the second floor.

"Inside lights to twenty percent. Outside lights to twilight." The computer that guarded his place already knew he was there from his prints, and picked up on his voice pattern after a brief pause. Soft, recessed lighting awoke, illuminating the large open room from kitchen area to comfy, living room couches. Outside, more lights bloomed, warming the part of his home that was his pride and joy. Joshua opened one of the sliding glass doors and stepped out onto the exterior balcony overlooking the large patio and pool area one story below.

Taming the natural spring flowing out of the heart of the mountain hadn't been easy. The tear-drop shaped pool alone had taken over a year to construct. He'd finally come up with a gate system that allowed the water to fill the deep, man-made grotto that was the bulb of the tear-drop. The narrowing end lead away from the house, allowing the constantly flowing water to travel to the cliff's edge where it emptied in a six foot wide cascade into the main river some fifty feet below.

Joshua could feel the crisp, cool water calling him. With an effort, he turned away and went back inside. He had far more pressing things to do at the moment. He had questions, lots of questions, and way too few answers. Using another palm pad, he gained entry to his office—or his "nest" as the men in his unit had christened it.

"Lights at fifty percent. All computers active."

Along with the lights, monitors flashed on, blinking awake like a bunch of sleepy eyes. Lots of eyes. Adrian Bellinger, the NightHawks' communications expert, had gone into a fit of ecstasy when he'd first seen the bank of monitors and state-of-the-art computer system. Joshua grinned at the memory as he slid into the comfortable chair opposite the screens. Adrian's codename was Capella, after the star system with four suns. That was the minimum number of computers Adrian had running at any one time. Anything else was gravy, and being a good old southern boy, Joshua believed in lots of gravy. He pulled a wireless keyboard into his lap and started tapping keys. Three minutes later, his boss, Commander Caleb Aberashoff, appeared on the central monitor.

"Joshua. Good to see you. How are things at home?"

"Nice and quiet, same as usual."

"Really? I heard you'd already gotten in some target practice."

Joshua's senses sprang alert. Who did command have watching him? And more importantly, why? He took a stab in the dark. "I thought Kyle grew out of the tattle-tale stage years ago."

Abe, as the commander was often called, chuckled. "He said you'd say something like that. He said to tell you he's not regressing to his second childhood yet. He's just reporting in."

Joshua tensed. "What do you mean, reporting in?" Kyle had been out of the SO for six years now.

"I reactivated him last year."

That was news. And it really shouldn't have

29

been. Kyle was his best friend, for hell's sake. He'd been a member of Joshua's team. If he kept something as important as his reactivation from Joshua, did that mean Farrah didn't know either? The blasted idiot. If he wasn't careful he was going to lose her.

"Does his wife know about this?"

A smile flickered across Abe's lips. "Who do you think talked him into taking the assignment?"

Joshua fell back in his seat, feeling as if he'd just been sucker punched. Farrah's beloved oldest brother had died while in the Army, spawning her hatred for all things military. At least that's what he told himself when she'd "Dear John'd" him back in his boot camp days. Her love of life, her profession as a doctor, neither were compatible with someone who killed for a living. Whatever this assignment was, it had to be something cataclysmic for her to not only approve, but *urge* Kyle back to active duty.

"What's his assignment?"

"Nothing strenuous. He's just playing watchdog for me."

Watchdog—i.e. target surveillance. Who the hell could possibly be a target in Clear Springs?

"Who's he watching?" He had a right to know. This was his community. The only family he had lived here along with his friends and neighbors. Even bullies like the Wassiles were his mess to clean up, though the sheriff would probably disagree with him on that point.

"Kyle tells me you've already met her."

Ice water flooded his veins. Amy Sheridan. He'd known there was something different about the woman. But this? And Kyle had invited the woman to his house? Was he crazy? She'd be in striking distance of his family! He shoved the keyboard onto the desk and leaned toward the monitor. "What the hell is going on, Aberashoff?"

"Calm down, Joshua, it's not as bad as it sounds."

"Are you saying she's not a target?"

"No, she's a target all right. She's just not *our* target."

Oh, this kept getting better and better. "That's just as bad. Be a hell of a thing if whoever is after her takes out Farrah or one of the kids in the process. Kyle has lost his mind to agree to something like this."

Aberashoff's eyes hardened. "And if you think I'm cold-hearted enough to deliberately put innocents at risk, you don't know me half as well as you think. We know who's after Sheridan. That's why we put her in deep cover in Clear Springs, to hide her from him. That's also why I sent you home."

Joshua took a deep breath, trying to calm his racing heart. He wasn't in the habit of letting his emotions rule him. It was just that Kyle and Farrah were the only family he had. Of course, that didn't explain why his stomach twisted into a few extra knots as Abe's words sank in.

"She's been found."

"We think so."

He glared at his commander. "I think it's time you told me the whole story."

Abe's expression hardened. "I'll tell you what you need to know to do your job, same as always."

Anger made Joshua grind his teeth. He was well aware of the SO's stingy policy when it came to information. "And that job would be?"

"Number one, take over watchdog duty from Kyle. I've ordered him to step back from Sheridan. He isn't happy, but he understands the necessity. Number two, if the son-of-a-bitch traitor who's after her so much as shows his nose, you cut it off."

Joshua waited. Usually the words "catch" or "capture" came next, along with "bring him in." After several seconds of silence, he finally got the message. Whoever this traitor was, whatever he'd done, his life was forfeit.

"Understood," Joshua said.

"Good. I'm sending you a file now. Feel free to share anything in it with Kyle or the other Hawks as needed. And before you ask, yes, they've been put on alert. I don't want them flying in there all at once, but they're quietly relocating closer to Clear Springs as we speak. Their new locations are attached to the file. Whoever you need can be there within a few hours."

Joshua nodded. He'd go ahead and start calling the men in one at a time. "So why is Sheridan a target, and who wants her dead?"

"She's the woman who turned in the traitor responsible for the Brazil fiasco eighteen months ago."

A cold wave of anger battered at Joshua's calm. Fiasco was an understatement. No one knew for sure what had caused the Delta unit to take out the wrong target and touch off an international incident. The official report placed the blame on Delta's sniper, who'd assassinated not only the unit's leader, a man Joshua had known for years, but a Brazilian contractor whose death had cancelled a multi-million dollar defense deal. The repercussions had rippled up and down the chain of command, all the way to the White House.

And then nothing. Nada. No court marshal, no trial. The Predators, as Delta unit was known, were quickly and quietly disbanded. Even he had been unable to find out what had happened to them. And as for the sniper who supposedly had pulled the trigger in both cases? Well, no one had looked harder for that person than Joshua.

"I know Jonathan Tucker was a friend of yours. He did a damn fine job leading the Predators." Abe tapped a finger on the desk in front of him, the first sign of nervousness Joshua had ever seen him make.

"Do me a favor, Joshua, and set aside any personal feelings you might have for the next couple of weeks. I need you clear-headed."

"My head's always clear." No matter how difficult the assignment. He knew better than to let his emotions get in the way.

"Yes, well, just keep that in mind when dealing with Ms. Sheridan. She's more likely to hand you your balls on a platter than thank you if she finds out you're protecting her. Woman's too damn independent for her own good." Though his expression was stern, something twinkled in Abe's eyes.

Respect, Joshua decided, feeling the corners of his lips twitch into a tight smile. He'd assumed Amy had guts from the way she'd stood up to Chet. Finding out she'd placed her life on the line by turning in a traitor to her country only confirmed that assumption.

"Does Ms. Sheridan know she's being hunted?"

Abe rubbed a hand over his mouth a couple times—another nervous gesture. He was definitely hiding something. "She knows he'll come after her eventually, but she doesn't know how close he is. I want to keep it that way as long as possible."

"Why? Seems to me she has a right to that information since it's her life we're playing with." Joshua paused as another possibility came to him. "Unless you're afraid she'll bolt."

Abe snorted. "Sheridan? Not bloody likely. But you'll find that out yourself quick enough. Just stay close to her. Use any means necessary to keep her alive." A calloused finger jabbed in his direction. "If she dies, your ass is mine, Colby."

"Sounds like a personal problem."

"Let's just say that if anything happens to her

33

I'll take it very personally, and leave it at that."

Joshua cocked a brow, but said nothing. It was clear Aberashoff held Ms. Sheridan in high regard. The question was, why, and how much? It would be interesting to know. Maybe he'd dig into it later if he had the time. Find out why good ole Abe was keeping secrets.

One of his monitors beeped. Joshua opened the file and scanned the first page.

"I thought the Predators' sniper was code named the Raven. Says here the traitor is Adrik Velavich, aka, the Cobra."

"That's right. Velavich was their communications specialist. Put him in the perfect position to manipulate the information coming in and going out."

A ball of dread mixed with rage began forming in Joshua's chest as he read more. "He's been a member of Special Ops for ten years, Abe, and a com specialist for six." That put the Cobra in a very sensitive position. There was no telling what pies he'd had his fingers in.

Abe's lips thinned. "Believe me, we know, Joshua. We've already confirmed a dozen cases of tampering that can be tied back to his security codes. Most of them were very subtle. A word here, a phrase there. Nothing too elaborate. He knew exactly what he could do and still remain under the radar. We were lucky that half the time whatever he did had no impact on the assignment whatsoever."

"And the other half?" Like the job six years ago that almost cost Kyle his life?

"We haven't been able to tie him to the job in Cairo, if that's what you're getting at."

Maybe not yet, but something told Joshua they would. "How bad does Velavich want Amy?" It couldn't be any more than he wanted his hands on the stinking Cobra right now. He'd squeeze the truth out of him.

"Very bad. Not only did she pull the plug on his cushy cover, she gave us information on his personal accounts. Apparently, he was being well paid for some of his tampering. We froze assets in excess of four million dollars."

Joshua whistled. "Bet that hurt."

"Not enough. We hoped to cripple the bastard, but he evidently had an account Sheridan didn't know about. He dropped out of sight before we could run him down. That was fourteen months ago. Two weeks ago, he finally crawled out of his hole in London."

Things clicked inside Joshua's head. The NightHawks had been ordered to shadow a very low-level official on a visit to London two weeks ago. That boring, mundane job followed by the three week enforced leave order when they returned to Washington had his guys wondering what they'd done to earn such punishment. Joshua had asked, but hadn't gotten any answers. Now he knew it was just command's convoluted way of getting the Hawks where they were needed without anyone being the wiser—even the Hawks.

"What makes you think he has a line on Ms. Sheridan's whereabouts?"

"We're not sure he does. But he flew into the US using a fake identity six days ago. The HellHounds tracked him to New York and then to Atlanta. He booked a flight from there to Tampa, but never boarded the plane."

"They lost him?" That wasn't like the Hounds. Charlie Unit had some of the best trackers in the world on their team. His own tracker, Rashid, had spent a year training with them.

"Yes." A disgusted sigh. "Lost a Hound in the process. Bastard used cobra venom in a syringe."

Joshua cursed softly. He knew what the leader

of the HellHounds was going through. He'd lost three men of his own over the years. It always took something out of him.

"If Velavich shows up in your neck of the woods," Abe said pointedly, "do not, under any circumstances, communicate that information to anyone but me. The Hounds are understandably out for blood, and I don't want them complicating things by trying to take the Cobra out themselves. The NightHawks have sole responsibility for this assignment. Don't screw it up."

The screen went blank.

Joshua sat back, blowing out a breath. So, Amy had been involved with the Cobra. She'd discovered what he was doing, turned him in, and as a result put her own life in danger. Except for the bad judgment of getting involved with Velavich in the first place, he had nothing but admiration for her.

Staying close to her shouldn't be too difficult. She was already comfortable with Kyle and Farrah. Slipping his way into their circle of friendship should be no more difficult than nicking the cap off Chet's head—a little risky, but well worth the results.

Who are you kidding, Colby? Nothing is ever easy when a woman is involved. He knew that from experience.

He spent the next half hour reading the file thoroughly, paying close attention to the section on the Predators' individual team members. Here was the answer as to who they were and where they'd been stashed. Two were in the Atlanta area, and one lived near Tampa. He didn't for one minute believe that was coincidence. He started to red flag the information for further investigation until he saw the note indicating the three men were already being watch-dogged. If Velavich tried to contact, or worse, kill, any of his old team, he'd find himself in a sniper's crosshairs.

Speaking of snipers...

Joshua checked over the data again to be sure, but found nothing. Information on the Raven, the Predators' most excellent sniper-turned-murderer, was conspicuously absent. Not even a hint to identity or whereabouts. Maybe the rumors were true and the Raven had already been executed and buried. The commander hadn't said if he thought the Cobra and Raven were partners, but it would make more sense than assuming Velavich worked alone. Joshua made a note to ask Abe the next time they spoke.

If it was one thing he didn't like, it was loose ends.

In the meantime, protecting Amy had just become his first priority. After checking the attached file for the locations of his men, he started planning his strategy. It wouldn't be the first time he'd gotten close to a woman in the line of duty. But it would be the first time he really wanted to.

Chapter Four

The town of Clear Springs was like most other little North Carolina towns. Tucked into a valley fold, the quaint stone and wood buildings clung to the main street leaving most of the side roads to houses and yards. Only a quarter of the residents actually lived in town. The rest had homes scattered over the valley and up the various mountainsides.

The river bisecting the valley, called the Oscarlee by the natives, came from two sources, complete opposites in nature. One half, the Lee, meandered in from the north while the other, the Oscar, rushed down from the east. The two streams of water met south of the town, the calmer, northern branch passing just west of the main cluster of buildings before joining its more frenetic half.

Joshua lived on the eastern slope of the valley, almost to the ridge line. His home perched on the edge of a cliff overlooking the river rushing by below. Had there been a vehicle bridge at Kyle's garage he could have driven from his house to his friend's home in only a few minutes. As it was, it took him nearly twenty minutes to navigate the winding mountain road. Despite his intention to arrive early, he ended up being late.

The clock in his Jeep read six-forty-five when he finally took the last hair-pin turn up the mountain road and eased his Jeep onto Kyle's perfectly flat lawn. The level patch of thick green had been Farrah's only requirement for living on the mountain where her husband felt at home. She just had to have a flat yard, one you could turn around

38

on without falling off the mountain.

A dark blue mini-van sat in the yard a few feet from Kyle's custom built truck. Joshua didn't see any other vehicles, so he assumed the van was Farrah's. She'd had a small car last time he was home, but had mentioned she was looking into getting something bigger. With the arrival of a third child, it made sense to pick a van, he supposed, though it was hard to imagine Kyle driving one. The man had always been a maniac behind the wheel. He'd have to make sure to tease Kyle about it later.

He got out of his Jeep, wondering if Amy had decided not to come after all. Maybe she found out from Farrah that he was coming, too. They hadn't exactly parted on the friendliest of terms earlier, though he still didn't know what he'd said or done to cause her to shut down. The thought that she might want to avoid him bothered him more than he wanted to admit. And made him just curious enough to want to go looking for her to find out why.

A child's giggle made him pause on the wide front porch. Instead of knocking on the door, Joshua followed the infectious sound around the back to the little flower garden off the kitchen. He saw the children first, a little girl and boy, running in circles around a stone bench. A woman in a flowing, cream colored dress sat on the bench, her back to him. Without seeing her face Joshua knew it was Amy. He recognized the rich, dark brown hair tumbling in loose curls over her shoulders.

So, she had come, he thought, putting his pleasure at her presence down to the fact he could start his mission sooner rather than later. That didn't keep him from still wondering if she knew he'd also been invited.

He approached the garden stealthily, using his considerable skills to keep his presence hidden for the moment. He wanted to be in a position to see her face when she realized he was there. When he judged he was close enough, he leaned around a tree, intending to surprise both the children and Amy. It wasn't his fault he suddenly lost his breath as well as his reason.

Amy held a baby cradled in her arms, her head bent down toward the infant. The look of tenderness on her face hit Joshua with the weight of an Abrams tank. He'd never seen anything that shook him more—and he'd seen a lot in his thirty-five years. But nothing, absolutely nothing, had ever affected him like this.

His heart began to pound as she leaned over to nuzzle and kiss the baby's cheek. When she straightened, her lips spread into a soft, tender smile. She wasn't just cute anymore, he decided, she was beautiful. Heartbreakingly beautiful.

Her lips moved. Joshua wished he could hear what she said, but three-year-old Trevor and five-year-old Katrina were making too much noise. Just as well, he told himself. He didn't need to get tangled up emotionally with someone like Amy. Not when he was home only a couple weeks out of a year. She was the type of woman a man stayed home with.

Joshua shifted his attention to the kids. The baby must be Kyle and Farrah's newest addition, little Amber Lee. He was already familiar with the two hyper imps racing around, taking turns showing Amy leaves and bugs. The setting sun glinted off the hair of both children, bright blond with hints of red, just like their mother's. Seeing them brought a warmth to his heart. Farrah's children. Farrah's and Kyle's.

When he and Kyle left Clear Springs and entered the military, Farrah made her feelings on the matter quite clear. She'd broken things off with Joshua, graduated high school early, and promptly headed to college to become a doctor. A surgeon, of all things, with a little training in just about everything else. She'd moved back to Clear Springs the first chance she got, and had her practice pretty well established by the time Kyle was forced into early retirement after nearly getting his leg shot off.

The fact she and Kyle had fallen in love never ceased to amaze him.

Six years ago, if anyone had asked, Joshua would have told them Kyle Fagan would live and die a happy bachelor. The man loved women, and seemed too much of a rover to settle on just one. Now, here he was, not only married, but with a growing family.

Watching the little ones, Joshua completely forgot about hiding. He shifted his weight without looking—a stupid, wet-behind-the-ears mistake—and a twig snapped under his foot. Amy's head jerked in his direction. Her entire posture changed, going from relaxed to tensely guarded in an instant. Dark blue eyes pinned him with a look that again had Josh's sixth sense kicking into high gear. This time, he thought he understood why. Amy looked ready to flee...or fight.

He thought she would relax again when he saw recognition flash in her eyes. If she did, it wasn't by much. She still reminded him of a gun with a hair trigger, ready to go off at the slightest touch. He didn't know why, but that guarded look in her eyes bothered him. Just what was she so afraid of? Then Katrina and Trevor saw him. The two children froze, the echoing sound of their laughter fading quickly in the silence that followed. With uncertainty in their eyes they started edging closer to Amy.

Josh squatted immediately, his gaze settling on Katrina. "Hi, Kitty-Kat. Remember me?"

A few seconds passed before the child's face cleared. "Uncle Josh!" Kat squealed and ran over to throw herself at him. A sense of peace flooded him as

41

her small arms wrapped tight around his neck. He closed his eyes to savor the feeling. God, it was good to be home.

When he opened his eyes again he found Amy watching him, her head tilted slightly to one side. Curiosity had replaced the guarded look. Good. He'd take curious over scared any time.

Trevor watched him, too. The boy leaned against Amy's side, eyeing Joshua with suspicion. No surprise there. The kid hadn't quite been two the last time Joshua was home. How Kat had remembered him after over a year's absence was a mystery, one Joshua wasn't going to worry about. Just the fact she remembered him was enough.

"See, I told you he was okay."

Kyle's voice, filled with amusement, drew Joshua's gaze to the kitchen doorway. His friend stood behind a woman with a wealth of red-gold hair, both of his arms wrapped securely around her waist. He was smiling smugly while the woman's smile was simply...dazzling.

Joshua grinned back at the couple and stood, Kat still in his arms. "Of course I'm okay, why wouldn't I be?"

Farrah Fagan peeled herself out of her husband's arms. Shaking her head, she walked up to Joshua, put her hand against the side of his face, and stretched up to kiss him on the corner of his mouth. "Why not, indeed. It's good to have you home, Josh." She held out her arms toward her daughter. "Come on, pumpkin, time for supper."

The child dived for her mother. "Is Uncle Josh gonna eat with us?"

"Yes, he is."

The little girl glanced back at him. She put her face close to her mother's and whispered loudly. "Can I sit by him?"

Farrah glanced at Joshua, eyes twinkling with

laughter. "I think we can arrange that. Come on, Amy, let's get Amber in her crib and these two cleaned up. Josh, you and Kyle can finish setting the table."

"Yes, ma'am," Joshua said, giving her a little salute. He winked at Kat, causing the little girl to giggle.

Then Amy walked by. Floated, would be a better description. She moved smoothly, barely jostling the baby in her arms. She glanced at him once, her blue eyes vivid in the late afternoon sun, and he thought he saw confusion there. She paused next to Kyle long enough for the man to brush a kiss against his baby daughter's curls, then she was gone.

A tightness he was becoming all too familiar with returned to Joshua's chest. He took a deep breath, trying to breathe away the uncomfortable feeling. Jealousy, longing, hell, he wasn't sure what he was feeling, but he knew he didn't like it.

"Man, you got it bad," Kyle murmured, a definite smirk on his face.

Joshua started to frown, caught himself, and grinned instead. There were better ways to get back at his annoying best friend. "Of course I do," he said smoothly. "How can I resist that cute little smile and adorable giggle?"

His buddy frowned. "Amy doesn't giggle."

Joshua waited until he was standing right next to Kyle before he spoke. "No, but Kat does. I told you she and I had a thing going on." He waggled his brows and was rewarded by Kyle falling off the swearing wagon.

"Bastard." He punched Joshua none too gently in the arm. "Wait until you have a daughter of your own, then you'll know how it feels."

Joshua laughed. He started to say, "Not in a million years," but the memory of Amy sitting on that garden bench holding Kyle's second daughter in her arms had him backing up. The thought that he wouldn't mind one bit if Amy had been holding his baby daughter instead, wormed its way into his brain. The only problem with that scenario was that it was never going to happen. He lived and breathed Special Ops, a world of danger, intrigue, and sometimes, death. If Amy hadn't already gotten her fill of his world, she soon would. In fact, from everything he'd seen so far, she belonged in another world altogether. The same world Farrah lived in. A world he could only visit every so often.

Assuming he was that lucky.

Chapter Five

Inside the house, Amy breathed a sigh of relief. She'd known she was taking a chance coming to dinner with the Fagan's tonight. After finding out who Joshua Colby was, she should have stayed away. Far, far, away. But backing out without a good excuse would have been almost as bad. She didn't want to draw Joshua's attention any more than necessary. Unit leaders, the Harrier in particular, were good at putting two and two together without even knowing the full equation.

Helping Katrina and Trevor wash up gave her a few minutes to calm her nerves. Getting surprised by Joshua's sudden appearance had made her feel like she was deep inside enemy territory without a weapon to her name. Thank God for the baby in her arms. Little Amber had kept Amy from doing something stupid, something that could have given too much away. No one inside the SO was supposed to know where she was except for the commander.

Supper progressed with little fuss, considering the two excited children and the predator seated between them. Joshua divided his attention between Kat and Trev, but every once in a while his gaze would settle on Amy in a disconcerting manner. As if he knew who she was and what she'd done. God help her if he did.

No doubt he'd eventually get around to asking the usual questions. Where was she from? What had she done for a living before moving to *his* town and worming her way into *his* familial circle? He wouldn't be a unit leader otherwise. They tended to

45

be a bit paranoid to begin with and only got worse the longer they stayed on active duty. Simple survival instincts.

By the time the meal was over, Amy's nerves were wound tighter than Joshua's compound bow string. Her own survival instincts were telling her to get as far away from him as fast as possible. Unfortunately, running from trouble wasn't something she let herself do often. Once was enough, and look where that had landed her.

While Joshua helped Kyle and Farrah put the kids to bed, Amy strolled out onto the wide deck off the great room. The cool night was edging toward cold, the black spring sky clear of clouds and dotted with a multitude of stars like holes in a sieve. Somewhere out in the woods an owl hooted. The haunting call threatened to dredge up memories better left undisturbed.

Hurriedly she re-focused on the present, on trying to figure out exactly what game Joshua was playing. Watching him interact with the Fagans had been very educational, if a bit confusing. The only conclusion she was able to draw was that he was a consummate actor. The question was which role was the fake and which was the real deal—coldly efficient military leader or warmly affectionate uncle.

Could both be real? *Yes.* Just as easily as both could be fake. She didn't know him well enough to argue either side. That didn't keep her from wondering.

The owl hooted again. A hundred yards down the valley, a silent shadow skimmed the treetops; the night-time predator in search of prey.

"Happy hunting," Amy murmured.

Awareness skittered down her back. Even though she hadn't heard anything, she knew Joshua stood right behind her on the shadowed deck. She made sure to look surprised when she turned enough to see him, adding a little, "Oh!" With a touch of irony, she realized she was the one acting now.

"Sorry, I didn't mean to sneak up on you."

"No, that's okay." She smiled and turned back to the view of the star-lit valley, casually easing to the side as he came up beside her. "I'm surprised you got away so soon. Katrina didn't request her usual three books?"

"Four, actually. I'd forgotten how voracious she is. Good thing I'm a fast reader."

His fond chuckle drew Amy's curious gaze to him. He'd laughed a lot this evening, bantering back and forth with Farrah, groaning at Kyle's poor jokes, teasing Katrina and somber little Trevor. He seemed to fall into the role of uncle and best friend naturally. Amy realized the possibility that this side of him was all for show made her sad.

"Is something wrong?"

He was frowning. Amy looked away quickly, aware she'd been frowning, too.

"No, I'm fine." She knew she shouldn't ask, that she was only courting trouble, but she wanted to see what he'd say. "So what is it you do in the military? What branch of service are you in?"

"I'm in a unit attached to the Army. I handle logistics mostly, some personnel duties, a little troubleshooting now and then. Boring stuff, really. Nothing to write home about."

Honest enough descriptions of some of a unit leader's more harmless duties. Although saying Special Ops was attached to the Army might be stretching things a bit. Troubleshooter, indeed. Not that she'd thought for one minute he'd come right out and admit he was one of the most dangerous men in the covert op business.

Still, some perverse urge had her pushing for more. "Kyle said you travel a lot."

"Sometimes more than I want. What about you?" he asked quickly, turning the tables on her. "Do you do much traveling?"

"Used to. Not so much anymore." She could do vague with the best of them.

"Ever been to Europe?"

"I went to Spain once." Always stick as close to the truth as possible. Admit to one small thing to divert suspicion from the bigger picture. The fact that her one visit to Spain had been off the radar didn't matter.

"Really, what part?"

"The southern coast. The beaches are beautiful there." From what she'd seen flying in and out in the middle of the night, anyway.

He nodded. "I've seen them a time or two myself. What made you decide to settle down here in Clear Springs? It's a far cry from any beach."

Wow, talk about a subject change. But that was okay. The whole travel conversation was going nowhere anyway with both of them dancing around the truth. Amy suddenly felt like she had an unfair advantage because she knew what the truth was and he didn't. She had no intention of telling him who she was, however. Such a revelation would be a big mistake.

The fiasco of her last mission notwithstanding, the Raven had a well deserved reputation. The very few people who knew that reputation treated her with wary respect—a very distant wary respect.

That's why she'd kept her identity a secret from Kyle. She'd just started building the Raven's reputation about the time of Kyle's injury. It was a long shot, but Joshua might have mentioned the Raven's exploits over the intervening years. She couldn't see Kyle allowing someone like her alter-ego within a mile of his wife much less his precious children.

The Raven killed for a living.

She smiled at Joshua's question. "Pure luck." Considering he lived here, too, more bad luck than good. Or maybe, she thought suddenly, no luck at all. Aberashoff had been the one to suggest Clear Springs to her in the first place. He had to know this was Colby and Fagan's home town, the sneaky bastard. Odds were Kyle had been watch-dogging her from the day she moved in.

Amy shoved aside the possibility that the Fagans' friendship was only a way for Kyle to keep a closer eye on her. That kind of hurt would need to be dealt with in private. She waved a hand toward the quiet valley. "I came looking for peace of mind and this is what I found."

"Clear Springs can give you that, if it's really what you're looking for."

"You have something against peace of mind?"

He shrugged. "Different people look for different things all the time. It's what makes life interesting. I guess I just always thought a little peace of mind can go a long way. I love coming home, but I'm not sure I could stay here full time. Even with the Wassiles, there's not enough excitement."

"Yeah, I saw the bottle of hot sauce you dumped on your pasta at dinner. You like to live way too dangerously for my taste."

She saw a flash of white teeth by starlight. "What can I say? I like a little spice in my life."

She snorted softly. "It's not the sauce itself I was talking about, but the way you drowned Farrah's perfectly good pasta dish. You did see that look on her face, didn't you?"

He chuckled. "Why do you think I used so much?"

She laughed with him. They both stared out over the valley a moment before he said, "The trouble with looking for something different in life, something spicier, is that sometimes that something finds you first. Hard to go back to the way things were when that happens."

"Why would you want to? Go back, I mean." Did he really regret his choice of career?

Before he could answer, the sliding doors to the great room rumbled opened. "Well." Farrah exhaled a long breath as she joined them. "That went faster than I expected." Kyle followed, carefully carrying a tray of coffee cups. He sat the tray on a table, handed a cup to his wife and another to Amy.

"Your chocolate, mademoiselle."

"Why thank you, kind sir."

Joshua picked up a cup. "You don't drink coffee?"

"Only when I have to. My inner kid prefers chocolate, and I try to indulge her when I can." She surreptitiously studied Joshua's face as she sipped the dark liquid, savoring its heat as well as its taste. He seemed to be studying her in return. She hoped he didn't see too much. "I heard Amber crying. Is she okay?" Amy asked, trying to turn Joshua's interest to something else.

Farrah waved a hand. "I don't think she even woke up fully. Just needed a little pat on the back to settle her."

"Yep. That makes three little chicks safely tucked into bed," Kyle said. Amy watched him glance at Joshua, a look on his face she couldn't decipher. Joshua's lips twitched into a brief smile.

"So, Joshua, has Amy told you about her studio?" Farrah asked.

"Her studio?" Interest kindled in the man's eyes. Great, just what she needed.

"Yes, she's a photographer."

"*Amateur* photographer," Amy clarified quickly. Her hobby could hardly be called anything else.

"Sorry, but you sold several pictures last

month," Farrah pointed out. "That makes you a professional now."

"What kind of pictures?" Joshua asked.

Amy pointed toward the valley. "What else? And the pictures were sold at a church bazaar. I don't think they count."

"Of course they do. Everyone loved them."

"Yeah, her landscapes are great," Kyle added. "But you should see some of her wildlife shots, Josh. I don't know how she gets them."

"A very expensive zoom lens," she quipped. Not to mention the patience and stillness of a sniper. It was nice when her skills overlapped into something she really enjoyed.

"I'd like to see them. Where's your studio?" Joshua asked.

"Farrah was exaggerating when she said studio. I converted my basement into a darkroom. Speaking of which, I have film to develop in the morning. Not to mention Bors is probably going crazy wondering where I am."

"Bors is her dog," Farrah said quickly.

Another look passed between Joshua and Kyle. "I know," Joshua said.

Kyle burst out laughing. "I'll get my keys, Amy. No way are you walking back home tonight." He went into the house. Farrah followed with the tray of empty cups. Amy started to join them but halted at a touch on her arm.

"You walked here?"

Was it her imagination, or did she hear disapproval in those three words? "It's not that far through the woods. Only a couple of miles."

"What about Chet? Didn't it cross your mind at all that he could be waiting somewhere in those woods?" There was no mistaking the disapproval this time; quiet, bitten off words, lowered brows, censorious gaze. The man had intimidation down pat.

Instinctively, Amy started to draw away from him but stopped herself. He had no right to disapprove of anything when it came to her. She lifted her chin, the better to stare into his eyes. "Like I said this afternoon, I can handle Chet Wassile."

"Like you handled him today?"

"I *was* handling him, up until you raised the bar with your Robin Hood routine. So far Chet and his brothers have settled for verbally aggressive rather than anything physical. If that changes, I'll have you to thank."

"Me?"

"Yes, you. You embarrassed them today. They'll be looking to get back some of their pride, and it won't be you they go after."

"That was bound to happen eventually anyway. Talking your way around them might work the first dozen or so times, but sooner or later they'll up the ante. Pardon me for pointing out the obvious, but you're a woman. You can't take on three men at once."

Oh, couldn't she? The urge to show him just how wrong his statement was nearly won the fight with her common sense. She was so tempted she turned around right then and walked away. "It might surprise you what I can do, Mr. Colby." A week. All she had to do was avoid him for a week at most. SO units rarely took longer than a seven-day leave.

Inside the house, she gathered up the gym bag holding her running clothes. A large male hand closed over the strap. She tried jerking the bag away from him. He didn't budge. Instead, he just smiled.

"Do you really want to turn this into a tug of war?"

"Got the keys."

Both of them turned as Kyle came limping down the stairs. Farrah came out of the kitchen, meeting him at the bottom. Kyle swept his wife into his arms and kissed her quick and hard. "Back soon, love."

"I can take Amy home," Joshua said. He tugged on the bag again. Amy was so shocked by his offer, she let go of the strap. This was not good.

"You don't have to bother. Kyle can—"

"It's no bother. I drive right by your road on my way home, and I was going to turn in early tonight anyway. It's been a long day."

Before she could say anything else, Kyle spoke up. "If it's okay with Amy, I'd appreciate it, Josh. I didn't want to say anything, but my leg's aching like a son...like a bear," he finished, glancing quickly at Farrah. She nodded approvingly and stretched up to whisper something in his ear. Kyle's arms tightened and a wicked gleam entered his eyes.

Amy looked away, feeling herself blush. Not because of Kyle and Farrah's flirting, but because she should have noticed how badly Kyle was limping before. He'd favored the leg a little more than usual coming down the stairs. She should have driven tonight. It would have spared Kyle and her both. Now she was stuck riding home with Joshua in the confines of his Jeep.

"It's okay with me," she said quickly. The sooner she got home, the better. She hugged Farrah and Kyle and slipped out the front door. A moment later, Joshua joined her in the dark.

The inside of the Jeep was cold. The air, the leather seats, the metal buckle of the seatbelt. Everything combined to draw a shiver out of her.

"Sorry," Joshua apologized. "I'll turn the heater on in a minute. This should help in the meantime." He pushed a button. Several seconds later, Amy felt the seat beneath her warm. The change in temperature sent another shiver through her.

"Not better?"

"No, it's okay, it's getting warmer."

"Good. So, do you want to dance some more while we wait for the engine to warm up?"

"Excuse me?"

He turned his body toward her and leaned back against his door. She could see him swirl a finger around in the air between them. "You and I were twirling words around like a couple of kids at their first dance out on the deck. I just wondered if you felt like dodging some more questions."

"Like you weren't?"

"I said you and I, didn't I?"

"Yes, you did, and the answer is no. I think we've established that neither of us wants to talk about ourselves, so why don't we just leave it at that?"

He appeared to think that over for a few seconds. Then he shook his head. "Nope, can't do it. Call me curious, but I want to know more about you."

"Why?"

"Three reasons." He ticked them off on his fingers. "Because you're friends with Farrah and Kyle. Because my godkids seem to hold you in high regard. And because I liked the way you stood up to Chet this afternoon."

"I thought you didn't approve of the way I was handling him."

"I didn't say that. At the risk of drawing your fire again, what I said was that your method of handling the Wassiles wasn't enough. Standing your ground is good. I admire a woman who doesn't take any shit, if you'll pardon the language. But being strong can also work against you. The reason Chet has the hots for you is because you refuse to give in."

Amy gave him her most innocent, wide-eyed look. "Oh, I see. He's caught up in the thrill of the chase."

He nodded.

"So if I give in and let him have what he wants then he'll leave me alone. Is that what you're saying?" She wasn't sure but she thought she saw his jaw tighten.

"Hey, no twisting in the Jeep," he said roughly.

"What?" She'd been doing a pretty good job of verbal fencing, had been enjoying it, too, but he'd lost her with that remark.

He put the Jeep into gear and eased onto the mountain road. "You're twisting my words around, lady. I never said you should give in. In fact, I'd be disappointed if you did. Chet doesn't deserve a woman like you."

She tried to ignore the pleased warmth brought on by his comment. It was hard, though. Joshua had a deep, commanding voice, one that took on a sexy, seductive edge in the dark confines of the Jeep.

Allowing herself to be flattered by a man was how she'd gotten into trouble to begin with. She wasn't about to make the same mistake twice. And especially not with *this* man.

"Not that I disagree with you, but why would you say that? You don't know me."

"True," he said. "I've only known you a few hours. But there has to be something special about you. Kyle, Farrah, and the kids all like you."

"And you're just going to take their word for it?"

"Trust me, it's hard to argue with a house full of Fagans."

The easy smile curving his lips sent another rush of warmth through her. Damn, the man's lethal reputation didn't do him justice. She jerked her gaze back to the road ahead of them to keep from doing something stupid like smiling back. Maintaining a distance between them was critical, both to her peace of mind and her current living arrangements.

She didn't want to have to leave Clear Springs.

"Do you always let someone else make your

decisions for you?"

"I make my own decisions," he said quickly. "Always have, always will. Doesn't mean I can't take other opinions into consideration."

They didn't speak again until he pulled to a stop in front of her house. She took her time unbuckling the seatbelt, scanning the shadows for anything out of place. She couldn't afford to get caught off guard this late in the game. The touch of Joshua's hand on her arm startled her.

"Sorry," he said. His own gaze swept over the house and yard, lingering on the blackness of the woods. "Don't blame you for being a little skittish. Come on, I'll walk you to your door."

"It's okay. You don't have to do that."

"I don't mind." He opened his door and got out.

Amy fumbled with her own door handle and managed to climb out before he rounded the Jeep.

He shut her door and stood back, letting her lead the way.

She took one step and knew immediately something was wrong. Senses honed by several years of hard experience screamed at her that she was being watched, and not just by the man at her side.

She couldn't hear or see anything unusual, but something just felt…off. Her skin fairly crawled with the need to climb the nearest tree and hide.

Forcing herself to breathe normally, Amy hoped Joshua would think the cold night air was the reason she almost ran up the steps to her porch.

He stayed close to her. Protectively close, one might say. He kept turning to look at her except his gaze always slid just a little over her head to the thick woods to the east. It didn't surprise her at all that Joshua felt those prying eyes, too.

He placed a hand on her shoulder as they reached the door. "You go on in. I thought I heard something in the woods. Probably just an animal. I'll check it out before I leave."

Smooth, but she wasn't buying what he was selling tonight. "Don't patronize me, Joshua, I don't like it. If you think Chet's out there, just say so."

She didn't—Chet hadn't worked his way up to lurking in the dark yet. But letting Joshua think she did might allow her to talk him out of investigating.

If someone really was out there, she needed to find out who they were before Joshua did. She'd be happy to scream bloody murder and let him rescue her if it turned out to be a local. If that someone was from her past? Well, she wasn't a stranger to death now, was she?

"If it is Chet," Joshua said, "he deserves a good scare, don't you think? Don't worry, I won't hurt him. Much."

She let a little more of her irritation out. "I'd really rather you didn't confront him. I meant what I said earlier about your interference only making things more difficult. Joshua—"

She reached to stop him and grabbed air. He was down the steps without making a sound.

"Go inside, Amy. I'll take care of this."

Not even a civilian would have missed the command in his voice. Damn him, he was going to ruin everything. She swung around to unlock her door.

If she could get changed into her working clothes quick enough, she still might be able to get to whoever it was before Joshua scared him off, or worse, found him. She turned the door knob without thinking. The door jerked out of her hand as a dark shape squeezed through the opening to dart past her.

"Bors, hold!" Spinning around, Amy threw her hand out, automatically making the signals for *stop* and *hold position* even though Bors wouldn't see her.

He heard her, though, thank God. The verbal command brought him to a halt less than a yard from Joshua, legs and tail stiff, head down. The dog's attention was completely focused on the man he perceived as a threat.

Chapter Six

"Don't move, Joshua."

Staring at the silently snarling animal, Joshua thought Amy's suggestion had excellent merit. He now understood completely why Chet steered clear of her when Bors was with her.

What a monster. Three feet at the shoulder if he was an inch. The huge dog had a short, solid black coat, thick chest, heavy body, and paws the size of saucers. Not to mention a mouth-full of sharp teeth that would do a T-Rex proud. Tack on a couple more heads and he'd make a perfect Cerberus.

"This is my fault," Amy said, walking quickly toward him. "I'm sorry. I shouldn't have argued with you where he could hear. He's very good at picking up on verbal aggression."

No shit, Joshua thought, careful not to meet the dog's threatening gaze. At this distance, he wouldn't have a chance of snatching one of the three knives strapped to his body before Bors turned him into a Scooby snack. The dog was damned unhappy. So much so, Joshua automatically reached out to stop Amy from stepping between him and the angry animal.

Big mistake.

Bors took a step forward and growled, the eerie, rumbling sound freezing Joshua in place and raising every hair on his body.

"Bors! Hold!" Amy said sharply.

Every instinct in Joshua rebelled as she placed herself in front of him. He should be the one protecting her, not the other way around.

"Good boy," she murmured. "That's a good boy. Bors, this is Joshua. He's a friend, understand? Friendly."

The dog cocked his head to one side as if considering the concept. A moment later, the animal's entire body language changed, going from deadly sentinel to innocuous canine companion in the space of a happy bark. Tail wagging, Bors stepped forward to greet his owner, barely sparing Joshua a glance.

Amy squatted, giving her pet a hug and thumping his sides. She kept up a low murmur of praise, most of which Joshua agreed with even though he'd almost been on the receiving end of those sharp teeth.

"It's all right," Amy said over her shoulder. "You can move now." She sent him a teasing smile. "Though I would recommend you not use your 'I'm in command so do what I say' voice on me again. At least not until Bors knows you better."

"Recommendation noted." He glanced toward the woods. "I suppose whatever was out there is long gone by now. That dog of yours is enough to scare away anything, including Chet Wassile."

Her chuckle sounded a little on the wicked side. "Bors knows I don't like the Wassiles. As far as he's concerned, that makes Chet and his brother's fair game. He takes great delight in letting them know they're not welcome anywhere near me." She shrugged one slender shoulder. "Maybe that's why he shot out of the house. Maybe he smelled a Wassile in the woods, and you just happened to be in the way."

"Maybe," Joshua said, though he didn't think so. He squatted down next to Amy, careful to keep his movements slow. He started to hold out his fist. Amy caught his wrist.

"Let me."

He nodded, and she brought his fist up for the dog's inspection. The animal paused, glanced at Amy, then sniffed the offered appendage several times, his big black nose tickling the hairs on the back of Joshua's hand. Then a large, wet tongue rolled out, swiping once over his knuckles.

Joshua grinned. "Is that his seal of approval, or is he tasting the hors d'oeuvres?"

Amy laughed again, lighter this time. He liked to hear her laugh. The sound did something to him. Made him feel warmer somehow. Happier. He knew he couldn't get involved with her, but damn if he wasn't going to squeeze in every enjoyable moment he could while he had the chance.

"You've just been vetted. All tongue and no teeth mean you rank right up there with Farrah and the kids."

"What about Kyle?"

She stood, her gaze sweeping the surrounding woods before turning to him with a smile that kicked him in the gut. "Kyle got a couple of teeth. Of course, that was before Bors here learned his manners. Isn't that right, big guy?" She patted the big head affectionately. "Might as well take a quick run and do your business while you're out here," she told the dog. "Go on." She threw a hand out as if to shoo him on his way.

If he hadn't been watching the graceful move of that hand, Joshua would have missed the innocent flick of fingers that was anything but. He kept his eyes from narrowing in speculation, but his mind whirled, trying to come up with a plausible explanation for why Amy Sherridan knew Special Ops hand signals. Kyle sure as hell wouldn't have taught her, he knew better.

The dog responded to the *perimeter check* sign like a well trained operative. He huffed quietly, then spun around and set off at a fast trot, head up, nose scenting the air. The big black animal quickly blended into the surrounding darkness leaving Joshua alone with a very interesting mystery.

"Aren't you afraid he'll cross some scent and go chasing whatever it is out into the woods?"

"Not my baby. He's too well trained to let himself get distracted. He'll be back shortly." With another glance toward the woods, she turned and headed for her house at a brisk walk. Joshua followed more slowly. That sense of being watched had vanished, but he still had an itchy feeling between his shoulders. Someone had definitely been out there. The question was, who?

Looking for clues tonight would be a waste of time. He didn't have the mad tracker skills Rashid did. The NightHawks tracker, codename Griffon, could follow a week-old trail blindfolded. The Harrier, on the other hand, would have to settle for coming back during the day.

Amy paused on the steps of her porch. "Thanks for driving me home."

"No problem." He walked up the steps, stopping one down from her. The fact she didn't back up at all only reinforced his earlier opinion that she had guts. He leaned against the railing, wondering how far he could push her. "I don't suppose you'd like to invite me in. Maybe give me a tour of your darkroom. I promise to behave."

She gave a short laugh. "No, I don't think so. You're too much like the scorpion in that old fable. You know, the one who promises the frog he won't sting if the frog carries him across the stream? The scorpion ends up stinging the frog anyway because he can't help it, stinging is just part of his nature."

"So you think misbehaving is part of my nature?"

Moonlight highlighted the humorous twinkle in her blue eyes. "I don't think it, I know it. You forget

I've been around Kyle and Farrah for almost a year. Just about every story Kyle tells about his past misadventures include a certain Joshua Andrew Colby. The evidence is clearly undeniable. You reek of misbehavior, mister."

Joshua smiled easily. "In that case, have dinner with me tomorrow." He really didn't expect her to say yes. The only thing she knew about him was that he was friends with Kyle and Farrah. She didn't know *him*. Which, given his line of work, was probably a good thing. No doubt she'd run away screaming if she ever found out.

Instead of a clipped "No," and a door slammed in his face, Joshua was surprised at the sudden speculation in her gaze. His heart beat a little faster when she asked softly, "Why?"

He picked the light approach. "Because I think the playing field needs to be leveled. You know all about my misspent youth thanks to Kyle, but I don't know anything about yours. Not to mention, you owe me for the scare your dog gave me. Damn beast almost gave me a heart attack."

Smiling, not saying a word, she backed up the next step. He raised a brow and followed. "Retreating, Ms. Sheridan?"

"Just a matter of self preservation, Mr. Colby. Things are getting a little deep around here, if you know what I mean."

"Are you accusing me of exaggerating?"

"More like flat-out lying. I can't imagine the man who, as a boy, braved his neighbor's angry dogs to rescue a baby skunk, being afraid of my Bors. What did you name the little thing again? Patches, Patty...?"

Joshua feigned a grimace. "Panda. And Kyle evidently failed to mention the angry dogs were a pair of Yorkie Terriers."

"Ah, but size is relative. To a five-year-old, two

Yorkies in full battle mode should at least equal one Bors today."

He held up his hands in surrender. "Fair enough. Far be it from me to tarnish my tough-guy image. I take back the part about the heart attack. Everything else is true, however, so I still need an answer. Dinner tomorrow, yes or no?"

She continued to smile and backed up again, planting both feet on her porch.

He tsked. "Don't know if anyone's told you, Ms. Sheridan, but it's not a good idea to run from a predator. It tends to trigger their urge to chase you down." Slowly, deliberately, he put first one foot, then the other, on the next step up. Instead of backing away this time, she leaned forward, making him wonder who was really doing the chasing.

"A predator, Mr. Colby? I thought you were a—" She broke off, lips suddenly pressed together in a tight line, as if literally holding back her next words.

"A what?" he coaxed.

She blinked, smiled, and looked at him from beneath her lashes in a way that made his blood run hot. "A man who ought to know better than to try using intimidation on a woman he's just met. Really, I never would have expected you for the Neanderthal type. Chet, yes, but you?" Lips pursed in disapproval, she shook her head back and forth in a slow, playful gesture. The teasing look in her eyes brought to Joshua's mind a long, steamy night of naughty sex.

Get your mind out of the gutter, Colby. She's just a job. A target.

Targets, whether his or someone else's, were always off limits. *Always.* That was the one rule he'd never had any problems following. Until now, damn it. For the first time in his military career, he found his libido more than willing to toss the rule book out the window. Maybe it was because he hadn't been with a woman in months. Maybe it was the moonlight. But by the time he'd reined in his wayward thoughts his erection pressed against his jeans hard enough to be uncomfortable. He needed to leave. Now. Just walk away.

Some insane part of him rationalized his next move as part of the mission. He was assigned to protect her. What better way to do that than to stay close to her?

He stepped up onto the porch, using his size shamelessly to herd her back, right up against the wall beside the door. He leaned in close, watching her eyes, always watching her eyes. Not a trace of fear darkened the blue. No shadows at all except for the ones created by the chilly night surrounding them. If anything, she looked curious, expectant, with a little touch of amusement thrown in for good measure. A damn potent combination.

"I can't tell you how glad I am that you see the difference between me and Chet Wassile. Don't, however, make the mistake of believing just because I'm not a Neanderthal that you're safe."

Her eyes widened innocently. "Are you saying I can't trust you to be a gentleman, Uncle Josh?"

He chuckled and shook his head at her little girl impression. "Dirty pool, Ms. Sheridan."

"Of course. What else do you expect from a woman when you back her into a corner?"

"This." He took his time getting there, giving her a chance to say no. She didn't make a sound as he slowly settled his lips on hers. Somehow, even with the need to rush in and devour threatening to swamp him, he kept the kiss light, a meeting of lips only. Not until he felt her pouty lips quiver and part did he bring his tongue into play. Then he tasted her.

God love her, she tasted like a rushing mountain stream swollen with spring rain, pure, fresh, bubbling with life. He delved deeper, grinning inside and mentally licking his lips at the hint of hot chocolate teasing his taste buds. A small moan vibrated into his mouth, sending a fresh rush of blood to his groin, making his already hard shaft ache. Hell, he'd never been so ready to be inside a woman.

A low, canine huff accompanied by the puff of hot breath against his ass froze him just as he started to press closer. He lifted his head a little, feeling the lips beneath his slide into a sweet curve.

Amy whispered, "My boyfriend's back."

"Not funny." He nipped her bottom lip at the poor joke, then stepped back carefully. Turning, he found himself once again on the receiving end of the monster dog's intent gaze. This time, however, curiosity was mixed with the one-wrong-move-and-you're-lunch stare. Joshua slowly reached out to scratch behind the dog's ear. "Just being neighborly, big guy. No need to put me on the menu."

The dog huffed again, then moved out from under Joshua's hand to sit protectively at Amy's side.

Patting the dark head, Amy chuckled softly. "Something tells me he doesn't believe you."

"That's all right. I'll win him over eventually. I'm a patient man."

"Now that, I believe. And to answer your earlier question, yes, I'm free for dinner tomorrow."

"Good. I'll pick you up at six."

"Six it is."

He waited until she and Bors were safely inside before walking to his Jeep. Glancing back, he saw her standing at one of the windows, watching him.

Bors pushed his head under her hand, his big, dark eyes gazing worshipfully up at Amy. She glanced down at her pet as Joshua put his Jeep into gear, her love for the animal plain on her face.

A stab of something close to jealously made Joshua swear.

If he wasn't careful, he and Bors would have a lot more in common than a wide protective streak.

Chapter Seven

"Explain to me how Amy Sheridan knows Special Ops hand signals."

Lying back on a padded chaise, Kyle didn't so much as twitch as Joshua walked out of the dark a few minutes later. Instead of going home after leaving Amy's, he'd headed straight back to Kyle's, looking for answers. It didn't surprise him to find Kyle waiting for him on his deck.

Kyle's brows rose innocently. "Does she?"

"You know she does." He took the chair on the other side of the patio table and accepted the cup of black coffee Kyle poured from a thermos. The first hot sip burned a welcome trail down his throat, warming his insides. "I haven't read her entire file yet, but the only logical explanation is that she worked for the SO in some capacity."

"Yeah, that would be the logical assumption. It would explain how she got involved with Velavich, too, wouldn't it. Only there's no such notation in her file."

"You ask Abe about it?"

"Of course." Kyle gave him a disgusted look. "Old man blinked and told me not to worry about it."

Joshua took a deep breath and pushed it out noisily. "Damn it, I knew there was something he wasn't telling me." And he doubted Aberashoff would tell him any more than he had Kyle. If it didn't affect the job, Abe was the proverbial clam. There were other ways of finding out things, however. "I'll get Capella working on it. Abe may not think it's important, but I do."

"I was hoping you'd say that. Let me know what you find out."

"That depends," Joshua said slowly.

His friend scowled. "On what?"

"On whether you're going to continue to be an idiot."

"What the effin' hell does that mean?"

Joshua bit back a grin at Kyle's modified swearing and pointed a finger at his friend. "You and I are about to have words, bro. I don't care if Farrah begged you to take this assignment, you're playing with fire, and you know it."

His friend snorted. "Try telling me something I don't already know. But you know Farrah, when she gets something in her head, it's impossible to shake it out. Believe me, I tried."

Joshua grunted. He was all too aware of Farrah's stubbornness. "How'd she find out about the assignment in the first place?"

Kyle shifted on the chaise. If Joshua didn't know better, he'd swear his friend was actually squirming. Finally, Kyle snapped out, "Because of our blood pact."

"Our what?"

Kyle sighed gustily and ran a hand through his hair. "You remember that year you and I watched all those cowboy and Indian movies?"

Joshua wasn't in the mood for reminiscing, but he thought he saw where this was going so he said, "Yeah. We snuck a knife out of your mom's kitchen so we could slice our palms and become blood brothers." He held his left palm to the light. His scar was a lot longer than Kyle's. He'd been too excited at the thought of having a brother, even a pretend one, and the knife had slipped. Son-of-a-bitch wound had taken forever to heal.

"We swore never to tell anyone why we did it." Kyle rubbed his own short scar.

Joshua nodded. The secrecy had been part of their vows. "So, what does this have to do with Farrah?"

"After I came back home six years ago, she asked me about the scar. I swear I held out as long as I could, Josh."

Joshua widened his eyes and slapped his hand over his heart. "Damn, Kyle, I can't believe you broke our vow of silence after all these years. See if I ever ask you to sleep over again."

Kyle picked up the lid to the thermos and threw it at him. "Go ahead and laugh, idiot. You didn't have to watch Farrah cut herself because she wanted the same thing."

Joshua caught the lid and slid it back across the table. The image Kyle's words conjured sent a cold chill down his spine. Farrah, a knife, blood. No way was that a pretty picture. He shoved it out of his head and forced a grin. "She wanted you for a blood brother?"

"No, dumbass." His friend tilted his head back, looking up at the stars. "We were making promises to each other. Vows. You know, forever type stuff."

Joshua swallowed the wad of emotion building in his throat. No, he didn't know about forever type stuff. Not with a woman. But he could imagine. He could covet that kind of relationship with ridiculous ease.

"She liked the idea of sealing our vows by mixing our blood," Kyle continued, his voice going rough. "She figured it worked for you and me all these years, blood brothers forever, right? The blood thing kind of made our promises unbreakable in her eyes." He met Joshua's gaze. "I needed to give her that. Something unbreakable, something she knew would last."

Joshua didn't say anything as Kyle poured the last of the coffee into his mug. He drained it in two gulps and set the mug down. "Among other things, I promised her I'd always tell her if the SO ever wanted me back." He shrugged. "Didn't think they ever would, so it didn't seem like such a big promise at the time."

"Telling her about the assignment was part of the promise?"

"Yep, part and parcel. As soon as she read Amy's file, she started in on me. Threw me for an effin' loop. I was already primed to say no." He snorted softly. Joshua could hear the love in his voice when he said, "Damn stubborn woman wouldn't let up until I told Abe I'd take the assignment."

It was Joshua's turn to run his hand through his hair. "Didn't you tell her about the danger?"

"That's just it, there wasn't supposed to be any. Abe had the HellHounds tracking Velavich, and the clues they had didn't point anywhere close to the states. As soon as they got wind of his movements toward the U.S., Abe called you."

"He also told you to put some distance between your family and Amy. This dinner tonight, that ain't distance, Kyle."

Kyle grimaced. "I know. I'm working up to it."

"Working up to it? What the hell kind of wishy-washy answer is that? Damn, Kyle, if you'd pulled something like this while still in the unit, I'd have busted your balls."

Kyle swung his legs off the chaise and leaned over the table. He pointed at Joshua. "You want to be the one to tell Farrah she can no longer see the friend she's come to love like a sister because the woman's about to find herself on the wrong end of a bullet, go ahead, be my guest. I damn sure don't."

"That's a bullshit excuse and you know it." Joshua jabbed a finger toward the house. "Those are my nieces and nephew asleep in there. I'd like to see them grow up and have kids of their own one day.

This kind of business could get them killed. You need to back off. Better yet, take a couple weeks and get Farrah and the kids the hell out of the valley. Safer for everyone."

"Don't tell me how to protect my family."

"I will if I think you're doing a piss-poor job of it. Hell, I might even take over."

That quick, Kyle flipped the table over and lunged off the chaise, his fist aimed in Joshua's direction. Joshua knew he had it coming, but couldn't keep instinct from kicking in. He ducked, dived out of his chair, and kicked it at Kyle. He heard Kyle let out a string of dark blue swear words and grinned as he rolled to his feet. Knuckles slammed into his chin as he straightened, snapping his head back. Damn, he'd forgotten just how quick Kyle could be when he put his mind to it.

Joshua dodged another punch and went low, shoving a shoulder into Kyle's middle and taking him down. They hit the deck hard, bodies twisting, fists flying. An elbow caught him in the mouth, and he tasted blood.

"That's enough!"

Both of them froze, their gazes going to the lush female figure standing in the doorway leading to the great room. Farrah looked like she'd just crawled out of bed, her hair tousled, her curvy body wrapped in a thick robe. Hell, she even had fuzzy bunny slippers on her feet. Her face, however, was anything but sleepy. She marched out onto the deck and stood over them, hands on her hips.

"We're so busted," Kyle said.

His words, the same ones uttered at least a thousand times over the course of their misspent youth, made Joshua burst into laughter. Kyle stiffened, then quickly joined him. They rolled apart and lay on the deck, unable to do anything but laugh for a solid minute. By the time they calmed down,

Farrah had righted the furniture. Shaking her head at them in disgust, she disappeared into the house with the thermos and broken mugs.

"Think it's safe to get up now?" Joshua asked, wiping his eyes.

Kyle sat up slowly, wincing as he rolled his right shoulder. "Depends on how much she heard."

"I heard everything." Farrah stepped back onto the deck and shut the sliding glass door. She pointed at the window above them. "I cracked the bedroom window open when I went to bed. Now, if you two are quite through re-affirming your childhood bonds, I'd like to discuss the situation."

Joshua rolled to his feet. "There's nothing to discuss."

"Well, I think there is. Amy is my friend. I don't intend to turn my back on her no matter what this commander of yours says."

Joshua sent Kyle a warning look. If his friend didn't have the balls to explain things to Farrah, he would, friendship be damned. He'd rather have both of them alive and mad at him than dead. Kyle glared back, but finally heaved a sigh and held his hand out. Joshua took it and hauled him to his feet.

"Josh is right, sweetheart," Kyle said. He pulled Farrah into his arms and kissed her before she could disagree. "Remember, I told you part of my job would be following orders. That means when the commander says to back off, we back off. You don't have to worry about Amy. Joshua won't let anything happen to her, I promise. He's got the same wicked mad skills I do."

Her gaze slid to Joshua, her expression strange, as if she saw him for the very first time. He wondered for a moment just what kind of wicked mad skills Kyle was referring to. Deciding he didn't want to know, Joshua cocked a brow, daring her to disagree with her husband's assessment. Her lips twitched into a small smile. In a move so Farrah, she stuck her tongue out at him, making him chuckle. Heaving a deep sigh, she laid her head on Kyle's shoulder.

"I just can't help worrying about how Amy will see this. I don't want her to think we turned our backs on her."

"Baby, no—"

"She won't think that," Joshua said quickly. He leaned against the deck rail. "I saw her with the kids earlier, Farrah. I get the feeling that if she thought for a second she might be putting them in danger, she'd be the one to step away. Once this mess is taken care of, you and she will have plenty of time to sit down and smooth out any ripples in your friendship. In the meantime, as an active SO operative, Kyle is obligated to obey orders. No more dinners, no more lunches, and absolutely no trips into town together. As of tonight, Amy is off limits to both of you."

Kyle stiffened. "Now wait a god...blessed minute. No one said anything about me sitting this one out."

"I just did. If you want, I'll call Abe and have him make it official."

"Dang it, Josh, you're going to need help."

"I've got help coming. If you're a really good boy, you might even get to see a few of them when this is over. I doubt the guys will leave without the usual barbeque at my place."

Some of Kyle's aggression vanished, replaced by anticipation. Joshua felt a stab of pity for his friend even though he knew it wouldn't be appreciated. True, Kyle had Farrah and the kids, but like him, Kyle Fagan had lived and breathed Special Ops for too long not to miss it.

Farrah shivered. Kyle kissed her again and turned her toward the house. "Go back inside. I'll be in soon. And close the da…" He stopped, took a deep breath, and started again. "Close the window, please."

Farrah paused after opening the sliding door and turned around to send Kyle the sweetest, most come-hither smile Joshua had ever seen. Then she shot Joshua a stern look. "You're terrible for his vocabulary." Her gaze softened. "But I'm glad you're home, Joshua. I know you'll keep Amy safe." She closed the door and disappeared into the dark room.

Kyle came to lean against the rail beside him. They both stared up at the open window. After a long moment, Kyle called, "Farrah!"

Joshua heard a mutter before Farrah appeared and shoved the window closed. She glared down at them. As if they'd practiced, he and Kyle blew her a kiss at the same time. Her lips twitched into a smile, then firmed. With a toss of her head, she jerked the curtains closed. Joshua chuckled. "Stubborn, isn't she."

"You really have no idea."

"You do the half-swearing thing on purpose, don't you?"

The moonlight caught Kyle's wicked grin perfectly. "Can I help it if she believes in positive reinforcement?"

They both chuckled and moved back to the chairs. Kyle sat down with a groan and lifted his leg onto the chaise. Joshua frowned.

"Hope that fight we had didn't hurt it."

"That little tussle? Don't be insulting. Damn cold seeps into the muscles and ties them into knots, that's all. Have you figured out yet how you're going to keep an eye on Amy? Let me warn you, she's not a home body. Goes out in the woods almost every day, either running or taking pictures. Sometimes she camps out overnight."

Joshua's gaze drifted out over the dark forest.

Too many places for a snake to hide. "Does she take that monster with her each time?"

"Sir Bors?" Kyle's lips spread into another grin. "Met him, did you? Did he take a bite out of your ornery hide?"

Joshua snorted. "He rolled over and gave me his throat the instant he saw me."

"Yeah," Kyle said, still grinning. "Like I'm going to believe that crock of excrement. But to answer your question, yes, she does. Today was an exception. Which means following her without Bors alerting her to your presence is going to be a little tricky, even for you, you sneaky bastard."

"Yes," Joshua mused. So maybe instead of sneaky, he'd try a more direct approach. He'd already talked her into a dinner date. How much harder would it be to get himself invited for a romp in the woods?

A romp in the woods with Amy. Damn if that didn't sound like fun.

Chapter Eight

Joshua was on his third cup of coffee and second order of Marlee Borden's pancakes the next morning when the door to the café opened and the Wassiles walked in. Their hard, rough laughter came to an abrupt stop when they spotted him. He gave no sign he noticed the trio, but tracked their movements as they made their way to an empty table. Amy was right about one thing. The brothers weren't the type to let yesterday's encounter go unchallenged. Chet especially. Without even looking, Joshua could tell the eldest Wassile was winding himself up, getting ready to cut loose either verbally or physically. If the idiot knew what was good for him, he'd let Joshua finish eating before causing trouble.

The café's door opened again.

"Morning, Sheriff," Marlee sang out.

The rising tension coming off the Wassiles stuttered, then seemed to double. It had a different feel to it, though, less predatory and more wary. Joshua could appreciate the reason for the difference. In his late forties, Dan Penwell was a career law man, as good at his job as Joshua was his. He'd been policing the Wassiles for a long time. The three brothers knew where they stood with the sheriff. They didn't know Joshua. They had no clue that, of the two of them, Joshua was the most dangerous. He didn't always play by the rules like Pen had to.

"Morning, Marlee." Penwell's delayed greeting told Joshua the sheriff had probably taken a few seconds to assess the situation. "Seth," Penwell said, nodding to Marlee's burley husband behind the counter.

Seth nodded back. "Sheriff. You want eggs or pancakes this morning?"

"Just coffee today, Seth." Penwell's deliberate tread moved in Joshua's direction. "Chet, Franklin, Arnold, you boys ordering or have you already finished your breakfast?"

"We just got here, Sheriff, ain't even had a chance to order yet," said Chet.

"Yeah," said Arney. "You know how slow the service is here, Sheriff." All three men snickered.

"Well, enjoy your breakfast, then." Penwell stopped at Joshua's table. "I heard you were back in town, Joshua. Mind if I join you?"

Joshua picked up his coffee and waved to the seat across from him. He'd intended to drop by the sheriff's office after breakfast and speak to Pen about Chet harassing Amy. With the Wassiles a few tables over, that conversation would have to wait.

"You're out early," he said, reaching over to shake Penwell's hand as he sat down. He'd known the man all his life. Tall, solidly built, with a dry sense of humor that was hard to take if you didn't know him. Penwell kept himself in shape and would have looked ten years younger if not for the lines of worry and tension etched into his face and the gray streaking his short brown hair. He took his job very seriously.

The sheriff grunted. "Had a tourist run off the road before daylight this morning. I tell you they get worse every year. Thanks, Marlee." He picked up the cup the waitress set down.

"You're welcome, Sheriff." Looking at Joshua, Marlee lifted the coffee pot in her hand. "Need a top off?"

"Please." He nodded to her when she was done and watched her walk to the Wassile's table. With stiff politeness, she set down three cups, filled them with coffee, and took their orders. As she left, Joshua heard Franklin mutter, "Stupid old bitch." All three brothers snickered again.

Marlee Borden was just a few years over thirty and one of the kindest women he knew. He saw her back stiffen at Franklin's nasty comment. His anger at the three backwoods idiots threatened to boil over.

"Don't," Penwell said quietly.

Joshua's gaze snapped to the sheriff to find the man staring at him intently over the rim of his coffee cup. "Don't let those three goad you into doing something stupid. Verbal insults aren't worth the trouble."

Of course they weren't. That didn't mean Joshua wanted to let them get away with their rude behavior. Unfortunately, he wasn't in some godforsaken jungle where he could make his own rules. He was on Penwell's turf. He owed the man some respect. With a little effort, Joshua stuffed the anger back down again, letting the tension ease out of his shoulders.

Penwell's own shoulders dropped slightly in response. "So, how long will you be home this time?"

"Two or three weeks. Depends on if I get a call to come back to work. You know how it is."

Penwell nodded. Joshua watched from the corner of his eye as Arney got up and slouched his way to the café's jukebox. A moment later, a loud country song started blaring, something about fast cars and faster women.

Joshua took a sip of coffee, feeling Arney's hard gaze on him as the younger man returned to his seat. "My apologies in advance," he said to Penwell. The music was loud enough Joshua didn't worry about being overheard.

"For?"

"For whatever is going to eventually happen

between me and those three. It's going to cause you some paperwork at the very least."

Penwell grimaced. "You know how much I hate paperwork, Joshua."

"Yeah, I do, that's why I'm apologizing now. You might not be in the mood to hear me out later. It's going to happen though." He leaned forward over his empty plate. "I know about Chet harassing Amy Sheridan."

Penwell's brows rose, his surprise clearing the next moment. "Ah, Fagan. I take it you've talked to him already."

"We had dinner last night. Amy was there. I met her earlier, though, at Kyle's garage. She was out jogging without Bors and ran into Chet and his brothers."

A single swear word passed the sheriff's lips that would have done Kyle justice.

"I warned him to stay away from her. Damn it, that fool is going to make me file a restraining order on him yet. That'll mean a court date, more paperwork, and—"

"A waste of time. You know a restraining order isn't going to even slow him down."

"Hell, Joshua, I know that. But at least with the order in place, when he does step over the line I can slap his ass in jail."

Joshua ground his teeth. "After he hurts her, you mean."

Penwell's gaze locked on Joshua, his eyes seething with frustration. "You think I'm okay with that?"

"Then do something about it."

"Like what? I can't arrest someone for something they haven't done yet. The only other option is for Amy to hire a twenty-four hour bodyguard, and if you've met her you know that ain't likely to happen. Fool woman's as stubborn as Saul's mule. She thinks that dog of hers is enough, but eventually Chet's going to find a way around that animal and when he does..."

The song on the jukebox ended, forcing Penwell to stop speaking. Joshua didn't need the sheriff's words. His own mind could paint a clear enough picture, and he didn't like what he saw.

Another song started, this one a soft ballad about a man aching for a woman's touch.

Joshua sat, brooding over his nearly empty cup, only half paying attention as Penwell launched into an innocuous dialogue about the perils of flat-land tourists driving on mountain roads. There had to be a way to head Chet off, some way to convince the Wassiles that going after Amy was more trouble than it was worth. Having them hanging around would only complicate things if Velavich showed up.

It would have to be something big, Joshua decided. Chet and his brothers weren't the type to be put off by threats of arrest. All three had been in and out of jail more than once. No, a deterrent for them would have to be something more definitive, more personal. Something that clearly showed Amy was off limits.

Penwell's suggestion of a bodyguard wasn't a bad idea. In fact, it would fit in with his assignment quite nicely. Except Pen's assessment of Amy was correct. Joshua couldn't see her agreeing to let some strange man shadow her every move. Hell, even he didn't like the sound of that. Not unless he was the man.

As soon as the words formed in his head, Joshua heard the mental click of a plan falling into place. Damn if the Wassiles wouldn't come in handy after all. He could use them as an excuse to get close to Amy and solve the problem of Chet's harassment at the same time. The only obstacle to such a plan would be Amy herself. Normally he liked strong-willed women, but Abe was right, little Ms. Sheridan was way too independent for her own good. If he had any hope of gaining her cooperation it would have to be in a roundabout way. The more he thought about it, however, the more he liked the idea. And he already had the perfect opportunity to set his plan into motion.

He'd planned to take Amy to dinner at a restaurant in Asheville, someplace quiet, unobtrusive, and safe. Staying in town wouldn't be as safe, but it would work out better in the long run. The possibility they were a couple would spread fast among the gossips. The Wassiles would hear, and Chet would realize he'd have to go through Joshua if he wanted to get to Amy. The only problem would be making sure Amy went along with the gossip. He couldn't see why she wouldn't. It wasn't as if there would be any truth to the rumors. She would still have her freedom, and so would he. Once he explained things to her, she'd have to see the benefits. Of course, they'd have to be seen together often which would make his real assignment that much easier.

"You've got a strange look in your eyes, Josh. If you've got a suggestion, let me hear it. But I warn you, it better be legal. I'm still an officer of the law." Penwell's lips twisted a bit on the last words, as if he might sometimes regret the restraints his position put on him.

Joshua smiled in complete sympathy with the older man. "I was just thinking that there might be a way for Amy to have a bodyguard without her knowing about it."

Penwell's eyes narrowed with interest. "Oh yeah, how?"

"I'm taking her to dinner tonight."

Brown brows liberally sprinkled with gray flew up. "Damn, you work fast. Next you'll be telling me you and Amy are engaged."

"You and Amy are engaged? Oh, Joshua, I think that's wonderful!" Marlee exclaimed loudly.

Joshua stiffened. He hadn't realized how close Marlee was or that the jukebox had gone silent. Her excited voice flew clear across the café. He could see interested ears perk up, heads swiveling in his direction.

Chet Wassile's face darkened in rage.

"Now, Marlee..." Penwell began.

"That's okay, Pen." Joshua waved him to silence, his mind working furiously. This was even better, part of him argued. This way, his constant attendance on Amy would be more than accepted, it would be assumed. And when his assignment here was over and he went back to DC, Amy would still have the protection of their bogus engagement, assuming, of course, she decided to stay in Clear Springs. Penwell gave him a curious stare as Joshua said, "It's about time Amy and I let the cat out of the bag."

"Well I should say so," Marlee agreed, grinning from ear to ear. "I can't imagine how you two have managed to keep this a secret for so long."

"So long?" Penwell asked.

"Of course. That's why she moved here, isn't it, Joshua? You and she met while you were working overseas last year and when Amy had to come back to the states before you did, she came here to wait for you. Oh, I think that's so romantic."

Joshua didn't correct Marlee's assumptions. Damn if they weren't better than he could come up with on a moment's notice. She beamed at him, then jumped as the sound of a coffee cup smashing to the floor drowned out everything else. White ceramic shards skittered across the linoleum, making a trail between the Wassile's table and Joshua's chair. The café fell silent as a tomb.

Penwell slowly turned in his seat, pinning the three brothers with a "come to prayer meeting" stare.

"Sorry," mumbled Chet, glancing down and fumbling in his pocket. "I was trying to get Miss Marlee's attention for more coffee and the cup slipped out of my hand. I'll pay for it." He slapped some money on the table and got up. With sullen glances at Joshua, his brothers followed him out the door.

The buzz of conversations picked up before the door swung completely closed. Excited conversations from the sound of them. People kept glancing in Joshua's direction. Some even grinned and waved.

Marlee patted Joshua's shoulder. "Don't you worry about those three," she said. "Everyone knows Chet's been chasing after Amy like a rabid wolf. Now we know she's yours, we'll all keep an eye on her for you. Oh, and breakfast is on me today, sweetie. Congratulations." She kissed him on the cheek and left to get a broom.

Joshua met Penwell's eyes. "Don't say it," he warned.

The sheriff's lips twitched. "I knew you liked to live dangerously Joshua, but damn."

"Yeah, well, from Chet's reaction, I'd say my gamble has more than paid off already."

"He's pissed, all right. You realize that if he's serious about Amy, he's going to be coming after you to get you out of the way."

"That's the plan."

Penwell snorted in disgust. "Hell, Joshua, couldn't you come up with anything better than that? You know homicides generate ten times their weight in paperwork."

"Who said anything about a homicide?" Certainly not him. He didn't plan on killing anyone. Yet. Whether those plans changed depended on how stupid the Wassiles really were. "As long as Chet and his brothers behave—"

"It's not the Wassiles I'm worried about." Penwell chuckled. "Amy's going to sic that dog of hers on you the moment she hears what you've done. There won't be nothing left of you but scraps."

Joshua couldn't keep from smiling a little. He could already see the outrage on her pixie-like face, the flush on her cheeks, and the fire in her blue eyes. A rush of heated anticipation warmed his blood. "Speaking of which, I guess I'd better go talk to her."

"Yeah, you do that," Penwell agreed, still chuckling. "Wouldn't look good for the bride to break off the engagement before it even gets started."

Joshua ignored the jibe. He waved to Marlee and Seth, accepted several congratulations from the other patrons, and followed Penwell outside.

He was just thinking he needed to call Kyle and Farrah, too, when he noticed the king cab four-wheel drive pickup sitting across the street. Chet Wassile stared back at him through the driver's window, his face twisted into a murderous expression.

Joshua considered himself a man of honor. That didn't mean he wasn't aware of his own nature. When it came right down to it, he'd do whatever needed to be done to complete his mission. Right now, that mission had three salient points—keep Amy alive, kill the Cobra, and make sure Chet Wassile knew Amy was permanently off limits. He met Chet's gaze, stare for stare, letting his own predatory nature leak through the good-old-boy mask he kept in place when he was home. That part of him wouldn't think twice about killing and hiding a body in some dark ravine if that's what it took to keep someone he cared about safe.

No, deep down, he wasn't a very nice man at all.

It didn't take long for Chet to get the message. He looked away quickly, started the truck, and pulled out into traffic just slow enough not to warrant the sheriff's official attention.

"Remember when I said I wasn't worried about the Wassiles?"

Joshua blinked, slipping his mask back into place before facing Penwell. "Yeah?"

The older man's eyes stared knowingly into Joshua's. "I am now."

Without another word the sheriff turned and walked away, leaving Joshua with the uncomfortable realization that Chet wasn't the only one who'd just gotten a glimpse of the Harrier.

Chapter Nine

Amy couldn't stand it anymore. She just had to go for a run. She'd been stuck in her car since early morning, doing errands. Some of which probably weren't necessary, but, hey, anything to keep herself busy and her mind off Joshua Colby.

What had she been thinking? Getting involved with the Harrier, even temporarily, was as close to suicide as she was likely to get. Letting him kiss her had been a mistake, plain and simple, one she couldn't afford to make again. If she had any sense she'd call and cancel their date for tonight, only she'd forgotten to get his cell number. Common sense told her Kyle or Farrah would probably have the number but she hadn't made up her mind to call them yet. The fresh air from a run should help clear her head and give her a chance to figure out what she should do.

Amy dressed in comfortable jeans and slipped a sweat shirt over her usual tank top. The air outside was brisk, a carryover from the cold front that had moved in last night. Mindful of Kyle's request, she took Bors with her as she headed out. He was barely limping at all, and she planned to stay on the road. No rocks, no roots, no muddy little streams. Just a nice, short, easy jog to clear her head, but not enough to put a strain on Bors' paw. Not having to worry about where to plant her next foot gave her plenty of time to think.

Anyone associated with Special Ops knew why the leader of the NightHawks was code-named the Harrier. He was a hard, cunning, and relentless soldier. A lethal warrior. She'd seen for herself just how swift and deadly he could be with that bow of his. The Harrier wasn't harmless.

Yeah, try telling that to little Katrina. The child had climbed all over him like he was her personal jungle gym. Seeing Joshua with Kyle and Farrah's kids had really thrown her for a loop. She'd never imagined someone as hard core as the NightHawks' leader could be so tender. When he'd held little Katrina, there'd been love in the man's eyes. Love, for Pete's sake! Such a contradiction. And Farrah didn't seem to see him as some kind of lethal killer, either. She had to know at least part of what Joshua's job entailed since Kyle had been Special Ops himself before he'd been injured. Yet Farrah treated Joshua with warm affection, demonstrating clearly that while she loved her husband completely, Joshua still had a special place in her heart. A sentiment fully endorsed and echoed by Kyle.

Her first assessment had been correct. Joshua Colby was indeed a member of the Fagan family. Seeing them all together last night had put an ache inside Amy that she couldn't shake. Despite being included in their often rapid-fire conversations, Amy had never felt more like an outsider.

Maybe it was time to ease back from the Fagans. Nothing good could come from letting herself get too attached, especially to the children. Unfortunately, she had a feeling she'd already crossed that line.

Still, with Joshua home, she had the perfect excuse to distance herself from the loving family. She'd miss them—Kyle's silly jokes, Farrah's sisterly advice.

Amy was an only child. The closest thing she'd ever had to siblings had been the other members of her unit. They had looked out for one another, cared for one another, just like a family. Until one of her brothers-in-arms—a man she'd thought might actually be something more to her—had betrayed everything they believed in. Betrayed her.

Even after more than a year, the pain of that betrayal still had the power to hurt her.

The sound of a racing engine drew her from the painful memories. Some idiot was coming down the mountain, driving too fast from the sound of it. She signaled Bors to fall in behind her and moved to the shoulder of the road. The engine's roar became louder as the vehicle came around the curve behind them. Amy glanced back to make sure Bors was where he was supposed to be.

A surge of adrenaline hit hard when she saw the black Jeep. Harder still when the big vehicle crossed the solid yellow line to her side of the road. She wasn't sure she was ready for another round of Joshua yet. Then she noticed that instead of slowing down to pull alongside, the Jeep accelerated, heading straight for her and Bors. Her heart slammed into overdrive.

"Bors, here!' she shouted, slapping her chest. She let the big dog's lunge knock her back as she wrapped her arms around him. Her right shoulder slammed into the rocky ground. Sharp pain flared. Bors yelped. The Jeep's engine roared, sounding right on top of them. Desperately Amy rolled, tipping her and Bors over the edge of the roadway. Gravel showered them from the spinning tires as she and Bors fell through bushes.

Amy released her grip on her dog after their first tumble. The shoulder along this area was narrow, quickly giving way to a steep hillside thick with boulders, trees, and brush. Bors would do better by himself and so would she. She let herself roll down the hill a little, hoping to put a screen between her and the road. Then she reached out, grabbing at anything to slow her fall. The first few bushes tore right through her hands, shredding skin.

She slid several more yards before her grab at something stuck. The skinny sapling shook to its roots when her weight hit.

She didn't stay still long. Rolling and crawling as quickly and quietly as she could, she moved several yards to the side. A depression beneath the low limbs of a fir tree offered her cover, and she settled her aching body into the bed of prickly needles. Lying on her stomach, Amy didn't move for a long time.

She listened, ears straining over the sound of her own rapid breathing for any hint that someone might be coming down the hill after her. She didn't dwell too long on who that someone might be. She'd only seen one black Jeep Wrangler in Clear Springs.

Instead, she used the time to isolate the ache of bruises and sting of scratches from the possibility of more damaging injuries. About the time she decided nothing was actually broken, a cold nose nudged her ankle. Bors whined softly.

Amy rolled carefully to her side. "Good boy," she whispered as the dog crawled in next to her. She patted Bors once then gave him the signals for *Quiet, Watch,* and *Enemy.* Bors immediately sank to the ground. He sniffed, scenting the air while his keen, dark eyes stared through the fir tree limbs. The rumble of his silent growl beneath her hand was comforting. Amy took another moment to catch her breath.

After ten minutes of hearing nothing more threatening than a scurrying chipmunk, Amy signaled to Bors. The dog obediently backed out of their hiding place first. Amy joined him.

Careful to make as little noise as possible, she began climbing back up the hill. It took a long time. The aches were really starting to throb by the time she could see the road. She wasn't looking forward to the long walk back to her house. Added to everything else, Bors was limping again.

Just as they reached the edge of the road, Bors' ears lay back against his head. He froze, facing the same direction the Jeep had come from, his big black body stretched out like a bird dog on point. Amy hissed quietly. Waving him back, she slipped behind the trunk of a tree and waited. Her heart pounded. For the first time in a long time, she wished she had a gun in her hand.

Again she caught the sound of an engine before the vehicle came into sight. She recognized the red pickup, but held her relief in check. She had thought she recognized the black Jeep, too, and look where that had landed her. Poised for a second dive down the hill, she stepped from behind the tree. The truck slowed almost at once. Another few feet and it slammed to a stop, tires screeching.

"Amy? Amy, girl, are you okay? Good Lord, you look a mess. What happened?" Susan Haynes threw her door open and ran to Amy. The woman's face was wrinkled in genuine concern, anxiety radiating from her as her gaze left Amy for the surrounding woods.

"I'm fine, Sue, really."

"Are you sure? You don't look fine. What happened," she repeated.

The urge to keep the black Jeep to herself was strong. Amy flicked a hand signal, calling Bors out of hiding. A small distraction, but for Clear Springs' local veterinarian, it was enough. As soon as she saw him, Susan's attention focused on the dog.

"Oh my God, what happened to Bors?" She left Amy and moved toward the limping dog making little noises of sympathy. Amy leaned against the truck and watched Sue give Bors a quick, professional exam.

"A bruised hip or strained tendon maybe. I want to x-ray him to be sure there are no fractures. Want to come with me to the clinic?"

"Yes, please."

Sue helped Bors into a large dog crate in the bed of the truck while Amy climbed stiffly into the passenger seat. Amy let Sue ramble on the ride down the mountain, paying just enough attention to respond in the appropriate places. Mostly she spent the time replaying everything in her head, trying to make sense of what had happened.

Fact one—someone had tried to kill her using a black Jeep as their weapon. There'd been no hesitation, no swerving back and forth like there would be if the vehicle had been out of control. Whoever had been driving that Jeep had come around the corner, seen her, and headed straight for her.

Fact two—that wasn't the worst part. People had tried to kill her before. It wasn't something you got used to, but you learned to cope, to deal, to evade while planning on how to escape or kill them first. No, what made her insides feel like a lump of ice was knowing the Jeep that had almost hit her looked a lot like the one she'd ridden in last night.

That brought her to fact three—she didn't want to believe for a second that the man she'd let kiss her a few hours ago had just tried to kill her. But, really, how many black Jeeps were there in Clear Springs? She couldn't remember seeing one at all until yesterday. It was just too much of a coincidence. The possibility that Joshua was working with the traitor who wanted her dead sent a flood of ice water rushing through her veins.

Desperately, she ran through her memories again, trying to recall every detail. Trying to match the dark image from last night to the split-second one she'd gotten before her world had turned upside-down. Both vehicles were big, black, with a lot of shiny chrome. Both had over-sized tires. Both had snorkels for the engine. Both had a winch on the front and a roof-rack. Both had a side spotlight.

No, wait! Joshua's had a side spotlight. The other vehicle had...

Nothing.

Such a small difference, part of her said. It wasn't enough to rule Joshua out. The light could have been removed sometime between last night and a few minutes ago. Despite the valid point, Amy latched onto the discrepancy, using it as a springboard to examine something else about the incident that bothered her. She couldn't help but wonder why someone as experienced as the Harrier would use a vehicle for a weapon. He probably knew a hundred ways far more efficient, deadly, and sure, to take her out. Why would he try something so...amateurish?

He wouldn't, she decided. Joshua Colby, aka, the Harrier, was nothing, if not a professional. He had to be to do his job. That fast, relief swept through her. The sudden release of tension left her sagging against the seat, her eyes damp, her limbs feeling weak.

It hadn't been Joshua behind the wheel. She hadn't been betrayed again.

They reached the animal clinic and Amy helped Sue get Bors inside. While the vet x-rayed Bors' hip, Amy used the restroom to wash her hands and face and check her own damage. She'd gotten off lucky. If she'd been wearing her usual tank top and shorts, her arms and legs would be a mess. As it was, she'd have plenty of black and blue places by nightfall to go with her collection of angry red scratches. Only one place worried her. The back of her right shoulder had taken the brunt of her fall. Her shirt was ripped wide revealing abraded skin and several nasty scratches. There were even a few tiny pieces of rock embedded in her bleeding flesh along with a couple of thorns.

"You should really have a doctor look at this," Sue said when she examined the wound after finishing with Bors.

Amy tried not to wince as the vet picked out another piece of gravel. "Aren't you a doctor?"

Sue snorted. "You know what I mean."

Amy craned her neck to look at the wound. "Does it need stitches?"

"No, I don't think so."

"So what would you do if this was on Bors' shoulder instead of mine?"

The vet shot her a grin. "Clean it out, smear it with antibiotic salve, and snap a cone around his neck for a couple of days."

Amy laughed. "What say we forget the cone and slap a bandage on it instead? I promise not to lick the salve off."

"Deal," Sue said.

Amy was easing back into her torn shirt when she heard a vehicle drive up.

Sue glanced out a window. "It's just Dan Penwell. I told him to come by for some hairball remedy for his cats. He's got two, you know. Cats, I mean, not hairballs. Of course Pen wouldn't have any hairballs. I mean, really, that would be just silly."

Amy eyed the nervous woman. "Just when did you tell him to come by, Sue?"

"Five-thirty. I told him five-thirty." She pointed to a clock on the wall. "See? He's very punctual."

Amy sighed. "You called him while I was in the bathroom, didn't you?"

Sue gave her an apologetic look. "Please don't be mad. You and Bors are hurt and you wouldn't tell me how you got that way. I asked three times, Amy. You just kind of grunted and stared through the windshield. I was worried. I thought maybe you were in shock. I thought maybe...maybe you had a run-in with someone."

Amy sighed again. A run-in with Chet Wassile, Sue meant. The other woman stood there, twisting her hands together. "It's all right. I'm not mad." Amy hugged her. "And no, it wasn't Chet."

Sue's breath left her in a rush. "Oh, thank God. So what really happened?"

"Come on, I might as well tell this only once." She led the way to the front waiting room, arriving just as Dan Penwell closed the front door. He took in her bedraggled appearance at a glance. His frown grew darker.

"I'm fine," Amy said, cutting him off before he got started. "Just bruised and scratched a little."

"What happened?"

"Someone tried to run me and Bors down while we were jogging."

"What?" Sue exclaimed.

"Did you see the driver?" the sheriff snapped, all business now.

"No, I was too busy taking a nose dive down the mountain."

Penwell grunted. He took a small pad and pencil from his shirt pocket. "You're lucky you got yourself stopped before you rolled to the bottom. What about the vehicle? I'm assuming you didn't get the license. What about make and model?"

"It was a black Jeep Wrangler."

His pencil froze on the pad. Dark brown eyes pinned her like a fly to a wall. "Run that by me again."

"A black Jeep Wrangler. Oversized tires, front winch, engine snorkel, roof rack. If you need a visual you can track down Joshua Colby. This one looked almost exactly like his."

"Almost?"

Amy nodded. "The one that tried to hit me didn't

have a spotlight mounted on the driver's side. I know it's only a small difference, but believe me, even though I didn't see the driver, I know it wasn't Joshua."

Amy didn't know what made it so important for her to say the words. Maybe because she'd been repeating them over and over in her head, and somehow they just slipped out. Sue and the sheriff shared a startled glance before looking at her in surprise.

"Well, of course it wasn't Joshua," Sue said quickly. "We never for a moment thought it was." The sincerity in her voice made Amy curious.

"Why not? It was a black Jeep, just like Joshua's."

The vet gave her a patient look. "You know, I forget sometimes that you're not from around here." She patted Amy on her good shoulder. "It's okay, I can see where you might have gotten the wrong impression. Joshua is kind of big and can be a bit distant at times, but everyone who knows him knows Joshua would never hurt anyone."

Amy couldn't believe what she was hearing. *The man who'd run who knew how many wet missions, wouldn't hurt anyone?* Did Joshua have everyone in Clear Springs fooled?

Sue's phone rang and she excused herself to answer it. Left alone with the sheriff, Amy waited impatiently for his next question. Her body ached and a few wet wipes would never replace a hot shower. She wanted to go home.

Dan Penwell put his pad and pencil away and rubbed his face with his hand. He stared at her a long moment before asking, "Amy, have you talked to Joshua today?" His voice sounded funny. Strained.

"No, I haven't. I've been running errands all day. Why?"

The sheriff pursed his lips, deep lines forming

between his brows.

"You should talk to him as soon as possible. In fact, I think you should come with me over to his place right now." He held a hand out, motioning with his fingers.

"Why?" Amy repeated. She took a step back. The sheriff was acting very strange.

"No!" Susan said suddenly, her voice rising in disbelief. "You're kidding! Really? I had no idea. No, I don't know when the date is. She's right here. I'll ask her and let you know. Thanks for calling, Marlee."

Distracted by the one-sided conversation, Amy didn't see the quick hand that closed around her arm. "Amy," the sheriff said, urgently. Before he could say anything else she was enveloped in one of Susan's fierce hugs.

"Amy, girl, congratulations," Sue gushed. "I can't believe it. How in the world did you keep something like this to yourself for so long?"

Amy wiggled her way out of the hug, helped in part by Penwell still holding her by the arm. "Congratulations for what?"

"On your engagement, of course. My goodness, this is so romantic. Have you and Joshua set a date yet?"

Amy froze. Her engagement? To Joshua Colby?

Sue plowed on, oblivious to Amy's sudden lack of movement, her expression changing to one of concern. "Oh my goodness, Pen, did you call Joshua to tell him about Amy's accident? I don't have his number but I'm sure Kyle does. I can call—"

The sheriff broke in. "No, that's all right, Sue. I've talked to Joshua. In fact, I'm taking Amy to him right now." He tugged on her arm.

"Wait," Amy said, freeing her arm with a quick twist. "Sue, who told you Joshua and I are engaged?"

"Marlee Borden." Sue's eyes widened suddenly.

"Oh dear, she said you and Joshua were keeping it a secret. She overheard Pen and Joshua talking about it this morning at breakfast, and, well, Joshua said it was time to let the cat out of the bag, so to speak. Don't tell me he didn't check with you first?"

Amy ground her teeth. "No, he didn't." She turned to the sheriff, not caring if he saw how angry she was. Apparently, he was in on whatever wild scheme Joshua had cooked up. That made him a target.

"You and Joshua discussed our *engagement*? Don't you think it would have been wise to include me in this little conversation?"

The sheriff met her gaze evenly, impressing her despite her irritation with him. "Joshua left right afterward to talk to you. Guess he didn't catch you before you left on your errands."

Susan patted her arm. "Now, Amy, don't be too angry with Joshua. Men just don't have it in them to be able to keep secrets like us women. Don't look at me like that Dan Penwell. Amy's been with us for a good year now and never breathed a word. Joshua couldn't even keep quiet for a day. I don't blame you one bit for being upset, Amy. You go on and let Pen take you to Joshua." She winked broadly. "Rant a little, rave a little, give him a good scold and then forgive him. The makeup sex should be phenomenal."

Amy couldn't keep from blushing if her life depended on it. She didn't doubt for one minute that sex with Joshua would be phenomenal. The man was attractive, his body sexy, and from the brief sample she'd had of his technique before Bors had interrupted them last night, he knew how to please a woman. Not that she had any intention of finding out for sure.

Makeup sex? Hell, he'd be lucky to be able to have any kind of sex by the time she got through with him. Not all the color in her cheeks was from embarrassment.

She pasted a smile on her face and let Sue hug her. After promising to pick up Bors the next day, she walked calmly out of the clinic. Never once did she look at Dan Penwell, not even when he opened the passenger door of his patrol car for her. Smart man that he was, he didn't say anything until they were on the road.

"It's for Chet's benefit, Amy. Joshua thought Chet would back off and leave you alone if he knew you were already spoken for."

She drummed her nails on the armrest, staring out the side window to keep her eyes off the shotgun in the rack by her knee. "That doesn't make it right. He did this without asking me, without saying a single word to me. Damn it, I only met the man yesterday." She clamped her lips together to keep from screaming. How dare he walk in and try to take over her life by fighting her battles for her?

"He said you and he had a date tonight."

Her head snapped around. "Not anymore."

"Amy—"

"Stop the car, Sheriff."

He blew out a loud breath. "Amy, listen—"

"Am I under arrest?"

The car slowed. "I could arrest you for your own protection."

"If you want to protect someone, I suggest you go arrest Joshua." She opened the door while the car was still rolling. Penwell swore and slammed the brakes hard. Amy shot out, ignoring his calls to wait. She needed to get away. She was so mad she was about to explode and didn't want Penwell to get caught in the fall out. Joshua, however, was another matter.

She set off up the mountain, breaking her own trail until the brush thinned. Half an hour later her path cut across an animal trail and she fell into it, not caring at the moment if it belonged to deer or something with claws and teeth. She had claws and teeth, too, as a certain high-handed harrier hawk was about to find out.

Chapter Ten

It was almost dark by the time Amy reached Joshua's cabin. She was hot and sweaty and still mad as hell. Evidently, letting Joshua get away with the bow incident had been a mistake. She should have told him then that she didn't want or need his help. She could fight her own battles, damn it. She didn't need anyone, least of all someone who wouldn't be hanging around long, putting in his two cents worth. Of course, telling everyone he'd been secretly engaged to her for months was a lot more than just two cents worth of interference. This was going to cause her no end of trouble.

She ran up the steps, and started pounding on the door. "Joshua Colby, you come out right this minute! I've got a few things to say to you and you're darn well going to listen. Joshua!" She stepped back and waited.

Clenching her fists, she gave the door a good hard kick before stomping off back down the steps. She started muttering cuss words she rarely spoke aloud when she saw that his black Jeep was missing from beneath the pole barn. So, he wasn't home. Probably avoiding her. Well, too bad, she'd just wait for him.

Wanting to wait out of sight so she could ambush him when he got out of his Jeep, she headed for the back of the cabin. She plopped down on the back steps, rested her arms on her knees and her forehead on her arms.

Two minutes later, she realized her mistake. Moving had kept her muscles warm, kept her from feeling how sore they were from her tumble down the mountain. Every ache and pain, however minor, made itself known with glaring clarity. Groaning, she forced herself to stand, then walk. She needed to keep moving, otherwise she wouldn't be in any shape to teach Joshua a lesson once he decided to show up.

She paced from porch to tree line, then back to the porch. It took her three circuits to catch the faint sound of splashing water coming from beyond the trees. Curious, she pushed her way into the woods. She didn't think the eastern branch of the river cut through this high up. Maybe it was a spring-fed stream. There were several of them scattered throughout the valley. A little cool water would definitely be welcome.

The dense trees thinned almost at once, giving way to a narrow swath of low brush and bare rock. Surprised, she came to a stop. She hadn't realized Joshua's cabin sat so close to the edge of the cliff. Clear Springs valley spread out below, the view enough to take her breath away. Riveted by the sight, the photographer in her crying for her camera, it was a full minute before she became aware of the glint of water just below.

She eased closer to the edge and looked down. Despite the rocks and sand covering the bottom visible through the crystal clear water, the large, tear-drop shaped pool couldn't possibly be natural. Not with the areas of bare, flat stone extending out from both sides, looking for all the world like a custom-made patio. A second look showed her deck chairs and a table in the same slate gray as the stone. She tried to see more, but her view was blocked by a wide stone ledge a little more than half-way down.

Burning with curiosity, Amy walked to the left to get a better view. Sunlight glinted off something smooth and shiny set into the mountainside. Glass.

A wall of tinted glass. The dark surface started about twelve feet from the top of the cliff and extended down at a slight angle to the ledge in one smooth, uninterrupted flow. Admiring the craftsmanship and design, Amy spotted some steps leading up from the ledge, seemingly carved right into the cliff face. With a little searching, she discovered where they began.

One foot on the top step, she glanced back toward the cabin. Joshua might be home any minute. But which home? Something told her that tiny cabin of his was nothing more than a decoy. This hidden mountain oasis she'd discovered was Joshua's real house. Built into the cliff face, it extended at least three stories below the level of the cabin. He probably wouldn't appreciate her trespassing in his private domain.

Too bad. Why should she worry about what he thought? He'd obviously given no consideration to her feelings before linking them together in a mock engagement.

She negotiated the steep steps down to the ledge that turned out to be an elegant stone balcony. Cupping her hands around her face, she pressed against the warm glass wall. The dark tint made it impossible to see details. All she was sure of was that the room on the other side was deep and wide, and extended up another story.

The setting sun hot on her back, Amy turned and walked out to the edge of the balcony. There was no rail, and the middle of the balcony extended out over the pool. She wondered if Joshua ever dove into the pool from here. She would, assuming the pool was deep enough.

Off to the right, a second flight of stone steps left the balcony and curved down to the flagstone patio. Amy gazed longingly at the water sparkling in the large pool. The pool's rounded end began not that far from the house. Water boiled up slightly in the middle. Through the ripples she could just make out what appeared to be a grill set into the sand and rock bottom. She'd been right, it was a spring. Her admiring gaze followed the flow of the water to the teardrop's narrow point. It looked like the water spilled right over the edge of the cliff.

She glanced back at the house set into the hillside. The wall of tinted windows that she'd bet money was bullet proof was framed by several smooth logs of dark wood. Across the top logs, the word "REFUGE" was carved in big, bold letters.

Refuge? Okay, she'd buy that. Though Aerie might be more appropriate. The view of the valley from anywhere inside would be magnificent.

Her gaze shifted back to the patio. But a pool? Who would have ever thought the man would have a spring-fed swimming pool in his backyard?

The sparkling water made Amy even more conscious of her over-heated body. The hike from Penwell's car to Joshua's house was rough, and she'd taken most of it at an angry run. The water called to her, promising relief. Tall trees flanked both the house and the pool, screening the area from prying eyes without obscuring the view. It was outrageously gorgeous and sinfully restful.

She was headed down the steps to the patio before she realized it. She paused half-way down, glancing nervously at the house. *He's not here, stupid*, she told herself. If he was, the Jeep would be here, right? He would have heard her pounding on the door and screaming at the top of her lungs, right? There was no way to tell when he'd be back.

Having convinced herself, she ran down the last few steps, carefully stripping off her top as she went. Her shoulder was sore, a few sharp twinges shooting from the wide scrape next to the strap of her sports bra. The pain wasn't nearly enough to keep her from enjoying a dip in Joshua's pool. He owed her that much.

A few seconds later and socks, shoes, and jeans joined her shirt on a lounge chair. She reached back to carefully peel off the bandage Susan had slapped on. Dried blood stuck to the gauze and Amy hissed as it pulled away from her skin, opening the shallow wounds. She twisted around to see how bad it was. Blood seeped from the deepest scratches, already creating thin red lines. She hesitated, then thought, what the hell. The current from the spring should clear the blood from the water and the cold would help slow the bleeding. She placed the bandage carefully on the table to keep it dry and walked to the edge of the pool.

She dove into the water and came up gasping, as much from the slap of cold against her heated skin as the zing of pain from her shoulder. Setting the pain aside, she started swimming. Nothing, she decided, had ever felt so good.

Her face still felt too warm from her run and she flipped over onto her stomach. She spread her arms and legs in a dead-man float. Lifting her head, she took a deep breath, then relaxed into the water's embrace. After a few seconds, she began releasing little trickles of air through her nose. Her body adjusted to the shift in buoyancy, settling deeper and deeper into the water. Floating like this reminded her of flying in her dreams. She loved the peaceful sensation, and had trained herself to stay under for up to four minutes, five if she remained completely motionless. There was no need to push herself that far tonight. She'd rise at four minutes, maybe do another four before she got out. It just felt so good to be surrounded by the cool water.

****

Joshua turned off the engine with an irritable twist of his wrist after parking his Jeep. He'd been one step behind Amy all day. If he didn't know better, he'd think she was avoiding him on purpose. For a moment he just sat there staring through the trees at the sun setting over the tops of the low mountain range across the valley. It should have given him a sense of peace, like it always did, but for some reason he had the niggling feeling that all was not right. He realized the uncomfortable feeling had been creeping its way up between his shoulders ever since he'd turned off the main road. Probably Amy wishing he'd dropped off the side of the mountain, he told himself grimly.

She had to have found out about his claim of being his fiancée by now. With her strong, independent spirit, she was bound to take the idea badly. But he'd had little choice. Chet wanted her. It didn't matter that she'd told him no on more than one occasion. Joshua knew the man. If Chet ever realized he'd have to take her by force if he really wanted her, he would and worry about calming her down later. Except now, Chet knew Joshua had claimed her. That probably wouldn't stop him completely, but at least now he'd have to come after Joshua first.

He rubbed the back of his neck a few times, trying to get the hairs to settle down. The thought that maybe Chet had already taken the bait tripped through his mind setting off a dozen warning buzzers in his head.

He looked around at his cabin and yard again, scanning for anything unusual or out of place. Everything seemed normal enough. Still, he was on full alert as he slipped out of the Jeep. He walked to the edge of the yard where he paused to listen.

An eagle's lonely call echoed over the valley followed by the frantic scurrying of chipmunks diving for cover. Up in the trees, cardinals and jays took turns calling back and forth. The normal sounds of nature were reassuring. Slowly, bit by bit, the bunched muscles in his shoulders finally relaxed. Maybe he was just imagining things.

The sunset drew him to the cliff. He didn't plan to stay long since he still had to find Amy, so instead of going through the cabin, he took the narrow trail through the woods and descended the steps to the stone balcony. He stopped at the edge, watching the last rays bathe the sky with streaks of orange, pink, and gold. The approach of darkness triggered the solar sensors he'd turned on yesterday. Pale lights bloomed below, some scattered around the patio, others in the pool itself. When the sun had slipped completely out of sight, Joshua glanced down at his man-made oasis.

The half-naked body floating motionless at the bottom of the pool sent his heart into overdrive. Then the frantic hammering slammed to a complete stop as air left his lungs in a rush. He recognized that halo of dark hair.

He tore off his jacket as he sprinted to the center of the balcony hanging over the pool. When he noticed the trail of blood drifting up from her shoulder, he let out a string of curses Kyle would be proud of. Knowing he was too late—he'd wasted precious time wandering around his cabin—he launched himself from the balcony. The cold water didn't even register as he kicked to reach the bottom. He was too cold inside, too sick with the knowledge that he'd failed his mission. Failed *her*.

Grabbing hold of Amy with both hands, he twisted and shoved off the bottom. He didn't realize she was fighting him until they broke the surface, both of them gasping for air. Nails raked his arm just as an elbow flew back toward his face. Joshua ducked his head and let her go. She twisted around, swiping the hair out of her eyes, and glared.

"Just what in blazes do you think you're doing?"

she demanded.

The outrage in her voice was the sweetest sound Joshua had ever heard in his life. He even welcomed the angry fire flashing in her blue eyes. God, she was beautiful. And alive!

He couldn't help it. With a powerful kick, he closed the distance between them and captured her head between his palms. Pulling her close, he crushed her lips beneath his.

She instantly stilled.

For all of three seconds Joshua lost himself in the moment, in the feel of her soft, wonderfully alive lips. Then a subtle shift in her body warned him things were about to get violent. He braced himself just before her feet caught him low in the stomach. He winced, her toes digging in perilously close to his personal property. She used his body like a spring board, pushing away from him while shoving him under. She was half-way across the pool when he came up for air.

"Amy!" He dove after her, a cold anger growing inside him. She still had blood dripping from her shoulder.

"You stay the hell away from me, Josh Colby. Just because I was using your pool doesn't give you the right to maul me." She braced her arms against the lip of the pool, easily lifting her body out.

He snagged her around the waist and pulled her back in. They went under again. She tried to turn as they surfaced, but he crowded her against the side of the pool. In rapid succession he dodged a backwards head butt to his face, an elbow jab, and a kick to his groin. He pinned her legs with his, captured her wrists, and plastered his body against hers until she had no room to maneuver or gain leverage.

"Be still, Amy, you're hurt. How'd you get hurt? Who hurt you?"

Silence. Of course she insisted on being difficult.

Joshua shifted his hold on her wrists, holding both in one hand and freeing the other so he could examine her shoulder.

The sight of her blood leaking from torn skin sent a red haze of anger over his eyes. He felt like slamming his fist into something, or better yet, someone. Only the fact that the wound looked like nothing more than a bad abrasion and not the bullet hole he'd first imagined made it possible for him to calm down at all.

He ran his fingers lightly around the tender flesh marred by the deep scratches. They'd been tended by someone. Cleaned and slathered with ointment, some of which still clung to her skin.

The gut wrenching fear wasn't gone yet, not completely, but with his body pressed against her bare skin, fear was quickly being replaced by an altogether different feeling. One that was almost as uncomfortable in their present circumstances. Her breathing sounded as ragged as his.

"Who hurt you?" he demanded again.

"Let me go, Joshua." She turned her head to look at him over her shoulder. Joshua almost groaned. Her kissable lips were only an inch away. No way could he resist that.

He met her angry gaze, not bothering to hide his intent. Whatever she saw in his eyes caused her ragged breathing to catch. When it started again, her breaths were a little slower, deeper, and almost silent. Like a wild animal trying to hide from a predator. Except, right now, she had nowhere to run.

He leaned forward slowly, never taking his eyes off her. The kiss was slow and languid, with barely any tongue. Not what he wanted, but he sensed anything more would trigger her fight or flight instincts again.

He broke the long kiss, then went back for one, two, three, quick ones before raising his head. "Tell me who hurt you, sweetheart."

The corners of her lips curved up slightly. "Pretty interesting interrogation method you have there. Does it usually get the results you're looking for?"

"Every damn time."

Some of the humor left her eyes. "Hate to break your perfect record, but it isn't working *this* time."

"It is if you want out of this pool."

"What?"

"You heard me. We're not moving until you tell me how you got hurt. Now, I can stay in here for about three days if necessary. How about you?" The water was about 70 degrees right now, but would get colder as the night progressed. He doubted she could last more than an hour.

Her gaze narrowed. "If I didn't have better things to do..."

"Yes?"

She blew out a deep, exasperated breath. "It was an accident, okay, just a stupid accident."

"What kind of accident?"

"Nothing that need concern you." She tried to wiggle free again. Despite the cold water, his body reacted to the sweet friction of her backside brushing back and forth against him. She had to have felt his sudden interest because she immediately stilled.

Joshua closed his eyes, fighting to gather what little self control he had left. Erotic pictures of what he'd like to do to her fought back, flashing through his head.

Amy naked, stretched out on the warm flagstones, lean legs dangling in the pool, him standing in the water, his face buried between her legs...

Amy naked, bent over the cushions of a deck chair, him behind her, pumping in and out of her sweet heat...

Amy naked…

A shudder shook his body, and he bit back a groan. Damn it all to hell, he knew better than to let his imagination run wild. He had to remember that although he was home, he was working. Amy Sheridan was just another mission. He couldn't allow her to be anything more.

He felt her body begin to tremble and opened his eyes. Her head was bowed over the edge of the pool.

Shame filled him. How the hell had he let things get so out of hand so fast? He released her wrists. Other than the slight trembling of her body, she didn't move. He ran a shaky hand over the wet silk of her hair, trying to calm them both. He had to pull himself together, marshal his arguments. Convincing her to accept their fake engagement wasn't going to be easy, and he had a feeling he'd just made it all that much harder.

"Come on," he said gently. "Let's get you dry."

He swung her up in his arms and deposited her on the flagstones. She rolled right out of his arms and to her feet in one smooth motion.

Damn, the woman moved as fluidly as the water dripping from her body. She walked away and Joshua pulled himself up and out. Standing, he began unbuttoning his wet shirt, all the while keeping an eye on her.

Hell, he couldn't look away. Her soaked underwear didn't leave much to the imagination. The hard little nipples of her breasts were like twin mountain peaks pushing up from the smooth plain of her wet sports bra. His gaze shot to the junction of her legs. Her white panties were almost transparent yet he couldn't see a hint of dark thatch. Did that mean she was bare?

The rush of naked lust kindled by that thought hit him like a sniper's bullet, unexpected and deadly. For a moment, he couldn't breathe.

When she started to pull her clothes on he cleared his throat. "There's a towel in the bin behind the chair."

She paused, then went to the storage bin and pulled out a towel. Paused again, and pulled out a second towel, which she flung at him. He caught it before it slammed into his face.

"Thanks."

"You're welcome."

"We need to talk."

"You think?"

Joshua wanted to chuckle at her thick sarcasm, but held it back. He could sense she was still pretty angry with him. Draping his wet shirt over the back of a chair, he said, "Come inside."

She froze with her back to him, the towel over her head as she dried her hair. She flipped back a corner of the terry cloth and looked at him over her shoulder. "Why?" Her narrowed eyes were full of suspicion. He didn't blame her.

"Because we need to talk and we'll be more comfortable inside. Because I have a robe you can wear while we toss your clothes in the dryer. Because I promised you dinner—"

"I'm not going out with you."

"Did I say anything about going out? We'll eat here."

Her brows shot up. "Eat what?"

Such a loaded question. Joshua literally had to force his mind out of the gutter where it had happily fallen...again. "Steak, baked potato. Behave yourself and I might even throw in dessert."

She glared at him, but didn't say a word. After wrapping the towel around her body, she snatched up her clothes and marched up to him until he could feel her warm breath against his bare chest. His cock, on its way down, immediately perked up.

"Fine. After almost drowning me, you owe me a

steak dinner. *With* dessert. And don't expect me to do any of the cooking or cleaning up."

"Now you're being funny." He reached out and rubbed a lock of her hair between his fingers. "Why on earth would I let you anywhere near my carving knives? I'll admit I haven't handled things today with my usual finesse, but I'm not a complete idiot."

She knocked his hand away and stepped back.

He could tell she was fighting not to smile. Her lips finally won the battle, but it wasn't the same smile that sucker punched him every time. In fact, coupled with that little glitter in her eyes, he immediately went on alert.

"That's debatable," she said. "If you think a little food is going to get you off the hook for our *fake* engagement, I'd say your complete idiocy is pretty much a given."

He rubbed the bridge of his nose. "Ah. Heard about that, did you?"

He turned toward the house, hoping she'd follow so he wouldn't have to throw her over his shoulder. He watched her reflection in the wall of windows, breathing a little easier when she started after him.

"Yes, I heard. And I'd like to know what the hell you were thinking. Is this some crazy, back woods custom I'm not aware of? One kiss and you think we're engaged?"

He unlocked the door with a press of his palm to the ID plate. "No," he said, holding the door open for her. "It's a bit more complicated than that."

She must have heard the seriousness in his voice, because she stopped right next to him, her gaze searching his face. "I'm not going to like this, am I?"

He placed a hand on the small of her back and nudged her inside. "Probably not at first. But you're smart. I'm hoping, with a little time, patience, and a slice of cheesecake, you'll see the merits of keeping up the pretense. At least for a while."

"I don't like lying to friends."

"Neither do I. But we both know life isn't perfect. Sometimes lying is necessary." He pointed as he started up the stairs to his room. "You can use that bathroom. There's a robe in the left-hand closet and a washer and dryer in the right. Feel free to take a hot shower if you want. It'll take a few minutes for me to change and get the steaks ready for the grill."

He didn't wait to see if she took him up on his offer. He had to trust her some time. Besides, if she tried to leave, she'd find the door locked. All the doors. And he had no intention of deactivating the house locks until she fell in with his plans.

Well, maybe not all his plans.

He had no business working out scenarios where he could get that lithe little body of hers pressed up against him again. Preferably with both of them naked. He needed to shove such designs into a mental drawer and label it OFF LIMITS, because that's what she was. Totally and completely off limits.

Yeah, try telling that to his dick.

Chapter Eleven

Amy stayed in the shower a long time, trying to get her thoughts in order. Nothing had gone as planned. She hadn't found Joshua and lambasted him for making a decision concerning her that he had no business making. Oh, no, he'd found *her*. Not only that, but he'd found her half-naked in his pool. She'd been in a vulnerable position, a situation she hated with a passion.

But he hadn't taken advantage of her. Not really. Oh, he'd pushed and pulled her around a bit, threatened a little. Kissed her. But, all in all, she thought he'd shown remarkable restraint under the circumstances. In fact, she was surprised to find herself a little...disappointed. He was nothing like what she expected.

Of course, the night was still young. There was plenty of time left for him to live up to his ruthless reputation. Which meant she needed to live up to hers. The Raven was known for being stubborn when it came to getting what she wanted. And Amy wanted answers.

The smell of baking bread hit her when she opened the bathroom door a few minutes later. She breathed in the yeasty smell, trying not to whimper. Fresh baked bread was one of her weaknesses. Amy followed her nose to the brightly lit area at one end of the great room.

The open, slightly elevated space was split, kitchen to the right, dining to the left. Everything in the kitchen was shiny stainless steel. The appliances, the cabinets, the counters. The only color was the red pots hanging from hooks over the center island and the wine in the two glasses in Joshua's hands. He held one out to her as she took the three steps up and into the kitchen. "Truce?"

She'd already decided a cease fire was probably a good idea. The dip in the pool and the long shower had given her temper time to cool. Logic told her Joshua would have to have a damn good reason for starting the engagement rumor. The Harrier wasn't known for irrational behavior.

"Truce," she agreed, accepting the glass.

His answering smile sent a strange fluttering through her stomach. Oh, hell no. She wasn't going there.

Taking a sip of wine, she moved to the other side of the island, away from temptation. That first sip surprised her. Instead of something strong and full-bodied, the wine was a light, sparkling merlot, chilled, just the way she liked it.

"This is good."

He tossed her a grin. "Glad you like it. Find a seat and enjoy. Dinner will be ready in a few more minutes." He set his wine down and moved to an indoor grill where two steaks sizzled. She wiggled up onto one of the tall chairs at the island bar, watching him check on the food.

"While we're waiting," he said, going over to an industrial-sized refrigerator and pulling out the makings of a salad. "Would you please tell me how your hurt your shoulder? Don't know if you could tell looking in the mirror, but that whole area is already black and blue. Looks like you took a pretty bad fall."

Amy twitched the shoulder in question, wincing a little at the pain. She'd found a first-aid kit under the bathroom sink and doctored the scrapes as best she could before applying another bandage. And yes, she'd seen the multi-colored mess along with a few other bruises she hadn't been aware of earlier.

Joshua glanced up at her from chopping tomatoes. "Amy?"

She drew in a deep breath and blew it out slowly. Penwell would probably tell him anyway. "Bors and I went jogging—"

"Did you meet up with Chet?"

"No, it wasn't Chet—"

"Someone else attacked you? Who was it?" He leaned toward her, completely ignoring the vegetables, his knuckles white on the handle of the knife.

Tired of his interruptions, Amy slapped a hand down on the steel counter. "If you'd let me talk for more than a second at a time maybe I could tell you I don't know who it was because I didn't see the driver of the black Jeep Wrangler that ran me and Bors off the road." With a huff, she sat back in her seat and crossed her arms. Damn, the man could push her buttons.

His eyes narrowed, sending a shiver down her spine. Every nuance of his body told her Joshua wasn't in the kitchen with her anymore. The Harrier was.

"Details," he snapped coldly.

"It's none of your business."

He deliberately laid the knife on the counter and rounded the island slowly, never taking his eyes off her. Every move of his body was smooth, every step the glide of a predator on the hunt. A thrill ran through her at his approach. Talk about pushing buttons.

He came to a stop, the tee shirt covering his rock hard stomach brushing her knees as he leaned over her, caging her, his hands gripping the arms of her chair. "You will tell me everything I want to know, and you'll do it now."

"And if I don't?"

The smile he gave her sent a rush of heat through her, pooling low in her belly. "You only got a taste of my interrogation methods outside. Do you really want more?"

The sudden jolt of desire hit Amy right between her legs, making her throb. She could feel herself getting wet. For a few insane seconds, she was actually tempted to make him follow through with that threat. Without conscious thought, she found herself leaning forward slightly, her eyes locked with his.

Something over near the ovens buzzed loudly. Other than a slight tightening around his eyes, Joshua didn't move from his position over her. The repetitious sound, however, jerked at Amy's awareness enough for her self-preservation to kick in. Dear God, she was almost begging the man to kiss her.

She reversed direction at once, leaning back in the chair. "Sounds like the food is done." When he still didn't move, she said, "I like my steak rare, please, not burnt to a crisp."

"I have more steaks."

"Why are you being such an ass?"

"Because it's my nature." His lips finally smiled, but the hardness of his eyes didn't change. "Last chance, sweetness. Don't make me get rough."

The timer continued to buzz emphatically. Amy licked her lips. She could push more, but didn't see that doing so would get her anywhere but in trouble. Especially when his dark gaze shifted to lock on her lips. "All right," she said, wincing inside when the words came out sounding like a husky surrender instead of a damn-it-to-hell compromise. She cleared her throat. "I'll give you the not so gory details while you're rescuing my steak."

"You go first. I promise to keep the interruptions to a minimum this time." He straightened, but waited until she started talking before moving toward the ovens.

"As I said, Bors and I went for a run. We stuck to the road to keep the strain off his paw. About a mile from the house I heard a vehicle coming up from behind us. It was a big black Jeep, just like yours." She paused, thinking he'd interrupt her at that point, ask her a question, confirm that it wasn't him, something. But he didn't say a word as he worked at plating the food. He just nodded for her to continue.

"By the time I realized the vehicle was crossing the center line and accelerating, I had just enough time to grab Bors and throw us both off the road. We tumbled a bit, got ourselves stopped, then climbed back up."

He looked at her sharply, but still didn't say a word. He didn't have to. The look in his eyes said it all for him. Amy shrugged. "I'm not a fool, and the road was the fastest way home. I made sure to wait a while to see if anyone was coming down to finish the job before moving. The road was empty when Bors and I got to the top. Susan Haynes drove up a minute later. Bors was limping, so we went with her to her clinic. She called the sheriff, who showed up about the same time Sue got the gossip call about our supposed engagement."

She tried to give him the evil eye at that point, but he had his back to her, setting a covered bread basket and two small bowls of salad on the dining table next to their filled plates. Amy snagged both wine glasses off the counter and slipped off her chair to join him. She thought she'd moved without a sound, but he didn't seem surprised to see her standing so close when he turned around. He took their glasses and added them to the table before helping her into her seat.

"How did you know it wasn't my Jeep?"

"What makes you think I do?"

****

Joshua glanced sharply at Amy as he sat down. He wished he could see past that cool façade of hers. Past that politely inquisitive gaze and into her mind. Did she really think he'd try to kill her?

He snorted to himself as he shook out his napkin, realizing he already knew the answer. "Because I seriously doubt I would have found you taking advantage of my pool if you thought for even a second that I tried to kill you. Admit it, you'd have been waiting for me with a gun in your hand, ready to make me pay."

He cut a bite of steak and shoved it into his mouth with a sense of satisfaction. Any woman who'd spit in the Cobra's eye by turning him in would have no trouble taking up for herself.

He looked up, expecting to see Amy nodding in smug agreement. What he saw instead almost made him choke on his food. What the hell?

Amy sat rigid in her chair, arms wrapped around herself, as if trying to hold herself together. Her face was drained of color, as white as the robe engulfing her body. Her blue eyes were closed.

Joshua set down his knife and fork. "Amy?"

She didn't move.

"Amy!"

Her body jerked. She drew in a deep breath, as if she hadn't been breathing before, and opened her eyes. "Excuse me," she said, carefully unwrapping her arms and laying her napkin on the table. "I'm not as hungry as I thought." She stood.

Joshua was around the table before she could take more than a step, his hands going to her shoulders to stop her.

"Amy, what's wrong? What did I say?" It couldn't be because he'd nailed her character.

She shook her head, still refusing to look at him.

"It's not your fault. It's just...I don't like guns."

Her quiet words shocked him. She didn't like guns? That whole frozen in her chair, bloodless face, and shivering body was because she didn't like guns? As Kyle would say, not effin' likely. There had to be more to it. And Joshua bet he knew what. "Velavich."

She gasped, her head whipping up so she could look at him. "How do you know about him?" she whispered.

Joshua mentally cursed a blue streak. He hadn't realized he'd spoken the bastard's name aloud. Now that he had, there was no taking it back. He'd have to come clean.

"Come on, let's sit on the couch. We can warm the food up later."

He was glad she didn't fight him when he led her to the great room. This was going to be bad enough without another physical confrontation. He settled her into a corner of the comfy leather couch and took a seat a full foot away from her. She tucked her legs under her, looking like a kid huddled inside the over-sized robe.

"You know Velavich was part of a unit in the Special Ops division of the military."

She nodded slowly, her eyes wary. "Commander Aberashoff debriefed me."

A personal debriefing with the head man? Unusual, but in this case, not unexpected. It wasn't every day a unit was disbanded.

"Yeah, well, I'm the head of another one of those SO units. Aberashoff sent me here because Velavich is on the move."

She stiffened a little, but he didn't get the hysterical response he expected. Her only reaction was to dip her head so he couldn't see her eyes.

"You think he's coming here." The soft words were a statement, not a question.

121

Joshua leaned forward. The urge to take her in his arms and soothe her was a steady beat pulsing through his body. "We don't know for sure. All we know is that he's in the states. The unit tracking him lost him in Atlanta. That's too close for comfort.

"The commander sent me here to keep an eye on you until we can confirm Velavich's whereabouts. If he does decide to show up here, you'll be well protected, Amy, I promise. My men are coming in to help. He won't get anywhere near you, sweetheart."

Head still bowed, she said, "That's the reason for the fake engagement."

"Not entirely."

Her head snapped up. There was some fear in her pretty blue eyes, but not as much as he'd expected. There was something else, too, but he couldn't place it. "Then, why," she demanded. "It makes no sense. You'd have been more effective as a guard if Adrik didn't know about you. Why put yourself out in the open?"

"To keep Chet from making a dumb-ass mistake. The idiot never knew when to take no for an answer. If he thought you were already taken, maybe he'd get the message and leave you alone."

Her look turned incredulous. "You set yourself up as a target for a trained killer just to try and scare off a bully? Are you out of your mind? You just put two targets on your back instead of one. What kind of strategy is that?"

Joshua felt himself flush a little. Put that way, it did sound kind of stupid. Not at all his usual sound planning. But then, he hadn't been thinking straight from the moment he'd met her. "Hopefully the kind that'll keep you safe even after I've taken care of Velavich and gone back into the field. As long as you keep the rumor going, Chet should leave you alone." He forced himself to shrug. "When you do meet someone you're interested in, just tell everyone you asked me to change jobs so I could be home more, and you broke it off with me when I refused. Believe me, they'll understand. That'll leave you free to be with whomever you want."

He had to stop speaking at that point. For some insane reason, the thought of Amy being with some unknown man made him see red.

Her laugh sounded far too brittle. "Well, damn, Joshua. You've thought of everything, haven't you? Got my whole life planned out for me. Looks like all I have to do is sit back and enjoy the ride."

"I'm trying to keep you alive."

She came out of the corner in another of her fluid moves, one second curled into a tight ball, the next leaning so close to him he could smell his soap on her skin. It was all he could do to keep his hands from reaching out and pulling her into his lap. She would feel so good there.

"This may come as a shock to you, but I can keep myself alive. Been doing it for years. Go back and tell my...dear friend, the commander, that he's a little behind the times. I haven't needed a babysitter since I was ten."

He couldn't have stopped himself from grabbing her when she started to get up if he'd wanted to. The little spit-fire was being totally unreasonable. Just because he hadn't consulted with her, she was willing to take a risk with her life? Not if he had anything to say about it.

He flipped her around and had her stretched out on the couch under him before she could even gasp. She fought, but not, he thought, as hard as she could have. After several misses, he succeeded in grabbing her wrists, pinning her arms over her head. He pressed his legs and hips into her trying to keep her still. The bottom of her robe fell open in the struggle, freeing one of her legs. He tensed. If she knew anything about fighting, there were several different ways she could cause him pain with just her foot alone. But as soon as her leg curled around his, putting her heel in the perfect strike position, she stilled. She stared up at him.

He checked her eyes for fear, thinking it would be a good thing if she were a little afraid of him this time. Fear would make her more malleable. Even though the thought of being anything remotely like Chet Wassile made him sick to his stomach, he'd bully Amy into falling in with his plans if he had to.

But the emotion swirling in her eyes was a long way from fear. Blood started pounding in his ears, a flood of it rushing straight to his groin. Damn if she wasn't as turned on as he was. He ran his tongue across his bottom lip. "I want to kiss you."

She stared at his mouth. "More interrogation? I've told you everything already."

"I doubt that. But, no, no interrogation. Just a kiss."

"There's no such thing."

She was probably right. He dropped his head anyway and brushed her lips with his. Once, twice.

Her warm breath rushed out over his skin, effectively setting him on fire. With a low groan, he settled his mouth over her parted lips and licked his way inside. She tasted even better than he remembered. Fresh, like the first snow on the mountain in winter. Hot, like the fiery sky of a summer sunset. Everything about her whispered home to him.

****

Amy knew she should push him away. Her common sense screamed that she needed to leave. Not just his house, but the entire valley. She should be putting plenty of distance between her and Joshua before it was too late. Before he hurt her worse than Adrik had. But she also knew she wasn't going anywhere. She was sure he'd walk away from her once he found out she wasn't the same as Farrah—innocent and pure and harmless. But right now, he wanted her. And heaven help her, she wanted him right back.

He started to raise his head, his body tensing, as if he was going to get up. Amy wanted to growl. He was so not going to get her all hot and bothered and leave her hanging. She tightened her leg around his hip and grabbed a handful of dark hair at the same time to pull his mouth back to hers.

He grunted in surprise, but caught on quickly. The man was definitely fast on the uptake. His tongue began stroking repeatedly into her mouth.

After a few breathless seconds, his hips picked up the motion. Advance and retreat, advance and retreat, each move nudging aside her robe a little more until she felt the roughness of his jeans against her most sensitive skin. The sensation was so damn sexy her hips bucked on his next down stroke, seating the hard, denim-covered length of him right between her wet folds. Both of them froze.

Joshua raised his head, his hot gaze locking with hers. "How far do you want this to go, Amy?"

Chapter Twelve

Amy nibbled on her bottom lip, giving Joshua's question serious thought. His eyes shot to her mouth, and his body jerked a little, but held steady. She could feel his locked muscles straining, and felt a rush of admiration. He could have easily kept going.

A button flicked open, a zipper tugged down while he was kissing her, and he'd have been inside her. She probably wouldn't have stopped him. Correction, she definitely wouldn't have stopped him. But he'd stopped all on his own, giving her the power, acknowledging her right to shut him down. Only problem was, if she did that, she'd be shutting herself down, too.

"Amy?"

Guess she hadn't learned her lessons as well as she thought. "Condom?" she asked, wishing it wasn't necessary. Unfortunately, she knew exactly where she was in her cycle—an old habit from her SO days. Having unprotected sex for the next week would so be tempting fate.

Joshua's eyes closed, his head dropping until his forehead rested against hers. "I don't bring women here."

Meaning there wasn't a condom for miles.

Amy struggled with herself, knowing what her next move should be and wishing it could be different. She didn't want to give this up. She'd never been a slut puppy. Her entire list of sexual partners could be counted on one hand. And she hadn't been with anyone in over a year. Not to

126

mention, Joshua was the only man who had ever stirred her up like this, enough to make her feel like she was riding the edge of a whizzing bullet. To hell with safe, she wanted relief.

As if sensing her inner argument, Joshua raised his head, one hand coming up to caress her cheek. "Shhh. It's all right, Amy. I can still make this good for you. But you'll have to trust me."

Trust him? Amy groaned and squeezed her eyes shut. Of all the things he could ask her to do, it had to be the one thing she wasn't good at. Putting herself in someone else's hands again was a leap of faith she wasn't ready to take yet. Maybe not ever.

But when Joshua started to shift his weight off her, Amy's arms and legs latched onto him before she knew what was happening. Her heart might not be ready to trust again, but apparently her body was. She ground herself against his hard length.

"Amy! Shit!"

She opened her eyes to find him staring down at her, his face suffused with a hunger that sent a flood of heat through her. "If that isn't a yes," he growled, "you've got about one second to say so."

"Can you finish us with just this?" She rolled her hips into him again to demonstrate.

Air hissed through his clenched teeth.

Amy fought back a grin as affront mixed with the lust on his face. He must have seen the laughter in her eyes anyway because he dipped down and nipped her bottom lip as punishment.

"That depends," he growled.

"On?"

"On how wet we can get you."

Shifting a little to the side, he leaned his weight on one arm and slid his free hand down her body. He paused to tug the tie at her waist loose so he could brush her robe open. His hand felt hot against her skin, and slightly rough. His eyes never left her face, even when those calloused fingers of his finally reached her mound. Amy loved the way the lust surged in his eyes the moment he realized her intimate skin was completely hairless. He evidently liked the fact she was bare

"Damn, woman," he breathed. His questing fingers caressed her from thigh to thigh then dipped all the way down to her ass.

She parted her legs wider and lifted into his touch, feeling his hard shaft throb against her hip. He licked his lips, as if anticipating putting his mouth where his hand was.

His fingers slid back up her crack slowly, parting her inner layers. One smooth stroke and his hand was drenched. He groaned and pressed into her with his finger while thumbing the nub of flesh at the apex of her slit. Pleasure exploded in her body. She arched into his touch, unable to hold back a moan.

"That's right, baby. Just lay back and enjoy. I'll make this good for you, Amy, I promise."

He added a second finger just as he kissed her, a slow, penetrating assault that she was more than ready for. Tongues dueled, teeth nipped. She ran her hands down his back, feeling the shift of tense muscles beneath his shirt. Part of her wanted to feel bare skin while another, the more erotic side of her she never realized she had, got off on knowing she was naked while he was fully clothed. She settled for digging her nails into the material of his shirt. When he groaned and kissed her deeper, she almost purred with satisfaction.

He finally broke their kiss. Both of them drew in ragged breaths while his lips slid over her chin to her neck. She sucked in a shuddering breath and tipped her head back to give him better access. He paused at the base of her throat, licking and sucking, perilously close to leaving a mark she knew would be impossible to hide, much less explain. She tensed, unable to decide if she wanted to push him away or pull him closer. Before she could make up her mind he moved on, sliding down her body to her breasts. He hovered there, simply staring at her.

"What?" she asked. Her average B-cup breasts were far from spectacular. Certainly nothing to cause that look of awe on his face.

"You're absolutely beautiful." He cupped his free hand around one breast almost reverently. "Perfect," he whispered, leaning down and tonguing her nipple. The long, slow swipe sent a jolt through her body like an electric current. He smiled up at her. "And sensitive."

Before Amy could do more than nod, he was on her, his tongue moving in time to his thrusting fingers. First slow laps, then faster flicks, then back to slow laps again. Every once in a while his teeth would come into play, the little bites serving to heighten her pleasure. When he finally sucked the stiff nub into his mouth, Amy cried out, arching completely off the couch and sinking her hands into his thick hair to hold him in place. Her orgasm rushed toward her, only to back off when he switched to the other breast to start the process all over.

"Joshua! Please!"

"Soon, sweetheart, soon." He captured her hands and pushed them into the couch cushions. "Dig in here and don't let go. You're going to need something to hold on to, and I need my hair."

She didn't have time to wonder what he meant before he added a third finger to the ones already pressing inside her. He picked up the pace, his thumb sliding against her sensitive skin with each strong stroke.

Amy couldn't hold still. Her hips pushed up, meeting the hard thrust of his fingers, feeling them reach deep inside her, filling her, caressing her. "Ah, Joshua!"

"That's right, baby, let go, ride my hand. I swear I won't ever let you fall."

His words wrapped around her, giving her such a sense of security that for the first time since Adrik's betrayal Amy gave herself into another's keeping. She did as he said and rode his strong fingers, every nerve in her body awash with the building pleasure. She was even able to keep her hands where he'd put them right up until she reached the very edge of her orgasm. When it finally broke over her, she grabbed him with both hands, pulling him close so she could bury her face in his shoulder as she shuddered and gasped. And cried.

She didn't want him to see her tears. He would demand to know why she was crying and she didn't want to spend time trying to explain. Not now. She wasn't even sure she could explain. The emotions inside her were too mixed up for her to make sense of them. She'd think about them later, sort them out, and put them all in the right boxes.

For now, all she wanted to do was bask in the hazy afterglow of pleasure.

His hand moved between her legs, petting her, making her jump.

"Easy," he said pressing a kiss to her temple.

Amy sighed and snuggled into him while surreptitiously wiping away the evidence of her tears on his shirt. Joshua chuckled softly.

"Careful, I can almost hear you purring."

She bit back her first response. Telling him that ravens didn't purr would have opened up a whole line of questioning she wasn't ready for. From the way he'd explained about Adrik, she didn't think Joshua knew exactly who she was yet. She'd have to tell him eventually, but again, now wasn't the time.

She gave him her best imitation of a purr and

released her tight hold on him so he could pull back. He chuckled again then stopped abruptly. Either she had missed a tear or two, or he'd noticed his shirt was damp.

"Are you all right?" he demanded.

She placed her hand on his cheek. "I'm more all right now than I've been in months, and that's all I'm going to say on the subject. I need you to be able to get your head in the Jeep to drive me home later."

The serious look didn't leave his face. "I promised to take care of you, not make you cry."

"You took very good care of me. Now it's my turn to take care of you."

"You don't—"

"Yes, I do," she said firmly. Reaching down, she made quick work of the button and zipper of his jeans, giving him no chance to draw back. She shoved the material down just enough for his engorged penis and heavy balls to fall into her hands. Joshua sucked in a harsh breath, muttering a low curse.

"Mind telling me what you're planning?" He sounded strained, ready to break.

Amy caressed his sensitive flesh. "You'll see. For now, I want you to stroke yourself with the same hand you used on me."

He raised a brow, but did as she asked. She watched him a moment, enjoying the flutter low in her belly at the sight of his large hand wrapped around all that hard length. He in turn, seemed to like her watching him. Who would have thought the Harrier had a bit of exhibitionist in him?

Amy shifted her gaze to his face, smiled sweetly, then reached down between her legs. Joshua's eyes snapped to where her fingers dipped between her folds, scooping out the juices there. His breath shot out in a rush and his hand stilled and squeezed. From the look on his face, she could probably get him to come just by letting him watch her masturbate. But that wasn't the way she wanted to bring him off this time.

She pulled her hand free and brought it to his cock, smearing the wetness along its length from tip to base. His hand fell away, letting her have complete access.

"Is this going where I think it is?" His voice sounded harsh and hopeful at the same time.

"Maybe, maybe not." She dipped between her legs again and rubbed the resulting juices on the inside of her thighs. "Have you ever heard of *intercrural* sex?"

****

When Joshua realized what Amy had in mind, all he could think was, *Oh. Hell. Yes.*

He positioned himself over her as she brought her legs together. Fitting the head of his cock to the top of the cleft created by her closed thighs, he slowly lowered his hips. The broad head slipped in easily. The sensation of Amy's warm, wet flesh surrounding him, inch by slow inch, crawled up his spine like slow torture. He drew back and thrust in again, slow, deep. The way her outer lips kissed his cock each time it glided against them made him long to change the angle of his thrusts. A little shift would be all it'd take for him to slip inside her.

The fact he was so close, yet forbidden entrance, only served to jack up his desire.

"Tighter," he said, squeezing his knees against the outside of her legs. "Hold me tighter."

She crossed her ankles.

"Shit." His rhythm faltered. Then he thrust faster, harder, the head of his cock punching through to the soft, supple leather of the couch. He leaned down and took her mouth, his tongue penetrating her the way he wanted to do with his cock.

He felt her tug the back of his shirt up. Hot fingers danced along his bare skin, wiggling their way beneath his jeans to grip his ass. It took him a moment to respond to their demands, to realize she wanted him to shift his body forward. When he did, he slipped more firmly against her wet folds. Now, every time he moved up and down, his cock rubbed with more pressure against her sensitive flesh. Such a dangerous position. If she tilted her hips at all, he'd be inside her, condom be damned. He slowed, not wanting to risk damaging her trust.

She turned her head, breaking their kiss. "Don't stop. I want to feel you come." Her mouth opened wide over his stubbled jaw and she bit him. The firm press of her teeth against his skin coupled with her words was like a jump-start to his waning desire. He could feel his orgasm building at the base of his spine, sliding into his balls just the way her tongue slid down his neck.

Hungry little moans started at the back of her throat. Her body tensed beneath his. Then the muscles of her thighs began to clench in time to his thrusts. Realizing she was in the midst of another orgasm sent his own release boiling over the edge.

He came, unable to hold back a harsh cry as wave after wave of pleasure pummeled him. He tried to pull back to keep his semen away from her opening, but between her clenched thighs and her hands pressing down on his ass, it was a losing battle.

He shuddered through the last fiery pulse before collapsing, barely keeping all his weight off her.

"Mmm," she murmured.

Soft hands stroked languidly up his spine. He just managed to hold back a shiver. Opening his eyes, he found her staring up at him.

"Was that as good for you as it was for me?" she asked with a cat-in-the-cream smile.

"Minx." He shifted to the side and glanced down at the mess he'd made between her thighs. Just the sight of his seed on her skin made his softening cock twitch. Looking back to her, he bent down and pressed a kiss to her lips. "If it was any better, I'd have to replace this couch instead of clean it." And if she ever found out just how much she affected him, he'd be in a world of trouble.

She chuckled, the sound vibrating all the way though his chest where their bodies met. "Good. Then I'll leave you to clean up while I take another shower.

He sat up, tucking himself back in his jeans as she stood. She wrapped the robe around her body in a movement that was neither slow nor fast. Not embarrassed, but no longer in the mood to play, either. She didn't even glance at the wet spot on the couch before she left.

Joshua sighed and went to the kitchen, wondering just how badly he'd screwed up. Never in his life had he slept with someone he was supposed to be guarding. If one of his men were to pull such a stupid stunt, and Joshua found out about it, he'd bust them so far below private they'd never see NCO status again.

He tried to figure out how things had gotten so off course while he cleaned the couch with a damp cloth and a couple of sanitizer wipes. "Colby, you're an idiot," he muttered. "Completely certifiable." He'd evidently taken too many shots to the head somewhere along the way. The only good thing to come out of this was the possibility that Amy might feel a little more inclined to go along with the whole engagement thing. Or not.

When she came back out of the bathroom a few minutes later, he had their steaks and vegetables warmed up and back on the table.

"Thanks," she said, smiling and sitting across

from him. She wore her own clothes. Joshua tried not to frown at the small rips and stains still visible. The reminder of her close brush with death sent a chill through him. The driver had to have been Velavich. Chet wanted her alive, not dead, and there wasn't a third player in this deadly game that he knew of. He would have to keep a far closer eye on her than he'd intended. At least until his men got here. Three were due to arrive tomorrow. He'd already worked out a surveillance schedule designed to keep Amy covered twenty-four-seven. If Adrik Velavich so much as sneezed in her direction, he'd be in a NightHawks' crosshairs.

The silence between them stretched into something almost companionable while they ate. Joshua was content to watch her devour the food he'd prepared. Plenty of time to get back to their verbal sparring match later.

"You're a good cook," she said, finally setting her fork down and picking up another roll. She bit into the bread with obvious relish.

Joshua shifted in his chair with a mental curse. He really shouldn't be thinking about how good those even white teeth had felt against his skin. "I'm glad you enjoyed it."

After another long silence, she brushed the crumbs from her fingers and leaned back in her chair. "All right."

"All right, what?"

"All right, I'll go along with your preposterous engagement scenario."

Joshua smiled, feeling an absurd sense of relief. "Considering the rumor has no doubt already spread the length and width of the valley, I think you've made a wise decision."

She snorted softly. "Believe me, I realize how fast news travels here. It's not the reason I'm going along with your ridiculous plan. If I wanted to, I could deny I ever met you until yesterday."

"You could, but no one would believe you."

"Why not?"

"Because everyone knows I never lie."

She blinked. "You really are delusional, aren't you?"

He rose and took their empty plates to the kitchen. "I've been called that on more than one occasion, but never by anyone in Clear Springs."

"Well, you have now."

He turned around in time to catch the rest of the dirty dishes she shoved into his hands.

"If you're such a big shot unit leader, why couldn't you come up with something a little more believable?"

"You wouldn't say that if you'd been in the café this morning. I'm not the one who made up the part about our whirl-wind courtship abroad and you moving into my home town to await my return."

"Are you trying to tell me the rumor started itself?"

"Practically. That's what makes it such a good cover. There's enough of a romantic element to appeal to every female in the valley."

"What about the men? I doubt there's a romantic bone in Chet's whole family, much less his own body."

Joshua stepped toward Amy and placed his hands on the counter on either side of her, caging her with his larger body.

She didn't move, didn't blink. The only acknowledgement to the aggressive maneuver he could see was the quickening flutter of her pulse just beneath the skin of her throat.

She met his gaze without an ounce of fear. A reaction he found incredibly sexy. Most women cringed when he was this close.

Keeping their gazes locked, he leaned down

until only a breath of air separated them.

"Sweetheart, one look at you and there's not a man alive who wouldn't believe I chased you half way around the world to make you mine."

Chapter Thirteen

Amy stopped herself from licking her suddenly dry lips, certain Joshua would see the move as an invitation. Not that she'd mind kissing him again.

That was the problem. She'd already crossed the invisible line she'd drawn once. Quite magnificently, in fact. Doing so again wouldn't just be foolish, it would be what her father called "a serious breach of conduct resulting in disastrous consequences." There was a shorter two-word phrase he sometimes used that meant the same thing, but he tried not to cuss in her presence.

The urge to forget about warnings and lines and possible disastrous consequences grew with every breath she took. All she could smell was Joshua. All she could see was his face hovering over her. All she could hear was the pounding of her heart, the rush of blood in her ears, the—

Three loud beeps came from the phone on the kitchen wall. The fire in Joshua's eyes flickered and died, instantly replaced by concern. Without a word, he straightened and crossed to the phone.

Amy took a deep breath, every tight muscle in her body sagging, though in relief or disappointment she wasn't sure.

The tension ratcheted right back up when Joshua snatched up the phone and snapped, "What's wrong?"

His concern drew Amy closer to him out of reflex. Unable to hear the person on the other end clearly, she watched Joshua's face. The sudden shift from stern worry to wincing chagrin sparked a grin that Amy didn't bother to hide.

"Calm down, Farrah. Yes, I'm all right. No, she didn't kill me. No, you can't kill me, either." He glanced at Amy, hot, brown eyes daring her to say something. "Just put Kyle on the line," he continued, "please, honey? I promise I can explain it to him in two seconds, and he can spend the rest of the night explaining it to you." He heaved a sigh, meeting her gaze longer this time. "Yes, she's here, and no, you can't talk to her right now."

The voice on the other end rose in volume.

Amy stifled a laugh behind her hand when Joshua's eyes widened in shock. He took the phone from his ear and gave it such an astonished look, she laughed outright. He covered the mouthpiece with his hand and shook his head sadly. "And here I thought she'd be the one to influence Kyle."

"Never underestimate a woman's vocabulary," Amy warned him. "Just because we don't cuss like a sailor every chance we get, doesn't mean we don't know how to use the words when we need them."

He grunted and carefully put the phone back to his ear. "Kyle? Where the devil did she learn to talk like that? Never mind, I already know. I hope my godkids aren't in the same room with you two."

A long pause ensued, during which Joshua closed his eyes and pinched the bridge of his nose. Almost a full minute later, he said, "Are you finished? Good. Now listen up. This is a classic S-3 and I'm running a C-13. Explain it to Farrah and get her off my back. Scenario will run indefinitely—

Indefinitely, Amy mouthed, raising her eyebrows. S-3 was guard detail while C-13 constituted a plausible cover story, i.e. their fake engagement.

"Yes, I said *indefinitely*. You of all people should understand why."

She wasn't sure if he was speaking to her or

Kyle and decided it didn't matter. She'd end his little C-13 just as soon as they neutralized Adrik and Joshua left town. If that meant she had to up her game with Chet and the boys, then so be it. She'd learned the hard way not to rely on anyone but herself.

"What you don't like isn't my problem," Joshua said sharply. "Just talk to your wife, will you? Oh, and I requested some hard copy files and gave them your address. When the courier shows up, don't shoot him.... Because your place is easier to find than my cabin, goofus. I'll come by the garage around noon to pick them up."

He hung up the phone, not quite slamming it into the cradle.

"Soooo," Amy said, drawing out the word. "I take it Farrah's upset."

"Oh, yeah, I think you can safely say she's not happy. At first, she thought you'd kept the engagement from her."

"What?" She started to say she didn't keep secrets from friends but caught herself before lying. Not telling Farrah and Kyle about her dangerous past was definitely keeping secrets.

He held up a hand. "When Kyle told her it was probably a cover so I could guard you, she set her sights on me."

Better him than her, but..."Why is she mad with you?"

"Because she didn't know you'd be in on the plan."

Comprehension dawned. "Oh, I see. She thought you might be playing with my feelings."

Joshua made a disgusted sound. "Exactly. She flew into full mother hen mode before Kyle could explain things. Hence, the emergency call."

Amy smiled. "Good to know I've got someone on my side." She leaned back against the counter, trying not to bask in the warm feeling unfurling inside her. It had been a long time since anyone had her back.

Joshua scowled at her. "Don't let it give you any ideas. I'm holding you to your word."

"Fine. Hold away. Just so long as you can drive me home while you do it."

"About that..."

The look on his face snapped her food-relaxed senses to attention. What was he up to now? "What? Don't tell me something's wrong with your Jeep."

"No, Jeep's fine. But considering your near miss today, I think it's a good idea if you stay here tonight."

Amy stared at him, trying to keep from panicking. It took every ounce of willpower she had not to glance at the couch. *An entire night with Joshua Colby?* She wasn't sure she could survive the pleasure. Then her common sense kicked in its two cents worth, bringing that line of thinking to a screeching halt. *Don't be ridiculous, that's not why he's asking you to stay. This is strictly business. Guard duty. He's certain to be in SO mode.* Which actually did nothing to make her feel any better.

An entire night with the Harrier?

"You've got to be kidding. You want me to stay *here*? In *your* house? With *you*?"

He shot her an exasperated look. "You make it sound like I'm asking you to give up your first born. I just want you to stay here where it's safe." He crossed the room and put his hands on her shoulders. "Listen, what happened earlier...that was both of us scratching an itch, nothing more. I'm not expecting anything else to happen between us, so if that's what's bothering you, you can relax. You'll stay in one of the bedrooms down here, I'll be in my room upstairs, and never the twain shall meet."

Amy buried the small stab of hurt his words

caused under a mound of anger. Did he think she was an idiot? Of course their little couch session was just a mutual scratching of itchy libidos. How could it be anything else? They'd only known each other two damn days.

Time enough to get engaged Harrier style.

She knocked his hands off her shoulders and stepped back. "That's not what everyone else is going to think if they find out I stayed here all night."

He had the gall to shrug. "Consider it part of the engagement ruse. Now that it's official, no one will think twice about us spending the night together. In fact, it might look suspicious if we didn't. Especially when word gets out about your accident. Everyone who knows me is going to expect me to be a little over protective."

Amy bit back a frustrated groan. Of course that little tidbit would be making its run of the rumor mill, too. It wasn't as if she'd remembered to swear Sue and the sheriff to secrecy. Heck, even if she had, things like a small case of attempted murder had ways of eking out into the public sphere.

Face it, Amy. You've been out-maneuvered.

Chapter Fourteen

Joshua shifted the Jeep into park outside Amy's house the next morning. The long sleepless night had done little to improve his mood. Amy's temper seemed equally on edge. He ignored the glare she shot him when he switched off the engine.

"I told you I can look after myself. I'm just going to drive over to check on Bors and come straight home."

Stubborn woman. Joshua opened the door and got out without saying a word. He'd been biting his tongue all morning to keep from raising his voice. Not that she'd done anything to deserve his bad temper. It wasn't her fault he'd tossed and turned all night, starting awake at every damn creak and groan his house made. Oh, wait, yes it was. If she hadn't been sleeping downstairs, he wouldn't have left his bedroom door open, something he never did when he slept.

He told himself that he left it open last night so he could hear if she needed anything. It was only when he came downstairs and stood outside her closed door that he admitted to himself he'd left it open in case she decided to join him in his bed. Like that was ever going to happen. She hadn't argued with him for an instant when he'd dismissed their encounter on the couch. But then, why should she? He'd been right. It had meant nothing.

And if you tell yourself that often enough, maybe you'll believe it.

She slammed her door and glared at him over the Jeep's hood. "You're not going to listen to reason, are you?"

He took a deep breath to give himself time to rein in his less professional emotions. Not an easy task. Seeing her standing there with the heat of battle in her eyes and the morning sun shining off her raven dark hair made him wish for things completely unprofessional. Damn if last night hadn't lit a fire in him that refused to go out. He needed to get properly laid. Soon! Maybe then he'd get back to thinking with his big head instead of his little one.

"I could say the same to you," he said, proud of his practical tone. "Reason suggests a suitable amount of caution. You don't know where or when Velavich is going to strike next. For all we know, he might have you in his sights right now."

She preceded him up the walk, digging the keys from her pocket. "Don't be so melodramatic," she tossed back. "You can't even be sure he's within a hundred miles of here. Besides, if he's spotting us with a scope, it's you who should be worried, not me."

"You sound pretty certain of that."

She stopped with her hand on the doorknob and met his gaze, a wealth of worry clouding her blue eyes. "What I did to Adrik he took personally. He's going to want to make his revenge just as personal. Shooting me from a hundred yards away or even a hundred inches isn't going to be enough. Believe me, I know him. Nothing will do but skin to skin. However, that doesn't apply to you or anyone else who gets between him and me. He'll take you out, Joshua, without a second thought."

"I'm not that easy to kill."

Something dark flashed in her eyes. "Given the right weapon and enough time, everyone is easy to kill." She turned the door knob and went inside.

Joshua followed her, still not sure what he'd seen in her eyes. Fear, yes. She had good reason to be afraid. But there'd been something else, too. Something he would've called regret if he didn't know better. Maybe she was sorry she hadn't caught on to her ex-lover sooner. There was no telling how many innocent deaths Velavich was responsible for before she blew the whistle on him. And not all of them involved Velavich pulling the trigger.

Amy went directly to one of the kitchen cabinets and opened the door. Inside, Joshua saw a security pad with a blinking red light. She punched in a code and the light began flashing yellow. She punched in another code, and the light finally switched to green.

Recognizing the system, Joshua stepped back as she left the kitchen and went straight to the front door. The pad there was located inside a small table. The light was already green, and when she punched in another code, that light switched straight to red.

He raised a brow and leaned a shoulder against the wall. "Impressive security." Which was a vast understatement. The system was a top level SO design usually reserved for heads of state. Someone had to have called in a lot of favors to get it installed in Amy's house.

Amy shrugged. "It does its job." She lowered the lid of the table and tossed her keys on top. "Since you're here, you might as well make yourself at home. I shouldn't be long." She entered a hallway that presumably led to her bedroom.

The thought of her stripping out of her clothes was enough to send a rush of blood right where he didn't need it. He winced and used his hand to shift things around. Damn tight jeans. If Kyle could see him now, he'd laugh his fool head off. He definitely needed something to take his mind off the memory of Amy naked...beneath him...coming...

Shit!

Limping toward the kitchen, he raised his voice. "Mind if I make some coffee?" He'd had two cups before they left his house, but another one wouldn't be over his limit. When Amy didn't answer right away, he figured she must have closed her bedroom door and couldn't hear him. Smart girl. Not that he would have peeked or anything, but hey, he was only human.

He stepped back into the living room and headed for the hall. "Amy?"

She stood in the open doorway of a room, facing inside. One look at her complete stillness and lack of facial expression and his protective instincts soared through the roof. He pulled a handgun from the holster under his arm and moved silently down the hall, stopping just short of the opening. He tried to get her attention, but she wouldn't look at him. Her face was completely white, eyes devoid of anything but shock.

He cursed to himself and did a quick head bob around the doorframe to scan the room. Dresser on the right. Highboy on the left. Bed opposite the door. One nightstand to the left of the bed with lamp, clock, and book. A mirrored door in the wall to the right of the bed that might lead to a closet, and an open door on the left that definitely led to a bathroom—no windows—which he found both unusual and very telling.

Other than the furniture, the room appeared empty.

He eased past Amy and checked the closet and bathroom, just to be sure. It wasn't until he came out of the bathroom that he paid attention to the dress lying on the bed. It was the same creamy lace dress Amy had worn to Kyle's house two nights ago.

Except now there was a big fat bloodstain circling a hole the size of a large caliber bullet over the left breast.

****

All Amy could do was stare at the ruined dress

laid out neatly across her bed. A cold shiver snaked down her spine. Adrik had been in her house.

He'd been in her house!

How? When? Why hadn't the alarm tripped?

What if she'd been here alone?

She started to shake.

Joshua's strong arms wrapped around her, pulling her flush against his body. She grabbed onto him, burying her face against his chest, allowing herself this one moment of weakness. This would be the last one. The last time she was caught off guard by one of Adrik's malicious tricks. She knew his fondness for head games only too well. She'd seen him play them on others more times than she could count. Now he played them on her.

"Hush now, sweetheart, it's all right. He's not going to lay a finger on you, I swear. Damn it, Amy, please don't cry."

It wasn't until she focused on Joshua's words that she realized she was indeed crying. The tears came silently, a steady stream that soaked Joshua's shirt and skin. Angry tears. The absence of sobs was a dead giveaway. That was always the way she cried. Silent and angry, or heart-broken and sobbing. There wasn't much in between.

She couldn't find the words to explain the difference to Joshua. Not right now. All she could do was soak up the comfort he gave her—he soothing motion of his strong hand moving up and down her back from waist to nape, the fervent promises he whispered into her hair, the protective way he cradled her against him. She was grateful for every degree of warmth and every ounce of strength. Glad, for once, that he'd ignored her wishes and insisted on coming into the house with her. She could have faced this latest trial alone but was infinitely glad she didn't have to.

Slowly, her anger turned from hot tears to cold

resolve. It was time Adrik paid for his crimes. All of them.

She drew in a deep breath and let it out. Drew in another—and recognized it as a stalling tactic. Leaving Joshua's embrace was a lot harder than it should be. She finally stepped back, feeling the loss of more than just his warmth as his arms dropped away from her. She sniffed and blotted her face on her sleeve. "Sorry. Didn't mean to leak all over you."

"It's okay. As long as you don't blow your nose on me, we're good."

Remarkably, his words caused her lips to twitch into a small smile. She looked up at him, intending to tease him back, and her smile froze. Despite his light words, he looked ready to kill someone.

Abruptly, he turned away. "Stay here while I check the rest of the house."

Amy let him go. She could have told him Adrik was long gone, but knew he wouldn't listen. He was in full Harrier mode, protective and deadly. Instead, she moved to the bed. The dress was one of her favorites, *was* being the operative word. There was no salvaging it that she could see—not from the hole and not from the dark red stain that experience told her was indeed blood. Human or animal was the only question. Her gaze traveled down the dress. Part of the skirt was folded at an odd angle over the front and she twitched it back into place. Fresh anger filled her at what she uncovered.

"I'm going to kill that sick son-of-a-bitch!"

Joshua was in the room in less than two seconds. "What's wrong?"

Amy blinked rapidly to hold back the tears of rage. She silently pointed at the long sticky strings of semen darkening the lace.

Joshua froze. He seemed to stare down at the dress a long time. "I'll kill him for you."

The promise of death in his voice jerked her gaze

to him. A cold shiver slithered down her spine. She really should have kept this bit of disgusting evidence to herself. Touching his arm, she found the muscle beneath the sleeve of his jacket rock hard. It was if he held himself tightly in check, a cocked hammer ready to slam down with punishing force. God only knew what would release his trigger.

He started folding the bedspread in on itself, wrapping up the dress. She helped him.

"I take it we're not calling the sheriff about this."

"No," Joshua confirmed, "we're not. Dan and his men aren't equipped to handle someone like Velavich. I don't want them getting in the way or getting themselves killed. Like you said, anyone between you and dear old Vellie will be a target. I've got someone coming in today who can process all this and tell us for sure if it was Velavich."

"Who else would it be? Chet doesn't have the know-how to circumvent my security, nor does he have a reason to want me dead." She helped him stuff the bedspread into a garbage bag he brought from the kitchen.

"I just want to be sure." He laid a hand against her cheek. It took every bit of strength she had not to lean into it. She met his gaze, the dark brown of his eyes as deep and hot as melted chocolate. "I don't care who it turns out to be," he said. "Whoever it is, they're not going to get the chance to do this again. I promise." He leaned down and kissed her. Softly, sweetly, as if she was the most precious thing in the world. His unexpected tenderness burned its way deep into her heart. Feelings she never thought she'd have again stirred, bringing with them a sense of alarm.

Oh, my gosh, I'm falling for him.

Before she could react to her panic, he pulled back and stepped away. "You need to pack enough to last a few days. You're not coming back here until this is over."

Her first response, after she finally reined in her falling heart, was to dig in her heels. This was her home. The first real home she'd ever had, truth be known. She and her mother had moved around like a pair of restless vagabonds while she was growing up—six months here, three months there, never more than a year anywhere until her father found them. Then it was bouncing back and forth between Europe and North America until she turned eighteen and joined the US military. Which, of course, meant more moving around.

Even when she'd moved to Clear Springs, she hadn't intended to sink her roots so deep. Now she hated the thought of leaving her home vulnerable. Heck of a time for her nesting instincts to kick in. Fortunately, even after months of playing civilian, her SO training had no trouble overriding such distracting sentimentality. Her home base was compromised. Of course she couldn't come back—not until she neutralized the threat.

"All right."

She grabbed her suitcase from the closet and started shoving in clothes. She didn't even bother asking Joshua where she'd be staying. It would be with him, so he could keep his NightHawk eyes on her. Not the ideal situation, considering her current emotional state. Not if she wanted to come out of this mess with her heart intact. But she really had no choice. Whoever she stayed with would be in danger. Who better to deal with that danger than the most dangerous man she knew.

Chapter Fifteen

Joshua didn't bother hiding his grin as yet another person bore down on him and Amy. He hadn't exactly planned to take her into town this morning, but after leaving Amy's house, he'd headed straight for downtown Clear Springs. One reason was to get her mind off Velavich and that damn dress, and the other was to cement their cover story. If Velavich was sniffing around, Joshua wanted him to know without a doubt that he had Amy under his wing.

She'd still been in shock when Joshua helped her out of the Jeep. He knew, because she didn't protest when he started walking arm-in-arm with her down Clear Springs' main thoroughfare. She'd come out of her daze before they'd gone half a block. Hard to stay locked in your head when people kept stopping to give you hugs and good wishes on your engagement.

"I hate you."

Joshua just grinned wider at her harsh whisper. Not exactly the three words a man wanted to hear from his new fiancé, but he'd take a little bitchiness over tears any day. He patted the hand curled around his arm, timing his "That's nice, sweetheart." comment with the arrival of their latest well-wisher.

Nails dug into his skin. Then she was smiling and shaking hands, slipping into her role as his blushing-bride-to-be with an ease that surprised him. Damn if she didn't make every word, every caress, every loving look she sent his way, seem real. Woman had a gift for acting, no doubt about it. If not

151

for that little "I hate you." which held all the promise of a knife between his ribs, he might be tempted to believe their cover story himself.

With all the stopping and chatting, the two block walk to the Borden Café took a good thirty minutes. The lunch crowd wasn't due for another hour, so the café was nearly empty when they arrived. After the initial round of congratulations and hugs, Joshua ushered Amy to a back booth where they had a little privacy and a good view of all the exits. Marlee took their orders, smiling non-stop, and brought iced tea for him and a diet soda for Amy. As soon as she walked away, Amy heaved a disgruntled sigh.

"I hope you're happy. You couldn't have been more obvious if you'd painted a target on your back."

"I already had one, remember?"

She ripped the paper off her straw and jammed the plastic tube past the ice in her glass. "Not the same thing. Chet's a complete amateur. A man of your abilities could have handled his attempts on your life blindfolded. Adrik's different. He won't come after you with a knife or gun. Those aren't his weapons of choice."

"He likes to use poison."

"Yes. And he's very good at slipping it to someone when they least expect it. You'd be wise not to eat in public or even buy anything locally." She suddenly reached out and pushed both their glasses to the center of the table. "We shouldn't even be here. We should—"

He laid a finger over her lips. "Don't get worked up. I read his file. He's not going to come after me right away." He picked up his glass. Alarm flashed across her face, her hand shooting forward to wrap around his wrist. "It's all right," he said, gently prying her fingers loose. "Trust me. This won't kill me." Her expression briefly twisted into one of pain before smoothing into something distant, cold, as if she'd just flipped a switch and turned her feelings off. She leaned back into the booth's corner. When she spoke, her voice was as passionless as the mask she now wore.

"Go ahead, be an idiot. I'll be sure to tell Aberashoff to put that on your headstone."

He still held her hand and gave it a squeeze to reassure her. She tried tugging free, but he didn't let go. Couldn't. He didn't like this new act of hers or the distance, both emotional and physical, she was trying to put between them.

The only thing that seemed real was the trembling of her cold fingers in his grasp. She might act like she didn't care if he dropped dead, but her body said otherwise. Holding her gaze, he took three long swallows of ice cold tea before setting the glass down. Then they just sat there, staring at each other as the seconds piled up into minutes. Neither of them moved until Marlee set their lunches in front of them.

"Enjoy, you two."

"Thanks, Marlee," he said, still not looking away from Amy. Her cold mask had slipped as the minutes passed. The worry in her sky blue eyes touched him deeply. Part of him ate it up like it was his last meal, the other part wanted like hell to make it go away, to fix it so she'd never worry about anything ever again.

"See," he said when they were alone again. "No blurring vision, no pain, or shortness of breath." He moved her glass closer to her plate. "And like you said, he won't poison you. Not personal enough, right? So we're both safe today."

"Are you sure you're all right?"

He caught movement from the corner of his eye. One of the male patrons headed their way, probably going to the restrooms down the hall. Joshua

153

released her hand and slipped an arm around her shoulders, pulling her close. "Of course I'm all right, sweetheart. I'm marrying the most wonderful, sexy, talented woman in the world. Why wouldn't I be?"

Amy smiled at him angelically until the man passed. Then she wiggled in her seat as if getting comfortable, deftly elbowing him in the ribs in the process. "Behave, *sweetheart.*"

Joshua grunted through his smile and let her put a few inches between them. For all the subtly of the movement, that elbow jab hadn't been gentle. He'd have a nice bruise tomorrow.

"I am behaving, *darling*. If I weren't, you'd be sitting in my lap instead of beside me."

She dipped her head, but not before he caught the pink on her cheeks. "Don't be ridiculous. We're in a public place."

"Newly engaged couples are expected to cuddle."

"Sitting side-by-side is cuddling. Sitting in your lap would be…"

Heaven, he thought. Or hell. Or both.

She cleared her throat. "Inappropriate," she finished. "For more reasons than one."

He reached out, placing a finger beneath her chin before she could bite into her sandwich. With a little pressure, he tilted her head up until he could look into her eyes. "Nothing between us would be inappropriate." For a brief, mad moment, he swore he saw longing in her eyes. A reflection of his own?

"Maybe," she whispered.

Her response made his heart beat faster until she continued. "But only if we were really engaged, and we're not. This isn't real."

"Do you wish it were?"

Shit, did he ask that out loud? The shock on her face said he had. Damn. If he wasn't careful, she'd run screaming out of the café and all the morning's acting efforts would be for nothing.

"Sorry. Forget I asked that. Didn't mean to make you uncomfortable." He released her and bent over his plate, wishing like hell Velavich would walk in the door right now. He'd even welcome the brothers Dumb, Dumber, and Dumbest. Anything to save him from making a complete ass out of himself.

Oh, wait, too late, he already had.

****

Her head still spinning, Amy watched Joshua bite into several french fries at once. Before those were gone he bit into the burger, added more fries, then took another bite of burger, as if trying to keep his mouth filled with food instead of words.

She wanted to punch him. How dare he ask her such a provocative question out of the naked blue then turn around and take it back? Her mind had pounced on those five words with a vengeance. *Do you wish it were?* Why would he ask her that if he wasn't thinking along those same lines? And if he was.... The memory of their interlude together on his couch popped up—every wonderful, wicked moment in clear focus.

Did she want it to be real? Hell, yes. But she was honest enough to know it wouldn't work. Not long term. Too many complications.

But short term?

Thanks to the couch time, the possibility was already on a fast track, racing through her mind like a bullet train. Though, by the way he was concentrating on his food, Joshua had already derailed and buried the idea under a mound of common sense.

Normally she'd be cheering him on. Today, though, things were different. The sight of that blood-stained dress had sharpened Amy's vision, focusing it on one important fact. As much as she wanted to come out of this alive, the possibility existed that she wouldn't. That kind of realization had a way of lowering barriers and flicking off all kinds of safety switches.

Part of her had to have known that last night, or the heavy petting session would never have happened. Now her brain had caught up to her body. As long as she held on to the fact that all this was just a temporary diversion, she'd be okay. More than okay. A little play time with Joshua sounded like fun.

She waited until he had the burger in his mouth then said, "If it was real, I'd definitely be open to sitting in your lap." Choking noises ensued. She kept her smile to herself and her eyes firmly on the BLT sandwich in her hand, waiting to see if he'd take her bait.

He took a long drink before clearing his throat. "Would you now?"

She chewed up a bite of sandwich before saying, "Yes."

Something wicked flashed in his eyes. He lowered his voice. "Which direction would you face?"

"Toward you, of course."

He shifted a little in his seat. She felt like shifting, too, but held still despite the sudden throb between her legs. Things were getting interesting.

"You'd straddle me?"

She nodded and took another bite of sandwich. He finished off his glass of tea. Marlee immediately showed up to top off their drinks. Amy waited until she was gone before elaborating, never once lifting her eyes from her food.

"I'd move slowly, lifting my leg over your lap and sliding my knees along your thighs. Then I'd scoot up until I could feel you hard between my legs."

His voice bordered on a growl while he demolished a couple of french fries between his fingers. "Where would your hands be?"

"On your shoulders first. I'd dig my fingers in

until you felt my nails. Then I'd slide my hands up your neck and into your hair."

"My hands would be on your back—"

"No," she corrected. "They'd be on the table."

"I want to touch you."

"Later."

From the corner of her eye she saw his big hands clench into fists. Then they opened and settled on the table on either side of his plate, palms down, fingers spread wide.

"All right," he said huskily. "But I want kisses."

So did she. "Yes. Kissing would be good. I'd run my tongue back and forth over your lips. You have a very sexy mouth, Joshua." She flicked her tongue out and ran it along the seam of her sandwich in case he was looking, then licked her lips.

His quiet swearing sent a kick of lust through her stomach.

"I'd open my mouth and suck your tongue inside," he warned.

"I'd lick your tongue—"

"I'd lick you back. I'd go all the way inside your mouth and taste everywhere, drink you in."

"When you did, I'd rock against you—"

"Bloody—"

"Again and again."

"Hell!"

The word came out a little louder than a whisper, and they both froze for a few seconds. Then they made a show of eating something, drinking something, all the while panting like a couple of marathon runners. Amy crossed her legs and squeezed her muscles, trying to ease the ache.

"Oh, no you don't." His hand settled on her thigh, pulling until she uncrossed her legs.

She bit back a groan. "Why not?"

"Because we're not through. You started this and you're damn well going to finish it."

Yes, she'd started it, but she'd intended to tweak his libido, not her own, damn it. Now all she could think about was the orgasm hovering just out of her reach.

"Better hurry," he said. "Lunch crowd will be rolling in soon. Just so you know, we're not leaving here until this is done no matter how crowded it gets."

The warning in his voice was enough to make her look at him. When their eyes met, she almost went up in flames. The fire in his dark eyes burned bright, urging her on. Finally, she whispered, "I'd moan for you."

"Damn right you would. I want my hands free. I want to grab your ass and hold you tight against me as I grind into you. Can you feel me?" His eyes dropped to her lap. "Right there?"

"Yes." And she almost could. "Too many clothes."

He nodded. "I'd unfasten your jeans and push them down just enough to get my hand between your legs. I'd stroke you with my fingers—"

"God, yes—"

"I would stroke inside, deep inside. One finger, two—"

"Three," she gasped. "Three."

"For a little while," he agreed. "Just until I sucked both of your nipples into tight little buds right through your shirt. I'd bite them, too. You'd like that, wouldn't you?"

Her hips jerked in answer. "Yes. I'd ride your fingers while I held your head to my breasts with one hand and stroked your cock with the other." Her gaze dropped to his lap this time, and she saw the huge bulge behind his zipper straining to escape.

"Open my jeans."

Her gaze flew up to his face. "What?"

"I'd tell you to open my jeans. You'd reach in and pull me out."

She shook her head. "Wouldn't have to. You're so big, you'd fall into my waiting hand. I'd squeeze you and run my thumb over your slit."

His mouth snapped shut, jaw turning white while the rest of his face flushed with color. Air rushed in and out of his nose. Teeth ground. "Almost there, sweetheart."

Amy wanted to reach for him, touch him. A single touch, and they'd both come. Instead, she leaned a little toward him and dropped her voice even lower. "You'd remove your fingers, and I'd rise up on my knees just enough to slide the head of your cock into my wet opening."

He groaned quietly, and she kept going. "I'd run you back and forth, back and forth, until you were dripping wet with my juices. Then I'd slowly lower myself, drawing you deep inside me, scooting closer and closer until you were all the way inside, all the way to your balls. Then I'd squeeze my muscles around you."

The table creaked. Joshua's stiff posture and white knuckled grip nearly sent her over the edge.

"What would you do," she whispered.

Harsh, strangled words slipped from between his clenched teeth. "I'd slide in and out of your wet heat. Slowly at first, then faster and faster. I'd lift you up and bring you down to meet my thrusts. Harder. Deeper. I'd rub your clit every time. I'd make you feel so good you'd—"

"Come." And she did.

Pleasure surrounded her, swamping her until she wanted to cry out. Amy bit her lip, somehow managing to hold the moans down to a soft whimper. Her eyes wanted to close in bliss, but she wouldn't let them. She didn't want to look away from Joshua.

Beside her, his big body trembled.

Soft hisses, muttered swear words, she realized, were all that passed his lips. They held each other's gaze long after their bodies stilled.

Marlee Borden's arrival at their table jolted Amy back to reality. The waitress leaned down to collect their dishes, chuckling softly. "In case you're wondering, there's a bet going on about how much longer you two love birds are going to sit here making goo-goo eyes at each other."

Unable to meet the woman's amused gaze, Amy ducked her head. Embarrassment flooded her cheeks. Dear Lord, she'd just had phone sex without the phone.

In public!

Joshua's deep, husky laugh sent a gaggle of goose bumps running up her arms. "We were just leaving, Marlee, thanks." He pulled a couple of bills out of his wallet and handed them to the waitress. "Keep the change."

Then he stood and held a hand out to Amy. It was the challenge in his eyes that got her moving. If he could stand up and act like nothing happened, so could she.

Now if only her legs would just engage and stop feeling like a pair of wet noodles.

Thank God the walk back to the Jeep didn't take long. Joshua kept them moving, excusing them to the occasional well-wisher as quickly as possible.

Amy let him do his thing, wondering if she'd just made the second biggest mistake of her life. After thinking about it, she wasn't even sure he'd come. There was certainly no damp spot visible on the front of his jeans.

After he helped her into the Jeep and climbed in the driver's side, Amy asked calmly, "Where to?"

"Home first, then Kyle's garage. I need to pick up those files."

"Why not pick them up on the way to your cabin?" It didn't make sense for him to go all the way home only to double back down the mountain.

"Because," he said, tossing her a wicked grin as he eased into traffic, "as much as I enjoyed what just happened, I don't think you'd appreciate Kyle knowing about it."

Her cheeks warmed again. "How would he—"

She broke off as Joshua pinched his shirt right above his belt and pulled it out a little. Only then did she see the wide damp spot creeping up the fabric. Holy hell, the man's penis had been right under his belt when he'd come. That's why she hadn't seen anything lower on his jeans.

"How lo—" She snapped her mouth shut on stupid question number two. She'd had him between her legs last night and intimately knew just how long he could get.

Peeking above his waistband? Not a problem. She quickly looked away, but not before she caught his satisfied smirk.

Damn if she didn't have to bite the inside of her mouth to keep from grinning back at him.

Chapter Sixteen

Joshua couldn't stop the buzz zinging through his body. He was riding a definite high, and the woman sitting next to him was responsible.

She also sucked that high right out of him when she said, "You can drop me at the clinic on your way home. I want to check on Bors."

Like hell. "I don't think so."

"That wasn't a request."

"Good, because it's not happening."

She twisted sideways in her seat to face him. He could almost feel the essence of her anger swirling on her side of the cab. "Look, I get that you're supposed to bodyguard me. I even understand why you took me to the café. But we don't have to stay joined at the hip."

He slanted a glance in her direction. He doubted she understood about the café thing at all, including their little verbal petting session. It took a good amount of trust to do something like that, especially in such a public place.

"Hmm, joined at the hip. Interesting choice of words considering what just happened."

Okay, so he was being a bit of an ass but couldn't help it. He liked the way she blushed, how the color started almost in the center of her cheeks before blooming outward. The delicate pink made her blue eyes seem deeper, sexier—a perfect blend of innocence and sensuality.

"Get over it," she snapped. "You know what I mean. I like my freedom—what little I have left. You can just forget about taking over my life. I've agreed to every other demand you've made, including, the engagement and sleeping at your place. The least you can do is grant me a couple hours leave to check on my pet. And before you open your mouth, I know perfectly well that you wouldn't sit still for this kind of treatment. Don't be a hypocrite and expect me to."

She crossed her arms, the perfect punctuation to her "I-dare-you-to-disagree-with-me" glare. Damn it, he wanted to disagree. He should. But even he couldn't see how spending a couple of hours sitting with her dog would cause a problem. She'd be safe as long as she stayed inside the clinic with Sue. The woman was the only vet in the valley. People came in for appointments all the time. Velavich wouldn't risk waltzing in and taking Amy in front of an audience. And Chet had no way of knowing where she was.

He glanced at her again. The little minx had a smirk of her own going. Probably already guessing she'd won. Didn't mean he had to like it.

"Shit!" The word shot out of his mouth as sharp as a knife, making her jump. Joshua felt the distance between them widen. He rubbed a hand across his mouth, wishing he could take the swear word back. How had they gone from having their mental hands all over each other to this kind of don't-touch-me so fast? "Fine," he said, fighting for calm. "You can have your couple of hours. But I want it on record that I think this is a hell of a bad idea."

****

Amy held her temper, reminding herself that Joshua wasn't working at being an ass on purpose. He was simply being true to his nature. As a unit leader, he wouldn't like anything going against his own plans. She still couldn't believe she won this argument without resorting to violence. Then again, maybe he was still feeling a bit mellow from the phone-less sex. She'd have to keep that technique in mind. Might be worth a little judicious experimentation later.

Only three vehicles were parked in front of the clinic when they drove up. The truck was Sue's. Amy also recognized the little compact car belonging to Sue's part-time receptionist/assistant, Connie. The other vehicle was a minivan she'd never seen before.

Amy saw Joshua take in the almost empty lot and knew he was about to change his mind. "Thank you," she said just as he opened his mouth. She punched as much sincerity into the two words as she could. No smugness here, Mr. Harrier. Just an appreciative little woman who knows the big bad soldier could change his mind in a heartbeat. She gently touched his arm for good measure. "I promise I'll wait here at the clinic until you get back. Take your time. I'll help Sue with her patients if I get bored."

He muttered something under his breath and shook his head, but got out of the Jeep. Amy stayed where she was, waiting patiently while he did a quick search of the surroundings before coming around and opening her door for her. Not her usual behavior, but hey, she could do docile if the situation warranted. Not to mention, she knew how to choose her battles.

She still had to reassure him three times that she'd stay put before he finally got back in his Jeep and drove away. Thankfully, there was no one in the waiting room to witness her subservient behavior. Nor was there anyone in the small receptionist area.

Amy waited a moment, sure that the buzzer set off by opening the clinic's door would summon someone.

"Sue?" Amy called as she gave up and made her way to the back. "Connie?" A powerful bark answered her. Grinning, Amy followed the sound to a long room of kennels. A wide aisle led past the cages to a door at the far end that opened into a fenced area out back. The first kennel held a hyper Jack-Russell happily bouncing off the walls of his cage. An older black lab curled up on a pallet in the next pen studiously ignored the terrier's frenetic display. Amy glanced down the row, but didn't see any other animals from where she was standing.

"Bors?"

His deep *woof* drew her to the kennel on the end. She'd expected her baby to be at the cage's door, nose pressed tightly against the chain-links, eager to get to her. Instead, she found him facing the kennel's door leading to the outside run. His stance was stiff, hackles raised. A continuous, low growl rumbled from his throat. The door was closed, so Amy couldn't see what had him spooked. Bobcat, maybe. Bors hated felines with a passion.

"Bors? What is it big guy? You smell a kitty?"

The dog ceased growling and gave her a quick glance over his shoulder. Then he faced the door again and took a stiff-legged step forward. Thick, black lips drew back over sharp, white teeth in a silent snarl.

Amy froze with her hand on the kennel latch. Warning tingles danced down the back of her neck, raising hairs. Whatever was outside that door wasn't a bobcat, wasn't even an animal, not the four-legged kind, anyway. Bors only snarled at people.

All the doors to the runs had a small window in the upper half. Amy quietly moved into the kennel next to Bors. Standing to the side of the window, she looked out, first to the left, then the right. All she saw were empty runs and beyond them, an open stretch of grass, equally as empty. After that, the woods took over, thick with bushes, trees, and low-hanging limbs. It was impossible to see if anyone was out there.

Bors whined. Amy looked over to find him facing

her now instead of the door. The snarl was gone, as were the raised hackles. His tail waved slowly back and forth, picking up speed the moment she faced him.

"Woof!"

Amy drew a deep breath and let it out. She knew his barks. This one wasn't his there's-an-enemy-nearby bark, but his where-have-you-been-I'm-glad-to-see-you bark. Apparently whatever, or whoever, he'd smelled was gone. "You know," she said, walking out of the empty kennel, "it would help a heck of a lot if you could learn to talk."

She let him sniff her hand through the fence. His long tongue rolled out and wet her palm. Laughing, she rubbed his slobber on her jeans. "Hang tight for a minute, sweetie. I need to find Sue before I let you out."

Maybe she and Connie were in the x-ray room and hadn't heard Amy's call.

She turned to retrace her steps into the heart of the clinic just as the outside door at the end of the hall rattled on its hinges. Amy spun around. Something large thumped against the door again, trying to get in. The doorknob twisted. Amy's heart shot into overdrive.

What if it was Adrik? She didn't have a single weapon on her. The knife she usually carried was in her pack in Joshua's truck. A blatant bit of stupidity she easily blamed on her new bodyguard. Damn man had a way of making her feel safe when he was around.

She looked for another weapon. An animal control stick hung by its noose next to one of the cages. She reached for it just as the door jerked open.

"Get in there you beast."

Tension drained out of Amy at the sound of Sue's voice, leaving her feeling oddly light headed.

Her eyes widened as a mammoth St. Bernard lumbered through the doorway.

"Oh," Sue said, catching sight of Amy. "Jeepers, girl, you scared me."

"Sorry." Amy backed up to give the huge animal plenty of room. "Who's the four-legged wookie?"

Sue laughed. "His name's Samson."

"Okay, makes sense I guess." She eyed the dog's wealth of hair and heavy muscles. "Who owns him?"

Sue laughed again as she maneuvered the dog into an empty kennel, unclipped the leash, and secured the door. "You're not going to believe this, but his owner is a woman named Delilah."

Amy grinned. "You're kidding."

"Nope. Delilah Rehnquist. She's here visiting some friends in town. Brought good old Samson here this morning so she and the friends could ride over to the next valley to visit some other friends for lunch. That's her van out front."

"Where's Connie? I didn't see anyone when I came in."

Sue grimaced. "She came down with something after she got here this morning. Her sister picked her up to take her to the doctor. Said someone would be by later to get the car. With me being the only one here and not knowing how Samson was going to take to being left with a stranger, I called and rescheduled this afternoon's appointments."

"Would you mind some company? Joshua dropped me off and won't be back for a couple of hours."

"Not at all," the vet practically gushed, her face lighting up with a smile.

Something told Amy her friend's happy expression had less to do with the offer of company and more with the mention of Joshua.

"You know you're welcome anytime. This'll give us a chance to have a nice, long chat. I'm dying to know how you and Joshua met. Knowing him, I bet it's a hoot of a story." She linked their arms and Amy let the woman pull her along, praying for a way out of the mess she was in. She hated lying, even when her job required it. Lying to Sue, who Amy considered a friend of sorts, was not something she wanted to do. There had to be a way out of this.

The phone rang just as they entered the clinic. "Shoot," Sue said. "Hang on, I'll be right back." She hurried down the hall to the reception area. Amy followed, wondering how much harassing she'd get if she called Joshua to pick her up early. He'd laugh at her for sure, but at least she'd be spared the coming interrogation.

Still trying to pick between the lesser of two evils, Amy entered the reception area. Sue had her back to Amy, but swung around with a gasp. The horrified expression on her face sent a rush of chills across Amy's skin.

"Where exactly did you say?" The vet waved frantically, making writing motions. Amy snagged a pen from a cup on Connie's desk and took it to her.

"Yes, yes, of course." Sue scribbled hurriedly on a note pad. "I'll be right there." She slammed the phone down.

"What is it?"

"An accident on the other side of the valley. A livestock trailer jack-knifed, hitting a van carrying a family of four and their three dogs. It's bad, Amy. I have to go."

"Of course you do."

Sue ripped the note off the pad, then glanced at the clock and frowned. "I'll have to leave a note for Samson's owner. She's due to pick him up in an hour."

Amy put her hand on the woman's shoulder. "It's okay, Sue. I've got nothing to do for the next couple of hours. You go ahead. I'll be right here when

Delilah comes for her Samson. I'll even feed and water your patients and lock up when I leave."

Sue's shoulders sagged in relief. "Oh, Amy, honey, that would be great. Ms. Rehnquist paid this morning, so you don't have to worry about collecting any money. In fact, you can consider Bors' bill paid in full, too."

Amy tried to argue about the bill, but quickly gave up. Sue was adamant, and anything Amy said just rolled off the woman like water off an oiled gun barrel. After helping Sue gather supplies and seeing the vet on her way, Amy went back to the kennels to let Bors out. She took him to the large front waiting room so she could see when Samson's owner arrived. Watching for any hint of pain in her pet, she ran him through a routine that was half-play, half-work, designed to reinforce the list of silent commands she'd taught him. The office phone rang in the middle of *crawl and hide*. Amy signed for Bors to stand down, scratching his ears and giving him a couple of thumps on his side as she passed him on the way to the desk. A glance at the wall clock surprised her. Almost an hour had passed already. Samson's owner would be here soon. She picked up the phone.

"Haynes Animal Care. Can I help you?"

"I'm going to kill someone!"

Amy winced, jerking the phone away from her ear, certain she'd heard wrong. The gentle little veterinarian who loved all living things, especially animals, had not just threatened to murder someone. She eased the phone back to her ear.

"Sue, calm down. Tell me what's wrong. Is the accident worse than you thought?"

"That's the problem," Sue complained, "there is no accident. I've been up and down this road twice and haven't seen a darn thing. I even called the sheriff's office. No one's reported so much as a

169

dented fender today." Her irritated huff sounded like a windstorm through the phone line.

The call was a prank? Talk about cruel.

"Who would do something like this?"

Another huff. "I don't know, but if I find out, their parents won't have to worry about disciplining them. I have access to fleas. Lots and lots of fleas."

Amy grinned. What an apt punishment. "Are you on your way back?"

"Yeah. Has Samson's owner showed up yet?"

"No, but I imagine she'll be here soon."

"Okay, see you in a bit."

Amy hung up. She started to walk back to Bors, but stopped and stared at the phone. A crank call. Probably some irresponsible kid's idea of a joke. No reason at all to think it had any connection to Adrik. Still...

The sound of a car door and voices outside interrupted her musing. She shook her head, firmly closing the door mentally on the string of "what ifs" that had suddenly presented themselves. Damn if she'd let Adrik make her look for shadows in every little thing. She moved to a window just in time to see a car drive off, leaving a woman standing beside the van. Samson's owner.

Amy called Bors and led him back to his kennel. As soon as she took out Samson, Bors started barking. She met her dog's reproachful gaze, giving him the sign for *silence*. He quieted immediately, though he cocked his head with a betrayed look in his big brown eyes.

"Hang tight, buddy," she told him. "I'll be back soon and we'll go outside so you can run a bit." He whined softly.

After taking possession of Samson, his owner, an attractive, middle-aged woman, seemed in no hurry to leave. The woman was a talker, chatting non-stop about her trip to the next valley as if she and Amy were long-time friends. Anxious to get back to Bors, Amy slowly eased toward the front door, woman and dog blithely following. As soon as she opened the clinic's door, setting off the buzzer, Bors started barking again.

Strange. It wasn't like him to disobey a *silent* command. Of course, the Jack Russell's sharper yipping had started up, too, which could have set Bors off. When the Lab joined in, Samson wasn't far behind. The St. Bernard's deep, bass woof shook the ceiling tiles.

Looking both irritated and apologetic, Samson's owner quickly hustled her pet out the door and into her van. Another vehicle pulled into the parking lot as the pair left. Amy walked outside, muffling the on-going three-dog symphony by closing the door. She spent a few minutes talking to Connie's sister while the woman's husband retrieved her car.

"Connie will be fine," her sister said. "Just a bad case of the flu."

"That's great. Tell her I said hi, will you? I need to get back inside before Bors and his buddies bark the clinic down."

Connie's sister stuck her head through the open window, tilting it to one side. "You must have great hearing. I can't hear a single bark."

Amy listened, realizing the woman was right. The dogs had quieted. Not even a stray yip from the Jack Russell. "Huh," she said. "Guess they finally stopped."

Waving goodbye, she stepped back, watching uneasily as both cars drove away. As soon as they were out of sight, she headed back to the clinic, surreptitiously scanning the surrounding woods. The dogs' spate of barking followed by complete silence bothered her, like a target she'd been studying for days suddenly doing something out of character. Unease crept its way up her body with each step to the clinic, hair rising on the back of her neck.

She should have felt better inside the clinic with the door locked, but didn't. Goose bumps continued to chase each other up and down her arms. She tried rubbing them away without success. Something definitely had her sniper senses screaming a warning. But what?

She had two choices, stay in the dubious safety of the clinic or go outside and find out what the problem was. Barricading herself in the kennel with Bors until Joshua arrived was out of the question. Sure, it was probably safer, but it wouldn't do for him to find her cowering inside. He'd take one look at her, know she'd been spooked, and never let her out of his sight again.

That only left option two.

Excitement stirred, pushing aside the unease. Practicing her tracking and stalking skills while taking pictures didn't compare to actually using them in a potentially dangerous situation. It had been a while, not that she was hoping for trouble. The quick trip out the back for a perimeter check would just be to settle her nerves, nothing dangerous, just a nice, easy sneak through the trees. Besides, she didn't want Sue coming back into trouble.

As soon as she pushed open the door to the kennels, Amy knew her decision had come too late. The back door stood wide open. So was the door to Bors' cage. Her dog was nowhere in sight.

A whine from the Jack Russell's cage drew a quick glance. The little dog cowered inside the dog house at the back, body quivering. Something had frightened him.

The black Lab was still out, but lay in a corner, gaze fixed on the open door. A silent snarl curled his lips back over his teeth.

Amy stepped back toward the main clinic. She

wasn't a fool. Bors wasn't able to open doors by himself. Someone had taken him—someone who wanted her to follow.

Was it Adrik?

She didn't know and wasn't about to walk into a trap to find out. Time to call for backup.

She took another step back, reaching into her pocket for her cell phone.

"Now, now, no need for that."

A hand closed on her wrist. Chet's arrogant voice actually made Amy feel a little better. She could deal with the Wassiles a lot easier than she could with Adrik. As far as she knew, the brothers didn't want her dead.

Of course, she could be mistaken, she thought, as Chet's other hand came into view. The blade of the long hunting knife gleamed in the fluorescent light from overhead. Amy tensed. She could still take him down, but not knowing where Arney and Franklin were bothered her. Did they have Bors?

His hand tightened painfully on her wrist. "Don't even think about it," he said, the words uttered more harshly than she'd ever heard coming from him. The knife shifted closer to her throat.

Amy turned her head carefully, meeting his gaze over her shoulder. Chet's sharp features weren't tempered with his usual half-mocking, half-coaxing smile. His expression was harder, meaner, his eyes tight with anger.

"Where's Bors," she demanded.

He inched closer to her, his body crowding her into the wall, brushing against hers. Revulsion joined the anger building inside her, making her want to gag. It didn't help that his heated breath, tainted thickly with beer, wafted into her face when he spoke.

"Don't you worry about him. Frankie boy has your pup nice and safe." He tsked. "Too bad about his little accident. Knew you'd show up here eventually to check on him. All I had to do was have one of the boys watch the place and call me when you showed up. Took a chance on calling that fake accident in to the doc, but it was worth it to get you alone." He removed her hand from her pocket and dug into her jeans, taking his time fishing out her phone. Dark eyes gone almost black dared her to stop him.

Amy held herself sniper still. Something had cranked his aggression into overdrive. Probably the fake engagement. She'd warned Joshua his interference would escalate things. But even she hadn't imagined a straight out physical attack.

Unless she was badly mistaken, Chet Wassile walked an edge, teetering one short step away from violence.

Chapter Seventeen

"What do you want, Chet?" Amy kept her tone even, hiding the adrenaline-laced emotions racing inside her. Maybe she could talk him out of whatever he planned.

In answer, he pushed his body hard against hers once, then stepped back.

Amy turned slightly, keeping her shoulder facing him, waiting for his next move. She was torn between keeping him talking until Joshua arrived, and getting him to leave before Sue returned.

Chet shook his head. "All this time," he muttered. "All this time I've gone slow because I thought you were special. Pure. Only you're not, are you? Been around the block more than a couple of times, so I hear." He reached out and rubbed a lock of her hair between his fingers before giving it a sharp jerk.

Amy fought not to deck him. She wasn't sure what he was talking about. "You're starting to annoy me, Chet. You should give me my dog back and leave while you can."

Chet grinned, though the smile held no trace of humor. "Annoy you? Honey, I ain't even got started yet." He snapped his fingers.

Amy's gaze was drawn past him at the sound of low, sharp cursing mixed with choked-off growls coming from outside. When Arney appeared in the doorway dragging a gasping and writhing Bors at the end of a control stick, Amy lost it. Damn it, she'd be lucky to get out of this mess without killing someone.

She shoved away from the wall, intent on setting Bors free, only to have Chet grab her arm. She twisted out of his grasp without thinking, not even looking at him. She'd deal with him later. When Arney looked up from torturing Bors and met her gaze, his eyes widened. He gripped the pole, jerking the noose around Bors' neck tighter.

"I'll kill him," he warned.

Yep, someone was going to die.

Something sharp stabbed into the side of her neck. Amy swung around, slapping Chet's hand away, but it was too late. Whatever was in the syringe still in her neck was fast-acting. She jerked the needle free and threw it at Chet just as the room started swinging and tilting like a wild carnival ride. The florescent lights overhead dimmed.

Amy took a step and fell against the door to an empty kennel. She clung to the cold chain-links, trying to focus her eyes on Arney as he dragged Bors out of sight.

No. Her dog. She had to reach him. Save him.

A dark voice whispered in her ear. "That'll calm you down." Chet's voice, she thought, though it sounded just as blurry as her vision.

She fought to keep her eyes open, but knew it was a losing battle. The drug was just too potent. Her lids drifted down, feeling impossibly heavy as she tried to lift them back up. She was going to be out soon. Totally out. Completely vulnerable.

A gunshot came from outside, followed by a sharp yelp. Bors!

Amy tried to take a step and felt her knees give way. Arms caught her, holding her so tight, she could hardly breathe. Something grabbed her chin, tilting her head up.

"Nice," Chet said, the word sounding to Amy like the hiss of a snake. "Stuff worked just like he said it would."

He? Who was he? Amy wanted to ask, but couldn't. With a sense of helplessness, she fell into a yawning black tunnel as the drug took over, desperately afraid of what she'd find on the other side.

Chapter Eighteen

"Incoming."

Joshua lifted his head at Kyle's call, realizing as he did that he'd been studying files and sifting data for a lot longer than he thought. It was almost time to pick up Amy. He rubbed his eyes and blinked several times as he straightened, stretching his stiff back muscles. Damn, he hoped the new arrival was Rio.

The unit's newest member wasn't familiar with the area, so when he'd called earlier, Joshua told him they'd meet at Kyle's. Good thing he'd come in early. Trying to find a needle in a haystack went a lot faster with more than one set of eyes.

Joshua pushed back from the desk and stood, walking quickly out to meet up with Kyle in the main part of the garage. The sound of the approaching motorcycle, rumbling like the four-stroke growl of an angry bear, had him grinning. That had to be Rio's Harley.

They made it to the open garage door as the big black machine prowled into the parking lot. The rider brought the Harley to a stop and switched off the heavy thumping engine, planting the kick-stand before he pulled off his helmet.

Kyle gave Joshua a sideways look. "Drafting them a bit young these days, aren't you?"

"Don't let that curly hair and pretty face fool you. They don't come any meaner or slicker when it comes to hand-to-hand. Besides, he's a full year older than you and I were when we first joined the SO."

"Makes you feel old, don't it?"

"Every damn day." Joshua strode forward, meeting Rio as he swung a long leg over the bike. He saw the kid start to snap to attention and threw out a *hold* sign as he extended his hand. "A shake'll do." He caught the slight flush under Rio's tan and wondered if he'd really ever been that young.

"Sorry, Cap, force of habit."

"No problem." He indicated Kyle. "Want you to meet an old friend of mine. This is Kyle Fagan."

A cocky grin split Rio's face as he shook Kyle's hand. "A pleasure to meet you, sir. I've heard a lot of interesting stuff about you."

"Interesting. Is that what they're calling it these days?"

"Yes, sir," Rio said. "Well, that, and a few other choice adjectives."

"Uh-huh. Do me a favor, kid. Knock off the 'sir' bit or you'll discover just how accurate some of those adjectives are. Only my children call me sir."

"Fair enough. As long as you don't call me *kid* again I think I can remember to leave off the *sir*."

"Deal," Kyle said.

Rio turned back to Joshua. "So, I'm the first one in?"

"Yeah," Kyle said, cutting off Joshua's reply. "You can always tell the eager young shits from the—"

"Old farts?" Rio supplied smoothly.

Kyle grinned and nudged Joshua's shoulder. "He'll do."

Joshua snorted. "Well, now that we have your approval out of the way, how about letting us get back to work? You, too. We can use the help."

"Me?" Kyle's brows shot up. He slapped a hand to his leg. "I'm disabled, remember?"

"Nice try, goofus, but you don't read or think with your leg. The Commander said he reactivated you. That means as a unit leader, I can draft your

179

ass into service anytime I please. The Cobra isn't just going to slither up and tell us what he's planning. We have to find him before he finds Amy. To do that, we have to sift through every bit of data we have."

Kyle scowled. "Last time I checked, data sifting was Capella's job."

"Boss is big on cross-training," Rio said with a grin.

"Since when?"

"Since you left and took your badass skills with you," Joshua snapped. "I don't like holes in my team. Now stop wasting time and get your shop closed. Sam, Ty, and Brick are on their way. You can trade gripes with them when they get here."

"Fine," Kyle grumbled. "But your ratty cabin doesn't have Farrah's cooking."

And Farrah was exactly why they weren't going to Kyle's house. She might not have kicked up a fuss about Kyle being re-activated, but Joshua wasn't about to shove it in her face. And having a group of modern-day warriors crowd into her house would definitely be shoving it. Kyle should know better. "True," Joshua said. "But I promise not to let you starve."

He led the way back to the garage. Behind him, he heard Rio say, "Goofus?", and Kyle respond with a phrase that was solid-blue-Kyle. Joshua chuckled. He was almost at the door when his cell phone rang. He pulled it out and flipped it open. "Yeah."

"Joshua, I'm so glad I got you. Is Amy with you?"

The woman's frantic question brought Joshua to a sudden halt. "Sue?" He waved to get Kyle's and Rio's attention and punched the speaker button. Sue's voice quavered though the mountain air.

"Oh, yes, it's me. I'm sorry, I'm just so flustered. Please tell me you picked up Amy and Bors."

"No, I haven't." He took a deep breath to keep

himself calm. No reason to worry yet. "When did she leave?"

"I don't know. I got a crank call about an accident involving some animals and had to leave. Amy stayed to watch the clinic for me. I talked to her not twenty minutes ago, but when I got here, the back door was open and there's no sign of Amy and Bors."

Okay, maybe he should worry a little. "Could she have taken Bors for a short run?" Kyle immediately shook his head. Joshua agreed. After the incident with the dress, Amy would know better. Still, it didn't hurt to hope her stubborn nature got the better of her and she and the dog were on an innocent jog. Anything was better than thinking the alternative.

"I don't think so, Joshua," Sue said, her voice trembling. "There's b-blood on the grass by the back door."

Hell, Joshua thought, forget worry, it was time to panic.

Kyle mouthed a string of cuss words and headed inside his garage at a limping run. Rio moved back to his bike without a word and started unfastening a heavy pack secured to the back. Joshua thanked God for good soldiers and better friends while keeping the panic rushing through his veins out of his voice.

"Listen to me carefully, Sue. I want you to lock up and sit tight. Kyle and I are on our way. Don't go looking for Amy, do you understand? You're not to go outside."

"Oh, Joshua, is it the Wassiles? Should I call Dan Penwell?"

Joshua thought about the sheriff while he got into the Jeep. Pen wouldn't be happy if he learned about this after the fact, but having the other man muck around now might be dangerous, for him as well as Amy.

"No, don't call Penwell just yet. Let me take a look around first." He closed the phone without giving Sue a chance to argue and started the vehicle. Rio hit the back seat and began removing rifle parts from his pack. Kyle slid into the passenger seat a second later, a beautiful stainless .45 automatic in his hand.

"Think it's Velavich?" Kyle asked.

"We're about to find out." Joshua slammed his foot on the accelerator. Despite the twisting roads, he stayed heavy on the gas, cutting the twenty minute drive to the clinic almost in half. The place looked deserted when they pulled into the parking lot.

Shutting off the engine, Joshua said, "Kyle, secure the inside."

"Josh—"

"Can it. We both know you don't move like you used to." He hated bringing up his friend's injury, but it couldn't be helped.

At Kyle's stiff nod, they exited the Jeep. Joshua covered Kyle until he was at the door. Sue opened it without him knocking. With Kyle inside, he sent Rio around the building to the right while he took the left. They met at the back door to the kennels, Joshua squatted to examine the small puddle of blood staining the trampled grass while Rio stood guard. More drops led off toward the tree line.

"Boot prints." Rio pointed to a nearby patch of bare ground indented by heel and toe marks. "Two sets at least."

Joshua nodded. "Do a perimeter check. See what else you can find."

"Will do." The young man moved off quietly.

Joshua rose and rapped a knuckle on the door. "Anything?" he asked when Kyle stepped out.

Kyle held up a black cell phone. "Found this in the hall outside the kennels."

182

The panic inside Joshua had long since turned into dread. "Yeah, that's Amy's phone." He plucked the device from Kyle's hand and slid it into his pocket.

"And this," Kyle said, holding up an empty syringe. "Sue says it's not one of hers. No way to tell what's in it without an analysis."

Joshua ground his teeth. Bloody bastards had drugged her.

"Could have been for Bors," Kyle suggested, his tone too tentative to give Joshua any comfort.

"We both know the odds of that." He was pretty sure the kidnappers hadn't wasted money on a sedative for Bors. A bullet was far cheaper.

He glanced at the blood, wishing he had the chemicals to prove his theory right then and there. "How's Sue?"

Kyle heaved a sigh. "Upset. She thinks if she'd been here whoever it was wouldn't have snatched Amy. 'Course, she's still thinking it was Chet. That's why she's pushing to call the sheriff."

"See if you can talk her out of it. If this is Velavich, I don't want the local law involved."

"Cap!"

They both turned to see Rio standing at the tree line. "Found something," he called, then headed back into the thick foliage.

Before Joshua could utter a word, Kyle broke into a limping run for the trees.

"Stubborn fool," Joshua muttered. He should have ordered Kyle to stay at the clinic. Instead, Joshua made sure he reached the trees first. There was no sign of Rio, but he had no trouble spotting the trail the younger man had noticed. It wasn't the few crushed blades of grass and bent twigs that gave it away, but the drops of bright red blood.

"Watch yourself," he ordered Kyle, shooting him a hard glance.

Kyle's eyes rounded innocently. "Yes, Mother."

Stifling the urge to punch his friend, Joshua eased into the woods. They'd gone about thirty yards when he heard soft growling. Pushing past some brush, he caught sight of Kyle squatting at the base of a large oak. Ten feet away lay a very pissed off Bors, the noose of a catch pole around his neck.

The big dog was conscious, but not by much. Joshua figured that was the only reason Bors didn't already have his teeth sunk into Rio's flesh.

"Not too friendly, is he?" Rio observed quietly.

Kyle snorted as he slowly moved up next to the dog. "Let's put a bullet into you and see how friendly you are."

Bors' growl deepened when Kyle touched him, but he didn't move. Joshua stayed back as Kyle removed the noose and checked Bors over with quick hands. He motioned to Rio. "Report."

"I think the dog was trying to follow them. His blood led me to their exit trail. Three separate tracks, one deeper than the others. There's a spot just inside the trees where one of them sat waiting for a few hours."

Some of the urgency making Joshua's skin feel too tight faded. He'd been braced to find one set of tracks, or worse, none at all. Finding three made it easier to breathe.

"Damn Wassiles," Kyle muttered.

Joshua agreed. He'd have Amy back and the three idiots who'd taken her—what was left of them—on Pen's doorstep before the sun set.

"There was a fourth man," Rio said.

Joshua's blood ran cold. He should have known this was too damn easy.

"Where?"

Rio stood and pointed to a tall, thick spruce growing a few yards along the back trail. "I think he watched everything from the branches of that tree.

He's good, Cap. Has training. I would have missed him except for the drills Rashid has me doing."

Joshua cursed. It had to be Velavich. The question is whether he was using the Wassiles to get to Amy, or just happened to be shadowing Amy when Chet and his brothers took her."

"Bad shit either way," Kyle said. "If he doesn't already have her, the Cobra now knows where she is."

"In that case…" Rio produced a small round tin from a back pocket. Holding up the container of camo paint, he said, "Guess it's time to take this hunting trip to the next level."

Joshua nodded grimly. Becoming just another couple of dappled shadows in the woods might give them the edge they needed. No telling what kind of backup Velavich had with him.

He motioned to Rio. "See if Bors will let you pick him up and carry him to the clinic. Kyle, you stay with Sue. If Amy should show up—"

"I know. I'll call you." Kyle pushed to his feet. He reached out and grabbed a hand-full of Joshua's shirt. "Go. Find her. Or Farrah's going to have both our asses."

Joshua nodded grimly. "Rio, grab my bow and quiver out of the Jeep and catch up to me."

"Aye, Cap," Rio said. He bent and hefted a limp Bors into his arms. The dog had either passed out or was dead.

Joshua hoped the former, but didn't have time to worry about the animal. His sole focus now was on finding Amy. Every second counted. They had to find her before her ex-lover decided to silence her for good.

Chapter Nineteen

Amy stubbornly fought her way to consciousness. Once there, she wished she could sink back into oblivion. Considering she'd been tranqued and was now hanging upside-down over someone's shoulder like a limp quilt, she'd forgive herself for that moment of weakness.

The boney shoulder of her captor dug into her stomach at each step. Between the pain and the side effects from the drug Chet had given her, she felt like she was going to throw up her toes at any moment. The pounding in her head didn't help matters. She swore it felt like an entire brigade was marching quick time through her skull. And she was beginning to have trouble breathing.

Despite the growing list of discomforts, Amy managed to keep her muscles loose. No sense alerting the Wassiles she was awake before she was ready. Her wrists were tied, but not behind her back. And she could tell her ankles were free. That meant the moment she got her feet firmly under her, she'd make Chet and his sorry-ass brothers regret putting their hands on her. And pay them back for killing Bors.

Amy shoved back the sharp, biting pain those words generated before it could sink its teeth in too deep. Oh, yes, they'd be very sorry for killing her pet. If she let them live that long.

Whoever was carrying her slipped, almost losing his grip on her. He righted himself with a jerk, slapping a hand to her butt to keep her in place. His sharp movement drove his shoulder deep into her stomach and shoved a moan out of her. She was really going to throw up if she didn't get vertical.

"She awake?" someone asked. Chet, she thought, though she wasn't sure. The anxious tone wasn't one she'd ever heard from him before.

"Hell if I know," her captor said. From the whine in his voice, she guessed it was Franklin. The hand on her backside squeezed. "She ain't moving around none yet."

Chet's voice dropped warningly. "Watch your hand, Frankie Boy. That's my woman you're fondling."

The hand vanished. "Shit, Chet, I was just makin' sure she's steady so I don't drop her." He shifted her a little and started walking again. "Ain't like she'd feel it if I did," he muttered under his breath.

"Want me to carry her a while?"

Even upside down Amy heard the hunger in Arney Wassile's voice. Evidently Chet did, too.

"You just shut up and watch our back trail like I told you."

"What for?" Arney grumbled. "Nobody knows we took her. Ain't no one comin' after us."

"Just do what I tell you. I ain't takin' no chances on leading anyone back to our cabin. You know what Mr. V said."

Amy's breath caught in her throat and her muscles locked involuntarily. Mr. V? V as in Velavich?

Franklin stopped walking. "Hey, I think she's awake."

The crunch of leaves under boots drew closer, stopping next to her. "Let's see." Hands lifted her off Franklin's shoulder. As soon as Chet flipped her over, Amy's stomach heaved. She retched and pulled away from him.

"Shit!"

Chet all but threw her to the ground as the BLT she'd had for lunch left her stomach in a bitter-tasting rush. She'd fallen near the edge of another drop-off, and leaned over as her stomach emptied—not to be polite, but to scan the sharp drop between heaves. She would need to put some distance between herself and the three brothers fast in order to pull off an escape.

The area below was rugged, but she'd been down rougher. Several young evergreens clung to the rocky hillside. Their springy tops swaying in the wind sparked a wild idea, as did the glint of water through the line of trees at the bottom.

When she was done cataloging the landscape, she heaved one last time, spit, and sat up, wiping her mouth with the back of her hand.

"Here."

Amy eyed the bottle of water Chet held out to her. Oh, how she wanted that water. Not just to wash her mouth out, but to guzzle down her parched throat. But the seal was broken on the lid. She couldn't risk ingesting anymore drugs.

"No thanks."

Chet shoved the bottle closer. "You need to drink."

Amy pushed slowly to her feet. Her head throbbed painfully with every heartbeat, but the dizziness was fading by the second. She met Chet's insistent gaze. "I said, no thank you."

Anger flashed in his eyes. She wondered if he'd try to force her and prayed he wouldn't. She didn't have her strength back yet. With a grunt, he shoved the water bottle back into the pack he carried. "Damn stubborn woman. Suit yourself. But I ain't offering it for free again. When you get thirsty enough, you'll pay whatever price I ask."

"Not likely."

He wrapped rough hands around her upper

arms and jerked her against him. "Oh, yes you will. And you'll like paying me, too."

Confronted with an enemy, Amy's SO training slipped into place as if the past year of civilian life had never happened. Determination buried all traces of her fear. Her expression remained bland, her muscles relaxed, though adrenaline thrummed through her body like a surge of electricity.

"Don't hold your breath, Chet. Oh, wait, I take that back. Go right ahead and hold your breath until the moment I like anything associated with you. It'll save me the cost of a bullet."

Somewhere behind them, Franklin hooted with laughter. "I think she just threatened to shoot you, big brother."

"Shut up," Chet snapped, never taking his eyes off her. If glares could kill, she'd be dead and buried. "I'm going to enjoy making you take back every one of those words, my bitch. Starting right now." With a vicious growl, he smashed his mouth against hers.

Anticipating his move, Amy snapped her lips tightly closed. She kept her eyes open, watching Chet's frustration build. He ground his mouth against hers, bruising her lips against her teeth while trying to force his way inside her mouth with his tongue. Unable to get where he wanted, he reared back and slapped her hard.

She let her head roll with the blow, clamping down on her body's reaction to the stinging pain. Damn if she'd show him tears. He wasn't getting that kind of response from her. Contempt, yes. Rage, absolutely. But tears, even angry ones, he'd see as a weakness. She was a lot of things, but weak wasn't one of them.

She straightened slowly, lifting her head to meet his furious gaze with a calmness she was far from feeling.

"If that's your idea of seduction I can see why

you're so hard up for a date that you have to resort to kidnapping."

He cursed, picked her up and shoved her hard against the rough trunk of a tree. He held her in place with one hand wrapped around her throat, the other dragging up the hem of her shirt.

"That's right, teach her a lesson, Chet," Franklin urged. "Damn mouthy bitch."

Chet grunted, fisting a hand around one of her breasts. "Mouthy I don't mind. Lots of uses for a mouth on a woman. Disrespectful, though, that's something else. Can't have a disrespectful woman teaching my brothers bad habits. So let's see if we can't put you in a more respectful frame of mind before we reach the cabin." He jerked at her sports bra, trying to reach bare skin, his brothers urging him on.

Amy made herself not fight him. With her hands tied and that damn drug still dulling her reflexes, three to one odds were a bad bet. She'd have to stick to talking her way out of this mess.

"You don't want to do this." The tight grip Chet had on her throat made her gasp the words. She was sure she'd have bruises later.

Chet grinned, evidently thinking he'd found the button to her fear. His fingers dug under the stretchy bra fabric and into her flesh.

"Hell, yes I do. Been dreaming about sucking your sweet tits raw for months now."

"Bad...idea...Chet."

He paused. "Why? You figuring on trying to stop me?" The rising lust in his eyes told her he'd like that. He was the kind of man who would like nothing more than to beat a woman into submission.

She swallowed pointedly. He eased his grip a little.

"Right now all you've done is kidnap me. You let me go, and you have a chance to disappear, free and clear. You take this one step further, and no matter what comes after, if I don't kill you first, Joshua will hunt you down. You know he will. And when he's through, there won't be enough of you left to bury, much less identify."

"Best listen to the woman."

The deep voice came out of woods, sending all three brothers scrambling to put their hands on guns.

Amy heard the quiet spit of three silenced rounds in quick succession. The first two bullets dug furrows in the ground inches from Chet's and Franklin's feet, making them freeze. The third slammed into the pine tree next to where Arney stood a few yards down the trail. He yelped and ducked, covering his head with his hands as bits of bark flew.

A long silence followed. Then a giant of a man stepped into view. Tall, broad-shouldered, he was dressed in dark green camo shirt and pants, and black military boots. A heavy-looking pack was strapped to his back. In his right hand was a Sig Sauer with a silencer while his left cradled a scoped rifle clipped to a strap across his chest.

"Shit, Chambliss." Most of the tension melted out of Chet and he straightened slowly. "What are you doing here?"

Chambliss gave Amy a good long look with cold blue eyes. A vague sense of recognition swept through her. She couldn't place the hard, square-jawed face topped in a blond buzz-cut, but she knew she'd seen him somewhere before. His clothes and gear screamed military. Maybe he was one of Joshua's Hawks? But then, how would Chet know him?

"Consider me your guide," Chambliss said.

Franklin dug a wad of masticated tobacco out of his mouth and flicked it into the bushes. He wiped his hand on his pants and his mouth on his sleeve.

"We don't need a stinking guide to find our own place."

"That's right," Arney said easing up to stand beside his brother. "This is our back yard, mister. Nobody knows it better than us."

Chambliss' square chin wrinkled, the slash of his mouth pulling down on both sides. He nodded grudgingly. "Could be you're right. Maybe you don't need a guide. But that's not the main reason I'm here. Mr. Velavich thought you might have a little trouble resisting certain…urges."

His cold, emotionless gaze settled meaningfully on Chet. "He wouldn't like that. At least, not until he's gotten reacquainted with the lady first."

Amy swallowed back the hot bile rising in her throat again. God help her, it was true. Adrik had finally found her. And now she knew where she'd seen Chambliss before.

Just before the catastrophe in Brazil, she'd been waiting for Adrik at a little bistro, stupidly eager to see him. She'd just sat down when she caught sight of him getting out of a car down the street. The car later drove past the bistro. Chambliss had been behind the wheel.

Anger tempered her panic. She'd wanted to meet the man who'd betrayed both her and her country again, but on her terms, not his. Bound and weaponless would only get her killed. She couldn't let this lapdog of Adrik's drag her back to his boss. Somehow, she had to get away before they reached the Wassiles' cabin. She stuffed her panic down and tried to slow her racing heart.

"Dear, sweet Adrik," she drawled. "How is my old lover?"

Chambliss tilted his head a fraction, as if he'd expected an entirely different reaction from her.

"He's doing well. Said to tell you 'hello.'" He

sucked a breath in through his teeth and gave her a toothy grin. "Man's got grand plans for you, sweetheart."

"She's mine!" Chet's arms caught her around her waist, pulling her tight against him.

Damn if she didn't feel like a bone caught between two dogs.

Chambliss' gun, aimed at no one in particular before, centered on Chet's forehead. "She has a lot to answer for to Mr. Velavich. You were told you could have her after he was through with her."

"Making deals with the devil, Chet?" Amy murmured. "Good way to get yourself killed."

"Quiet," he growled.

A thought occurred to her. She tipped her chin in Chambliss' direction. "You were driving the black Jeep the other day. The one that ran me and Bors off the road."

His eyes flickered with something close to fear. "I was aiming for the mutt. Didn't think you'd grab him and take a dive off the mountain."

"You nearly killed me. Bet dear old Adrik was pissed." Considering what she knew of the man, that was probably an understatement.

"Let's just say he made it clear he wants you in one piece."

His gaze shifted to Chet, eyes turning as hard as granite. "You, however, don't rate that kind of treatment. Push me, and you'll regret it. Assuming I let you live that long.

She felt Chet's indecision in the way his fingers dug into her waist. Knew he was going to back down when his grip relaxed.

"No need for any rough stuff. Your boss and I can discuss things when we get to him. Let's just do this like we planned."

Chambliss tipped the barrel of his gun down a couple of inches. "Wise choice."

Chet switched his grip from her waist to an upper arm.

Amy never took her eyes off Chambliss. Getting a weapon away from him would be next to impossible even if her hands weren't tied. Better if she swiped one from the brothers and took the big man out first.

As if reading her thoughts, Chambliss let his rifle dangle from its strap and retrieved a thin nylon rope from a side pocket of his pack. "Wrap this around her from shoulders to wrists."

Franklin laughed nervously as he caught the bundled rope. "Her hands are already tied, man. What she gonna do?"

"You'd be surprised, or more precisely, you'd be dead." He tipped his head to her in respect. "Even with her hands tied, she could kill you right where you stand. Isn't that right, Ms. Aberashoff?"

"Aberashoff? Who the hell is Aberashoff?"

Amy ignored Chet's question. Hearing Chambliss call her by the name of the man in charge of Special Ops hammered the last nail into her determination not to be taken to Adrik. No matter how strained their relationship, she refused to be used as a tool against her father. "I prefer Sheridan if you don't mind. It's my grandmother's maiden—"

She broke off, taking advantage of Chet's momentary confusion to jab an elbow as hard as she could into his belly.

Air whooshed out of his mouth and he bent over, releasing her in the process. A swift, hard kick sent him headlong into his brothers. All three men went down.

Chambliss shot forward, angling to the left to cut off her escape. Guess he forgot ravens could fly.

Amy spun around, took two running steps, and jumped, sending herself into a freefall over the edge of the cliff.

Shouts followed her, but thankfully, no bullets. She was banking on all of them wanting her alive. Even Chambliss wouldn't shoot unless he was certain he would only wound her. No matter what kind of deal Chet thought he had, good old Adrik wanted to kill her himself.

She hit the young evergreen she'd staked out earlier slightly lower than she wanted. There was less give in the trunk here, and her rough landing knocked the breath out of her. She scrambled to latch onto a branch with her tied hands, gasping for air as the tree swayed in a dizzying dance. Finally managing to secure a hold near the trunk, Amy swung her weight around. The top of the tree bent in an arc toward the ground. Again, not as much as she wanted, but she'd take what she could get.

The slender trunk creaked ominously under her weight. Amy waited as long as she dared before dropping the last few feet to the ground. Bending her knees, she tucked her body into a roll to minimize the impact. She came up running, keenly aware of her pursuers.

She could hear Chet, Franklin, and Arney shouting to one another, arguing. The one she couldn't hear was the one she had to worry about. If Chambliss worked for Adrik, he wouldn't just have a little training, he'd be the best in his field. Tracker, assassin, whatever. He was the one she had to elude.

She tripped as she broke through the last of the trees, barely managing to break her fall with her hands. More skin lost. A small enough price to pay, she decided, eyeing the rushing water she'd just missed falling into. The tumbling Oscar had never looked more dangerous...or more welcome. A fast river ride was just what she needed.

Amy pushed herself up and started running along the bank. Getting away was a priority. Getting away without drowning would be even better. She'd jump straight in if she had to, but with her hands tied together, she really needed something to hold on to. Fifty yards downstream, she found what she needed.

The river had cut the soil from beneath what was left of a lightning-struck tree, dumping the top of its blasted trunk into the water. The other half was held out of the water by a few dry roots. If she was very lucky, her weight would be enough to pull the whole thing loose, providing her with the raft she needed.

Amy heard a noise behind her. She glanced over her shoulder to see Chambliss charging toward her. The look on his face was the stuff of nightmares, made worse by a trail of fresh blood trickling down from a gouge in his forehead. His furious gaze shot past her to the tree, then jerked back to her. He raised his gun as he ran.

Amy jumped.

Ice cold water swallowed her, taking her breath. For a moment she was completely disoriented, at the mercy of the surging current. Then her sneakers scraped along something hard. She pushed off, aiming for where water met sunlight. She couldn't risk missing the tree.

Her head broke the surface. She choked and spit out water and sucked in air. The tree was less than a dozen feet away and coming up fast. Again, she picked the spot she wanted to hit and struggled to put herself in the right position. Luck was with her this time. Lifting her arms high, she grabbed a limb with both hands, holding tight as the rushing water sweep the rest of her body under the hanging trunk.

One tug, two tugs.

Dry bark exploded next to her hands showering her with sharp splinters. Amy ducked, but didn't let go. "Idiot," she snarled through chattering teeth.

If Chambliss broke her arm with a bullet, she'd

probably drown. She ducked her head and tugged one last time, lifting the bulk of her body completely out of the water. Brittle roots snapped, dropping the tree on top of her.

Amy gulped air just before she went under. She held tight to the tree, letting it push her down, ticking seconds off in her head out of habit. The old tree rose slowly to the surface, as if too tired to float. She kicked, trying to force it into faster water. When the current caught the trunk, pulling it into a roll, she held on, letting it bring her face into sweet air.

Blinking the water from her eyes, Amy looked back, fearing Chambliss would dive in after her. When she found him, he was still standing on the bank. The Wassiles were with him, though their reunion didn't look happy.

Chambliss had a hand wrapped around Arney Wassile's throat, the end of his silencer jammed against his forehead. Chet and Franklin were waving their arms and arguing for all they were worth.

Amy's lips tugged into a cold smile. So maybe Chambliss hadn't been the idiot who shot at her.

Just before the river took her out of sight, Chambliss turned his head in her direction. She would have waved if her hands hadn't been tied. Or maybe not. Between the stupid drug and the freezing water, she didn't have much energy left. She would have to leave the river soon or risk drowning.

Five minutes of rough and tumble later, Amy was so exhausted she could barely hold on. She almost sobbed in relief when she spotted the little stream spilling into the Oscar. *Thank God.* With a desperate lunge, she abandoned her makeshift raft. It seemed to take forever to kick and claw her way into calmer water. Numb with cold, she let the water buoy her while she crawled through the shallows to reach the stream. Little stabs of pain shot through her limbs every time she moved. Her teeth chattered constantly.

She didn't stop crawling up the little stream until she was out of sight of the river. Knowing a short rest was all she could afford, she pulled herself onto a rock barely out of the water. She worried at the rope around her wrists with her teeth as she caught her breath. The soaked fibers seemed to stretch a little when she pulled at them. Taking a deep breath, she pulled one hand toward her, twisting it back and forth as she pushed away with the other. She winced as her abused hand finally popped loose. More lost skin, but at least her hands were free.

She started to toss the rope away, stopped, and sighed. If Chambliss or the Wassile's tried to track her, she shouldn't make it easy for them. With a groan, she eased back into the chilly water. She worked her fingers under the edge of another rock, lifting it just enough to stuff the rope under it. Then she pushed down on the rock to seat it back into the mud. The fast running water would hopefully erase any trace of disturbance.

She stood and waded into a patch of sunshine. Getting her body out of the water helped, but she couldn't leave the stream entirely. Not yet. Maybe in another hundred yards.

The bottom of the stream was peppered with rocks. Amy stuck to them as much as possible to reduce the silt muddying the water. They were slippery devils. More than once she stumbled, barely keeping from falling altogether. At least the fast pace she set kept her warm.

When the stream started to narrow, the banks rising on both sides, Amy knew it was time to leave the water. An old rock fall provided the perfect exit. She picked her way over the jumble of sun-warmed boulders until she reached a thick patch of pine needles. Hopefully, the wet trail she left on the boulders would soon evaporate like she intended to do.

Concentrating on not leaving a trail helped keep her mind off how miserable she was. That, and planning on how she was going to get to dear old Adrik. The man had had entirely too much impact on her life the last year and a half. It was long past time for her to impact his for a change.

Chapter Twenty

"They're headed toward the river."

Joshua acknowledged Rio's observation with a sharp nod. They'd been following the Wassile's trail straight up the mountain for more than an hour. At first he'd been surprised by the direction. Then he remembered Chet and his brothers had a cabin hidden somewhere in the vast forest blanketing the range east of Clear Springs. No doubt they were taking Amy there.

Assuming Velavich let them keep her.

So far they'd seen no further signs of the fourth person. Of the three sets of tracks they followed, one was always deeper than the other two. They were carrying Amy, which worried him a little. She wouldn't submit to something like that without a fight. Not unless she was tied up or unconscious. Either scenario made him want to wring Chet's neck. Then again, as long as they had to carry her, the better chance he and Rio had of catching up to them.

Five minutes later, they came to the edge of a narrow meadow. The trail they followed merged with an animal track leading into the thick grass. On the far side, another tree covered ridge rose. Joshua hunkered down behind a screen of tall bushes to scan the rising land, hoping to catch sight of movement. His sixth sense, the one that had served him well on numerous missions, told him they were getting close. God, he hoped so. He needed to get Amy back like he needed to breathe. Despite his best intentions, she'd become extremely important to him in a very short amount of time. Keeping her alive and safe wasn't just about not failing a mission anymore.

Something moved in the trees at the very top of the ridge. He focused his mind and the binoculars, waiting for a better sighting. A slight form, definitely two-legged, slipped stealthily from cover to cover. Joshua's heart jacked into a faster rhythm. Amy.

Rio tapped his shoulder.

"I see her," Joshua whispered. He watched her make her way down the slope, flowing between trees and over rocks in that graceful way of hers. Only something told him it was more than just her natural grace. The way she moved, how she set her feet, let him know she wasn't leaving much in the way of a trail. Just one more skill that indicated Amy was more than an amateur photographer. Much more. But then, he'd already figured that out last night.

He searched the top of the ridge above her. Nothing else moved. Yet.

"What's the plan, Cap?"

Crossing the open meadow was out of the question. He wasn't afraid of Amy spotting them, but he was damn sure by the way she moved she was being followed. He'd just as soon keep the Wassiles in the dark about his and Rio's presence. Not to mention that fourth party. "We'll swing around the meadow and meet her at the base of the ridge." Then he'd send Rio and Amy back home while he took care of the Wassiles personally. The way he felt, there might not even be bodies for Penwell to fuss about afterward.

****

Amy skirted a fat spruce at the bottom of the hill she was navigating and froze. A beautiful grassy meadow, about thirty yards across, opened up before her. Crossing it without being seen would be hard, but not impossible. What made her pause, however, was the prickly awareness running along her skin like goose bumps. Slowly, she eased back into the spruce's needles, ignoring the thousands of tiny pin-pricks against her skin. Someone was out there.

She forced her breathing to slow, quieting the rush of air so she could listen. Leaves rustled, limbs creaked. No voices or footsteps broke the stillness. Not even a faint echo. Anyone else would have assumed there wasn't a soul for miles. The peaceful quiet only made Amy more nervous.

With the ease of long practice, she melted farther back into the tree's embrace, sideling through the thick branches with very little sound or movement. Reaching the thick trunk, she knelt on the carpet of old needles to make herself as inconspicuous as possible while she planned her next move.

That wild river ride should have put her several miles ahead of any pursuit. How had they gotten in front of her so fast? More importantly, who was it that waited so quietly for her to step into their trap? Couldn't be the Wassiles. Despite their self-taught skills and knowledge of the area, Chet and his brothers were like a back-woods version of the Three Stooges compared to men like Chambliss and Velavich.

And the Harrier.

Amy's heart jumped in her chest. The thought that Joshua might be tracking her made her limbs turn to jelly. If he'd somehow discovered she'd been taken, he'd probably just assume from the evidence that her kidnappers were the Wassiles. He wouldn't be expecting a professional like Chambliss, or worse, Adrik himself.

She needed to warn him.

She stood, only to have her common sense stop

her. She didn't know for sure that it was Joshua out there. Odds were not in his favor. He'd probably already discovered her missing from the vet clinic, but how would he know where to search for her? That meant her stalker had to be either Chambliss or Adrik.

It would be just like her ex-lover to play a little cat and mouse before re-taking her. The sick bastard. He was so like his namesake, lying in wait until his prey came within striking distance. She hated the thought of being anywhere near him again. He'd almost killed her the last time.

A slight noise at the top of the hill she'd just descended caught her attention. The heavy footfall came again, followed by another, and another. Then the snap and crackle of broken brush. It sounded like a herd of elephants coming down the hill, which meant Chet and his stupid brothers had caught up to her. Amy quietly let out a disgusted breath. Damn it. She'd waited too long to cross the meadow. Now she was pinned down in her hiding spot. And if those three were here, Chambliss couldn't be far away.

She'd have to—

An arm snaked around her from behind. A hand clamped tightly over her mouth. Amy didn't waste time on screaming. She leaned back to put her attacker off balance, then threw her weight forward, trying to roll him beneath her. Satisfaction shot through her when she succeeded, only to change to chagrin when her attacker's free arm and both legs wrapped around her, effectively trapping her. She had barely enough room to bring her hand around her hip, aiming for the tender sack beneath the hard bulge pressing into her ass.

"Careful, sweetheart, we might need those later."

Her squeezing fingers froze at the low, urgent whisper. Relief shot through her as she twisted her head around to be certain she hadn't imagined his voice, that the hard body wrapped around her was indeed Joshua's.

His face, dark with camo paint, loomed close to hers as he moved his hand from her mouth to cup her cheek. Dark eyes searched her face. "Sorry I scared you," he breathed.

Feet stomped nearby, almost on top of them. Amy held her breath. Beneath her, Joshua shifted slightly. Then the cold handle of a knife pressed into her hand. Her lips twitched as her fingers curled around the hilt. Other men gave women flowers and jewelry. Joshua gave her a weapon. Of course, it could always be argued that the danger of their situation precluded roses and diamonds. Still, if he thought he was getting the knife back later, he was going to be surprised.

The noise of the brothers faded. Joshua's tense muscles relaxed just a fraction, enough to allow her to turn over and press herself all along his length. His eyes widened in question just before she bent her head and kissed him, hard, deep, and not nearly long enough.

"Does this mean you're glad to see me?" The heat of his whispered breath warmed her face.

She put her lips next to his ear before whispering just as softly. "That depends on if we both get out of this mess in one piece. Adrik's here, in the valley. And he didn't come alone. He brought at least one man that I know of. How did you even know where to look for me?"

Joshua pressed a kiss to her ear, making her shiver. "Your knight in shiny black fur tried to follow you."

Tears sprang to her eyes and her empty hand flexed into a fist on Joshua's shirt. "Bors is alive?" She'd been so sure he was dead.

"Was when we left. Sue's taking care of him."

She kissed him again, enjoying the way his chest and neck muscles tightened, as if locking back an audible groan. His hips rose in a deliberate move, pressing the hard bulge of his erection between her open thighs while his hand pressed down firmly on her ass, increasing the contact. The resulting sensation sent a flood of heat straight to her core.

Amy swallowed a groan of her own. She knew they were being foolish. Indulging in a bit of sexual play with the threat of violence hanging over them wasn't the smartest thing either of them had ever done. But she couldn't seem to stop. She hadn't been completely sure of her escape earlier.

Joshua's presence took that fear away, leaving her feeling a bit reckless. The prospect of potential violence only served to make every sensation he created inside her feel sharper, more intense.

The snap of a twig broke their kiss, both of them going still. A bird called, the innocuous sound causing Joshua to relax again. He whistled back and helped her sit up. Another man crawled almost silently beneath the sagging tree limbs. Young, handsome, dark-haired and brown skinned, he had a quiet, deadly air surrounding him that she recognized instantly. His sharp gaze moved over her once before turning to Joshua. He kept his voice to a bare whisper.

"Four men. Three walking in the open, the fourth hiding for all he's worth. They're scattering, Cap. Don't think they know we're here yet. They don't strike me as giving up any time soon, though. Seem pretty determined to get her back. Not that that's going to happen, ma'am." He dipped his head and smiled, his white teeth in stark contrast to his camo-streaked face. Even whispered, his words carried a heavy southern accent. Feigned, or real, she wasn't sure, but his friendly assurance along with his confident body language helped release the tight ball of tension in her stomach. Here was another competent soldier, ex-SEAL, or ex-Ranger, like Joshua, though a few years younger. Definitely a NightHawk.

When she smiled back at him, the man punched Joshua lightly in the shoulder. "See, I told you she'd like me. Man, the things I have to do to meet a pretty woman. Paint my face, crawl through brush, chase bad guys. Next thing I know you'll be asking me to kill someone."

Joshua sent the younger man a quelling look as he began checking for movement outside their hiding place. "Amy, this ungrateful brat—"

"Brat?"

"—is Rio," Joshua finished, ignoring Rio's evident outrage. "He's going to take you out of here while I tie up a few loose ends." He said the words calmly, easily, as if he talked about running down to the store to pick up a carton of milk.

Cold settled in the pit of Amy's stomach. She knew what he meant to do.

"They didn't touch me, Joshua."

His head turned sharply, eyes fastening on the bruises on her cheek and throat.

"You know what I mean," she said, determined to make him see reason. As much as she wanted Chet to pay for hurting Bors, killing the Wassile brothers would be a mistake. Besides, she didn't want Joshua going after them alone. Not with Chambliss and Adrik out there somewhere.

"They attacked you, Amy. They're not getting a second chance. Just go with Rio, honey. I won't be far behind."

"No. If you're going to do this, take Rio with you. I can find my own way back."

"Not happening, sweetheart, so stop wasting time and just go."

"Damn it, Joshua—"

Voices called to one another, coming closer. Chet and the others were backtracking for some reason, making more noise than even they should have.

Joshua's expression hardened, the tender, hungry, emotions that had filled his eyes just a moment ago retreating as the predator in him took over. He nodded to Rio and started to turn away.

Amy shot a hand out and forced him to look at her. She was fighting cold, exhaustion, and the lingering effects of the drug. If it was anyone besides Joshua, she might have still argued, maybe even won. But this was the Harrier. A man used to barking out orders and having them obeyed. Not that that would have stopped Amy from arguing with him. But he was also a man with a reputation for taking on larger forces and coming out alive. He knew his business. She might not be able to keep him from doing what he thought he had to, but maybe she could give him an edge.

"Chet's got a gun stashed in his left boot and a knife in the right. Arney has a switchblade he plays with like a pro. He's also pretty good with that rifle he carries, so stay out of his sights. Franklin's so antsy he's libel to start shooting at anything that moves. He carries a small pistol tucked under his shirt at his back. The most dangerous is the one you won't see until it's too late. His name is Chambliss. He's had training. Maybe military. *Do not* get yourself shot or knifed."

Joshua didn't smile. He merely wrapped a large hand around the nape of her neck and pulled her in for another deep kiss. "Orders understood. Now get your pretty ass home. Rio."

"This way, ma'am." Rio touched her arm, drawing her through the limbs on the side facing the ridge. She forced herself not to look back.

Making use of every scrap of cover, she and Rio made it to the top of the ridge without being spotted.

They cut west along the tree line on the far side, giving the area with the meadow a wide berth. With all the running she did almost daily, Amy should have been able to match Rio's steady jog with no problem.

Damn Chet and his sneaky syringe. Whatever he'd injected her with had the characteristics of a bulldog, the effects lingering with a tenacity she simply couldn't shake. Though she'd been awake for more than an hour, she still felt like an overused battery, drained and powerless. She tried to keep her stumbling to a minimum, but the way Rio kept glancing back at her said she must not be doing a good enough job.

When their path took them into the shadow of a steep, rocky cliff, Rio slowed to a walk. Without a word, he pulled a bottle of water from his pack and handed it to her. Amy could have kissed him. Cracking the lid, she swallowed half the bottle before splashing some on her hot face.

Still walking, Rio tapped her arm and pointed to a pile of boulders up ahead that looked like they'd broken off from the cliff face a good decade ago.

"We'll rest a little behind those rocks."

Amy wasn't fooled by the *we* part. For all their running up and down the folded landscape, they hadn't covered more than a mile. Even considering the altitude, she could tell Rio wasn't that tired. She, on the other hand, was a mess. She'd managed to keep pace with him, but that was about it.

Between her ragged breathing and dizzy spells she was lucky to be able to stand, much less run.

"Thanks, I could use the rest." She glanced back the way they'd come. Their path had taken them to higher ground, giving her almost a bird's eye view of the land below.

When the first shots came, she jumped. She wasn't even aware Rio had snatched her back into the cover of the rocks until the echoes died. Three hard cracks followed by several softer ones; rifle, then pistol. Joshua had found the Wassiles.

Another rifle shot.

"Shit," Rio muttered. His eyes cut to hers apologetically. "Sorry, ma'am."

Amy decided she didn't like the look on his face. Something was wrong. "It would make me feel a lot better, Rio, if you went back and checked on him."

He shook his head, slapping a boyish grin on his face. "And here I thought you liked me. Do you know what that man would do to me if I disobeyed his order to get you to safety?"

"Looks pretty safe to me right here. All the fighting's down that way." They both looked down as more shots rang out. The feeling that something was wrong grew stronger, raising goose bumps. "That's not normal for him, is it?"

Her bodyguard didn't answer right away. When he did, he sounded just as worried as she felt. "No ma'am, it's not. Cap usually works quiet."

Amy grabbed a handful of Rio's shirt, shifting them both until she could look him in the eyes. "Listen to me, Rio. Despite letting myself get kidnapped, I can usually take care of myself. I'm not helpless. But I'm not stupid either. I'm not at full strength right now so I can't go back and help him. You can. Please! I promise I'll stay right here, safe and sound, out of sight."

Rio cursed as another rifle shot cracked the stillness. He shook his head. "If he doesn't kill me for disobeying a direct order, he'll court marshal me."

Her hands tightened and she all but growled, "If you don't go back and he dies, I'll do worse than kill you."

He met her gaze for a long moment until, finally, his lips twitched. "Looks like my ass is toast either way. Might as well make it count."

"You're going back?"

"It's suicide by Harrier, but, yeah, I guess I am. Damn, and I liked this job, too."

She patted his cheek. "Don't worry about your job. I've got connections even Joshua doesn't know about."

He snorted. "Doesn't matter what kind of connections you have, I still have to be out of my mind. But I heard what you said about the fourth guy and I agree. He'll stay hidden until Cap is occupied with the other three. Then he'll strike."

He gave her a hard look. "I need you to stay right here, understand? Just hunker down and wait until Cap or I come back to get you. You know how to shoot?" He swung his rifle off his shoulder and held it out to her.

She nodded, swallowing hard as she hesitantly took the gun in her hands. Instead of feeling repulsed, she was astonished at how good it felt as her fingers brushed the trigger guard. "It's been a while though." Fourteen months, two weeks, and three days, to be exact.

Rio grinned. "Just like riding a bike, ma'am. The safety is here. Flip it off only when you're ready to shoot. Not that I think you'll need to."

He paused. Amy could almost see the wheels turning in his head. Disobeying his commander was not something a soldier took lightly. Especially a NightHawk. If she let him stand there and think about it too hard, he might change his mind.

"Go," she said, snatching the two extra magazines out of his hand. "Like you said, I'll be fine."

He nodded once, his boyish features sliding into something harder, meaner. "If something should happen, ma'am—"

Amy cut him off roughly. She didn't want to hear about *something* happening. "Rio, shut the hell up. And stop calling me ma'am. You're starting to piss me off." She didn't wait to see his reaction, just started climbing deeper into the rocks.

"Amy?"

She turned back.

"More water and snacks, in case you get hungry," he said, tossing her a small pack. He was already running for the trees by the time she nodded.

Chapter Twenty-One

There were plenty of hiding places scattered among the rocks near the base of the cliff. Some would take a bloodhound to sniff her out. Amy ignored them all. Snipers always preferred the high ground. Not to mention, the higher she climbed, the easier it would be to spot trouble coming.

The two hundred foot cliff face looked sheer from far away. Up close, hand and footholds abounded if you knew what to look for. Amy took it slow in deference to her shaky muscles. She passed several useable ledges, continuing to climb until she was well above the tree tops.

There she found what she was looking for. The long ledge cut deep enough into the rock that if she pressed herself lengthwise against the back, only the eagles riding high in the thermals would be able to see her. A good hiding place. Only she didn't intend to stay completely hidden.

Sliding onto her belly, she turned perpendicular to the ledge. Then she scooted forward until she could see the valley spread out below through the rifle's scope. She scanned the thick trees and open spots, looking for movement. There hadn't been any more shots since Rio had left. Amy wasn't sure if that was good or bad.

A half hour passed. She ate a protein bar and drank sparingly from another bottle of water in Rio's pack. The food and water seemed to help. At least her hands didn't shake anymore. She was finally able to scan the landscape below without the view jumping and twitching. So far, she'd caught no sign of anyone.

Where the hell were Joshua and Rio? Why was it taking them so long to neutralize three idiots and one pro? Sure the odds were two to one, but they were NightHawks for pity's sake.

A flicker of movement along one of the narrow ridges caught her eye. She eased the rifle into place, used the scope, and started looking in earnest. A man slipped from tree to tree using limbs and brush for cover. She could hardly make him out. His clothing was dark. Joshua and Rio's clothes were dark, but so were Arney's and Chambliss'. Smothering a curse, she adjusted the scope, trying to get a better focus. The picture in the small circle with the black cross hairs sharpened.

Rio, she decided, remembering the dark bands of leather he wore around his wrists. She kept the scope trained on him until she saw his body freeze. His head tracked slowly, stopping when he faced her direction. There was no way he could see her, but Amy got the distinct impression he knew a gun was being pointed in his direction. Knew it, felt it, and didn't like it.

Holding her breath, Amy moved the cross hairs from his body. Her finger was outside the trigger guard, but she still checked the safety on the gun just to make sure. Shooting someone by accident, especially Joshua or Rio, was the last thing she wanted to do. All she wanted was to try to keep track of what was going on. She didn't mind being stashed someplace safe as long as she could keep an eye on things. Apparently the sniper's urge to watch over her team still burned inside her despite her efforts to bury it.

Amy grimaced, shifting her gaze to a clearing a few degrees to the left of Rio's position. She hadn't wanted to bury her instincts. Becoming an SO operative had been a dream come true. Ever since she could read, she'd devoured stories where the hero saves the lady in distress. Not once had she wanted to be the lady who got saved. She wanted to be the hero who fought the bad guy, the one who made it safe for everyone else.

It had been like a salmon fighting a rushing river for her to even make it into Special Ops. More than once she'd met with vehement opposition. Her mother, her trainers, and, at first, every member of the Predators Unit she'd been assigned to. Oddly enough, the only one who'd ever seemed to understand her deep-seated need to protect others was her father, a man she'd never set eyes on until she was fourteen.

And wasn't that a family reunion for the books.

Movement caught her attention. She focused on the bottom of a ridge where a rocky area stood out like a scar on the wooded landscape. Probably an old rock slide. As she watched, a man slipped out into the open. He took three steps and paused, sunlight glinting off the barrel of a gun in his hand. Her breath caught. She didn't even need to see his face to know who this was. Joshua moved with the confidence and grace of a deadly assassin on the hunt for his next victim.

As she watched, another man jumped out of the trees. He knocked Joshua's gun aside and came in low with the knife in his hand. Amy gasped, losing sight of them for just a moment as her hands shook in reaction to Chambliss' swift attack. By the time she juggled the rifle back in place, the two men were fighting in earnest. Joshua held the bigger man's wrist, straining to hold the knife away from him. Suddenly, he fell back. Amy's heart stuttered, then strengthened as Joshua rolled, catching the heavier man in the stomach with his feet and flipping him over. Both men scrambled up quickly. They circled one another, feinting, neither taking the bait. Big as he was, Chambliss was quick, and he fought dirty. All she could do was lay there and pray Joshua's training was better.

****

Amy was right, Joshua thought, Chambliss definitely had military training. And he was fast. Joshua blocked the knife and grabbed the man's thick wrist, fingers digging into nerves. The knife fell, lost in the shifting jumble of rock and shale as Chambliss made a grab for Joshua's throat. Joshua dodged. He and Chambliss traded a series of quick jabs and punches. Both of them soon had bloody lips and bruised knuckles.

A shout echoed over the valley, but Joshua ignored it. He kept his eyes on Chambliss, watching for a weakness, any opening. He blocked and struck back almost without thought, letting his training take over. Chambliss was methodical, but he liked patterns. He kept repeating the same moves, though the series he used was so long he probably took out anyone he usually fought before his opponent noticed the repetition. But Joshua wasn't just anyone.

Anticipating the next move, Joshua leaned to the side just enough for a hard, meaty fist to slide by. He grabbed Chambliss' arm, jerked, and soon had the man caught in an arm lock. Squeezing his arm around the man's throat, Joshua felt Chambliss stagger. He caught movement from the corner of his eye and twisted, thrusting Chambliss at the man bursting out of the trees.

Chambliss swore and threw himself to the side, his body sliding a few feet down the slope on the loose rocks. Arney Wassile ignored him and came at Joshua, slicing the air with that switchblade of his while grinning like an idiot. Chambliss was up in the next moment, scrambling back up the hillside.

Great, just great. A two for one. At least the only

gun was lost in the shale somewhere behind Joshua. He'd have to take out Arney first before he could get back to Chambliss.

But when the Wassile brother made a move toward him, a dark blur burst out of the trees and slammed Arney to the ground. Joshua barely had time to recognize the blur as Rio before Chambliss took advantage of the distraction. The bigger man's fist shot out, catching Joshua with a glancing blow on the chin. He spun with the blow, and flung a leg up to kick Chambliss back. Loose shale shifted beneath their feet, sending both of them sprawling. Joshua rolled over to see Chambliss scrambling across the pile of scree. When he stood up, he had the pistol in his hand.

There was nowhere to hide and too much room between them. Joshua knew he'd never reach the man in time, but he had to try anyway. He lunged across the intervening space. Chambliss knew he had time and took it. He raised the gun slowly, one side of his lips turning up in a sneer.

Joshua heard the echo of the shot a second after the side of Chambliss' head exploded. The impact of the bullet spun his body sideways, causing the bullet that should have taken Joshua square in the chest, to kiss the side of his arm instead. Joshua ignored the burn. Turning, he crossed the rock covered slope in quick strides to where Rio lay on the ground, shoving aside a very dead Arney. As the younger man crawled to his feet, Joshua grabbed his arm, almost jerking him off the ground.

"Tell me that was one of our guys. Tell me you ran into Ty or Brick and that's why you're here and not with Amy. Tell me she's with them!"

Rio's gaze went to Chambliss' body then back to Joshua. "Sorry, Cap. When all the shooting started, she got scared. Wouldn't go another step and insisted I come back to help you. I left her hiding at the base of that bare cliff to the west. I...gave her my rifle."

"Son of a bitch!" Joshua shoved Rio away and started running, automatically calculating the bullet's trajectory back to its origin. The angle had meant the bullet had to have come from tree top level or above. He burst through the trees, his eyes scanning the cliff as he approached at a dead run. He didn't see Amy, but he did see the tip of a rifle barrel sticking out over the lip of a ledge a hundred feet up.

Joshua felt like his insides were twisted into a dozen tight knots. This would kill her. She didn't have it in her to be able to take another person's life without a heavy backlash of guilt. Not his gentle Amy. Rio shouldn't have left her the rifle, he just damn well shouldn't have. The fact that if he hadn't, Joshua would be dealing with a bullet in his chest right now, didn't matter. He would have taken that bullet for her. Still would. Anything to keep Amy safe and sane.

He heard her muttering before he reached the ledge. She was lying on her back, one arm thrown across her face, the other still clutching the rifle. Everybody handled kill shock differently. Some threw up. Some fainted. A few crawled into a place in their own minds and rarely, if ever, came out again. Some lost the ability to tell friend from foe, which meant that if they still held a gun, they were a danger to everyone, including themselves.

"Amy? It's me, Joshua. It's all right. It's over. You're safe now." He crawled slowly onto the ledge.

More muttering, this time some of the words recognizable, enough anyway, to make him stop and blink in disbelief.

He rubbed a hand across his face deciding he didn't want to know where she'd learned such language. Hell, some of the words he didn't even use.

Carefully, he took another step. "Honey, you're doing an awful lot of swearing. That's not like you."

She let out a soggy laugh. "You've known me all of three days, Joshua. You have no idea what I'm like."

"I know enough." But the certainty of her words made him wonder what he'd missed.

Her head rocked back and forth. "No. You really don't." She dragged her arm across her face and started to sit up.

Joshua reached for her. She froze at his touch, then let him help her scoot around until her back was against the cliff. She crossed her legs tailor fashion. Joshua took careful note that she still held on to the rifle, cradling it across her thighs.

Joshua eased down beside her. He propped his arms on his bent knees and scanned the woods below, letting the silence between them lengthen. Rio would have called for cleanup by now. Joshua would let them take Arney's body, too. No sense in getting Penwell involved. The fact the Wassiles had hooked up with Velavich put them squarely under Joshua's jurisdiction as far as he was concerned.

Tracking down Chet and Franklin was going to give him a lot of satisfaction, but it would have to wait. Right now, Amy was more important. He hoped she'd start talking soon.

She sighed deeply. An encouraging sign. Then her words had him tensing up again.

"There's no easy way to say this, so I'm just going to spit it out."

Determined, Joshua met her sad gaze. No matter what, he'd see her through this.

"I'm the Raven."

It took a moment for her words to sink in. Understandable, since those were the last words he expected to hear. *I'm scared. I just killed a man. What happens now?* Any of those would have fit the

218

situation. But not, *I'm the youngest, most talented sniper in the SO. You know, the one accused of betraying her country and killing her commanding officer.*

He looked away from her and scrubbed a hand over his face. Bloody effin' hell. His first thought was that this was what he deserved for breaking his own rules and getting involved with a woman he was supposed to be guarding. Never knew what kind of secrets were in their closet. Then a bigger realization hit him. This one life-changing huge. His biggest reason for not becoming involved with Amy had just gone up in smoke. She was already part of his world. A big part.

"Why the hell didn't Aberashoff tell me?"

Amy shrugged. "The official report says the Raven killed Colonel Tucker. Everyone knows you and he were friends. Aberashoff probably didn't want you coming after me with that bow of yours. Not that I'd blame you." The sadness in her voice was unmistakable.

"You didn't kill Tucker." He didn't waste time with a question mark. She'd just proved she could kill, but everything he'd learned about her so far said she didn't do so without a damn good reason.

She met his gaze evenly. "You're right, I didn't."

"Was it Velavich?"

"I don't know. I wasn't there when it happened. Once I realized what Adrik had done, I went to Colonel Tucker. He sent me back to HQ by myself because we didn't know if anyone else on the team was involved."

"He confronted Velavich alone."

"But why? Why didn't he call someone he trusted? Why didn't he call you?"

"His unit, his mess. I would have done the same. Velavich must have gotten the drop on him somehow, though I find that hard to believe. JT was good."

Her head dropped back against the rock wall. "Maybe if I'd stayed, I could have done, I don't know, something."

"Did Velavich say who authorized the mission?"

Anger kindled in her eyes. "There was no mission, damn it. It was a setup, plain and simple. One I fell for hook, line, and stinking sinker."

"I read the file, Amy. You weren't the only one Velavich fooled. Your whole team fell for it, including JT."

She jammed a finger to her chest. "But I was the one who should have seen it coming. I was the one responsible. I was the one..." Her whole body sagged. "I was the one who pulled the trigger."

"You were following orders, doing your job."

"My job didn't include killing an innocent man in cold blood, Joshua. Rodrigo Estacada didn't deserve to die. He was a good man. I know, because I made a point of finding out everything I could about him afterwards. He wasn't a gun-runner. He didn't rape children. He was a decent man who loved his family more than anything else. Did you know his oldest daughter was due to deliver her first child two weeks after I shot him? That child will never know his grandfather thanks to me. And don't give me the speech about collateral damage. Estacada wasn't killed accidentally in pursuit of a higher purpose. He was murdered. *I* murdered him."

She closed her eyes and gulped in one breath after another as hot tears rolled down her cheeks. Joshua wanted to hold her so bad his arms ached. But she looked so fragile right then, so damn breakable, he was almost afraid to touch her. All it would take was one wrong word and he knew she'd shatter.

"So, you had Velavich so high on a pedestal all you could see was his dick."

Joshua caught the hand that came flying at him a split second before it reached his face. He'd taken a risk with the insulting remark, but at least he'd gotten through that wall of self-pity and guilt she'd wrapped around herself. He shifted his grip to her wrist, noting with satisfaction that instead of an open palm, she'd gone for him with a tight fist. His Amy didn't play around.

"Tucker always said you were a right bastard," she snarled. She tried to jerk her hand out of his grasp, but he wouldn't let her. In a show of strength he knew pissed her off even more, he brought her tight little fist to his mouth. Slowly, he kissed each white knuckle. "You aren't the first person to get blindsided by someone you cared about. Nor will you be the last. Slimeballs procreate just like the rest of us. We're bound to run into them from time to time. When we do, and they're lucky enough to knock us down, we pick ourselves up, fix what we can, and go forward."

She sat quietly for a long moment, just staring at him. Then she said, "I didn't hear anything in there about paybacks."

Joshua managed to wiggle some fingers beneath hers, coaxing the delicate digits to flatten against his palm. He rubbed the back of her hand against his check and smiled. "Sure you did, sweetheart. That's the fixing part."

"So how do you plan to fix the Cobra? And I'll tell you right now that pulling his fangs by locking him in a cage for the rest of his life won't be fixed enough for me."

"No, no cage. I was figuring on something a little more permanent."

"Cap?"

He'd glimpsed Rio trotting out of the woods toward the cliff earlier, so knew he was nearby. His presence on the ledge, however, was a surprise.

221

"Is she all right, Cap?" the young man asked as he crawled forward. "Do you need help getting her down?"

Amy answered before he could. "I'm fine, Rio. Thanks for asking."

Rio seemed taken aback by her calm answer. Then he sighed dramatically. "Boy, am I glad you're okay. Now maybe Cap won't beat me to a bloody pulp."

"I still might. You disobeyed a direct order, mister."

"Joshua, please—"

"No, Amy, he knew there'd be consequences. He was given charge of a civilian and put that civilian at risk by abandoning her."

A flash of something close to insult flashed through Amy's eyes. "I'm not—"

"Quiet," Joshua ordered. He didn't want her true status known yet. "This man is part of my unit and under my command, not yours. So, Lieutenant, what do you have to say for yourself?"

Rio stiffened to attention as much as his kneeling position on the ledge allowed. He executed a snappy salute. "Yes, sir, I disobeyed your order and abandoned the civilian under my protection, sir. Given a member of my team was facing four-to-one odds with the possibility of additional unknown enemy in the area, and given said civilian refused to go any further and would have fought me had I tried to force her—"

"Damn right," Amy put in.

"—I made a judgment call, which involved hiding the civilian in a place of safety and returning to assist my team mate."

Joshua waved a hand at their elevated surroundings. "This is your idea of a place of safety?"

"No," Amy said quickly. "It's my idea of a place of safety. You can't fault Rio for my preference for heights. And in case, you've forgotten this 'civilian' just saved your life. You owe me, Colonel Colby, and you know what payment I want."

Joshua fought back a grin. He so liked her temper. Made those eyes of hers flash and her cheeks flush. Just looking at her like this made his blood pump. Which was not a good idea at the moment. Chet and Franklin were still out there somewhere. So was Velavich. He needed to get his shit together and organize a search. Making Amy safe came first.

"Fine, he gets a pass on this one." He pinned Rio with a hard stare. "Only time, soldier. Disobey another order of mine and I'll ship your ass out so fast it'll take a solid week for the rest of your body to catch up. Understood?"

Another crisp salute. "Yes, sir, thank you, sir. I won't disappoint you again."

"Fricking Marine," Joshua muttered fondly, snapping off a return salute.

He felt Amy's fingers tighten on his, only then realizing that she hadn't even tried reclaiming her hand upon Rio's arrival. He returned the pressure, feeling something loosen in the vicinity of his heart. Such a small thing to give a man such big ideas.

"You know," Amy said. "You're the one who should be punished for disobeying an order."

Joshua looked at her in surprise. "Me?"

"Yes, you. I ordered you not to get shot, don't you remember? Rio, you heard me tell him, didn't you? I specifically ordered him not to get shot."

"Yes ma'am...uh, Amy...that's what you told him."

"Shut the hell up, Rio," Joshua snapped.

"But, Cap, she did tell you. I heard her say plain as day, don't get shot or knifed."

"You've got no room to talk, Rio," Amy said. She pointed to the makeshift bandage knotted around his thigh. "You let Arney put that knife of his into your leg, didn't you? I told you he knew how to use that knife."

Rio hesitantly pointed in Joshua's direction. "Actually, I think you were talking to..."

A noise from Amy—was it really a growl?—had the lethal soldier ducking his head and nodding instead. "Sorry, Amy. It won't happen again." Joshua felt a smile tug on his lips. The smile froze, though, when Amy leaned over Joshua, pulled Rio's head to her and kissed him on the cheek. Now it was his turn to growl. Amy's soft, husky voice didn't help.

"Thank you for your help, Rio. You've got a sweet rifle."

The only thing that saved Rio at that point was the shear panic on his face when he looked over Amy's head at Joshua. Joshua slowly raised his brows and made a point of looking over at the ledge and the hundred foot drop below. Rio shifted away from Amy quickly.

Joshua hid his smile and gently tugged his woman back under his arm. At the same time he removed the rifle from her lap and handed it to Rio. "Take your sweet rifle and go oversee the cleanup crew. I'm taking Amy home."

"Yes, please. I so need a hot shower." She sighed and leaned into him. At that moment, she was all soft female—the hard, competent sniper tucked away. Just knowing that side of her existed was enough to slap Joshua with his second biggest realization of the day.

He was falling in love with the Raven.

Chapter Twenty-Two

Amy stayed under the pounding spray of the hot water for a long time. When she finally made herself get out, she dried off slowly, feeling weak, drained, and kind of detached. Her mind kept replaying the instant Chambliss had pointed his gun at Joshua, and then jumped to Chambliss' head exploding. She didn't even remember thumbing off the rifle's safety much less making the conscious decision to pull the trigger. It had all been reflex. An automatic response to the driving need to protect Joshua that went beyond conscious thought.

And it scared the breath right out of her.

She threw the towel aside, angry with herself. God, she'd only known the man a few days. If she felt this way about him now, how much worse would it be in another week, a month? What would it do to her when he finally left her? And he *would* leave. Despite his grand cabin, she knew he didn't stay in Clear Springs for long stretches. He was too much a creature of action and intrigue to ever leave Special Ops. She could see him as the commander in a few years. Oh, he'd come back from time to time. Clear Springs was his home, after all, and she knew the value of that. He'd return once in a while to rest his mind and body. Why else would he name his cliff-side home *Refuge*? But he'd be gone again just as quickly. The man lived for the rush of a covert mission.

And Amy had left that life behind...hadn't she?

Sliding into shorts and a loose t-shirt, she shuddered, remembering the sound of her heart pounding in her ears after the kill shot. The sudden rush of emotion that had swept through her as she lay on the ledge had felt both familiar and strange. The sense of relief hadn't been what she usually associated with the completion of a mission. Satisfaction, yes, but never relief.

She could lie to herself, insist the relief was because Joshua was safe, but she hated liars.

She looked at herself in the bathroom mirror. Wide blue eyes stared back from a pale face framed with wet strands of dark hair. "You've killed again," she whispered to her reflection. She hadn't thought she'd be able to. Not after the horror that had filled her when she learned she'd taken the life of an innocent man. She hadn't been able to even touch a gun for months.

Despite her former profession, Amy didn't consider herself a cold blooded killer. She didn't go out looking for random targets. Except for Chambliss—and her one mistake—her kills had all been military targets, thoroughly researched and sanctioned. Chambliss hadn't been an assigned target, but there had been no doubt in Amy's mind that he had needed killing.

So did Adrik. She'd seen the evil in his eyes up close and personal. Joshua had his own particular demons—she'd looked deep into his eyes too—but compared to Chambliss, he was nothing less than a saint.

But all this was after-the-fact rationalization. She'd been faced with a situation that had demanded an instant reaction and she hadn't paused even a second to think things through. She'd just reacted.

And it had felt...good. Taking out bad guys, protecting others, those things were a part of her, ingrained in her DNA.

"Once a sniper, always a sniper," she whispered,

repeating her father's words. He'd tried to talk her into staying in the SO after Adrik's betrayal, urged her to "get back on the horse," but she hadn't been in any shape to listen. Not to him, not to her other team mates. She hadn't been in any shape for much of anything.

She'd been such a wreck. Hurt, ashamed, embarrassed, angry. God help her, she'd been so angry. The looks of pity from her team mates had almost crippled her. All she'd wanted to do was crawl into a hole and pull the dirt in after her.

But she'd come to Clear Springs instead, hidden herself in the deep woods and concentrated on just living one day at a time. It hadn't taken long for the quietness of those days to get on her nerves.

Thank God Bors had dropped into her life the day she'd taken her car to Kyle's garage. Things had changed after that. She'd made a few friends, albeit cautiously, and concentrated on her photography, a type of shooting that had nothing to do with guns. She was starting to enjoy life again.

Then Joshua had shown up and shot a freaking arrow between her and trouble.

Her new, well-ordered life spiraled out of control from there, and if it was one thing her sniper mentality couldn't stand, it was not being in control. Somehow, for the sake of her own sanity, she had to get that control back. She knew Joshua wasn't going to like it. He was as much a control freak as she was. Maybe more, she conceded.

Well, that's just too damn bad, she decided, running a brush ruthlessly through her wet hair. She wasn't letting herself get sucked into a relationship she couldn't come out of in one piece. Not again.

I will not be a victim again.

She came out of the bathroom ready for a fight. Joshua had shown her to an upstairs bedroom upon

227

arrival, one with its own bath. She'd been too exhausted to ask him about the change. She opened the bedroom door and paused, listening. Male voices. Joshua, Rio, others she didn't recognize. Padding barefoot down the hall she came out onto the balcony overlooking the great room. Joshua and Rio stood near the fireplace talking with three other men. Amy knew she hadn't made a sound, but all five men suddenly looked up, as if aware on some level they were no longer alone.

She started for the stairs. Joshua met her halfway.

"You should be resting." He raised a hand and tucked a damp strand of her hair behind one ear. His thumb hesitated over her bruised cheek before brushing across it lightly. The gesture was so tender, his eyes so full of concern, that all her anger just melted away. So much for fighting him for control, she thought sourly. Instead, she tilted her head into his hand and considered the fatigue of her body.

"I am tired," she admitted. "But part of that's probably still the drug Chet hit me with."

Tanned skin tightened across his jaw. Evidently he didn't like being reminded about what they'd done to her. She covered his hand with hers. "I'm okay. Stuff has a nasty kick, that's all. Besides, I want to call and check on Bors."

"I already have." His expression tightened a bit more, making her fear the worst. "Sue said he made it through the operation, but he's not out of the woods yet. We'll see after the next twenty-four hours. And before you ask, no, you can't stay with him. Sue's got it covered. She promised to call if there's any change." He turned and gestured to the three newcomers, probably hoping to distract her. "These are my men, Sam, Brick, and Ty."

Distraction indeed. Amy immediately focused her attention on the trio of NightHawks as she and

Joshua completed the descent to the bottom of the stairs. She would have been happy to just wave hello, but each man stepped forward. Sam was first, extending his hand. He was along the same lines as Rio, good looking, young, but his eyes filled with a wealth of experience. He moved with a deadly grace only another modern day warrior would pick up on. "Pleased to meet you, ma'am."

"I wouldn't call her that if I were you," Rio said quickly. "She gets testy." He shot her a playful smile, which Amy had no problem returning.

Still, she made a point of shaking her head sadly. "You're right, Joshua, he is a brat."

Rio's expression shifted to a mock scowl as the other men laughed. Amy laughed with them. "But he's right, too. It would make things easier if everyone just called me Amy."

"Amy it is." The big man named Brick stepped up. He was built a lot like his name, tall, square-bodied and solid. His skin was the color of gunpowder and his voice was deep and warm as a summer's night. "I'm the unit's blast tech. You need something blown up, just let me know."

"Geez, Brick, can you be any more subtle?" Sam muttered. "I swear the only word in your dictionary is 'boom.'"

"Naw, man, I got others." He ticked them off on his fingers. "Detonate, explode, flatten, obliterate, and my very most favorite, C-4."

"That's not a word."

"Is in my dictionary." He winked at her.

Amy laughed again. "Thanks, I'll keep that in mind."

She managed to keep her response light despite a sudden blistering wave of nostalgia. These men reminded her so much of her team mates. Loyal to each other, honest and honorable. Comrades. Friends. Damn, but she missed her guys. Monty's quick wit, Trey's sarcasm, Tao's practical jokes. And most of all, Jonathan Tucker's strong, guiding hand. He'd been the first of the Predators to really believe in her.

The third man stepped in front of her, drawing her away from such painful thoughts. "I'm Ty."

She shook his outstretched hand. Ty was full-blooded American Indian by the look of him. Bronze skin stretched over a hawkish nose and strong cheekbones. There was a faint line of ever so lighter skin just above his eyebrows that told her he usually wore his hair loose with something tied around his forehead to keep it from falling in his eyes. Right now the straight, raven black waterfall was tied back in a tail hanging well past his shoulders. Amy met the dark eyes shadowed by slightly prominent brow ridges and all her senses went on alert. They were too much like the ones she saw when she looked in the mirror. Not the color or shape, but the sharpness. The way he took in everything and everyone in the big room.

He's their sniper.

The realization came in a flash of insight, causing her pulse to miss a beat. If she could tell what he was, would he be able to see the truth about her in her eyes, too? Joshua hadn't turned away from her when she'd revealed she was the Raven. But she'd just saved his life, and he was under orders from her father to protect her. Would his men be as accepting? Or were they already convinced the Raven was a murderer, a traitor to everything they believed in?

"Come on," Joshua said. "Introductions are over for a while. You need to get some sleep." He urged her back up the stairs, his hand warm against her back.

Amy was only too happy to go along with Joshua's suggestion. Her mind was still a bit fuzzy, and she knew she'd need all her wits to deal with these men. She wanted to meet them on equal footing, not as an enemy and certainly not as a victim. She couldn't keep from glancing down at them as Joshua led her along the balcony.

Ty was the only one who watched her leave. He gave her an almost imperceptible nod. Oh, yeah, he knew what she was. Which meant if Joshua hadn't already told them, the others would know in the next few minutes. So be it. She knew she'd just been putting off dealing with the fallout of Adrik's betrayal when she'd let her father talk her into disappearing. Convincing everyone she was as much a victim as Colonel Tucker would take time.

Joshua led her down the third floor hall opposite from the room she'd just exited. "Why can't I use the same room I was just in?" she asked irritably.

"Because I've got more men coming, remember?" He stopped at a metal panel the size of a door set into the wall. It was a beautiful piece of artwork made up of one foot squares of different metals. Copper, tin, bronze, and something darker she wasn't familiar with. The patterns on each varied, some beaten, others punched and etched with intricate designs. Joshua drew her close until their bodies touched. "And because I'll feel better if you sleep here in my room."

In his room. *In his bed*. Amy couldn't hold back the warmth that flooded her body. Sleeping in Joshua's bed sounded like an oxymoron to her. She doubted there'd be any rest involved.

"You'll be safe here," he said, his gaze shifting to her throat. Dark eyes tightened as he lifted a hand and ran his fingers gently over the ugly bruises. The light touch made her shiver. His gaze shot up to her face, anger burning bright hot in the depths of his eyes. If she didn't believe he was upset *for* her and not *with* her, she would have been very afraid.

As the seconds passed, something else joined the anger. Something that had Amy's body responding on so many levels she had to force her eyes away or embarrass herself with a moan. The man was just too damn sexy for words. Not to mention the fact he had seduction down to an art.

So had Adrik.

She shoved the unpleasant thought away. Joshua wasn't anything like Adrik Velavich. She'd stake her life on it. Hell, she was staking her life on it, wasn't she?

With a mental wrench, she forced herself to focus on the metal panel. It didn't really look like a door. There was no knob, no handle, no way to open it that she could see. She touched the cool surface. "Is your bedroom behind here?" When he nodded, she laughed a little. "What do you use to get inside, a magic word?"

His lips turned up slowly into a smile. "More like a magic touch." He rested his hand against one of the squares. Less than two seconds later, the entire panel slid aside with a whisper of sound.

"Touch pad," she said. "Nice. Coded to accept only you?"

"At the moment, yes." He waved her into the dark room ahead of him. She stepped inside. Dim lights automatically began to glow around the edge of the ceiling. The first thing that struck her was that, just like her bedroom, there were no visible windows. The wall she knew faced the valley was a solid, unbroken expanse of smooth dove gray. No furniture set along its length. There were two more metal doors in the opposite wall with a bank of bronze panels between them. An immense bed dominated the room, draped in rich shades of bronze, gold, deep red, and slate gray.

Joshua walked around the bed to one of the doors. A quick touch of a finger and the metal slid aside. Another soft light came on. "Bathroom's here, the other's a closet. These are drawers and cabinets." He waved a hand at the bronze panels as he walked back to her. In the wall next to the bedroom door were several other metal squares. He touched one of them. A large rectangle of squares shifted aside to reveal a control panel complete with a view screen. He touched a few buttons on a pad and motioned her closer. He pointed to a series of buttons below the view screen.

"These are tied to cameras scattered around the place." He punched the first button. Views of the house, patio, and surrounding woods flashed by in quick succession. One came up, the kitchen, and the auto-view stopped.

Rio was there, rummaging in an industrial-sized refrigerator. Joshua touched another button and she could suddenly hear bottles clinking. She even heard Rio's welcoming sigh as he pulled out a cold beer. He thumbed the top off, the metal disk tinging when it hit the ceramic floor, and kicked back the bottle. After taking several long swallows, he lowered the bottle, paused, and belched loudly.

Amy couldn't help grinning at his look of satisfaction. She didn't realize how fondly she was watching Rio enjoy his beer until Joshua stabbed a button and barked, "Rio!" in a loud, growly voice.

To his credit, the young man in the kitchen hardly jumped at all at the disembodied voice. He tilted his head toward the ceiling. "Yo, Cap."

"You contact the other guys yet?"

Rio nodded, apparently aware of Joshua's camera system. "Rashe and Gage will be in by midnight. They'll call when they hit town."

"Good. Let me know when you hear from them."

"Aye, Cap." He raised the beer in salute before tipping it back again.

"And pick up that cap."

"Aye, Cap...uh, sir."

Amy covered her grin. Joshua just shook his head and returned to the keypad, punching in a long series. Another metal panel slid aside, revealing a smooth, dark square. "Put your palm here," Joshua told her.

Amy flattened her hand against the cool surface. "You do realize that having a palm-locked bedroom makes you seem a bit paranoid."

"You think?" He flashed a smile, then just as quick his expression turned serious. "Considering that, you might want to think about what my letting you in here means."

"I didn't ask to come in," she pointed out softly.

"Poor choice of words. It's not that I'm letting you in, I'm inviting you in. I want you here." Cupping her face with his hands, he leaned in and kissed her.

Amy could tell he tried to keep the kiss light. When her hands came up and fastened on his arms to steady herself, she could feel how tight his muscles were, how disciplined his control. And all of a sudden, she didn't want light. The hard kernel of desire Joshua had planted yesterday exploded like a piece of popcorn.

With a little moan, she deepened the kiss, sliding her tongue into his mouth to taste him. When he tried to pull back, she wrapped her arms around him and hung on, rising on her toes to prolong the kiss. He indulged her for a moment then twisted his face to the side.

Breathing hard, he said, "Amy, baby, we don't have to do this right now. You've been through too much. Give your body time to rest." His hands had shifted to her hips during the kiss.

The way his fingers bit into her said he didn't want to wait. So did the hard length of his erection when her fingers closed around him. The eager pulse against her palm sent a spike of raw hunger rushing through her to settle between her legs.

She could feel herself throbbing with need, getting hotter by the second, wetter. Pressing several kisses along his clenched jaw, she shifted close and stood on her toes again to whisper in his ear. "I'm fine. I want you, Joshua. I need you. Right now."

Chapter Twenty-Three

Joshua didn't bother trying to stifle his groan at Amy's words. His sly little minx knew exactly what she was doing to him. *Thank God she's so stubborn.*

Wrapping her damp hair in his fist, he tugged her head back so he could see her face. He was so hungry for her. Starving. The little verbal petting session at the café had done nothing but whet his appetite for something far more satisfying. Her abduction added a bite of desperation to his growing need that chose that moment to surface. He had to have her. *Now.*

With a growl, he latched onto her mouth. The hot, erotic taste of her shredded the last of his control. Blindly, he swiped a hand against the wall controls, somehow finding the one that closed the door. Still kissing her, he cupped her sweet backside in both hands and lifted her up. Her legs wrapped around him without hesitation. He shoved the hard bulge of his cock against her hot core, reveling in her needy moans.

Too many damn clothes.

He needed her naked.

Cracking his eyes open, Joshua somehow made it over to the bed. He crawled onto the mattress on his knees and leaned over, pressing her into the thick quilt as he scattered kisses over her throat. Hands tugged on his shirt. Her low, sultry voice held a note of command.

"Take this off. I want skin this time."

Since that was what he wanted, too, he had no problem obeying her. He let her pull his shirt over his head, then snagged the hem of her navy blue tee shirt and skimmed it up and off. Damn. No bra. How had he missed that?

He swooped in and took an entire dusky rose circle into his mouth. Amy cried out, arching her back while her hands pressed his head closer. Joshua felt like purring around the mouthful of soft flesh. He loved a woman who didn't mind letting him know what his touch did to her, who held nothing back. He flicked the taut nipple with his tongue, imagining doing the same to her clit, and felt her legs spasm around him.

"Joshua!"

He shifted focus to her other nipple, drawing it deep while fingering the first one. She writhed and pulled at his hair, trying to bring him back to her mouth. He chuckled and let her tug him up. "Impatient much?"

"Look who's talking." She fused their mouths together, as if she was as hungry for him as he was for her. He lost himself in the deep kiss until she twisted her lower body and shoved at his chest at the same time. He could have stopped her from rolling him over, but didn't, wanting to see what she had in mind. He didn't have to wonder long.

Once astride him, she started touching him, running her hot little hands all over his skin, stroking him, petting him, setting him on fire. He took it as long as he could, mesmerized by the look of pure lust on her face. When she raked her nails over his nipples, he almost came off the bed.

"Fuck!" He grabbed her wrists, careful not to hurt her.

"Yes, let's." She leaned down and kissed him again, her little tongue licking inside his mouth until he thought he'd go crazy.

He let go of her wrists and rolled her beneath him, one hand holding her in place while the other worked to pull down her shorts. In no time, he had her completely naked. Every inch of her toned runner's body bare for his enjoyment. He took a moment just to look at her.

Her lightly tanned skin wasn't flawless. Besides the numerous recent bruises, Joshua found scars. Most looked like a mish-mash of Morse Code sprinkled randomly over her body, the pale dots and dashes years old. Not so the three inch scar down her left side. He ran a finger across the puckered flesh.

"Adrik's going away present," she said, removing his hand. "I don't want to talk about him right now." She took his fingers to her mouth, sucking and kissing them one by one.

Joshua let the sensuousness of her actions calm him. Killing Velavich wasn't a job anymore. It was a driving need. Not just because the man had betrayed his country, taken innocent lives, and ruined a top-notch team. He wanted Velavich dead for daring to set steel to the flesh of this woman. For giving her more scars than the one visible on her skin.

He removed his fingers from her grasp and gently took her face in his hands, forcing her to meet his gaze. "I *will* kill him for you," he said, repeating the words he'd spoken at her house. This time, though, they were more than an offer. They were a promise.

She gazed up at him for a moment, then caressed his face. "Thank you, but I'm perfectly capable of killing the bastard myself."

Her matter-of-fact words called up an impossible grin from somewhere deep inside him. Didn't she know that if she kept showing him how strong she was, he'd never let her go? "That you are, Raven." He kissed her, and couldn't help murmuring, "My Raven."

He moved a hand down her luscious body to the

hot place between her legs.

The feel of her smooth skin there made his cock jerk behind his jeans. He'd always found a woman's tight curls sexy as hell, but damn if their absence didn't send his lust through the roof.

He easily slipped a finger through the bare folds, groaning when he met a wealth of slick wetness. He rubbed her as they kissed, circling the tight bud of her sex with his thumb as he dipped his finger inside her over and over again. Her hips soon bucked into his touch, the passionate response making him ache to be inside her.

When her hands closed on the fastener of his jeans, he levered his lower body up enough to give her room to work. The moment he spilled out into her waiting hands, he locked his muscles in place. The sensation of her cupping him, caressing him, was like a shot of pure adrenaline to his system.

"Joshua, please."

He rose up and shucked his boots and jeans as fast as he could. Returning to her, he took a moment just to drink in the sensation of lying against her bare skin. He'd kill for this moment alone, for the feel of her hands on his back, her breasts pressed tight to his chest. For the way her legs wrapped around his and her hips tilted up, welcoming him home.

With a groan, he shifted his hips, the head of his cock rubbing eagerly against her slick opening.

****

Amy's whole body burned. One push, and he'd be inside her, filling her, giving her everything her body craved. One push—

"Wait."

She couldn't believe her ears, could barely process the fact Joshua left her. The man just crawled right off the edge of the bed onto the floor. All she could think was that he'd better be dying.

Leaning up on an elbow, she called, "Joshua?"

His head popped back into sight, followed by the rest of him. He quickly returned and knelt beside her. Only then did he flash the foil packet in his hand.

"Oh." She hadn't even thought about protection this time. She narrowed her eyes at him. "I thought you didn't have any of those."

He grinned as he ripped open the packet and rolled the latex onto his thick erection. "I don't. I stole a couple out of Kyle's desk while at the garage."

"Kyle keeps condoms at the garage?"

"Apparently." With a quick move, he settled back into place between her legs. Amy groaned at the pleasure of just having him there. His weight felt glorious. "Now, where were we?" He nudged the head of his cock just inside her.

Amy gasped. "Right there."

"Mmm, yes." He started nibbling on her lips as he pushed in, slowly, relentlessly, every inch a torturous pleasure. He trailed kisses down her neck. "God, you're tight."

Amy could only nod and hold on. She knew this was going to be a little uncomfortable at first. She'd been celibate for over a year and Joshua was so...big. She bit her lip when the pressure touched on the edge of pain.

He must have sensed her discomfort, because he stopped and kissed her again. Then he began to rock his hips in a gentle motion. The subtle movement rubbed some part of him exactly where she needed it most and just like that, the pleasure far outweighed the discomfort. Her hips jerked up of their own accord, seating him fully inside her.

Joshua hissed and groaned, the erotic sounds sending a surge of lust through her. She wanted to wring those sounds of pleasure from him again and again. With that goal in mind, she clenched her inner muscles, grasping him, caressing him. His eyes flew wide.

"Damn, baby!"

He pulled out and thrust into her hard, sending pleasure arcing through her body like lightning. He did it again, and again, his momentum building like a runaway locomotive, his thrusts growing in speed and intensity until nothing held him back. Soon he was pounding into her, calling out her name, grinding out words of praise, of promise. "Yes, baby, right there, right there. You're so damn good. I'm going to make you come so hard."

Amy reveled in his possession. She met him stroke for stroke, digging her fingers into his shoulders, his back, his pumping ass. The wave of pleasure built and built until she was riding the crest. He had her so close, so...damn...close...

She came, unable to hold back a scream, realizing dimly that she didn't need to. With Joshua, she didn't need to hide who she was.

His hips jerked hard, once, twice, and Joshua threw back his head and roared as he came. The pulse of his cock deep inside her sent a wave of pleasure through Amy, coupled with something else she dare not name.

He wasn't hers. This wasn't forever. They were just two people thrown together by circumstances. Two people with a common goal. Once that goal was reached, they would each go their own way. Alone.

Still breathing hard, Joshua raised his head. "What is it?"

"What?" She hadn't said any of that aloud, had she?

"I felt you tense up, and not in a good way. Did I hurt you?"

His worry touched her. Forcing the tension from her body, she reached up and smoothed the wrinkles between his brows. Even then, the lines remained, evidence of the strain of his position.

"Nothing's wrong. Everything's right. As if you needed to be told."

Lips curving, he rolled to his side, taking her with him. "I have it on good authority that positive reinforcement is the way to go."

"Oh, really?"

"Yes, really. Works wonders every time."

She couldn't help reaching up and patting him on the top of the head. "Good boy."

He scowled and gave her a mock growl. "I was thinking of something a little more satisfying."

Amy giggled. "Sorry, I'm afraid I'm all out of dog biscuits."

He growled again and rolled back on top of her, his fingers dancing over her ribs. How had the man known she was ticklish? He soon had her begging for mercy.

They were both breathing hard even before his fingers found their way down to more interesting territory. Amy stretched and sighed, enjoying the glide of his touch against her sensitive flesh, the way her muscles quivered, sending little jolts of pleasure shooting deep inside.

Joshua's lips brushed hers, then slid along her jaw to her ear. "See, now this is more like what I had in mind. I like petting you."

Amy wanted to push her hips up against his hand to beg for more, but her tired body wouldn't cooperate. She gazed up at him through eyes half-closed. "Pet away. Just don't be offended if I fall asleep."

He chuckled, the movement of his fingers slowing into soft, languid strokes. "I don't mind petting you to sleep, baby. But when you wake up..."

His pause had her dragging her heavy eyelids open. The uncertain look in his eyes stunned her. This was the Harrier, a man with a reputation for making quick, hard decisions. A man with enough confidence to match a battalion.

"Once isn't enough. You know it and I know it. I'm going to want you again, Amy. Will you let me have you? Will you have me in return?"

After what they'd just shared, most men would simply assume she was theirs for the taking. Joshua asked. Her heart gave a crazy little flutter. Amy dragged a hand up and gently caressed his face.

"Condom?"

Something, she wasn't sure what, flared deep in his eyes. He silently held up three fingers.

Amy smiled slowly. "That might just be enough."

Chapter Twenty-Four

Joshua tucked several strands of damp hair behind Amy's ear. Flushed from a shower where they'd shared more than water, she looked positively bitable. "Are you sure I didn't hurt you?"

He'd gotten pretty rough more than once. One little bit of encouragement from her and his iron clad control simply disintegrated. She hadn't seemed to mind, but he was still worried. Hurting her was the absolute last thing he ever wanted to do. Keeping her safe, keeping her... Ah, hell, just keeping her was all he wanted.

And he was no closer to figuring out how he was going to accomplish that task than he'd been last night.

"I told you, I'm fine. I'm a lot stronger than I look." She pulled his head down. Petal soft lips still slightly swollen met his in a light kiss.

Even after having just had her, his body stirred. She was like a drug, turning him inside out with a simple touch. He pulled close, leaning in to deepen the kiss.

The intercom on the wall beeped. Again. Amy drew back, chuckling. "That makes an even dozen, I think."

Fighting back the urge to shoot someone, Joshua turned and slapped the wall unit off and the door open. He'd talked to Rio and the others not five minutes ago. It wasn't like them to act like a bunch of two-year-olds who needed their hands held.

The sound of an infant's cry rushing into the room through the open door washed away every

244

ounce of irritation, turning his insides to ice. He hurried to the balcony, Amy right beside him.

The great room below teamed with people, most of them surrounding one of the couches where a man lay, beaten and bloodied.

"Kyle!" Amy's strangled cry flooded Joshua with a rush of adrenaline.

He glanced around the room as they rushed down the stairs, a spike of fear tearing at his gut when he didn't immediately see Farrah. The shrill baby's cry drew his gaze to one of the spare bedrooms. There. The devoted mother would be with her children.

He stopped Amy at the foot of the stairs. "Farrah," he murmured, lifting his chin toward the bedroom. "Try to find out what happened. See if you can help with the kids. They know you."

Amy nodded, casting a worried look in Kyle's direction before she bolted toward the bedroom.

Joshua swore long and hard when he leaned over the back of the couch and got a good look at Kyle. His friend's face was a mass of bruises and blood. His body didn't look much better.

Gage, the team's medic, was trying to staunch a bleeding gash in Kyle's thigh while Ty worked on a stab wound on his shoulder that went bone deep.

"Bloody hell, who did this?" Joshua growled.

"Cap—"

He waved Rio to silence when Kyle's eyes popped open.

"Wassiles," Kyle choked out, his voice full of pain and anger. "Chet and Franklin." He reached up and grabbed a handful of Joshua's shirt, pulling him down with surprising strength. From the amount of blood coating his body, Joshua was amazed he was even conscious.

"I should have listened to you," Kyle grated. "Should have left the valley like you said. Velavich w-was with them. Son of a bitch attacked my family." He broke into a fit of coughing, releasing his hold and dropping back onto the couch.

Joshua grabbed his hand, letting Kyle squeeze through the fit while Gage and Ty kept working to stop the heavy bleeding.

When Kyle was through, he met Joshua's gaze, eyes filled with a mix of anguish and rage. "He hit Katrina, Josh. He fucking hurt my daughter!"

A red haze clouded Joshua's vision. Velavich was so going to die.

Kyle's body jerked as Amber let out a fresh squall. He tried to rise. "Farrah..." More than one hand held him down.

"Easy, easy," Joshua said. "Amy's helping her with the kids."

Kyle squeezed his eyes shut and rocked his head from side to side, face twisted into a grimace. "Farrah..."

The longing in that single word struck Joshua like a blow. He opened his mouth to call Farrah from her kids, but Kyle suddenly went limp against the cushions. Joshua beat back a moment of panic as he waited for the next breath. When it came, relief drenched him.

He shot Gage a questioning look. The medic calmly shrugged, though his fingers flew as he finished applying a pressure bandage to the wound he was working on. "You'll know when I do," Gage said. "Right now, he's holding his own."

He produced a knife and started cutting Kyle's bloody clothes from his body, rattling off a disturbing list of injuries along the way.

"Probable concussion, a broken nose, hole in his shoulder, one—" He pressed lightly on a faintly purple spot on Kyle's side.

Eyes still closed, Kyle flinched and groaned.

"Sorry, buddy, make that two cracked ribs.

Slashed thigh, miscellaneous bruises."

The knife flashed, removing the last of Kyle's jeans. Joshua sucked in a breath at the badly swollen knee. How the hell had the man walked out of his house much less driven his truck to get here?

Gage glanced up, his expression grim. "Won't know how bad some of the injuries are without x-rays."

Joshua nodded in understanding.

Gage tossed the knife aside and pulled a suture kit from his pack. "Sam, I'm going to need your expertise here," he called.

"Be right there." Sam headed for the bathroom to wash up. As their blade specialist, he knew every way imaginable to slice through someone's flesh. He also made it his business to know how to repair such wounds. A needle and thread in his hands were pure magic.

Joshua looked up and saw Amy standing just outside the bedroom cradling a sniffling Amber to her shoulder. Amy's eyes were huge, glittering with unshed tears and something else. Alarm.

"Cap—"

"In a minute, Rio."

He was stuck on Amy's expression, couldn't figure it out until he looked past her. Through the open doorway he saw Brick holding both Katrina and Trevor in his big arms. The children clung to the big man, a total stranger, when they should be clinging to their mother.

"Where the hell is Farrah?"

"She's not here," Amy said, the softly spoken words jerking his attention back to her.

"Not here?" He couldn't have heard right. Farrah's family had been attacked. Her child assaulted—he could see the bruise on Katrina's pale cheek from here—and her husband beaten half to death. Where else would she be?

With single-minded stubbornness, he refused to acknowledge the answer that stared him in the face.

"That's what we've been trying to tell you, Cap," Rio said. "It's just Kyle and the three kids."

The ice in his veins hit his heart first, then his brain. It was true. *Farrah was missing.*

Leaning over the couch, he slapped Kyle's cheeks until he roused. He had to do it twice more before his friend opened his eyes with any sense of awareness. Grimly, he gripped Kyle's chin, bent down until their faces were inches apart, and asked the question he was afraid he already knew the answer to.

"Kyle, where's Farrah?"

****

Amy stood just inside the bedroom door, listening to the heated conversation going on in the front room. Half of her was numb with fear, the other half a raging mass of anger. Adrik had taken Farrah Fagan. A bold move, even for him. He had to know Joshua would come after him with a vengeance. But then, he also knew Amy well enough to know she wouldn't risk sacrificing an innocent for her own skin. He knew she'd come, too.

What he didn't know was that she'd be coming to kill him.

The baby in her arms whimpered and squirmed. Amy forced herself to relax and tipped the bottle back into place. Thank goodness Farrah kept an emergency diaper bag in Kyle's truck. She'd have Amber asleep in another few minutes. A glance at the overstuffed chair where Brick was reading to Trevor and Kat told her she wouldn't have to worry about them either. Both children had latched onto the big man and didn't look like they'd be letting go any time soon. Her only problem would be getting past Joshua. She'd had to listen hard to catch his harsh whisper when Kyle explained Adrik's demand—Amy's life for Farrah's.

"No, absolutely not. We'll go up and get Farrah back, but I'm not putting Amy at risk. She stays here."

Silly man. Did he think he could order her around?

While Joshua gathered the men around the dining table and made plans, so did she. After burping Amber and laying the sleeping infant in the middle of the bed, she nodded to Brick and slipped out of the room. A couple of the men glanced her way, including Joshua. They quickly returned their focus to the maps spread on the table when she waved and headed to where Kyle lay swathed in bandages.

An IV pole stood at the head of the couch, two bags hanging from its hook. One held clear saline, the other blood. Each had a line running into one of Kyle's arms, pumping life-giving fluids into the badly beaten man. Amy's heart squeezed painfully at the sight of her friend. Lying there so still, his eyes closed, he looked defeated. Lost. Like half his heart was missing.

His eyes snapped open when she touched him, and suddenly he didn't look lost anymore. Impotent rage simmered behind dilated pupils, reminding her of a half-mad bull pawing for a fight without a matador in sight. They'd given him something for the pain. Something strong. Despite his determination, he'd be completely out soon. She knelt down beside him.

"Hi," she said.

Tears filled his eyes.

She grabbed a piece of gauze from the open kit by the couch and dabbed them away. "Shh, it's all right. The children are fine. Amber is asleep and Brick is reading to Trev and Kat."

White lines flashed along his tight jaw. "I

couldn't...I couldn't protect them."

"Farrah begged you to stop fighting, didn't she?"

He drew in a sharp breath. "How did you know?"

Because she'd come to know this couple well over the past year. Their love for one another was almost tangible. Amy brushed his hair off his forehead. "Because you're insane when it comes to protecting your family. You'd have fought for them to your last breath. Farrah wouldn't want that. She'd want you alive so you could rescue her." And only Farrah could have made him stop after Adrik hit Katrina.

Eyelids drooped as bruised and bandaged fingers dug into the leather couch. "Hell of a rescuer I turned out to be."

"Don't sell yourself short, tiger. You got your children to safety. Believe me, that'll be the first thing Farrah asks you when she sees you again. And you made it to the one person you knew could get her back. You didn't fail her." Amy gently tapped a finger on the splints taped around his bad leg. "You couldn't know he'd go after your weakest point once you stopped fighting. Take it as a compliment. He didn't want you teaming up with Joshua to come after him."

"Fuck his compliment. Want the fucking bastard dead."

"I know. I promise I'll take care of it after I get Farrah back."

Brows drew together and heavy eyelids lifted. "What?" he whispered.

"I said I'll take care—"

"You can't—"

She quickly covered his mouth to keep his agitated words from alerting Joshua. "Listen to me," she said softly. "I'm not what you think. I'm more than just the Cobra's stupid girlfriend." She took a deep breath. "You've heard of the Raven, right, the

Predators' sniper?"

A slight nod.

"Well, I'm the Raven." She saw the disbelief in his eyes and hurried on. "It's true. You can ask Joshua later if you want confirmation. I'm just sorry I didn't tell you sooner. I should have, I know. And I won't blame you if you decide…if you want me to stay away from your family after this is over."

He opened his mouth, but she quickly silenced him again. She'd understand if he thought she was too dangerous to be around his loved ones, but she didn't want to hear it yet. "I'm not going to tell you not to worry. All I want you to remember is this. You and Farrah have been the absolute best friends I have ever had. I won't forget, and I won't let you down."

She heard the sound of chairs scooting across the floor. Bending down, she pressed a kiss to Kyle's cheek. "I have to go now."

She rose and moved to the sliding glass doors without glancing toward the dining area.

"Amy?"

She waved blindly in Joshua's direction. "Just going outside for a minute."

"No, she's leaving. Stop her, Josh."

Damn it, Kyle.

Instead of going around the second couch in the living room, Amy leaped over it. One of the sliding glass doors was open a crack and she slammed it back, not caring if the glass shattered. Without pausing, she ran straight off the balcony, arching her body at the last second to slice into the pool below. She came up swimming hard for the waterfall.

Shouts erupted behind her. Joshua's voice rose above the others, yelling for her to stop. She didn't dare. After what he said, she knew he wouldn't allow her on this mission. And she had to go. She couldn't let Adrik hurt someone she cared about again, least of all Farrah Fagan. The woman was her friend, and Amy didn't have so many friends that she could afford to lose even one.

She'd almost reached the waterfall when she heard the shot. Water spurted up from the impact, close enough to splash her face. Shocked, she whipped around. Joshua and Rio, running along the side of the pool toward her, slammed to a halt. Both of them looked up to the second floor balcony. Ty stood perfectly still, the stock of a rifle snug against his shoulder. The silent sniper squeezed off another round. The shot hit the water near Amy's shoulder. Rio whipped out a pistol and aimed it at his teammate. She'd have to remember to thank him later.

"I don't know what you think you're trying to do, Ty," Rio barked, "but you damn well stop right now!"

Instead of adding his own order, Joshua turned back to her. She could see a kind of disappointed understanding mixed with the anger in his eyes. Maybe it did look pretty bad, her running out so suddenly. Cowardly, even. Especially since he didn't know what she planned to do. The idea that he could think she'd run and leave Farrah in Adrik's hands hurt, but only for a moment. He would understand later. And if he thought she was running away now, afraid for her own life, maybe it would keep him from coming after her.

She made another lunge for the waterfall. When it came this time, the shot didn't surprise her. The fact the bullet grazed her arm shouldn't have either. Nothing major, just enough to singe skin, but it stung like fire. Amy clamped her jaw shut to keep from crying out.

Joshua's loud swearing colored the air. "Stand down, all of you!"

Even without his shouted order she wouldn't

have hesitated to keep going. If he'd wanted to, that sharp-eyed sniper on the balcony could have put that bullet anywhere in her body. He wasn't trying to kill her, just slow her down so Joshua could catch her.

"Amy, stop! Baby, you don't have to do this. You don't have to be afraid. I'm not going to let Velavich get his hands on you, I swear!"

She snagged the lip of the fall and looked back. Joshua stood at the edge of the pool, poised to jump in after her. She shook her head, praying he'd understand—that he wouldn't end up hating her. "It's not Adrik I'm afraid of, Joshua." She pushed off with her feet, propelling her body up and over the edge.

The fall's not nearly long enough, Amy thought as the frothy water closed over her in a rush.

Chapter Twenty-Five

Joshua watched the woman he was coming to care about disappear over the falls. "Amy!" He lunged for the cliff edge. Hands caught him and held him back. He fought mindlessly until a hard-knuckled fist clipped him on the jaw, making him see stars. He shook his head.

"You can't catch her that way, Cap. Not if she swims half as fast as she runs."

Joshua dragged in several ragged breaths. He felt light-headed, something that had nothing whatsoever to do with running or fighting or getting hit in the jaw, and everything with seeing Amy run from him as if she was afraid of him. Afraid he'd trade her life for another. It made him feel like a monster.

He jerked his arms from the restraining hands and pushed past his team, going to the edge of the cliff. He didn't see her at first, and his heart missed several beats. Then, a dark head swam out of the churning water, and he was able to breathe again.

"Figured she'd be fast." Ty's rumble came from beside him. The lethal sniper stood empty handed, his body slightly tense, as if waiting for Joshua to make a move. Joshua obliged him, slamming his fist into the man's stomach in a rapid one-two punch. He finished off with an uppercut that lifted Ty off his feet before sending him to the ground. He stood over his teammate, his friend, and glared.

"You even think about pointing a gun in her direction again and I'll kill you."

"He was only trying to slow her down, Cap."

Sam held out a hand to Ty to help him up but the man didn't move to take it. He lay there watching Joshua. Probably waiting to see if it was safe to get up.

"I know," Joshua ground out. "I know what he was trying to do." He took a step back. "But mistakes happen. He could have hit her."

Ty slapped a hand in Sam's and hauled himself up. "I did hit her."

It took all three of them, Rio, Sam, and Gage, to keep Joshua from throwing Ty off the cliff. Gage finally got an arm around his throat from behind. "Calm down, Cap. We got too much to do right now. You can kill him later."

It was a struggle, but Joshua finally managed to get himself under control. He stared hard at Ty, a man he'd trusted with his life more times than he could count. All he wanted was get his hands around Ty's throat. "You son of a bitch. How bad?"

"Just a graze. Didn't do more than burn off a little skin. I was trying to scare her into stopping, but your woman doesn't scare easily."

Joshua barked out a bitter laugh and shook himself free of Gage's hold. "So you think she lit out of here like a cat with her tail on fire because she felt safe with us?"

"I'm not sure yet, why she left. But it wasn't because she was afraid."

"Wrong! She was terrified. And if she wasn't before, she damn sure is now. She's already been kidnapped once. Doesn't take a genius to figure she wouldn't want to be in their hands twice."

"We wouldn't have let that happen," Rio growled.

The younger man looked about as pissed off as Joshua felt. His green-eyed gaze fixed on Ty held a dark threat usually reserved for their enemies. After Ty's admission, Joshua almost wished he'd let Rio take that second shot at the sniper.

"No, we wouldn't." And if Amy was telling the truth about being the Raven, she had to know that already. SO units never sacrificed an innocent.

But she'd already been sacrificed once, hadn't she? *By one of her own team, no less.* Joshua swore softly. One night in his arms wasn't going to erase the fear left behind by that kind of betrayal.

"She knows how close I am to Farrah," he admitted. "That might have something to do with her decision to run."

Sam whistled. "She thought you'd trade her life for Farrah's?"

"That's a load of crap," Gage said. "We don't trade one innocent life for another."

"Not in a million years," Joshua agreed. "Not even if I didn't already love her."

Love. Wow. He'd actually said the word out loud. If he wasn't on the clock he'd be looking for a place to sit down right about now. Epiphanies had a way of making a man weak in the knees.

His stark admission seemed to startle everyone into silence but Ty. "Does she know that?"

The serious question shook Joshua out of his stupor. "Yeah, she does." He frowned. Or she should. God knew it was certainly what he'd meant when he'd spent the night with her in his bed. Usually his sexual encounters consisted of a quick tumble and a quicker exit, no strings attached much less emotions. But maybe a full night of mutual satisfaction interspersed with whispered conversations and soft touches didn't translate into the same thing for her.

"Then I think your assumption is wrong," Ty said. "She should know you wouldn't put her in danger. That means she has another reason for running."

Joshua slashed a hand through the air. "Doesn't matter." As long as her running took her away from

Velavich, he'd deal with her reason later. He headed to the house. "Right now, we concentrate on getting Farrah back alive."

They took the steps up to the second floor two at a time. Brick stood by the couch. The big man had a hand on Kyle's shoulder, holding him down. Kyle stared at him, eyes fever bright. "Sorry. Should've warned you sooner."

"No problem. We'll catch her. You just stay put. Try anything stupid and Brick has my permission to sit on you."

The big man grinned, then frowned when he realized what that meant. Joshua patted his shoulder. "Don't worry, if I need anything blown up, I'll be sure to call you. While we're gone, I want you to organize an evac for Kyle and the kids."

"I'm not leaving without Farrah."

He pointed a finger at Kyle. "You'll do as ordered."

Kyle ran a shaking hand over his face. "Damn it, Josh, you don't understand. I can't...I can't lose her."

Joshua thought of Amy facing someone as deadly as the Cobra on her own and had to fight back a surge of fury. "Believe me, I understand better than you think."

He caught Gage's eye and looked pointedly at Kyle's IV. He didn't want to take a chance on his stubborn friend doing something stupid. Gage tilted his head as if calculating, then nodded and pulled a syringe out of his pocket.

Satisfied, Joshua crossed the room to the door beneath the stairs. His armory.

"What if Ty's right, Cap?"

Joshua spared Rio a glance as he palmed the door open. "Right about what?"

"Well, Amy doesn't strike me as being stupid. She should know by now you wouldn't let anything happen to her. Not after everything we did getting her back the first time. She should know you'd insist she stay here, safe and sound. Hell, she probably heard you say exactly that. Maybe that's why she ran."

Joshua stared at Rio, feeling the blood drain from his face and his heart trip in panic. Hadn't Amy told him she was capable of killing Velavich herself? "Ah, hell, Rio, I hope you're wrong."

"What is it?" Ty asked.

Joshua let Rio explain. He was too damn mad. The sneaky little vixen. How dare she go after Velavich without him.

You were going without her.

Different, completely different on so many levels. He was taking backup. He had a plan.

"She's gone after Velavich herself," Rio said. "She knew Cap wouldn't let her come with us. That's why she took off."

Joshua snatched up guns and ammo, muttering under his breath. "Damn woman's got a sacrificial streak a mile wide." She'd probably give up her soul to save someone else.

"That's called honor," Rashid said, checking over the gun he'd selected.

"No," Joshua corrected harshly, "that's called stupid. Especially when she doesn't bother to check to see if I have a better plan." Damn it, why hadn't she trusted him?

Rio snapped a full magazine into his gun. "We going to stop her."

Joshua nodded. "I'd rather she didn't stumble into the middle of our operation. We'll try catching her at her cabin. She'll have to go there first. I doubt she'll try making it up the mountain barefoot, and her cabin's not that far downriver. We might even be able to get there ahead of her if we leave now."

The sling of a scoped rifle went over his shoulder. His bow and quiver of arrows were already in the Jeep. Snagging one of the pre-packed backpacks by the door, he left, the others right behind him.

Rio, Sam, and Rashid squeezed into Joshua's Jeep while the others piled into Gage's truck.

"Rio, you're on communications," Joshua said, starting up the engine. "Get in touch with the others while we're in route to Amy's and bring them up to date. Find out if Capella has found the Wassiles' cabin yet. Tell him if he hasn't, he's fired. Have him link the satellite feed to your laptop."

"Can he do that if he's fired?"

"He could do that even if he was dead," Joshua said. Capella was a freaking electronic genius. "I want to know every route to and from the Wassiles' cabin. I want an ID on everything with a pulse within a ten mile radius. We know Velavich brought at least one man with him. He may have more."

He had no intention of walking into a trap. Not with the lives of the two women he loved on the line.

****

Amy pulled herself out of the river and started jogging. She bypassed the trail leading to her house. Joshua wasn't stupid, and he wasn't slow. He'd probably already figured out her plan and was on his way to her place right now to stop her. Assuming he meant half of what he'd said last night—and she had no reason to doubt him—she could just imagine how angry he was with her right now. Here he'd gone to all the trouble of rescuing her from Adrik and she was headed right back into his hands again.

She winced as a stone dug into the arch of her foot. Good thing she'd planned ahead for just such an emergency as this. Another hundred yards brought her to the gnarled tree she was looking for. The ancient oak stood guard over a pile of moss-covered stones at its roots. The pile looked like they hadn't been disturbed for at least a hundred years.

Breathing hard, she dropped to her knees beside them and started heaving rocks aside. The waterproof duffle bag she'd stashed here almost a year ago was covered in dirt, mold, and leaves. Inside, the clothes, weapons, and other emergency supplies were double wrapped. They fell out into her hands as clean as the day she'd packed them.

She changed clothes quickly, then ran a fast check on the weapons before stuffing her pockets with ammo. The last thing she pulled out of the bag was a radio earpiece, the same kind issued to each special ops unit member. Amy stared hard at the small device. She could turn it on, call Joshua, and explain to him why she had to do this.

Oh, yeah, that would work. She'd be lucky not to get her ears blistered. Not to mention standing around trying to talk Joshua into letting her do things her way would give his human bloodhounds time to track her down. She tossed the radio on top of the duffle bag and stood. Farrah was in Adrik's hands because of her. No matter what Joshua might think, this mission was her responsibility.

Grimly, she settled the strap of her sniper rifle over her shoulder and headed up the mountain. It was time to kill again.

****

Joshua forced himself to stand still while Rashid combed the nearby riverbank and Rio circled Amy's yard, looking for any sign that she'd been here. They'd already searched the empty house. Sealed in a concrete vault buried under the floorboards of her bedroom was where Ty found her cache of weapons, the ones she refused to use again because she'd been tricked into killing an innocent man. The impressive collection appeared untouched.

He ground his teeth. Where the hell was she? Surely she wasn't stupid enough to waltz up that bloody mountain in nothing but shorts and a tank top and just turn herself over like some sacrificial lamb. If so, then neither she nor Farrah had a chance of coming out of this alive. Not unless he got to Velavich first.

"I got nothing," Rio reported. "Far as I can tell no one's entered the yard in the past twenty-four hours."

"It looks like she came out of the river okay," Rashid said, jogging toward them. "But her trail leads off to the north."

"She wouldn't come back here," Ty said softly. "At least, not to the house."

"What makes you so sure about that?" Joshua demanded, still angry enough with the sniper to want his hands on Ty's throat. "Other than shooting her, you don't know a damn thing about her." There hadn't been time for him to explain exactly who she was yet.

Ty shrugged a shoulder, his gaze never leaving the surrounding green woods. "I know she's smart. She'll have a plan in case of emergencies. Probably has a stash somewhere with clothes, food, traveling money. Maybe more than one." He turned his head, dark eyes locking on Joshua. "And if she's who I think she is, that stash will include weapons."

Joshua's stomach clenched as if someone had just punched him in the gut. Damn it, Ty was right. He'd still been thinking of Amy as a civilian. Hell, she was as well trained as any man in his unit. Of course she'd have a plan.

"And just who do you think she is?" Rio asked, his tone indicating he still wasn't happy with Ty. Joshua wasn't either, but he knew he'd get over it. Nor was he surprised to learn Ty had guessed Amy's secret. Snipers had certain characteristics in common. Sharp eyes that saw everything at once. A stillness when their body stopped moving that seemed just a bit on the unnatural side. He was surprised he hadn't picked up on the small tells himself and guessed the truth about her sooner. But then, he hadn't been looking for a sniper in his own back yard.

"Well," Rio demanded.

Ty didn't say a word, leaving the decision of whether or not to inform the others of Amy's identity up to him. Joshua couldn't see any reason not to at this point.

"Amy Sheridan is the Raven."

"The Predators' Raven?"

"Shit!"

"No way."

"Load up," Joshua ordered, forestalling any further comments. "I'll fill in the blanks on the way."

"You don't want me to follow her?" Rashid asked.

"No need. We know where she's headed. We'll make better time in the Jeep." Hopefully they'd get there first and have everything wrapped up before Amy even arrived. He didn't want her to have to kill again, and he sure as hell didn't want Velavich anywhere near her. He didn't know how he and Amy were going to work things out between them, but God knew he wanted the chance to try.

Chapter Twenty-Six

Amy slowly settled into the crook of a large tree, carefully positioning her rifle until she had a perfect view of the Wassile's cabin through the scope. She'd actually located the little mountain-top hide-away several weeks ago after hearing someone in town mention the Wassile's second home. Just a little exercise in deduction and tracking to keep her skills sharp. The only surprise was the fact she'd made it here ahead of Joshua.

A wide porch ran along the front of the cabin. The front door stood open. Placed on the porch in the center of the doorway was a rickety chair. Farrah sat there, her arms and legs tied to the chair's spindles. She'd been crying. Her red, puffy eyes constantly scanned the surrounding woods. She's afraid, Amy thought, but not necessarily for herself. She could easily guess Farrah's terror. The possibility Kyle would come limping out of those woods, beaten, bleeding, but determined to rescue the woman he loved. Thank God he was passed out on Joshua's couch.

Amy spent several minutes scrutinizing the surrounding area. Twenty feet away, Franklin Wassile was hunkered down behind a tree. The idiot faced the cabin, his back to Amy. She spotted four other men hidden more effectively. Adrik's posse, she assumed. Men like Chambliss.

Movement inside the cabin drew her attention. Chet, pacing back and forth like a cornered bear. She watched him for a while, trying to figure out where Adrik had parked his sorry ass. Inside the cabin, for sure. Waiting in some dark corner for her to get within striking distance. She had to wonder if his plan was to kill her outright, or try to take her alive. Either way, she knew he wouldn't let his hostage go.

Amy shifted location twice, trying to see as much of the cabin's interior as possible. With Farrah sitting out in the open, neutralizing all the players in the right order was imperative. Too long between shots would leave time for someone to put a bullet into their captive. So not an option. The four professionals outside would have to go first, then Franklin. That would leave an opening of only a few seconds for Amy to get inside the cabin and take out Chet and Adrik.

Come on, Raven, who are you kidding? Chet might hesitate, but not Adrik. Even if she knew exactly where he was, he'd have too much time to act. Farrah would be dead. Damn it, this just wasn't a one-woman operation. Someone was going to have to get inside the cabin and do Adrik first.

Unless she could somehow lure him *outside*.

Sound burst from some bushes off to her left. Crashing branches, dry leaves thrashing together, the cry of some kind of animal. Amy kept most of her attention focused on Adrik's men as something tore its way through the brush. The doe bounded into the cabin's small yard on spring-loaded legs and was gone in seconds. Amy barely noticed the terrified animal. Nor was her attention still on Adrik's men. Not with the quivering black arrow suddenly sprouting a scant six inches from her hand. Joshua had arrived.

Amy eased her head around, tracing the arrow's path back to a nearby tree. It took a moment to pick out Joshua's camouflaged face. His hand moved, the sharpness of his signals a good indication of his mood. Who would have thought you could yell using hand signals?

Change of plan! Fall back! Rendezvous! One-half klick south-west! Order!

Amy frowned, hesitating just long enough to let him know she didn't like taking orders. Which was stupid, since she took orders all the time. But this was Joshua. If she gave him an inch, he'd take a lot more than a mile.

His eyes narrowed. *Now!*

She glared back, but nodded, and started inching her way down the trunk. Five minutes and half a mile later she spotted the rendezvous spot. She walked in boldly, counting warm bodies as she passed them. Six, including Joshua. Perfect. Timing problem solved. Now she just had to convince the Harrier to let her play bait.

****

Joshua drank in the sight of Amy. The confidence in her walk, the competent way she cradled the top of the line sniper rifle in her arms. Gone was the delicate little civilian he'd met at Kyle's garage. Amy looked completely at ease in dark green fatigues and dripping weapons. At home. And wasn't that sexy as hell. Only the rapid pulse beating at the base of her throat betrayed her nerves. A feeling of pride joined the frustration and worry that had dogged him all the way up the mountain. She didn't want to kill again, but that hadn't stopped her from picking up a gun and charging up the mountain when she knew Farrah was in danger. Damn woman had even run out on him without even bothering to find out what he planned. Thank God he'd caught up to her before it was too late. She was safe, she was well, and from the flash in her eyes, she was pissed. Good, so was he.

She came to a stop six feet away, glanced around at his men, then met his gaze. "What do you mean there's a change in plans?"

"If you hadn't run, you wouldn't have to ask."

"Are you saying I should have waited and ridden up here with you?"

The challenge in her voice had him wanting to shake her. He settled for glaring instead. She nodded, as if his silence was answer enough.

"You don't have to do this," he ground out. "You don't have to use that gun in your hands."

Her fingers flexed around the weapon. "Yeah, I do. He's my mistake, Joshua. My target. I have to be the one to take him down."

"Can you?" Ty asked.

Joshua tensed. He couldn't blame Ty for asking. Everyone knew by now that the Raven and the Cobra had been romantically involved. Still, the urge to slam a fist into the sniper's face returned with a vengeance.

Amy slowly walked up to Ty until they stood toe to toe. "If you're asking if I'll be able to pull the trigger when the time comes, the answer is yes. I may not be active SO, but I'm still a soldier. I do what has to be done. And I advise you not to question me again. I might remember how bad that bullet of yours stung and decide not to wait until later to pay you back."

The sight of his diminutive woman threatening a man twice her size should have scared Joshua to death. Instead, that sense of pride exploded in his chest.

"Easy." He reached out to gently pull Amy to his side. Shocked the hell out of him when she let him. He fought back a satisfied grin. "Sam," he said, "give me a perimeter check. I don't want any surprises."

Amy turned away from Ty, as if dismissing him. When she took a step away from Joshua, he let her go. It was hard to think straight when he was touching her anyway.

"He's got four men stationed outside the cabin," she said. "Five, if you include Franklin."

"SAT image shows seven warm bodies," Sam corrected. He pointed to the screen of a laptop he'd pulled from his pack. "Five around the cabin, like she said, and two in a line, here and here, about fifty yards apart."

Amy moved until she could see the screen. "His escape route."

"Probably," Joshua agreed. "Not that he's going to get a chance to use it. Rashid, take out the farthest one away first, then his partner." He pointed to two red dots near the cabin. "Ty, these two are yours. Sam, this one and this one. Franklin is yours, Rio."

"Alive or dead?"

Joshua didn't hesitate. The Wassiles had thrown in with a traitor. That made them fair game. "Consider the brothers hostile."

Rio nodded grimly.

Amy shifted her feet, the movement drawing Joshua's attention. He met her eyes briefly. She had to know what his words meant. Would she object to Franklin's death sentence?

Instead of protesting, she merely raised a brow and changed the subject. "You do know there's no back door to this place, right? How do you plan to get to Chet and Velavich?"

Velavich, not Adrik. He wondered if she realized it was the first time she'd used the man's last name instead of the first. Very telling as far as he was concerned. "There's a window in the back room big enough for me and Gage to slip through." He could tell from the stubborn look in her eyes that wasn't what she wanted to hear. Too bad. He wanted to give this woman everything she wanted or needed, but damn if he was willing to risk her life to do it. Besides, he'd promised to kill Velavich for her, and he always kept his promise. "As soon as the shooting starts, I want you to go for Farrah."

"No."

"Yes, and don't argue with me or you're out of this altogether." She took another step away from him, blue eyes flashing angrily, her body tense enough to explode. Like hell she'd run from him again. Couldn't she trust him just this once? "One more step," he warned, "and I'll turn you over my knee." Oh, yeah, like that was going to work. Those beautiful eyes of hers blinked, then narrowed.

"You'll what?"

"You heard me." He pointed at her, hoping to forestall another display of insubordination. "Farrah knows you. She'll do what you say without hesitation. The quicker she's taken off the playing field the better."

She stood there glaring at him until Rio stepped up beside her and nudged her shoulder with his. "Better listen to him, *chiquita*. The Harrier never bluffs."

Her fingers caressed the rifle's trigger guard. "Neither do I. If you recall, I said Velavich is mine."

"So you think you're little vendetta is more important than Farrah's life?"

She stiffened, cheeks coloring as if he'd physically struck her instead of just striking a nerve. "Of course not."

"Good. Then we do things my way."

Up came that stubborn, thoroughly kissable chin. "Your way sucks."

Joshua heard a couple of low whistles and what might have been strangled laughs from his men. *Recon*, he signaled. *Five minutes.*

Five seconds later, he and Amy were alone. He closed the distance between them without once taking his eyes off her. She licked her lips. Her breathing picked up. So did his.

"In case you haven't thought of it," she said, "there could be another dozen men hiding inside that cabin. Damn lousy odds if you ask me."

Grasping her chin, he leaned down so close he could smell her sweet scent beneath the sweat and dirt. "Of course I've thought of it. Why do you think I want you to stay outside? I can't…I won't risk your life, Amy. Don't ask me to."

Her gaze went soft. "I can pull my own weight, Joshua, honest. Been doing it for a while now."

"Not a minute goes by that I'm not aware of that. My point is that there's no need for you to risk your life here."

"But you can risk yours? And Gage's? Why? Why risk anyone's when we have the perfect bait to lure Adrik outside?"

Joshua wanted to growl, both at her use of the bastard's first name again, and her suggestion. He knew damn well what kind of bait she was referring to.

"Hell. No."

She twisted her chin out of his hold.

If she'd stepped back, he would have grabbed her. Instead, she leaned toward him, one hand fisting in his shirt. "Why not? You'd do it if it was you he wanted. Or if it was Rio, or Sam, or Ty, you wouldn't be pulling this shit on them. Why me? And don't you dare say it's because we slept together."

He grabbed her shoulders, unable to keep from shaking her just a little. The woman was stubborn to the bone. "Have you forgotten about that lace dress? I sure as hell haven't." The thing had starred in his nightmares ever since. "How do you know he won't put a bullet in your chest the moment you step into that clearing?"

"Because the dress was just part of his game, a way to rattle me. Believe me, I know him. I know how he thinks. He wants revenge. And he takes his revenge up close and personal. That means he'll come out of the cabin if I show up alone and unarmed. He won't be able to resist." She sighed. "That should give you a clear shot."

The plan was far from perfect. Velavich might want her, but he wasn't stupid. He'd keep out of sniper range as much as possible. But even Joshua could see Amy's plan had a better chance of keeping Farrah alive. Despite his almost overpowering urge to keep Amy out of this mess, Joshua felt his resolve slipping. "What happened to 'Velavich is mine'?"

"You were right about Farrah being more important. I let my emotions blind me once, I won't do it again." She laid a hand on his cheek. "I can do this, Joshua. Please, trust me."

He took her hand and kissed her palm. "I trust you, sweetheart, I just don't want to lose you. So while I'll let you go in first, we'll still do it my way."

"Joshua—"

"Which means I'm still tossing a few NightHawks into the mix. Velavich isn't stupid. He knows Kyle will come to me for help in getting Farrah back. If you show up first, he'll expect me to be right behind you. I say we don't disappoint him."

A slow smile curved her lips. "Can't think of anyone else I'd rather have at my back."

Her husky words made it impossible for Joshua not to lean down for a quick kiss. Despite her tense body language, her soft lips yielded to his almost immediately. He stroked his tongue past her lips a couple of times, tasting her, before pulling back. The heat and longing in her gaze stirred his blood to a fever pitch. Damn if he didn't want her right here, right now.

The deliberate scuff of boots through leaves warned that his men were returning.

Later, Joshua told himself. And there damn well would be a later. He wasn't losing her now.

Chapter Twenty-Seven

Amy rubbed her palms down her thighs. She didn't know what else to do with her empty hands. She'd easily gone almost a year without even touching a gun. Now her palms itched to hold a weapon, any weapon. The thought of facing Velavich bare handed had her heart racing.

"You okay?"

"I'm fine." She didn't look at Joshua. If she did, he might see how nervous she really was and call a halt to things. Not an option. This was the best way, the safest way, to free Farrah. Nothing else mattered.

Okay, so she still wanted Adrik's head. *Traitorous bastard.* But sometimes sacrifices had to be made. She'd learned that the hard way.

Rashid ghosted out of the woods. "Ty's in position, Cap."

Beside her, Joshua nodded. "You've got five minutes to get into yours."

"Roger that." And he was gone, melting into the brush with hardly a sound.

The NightHawks had decided not to use their radios. As a com-tech, Velavich would know how to scan for their frequency. Slowed things down, but not by much. Joshua's men were very good at their job.

Joshua's hand closed over her arm. "You ready for this?"

"Past ready."

He let her go and she started forward, making her way through the woods without bothering to keep quiet. They needed Velavich's men focused on her. Though she couldn't hear him, she knew Joshua shadowed her.

Reaching the cabin, Amy stopped just inside the edge of the trees. The small clearing in front of the cabin wasn't very big, maybe thirty feet across and twenty deep, if that. Not a lot of room to maneuver. Dangerous, too. Stumps poked up through the thick layer of pine needles covering the ground. Some were old and ragged, slowly succumbing to rot. Others looked freshly cut, sap still dripping from the fatal wounds. All were trip hazards when you needed to move somewhere fast. No telling what other little surprises Adrik had added. Land mines, trip wires, the list was endless.

She took another step forward. To her left lay the remains of an ancient trunk. Moss and ferns covered its crumbling body. Would have made a great nature picture. Maybe when this was over she'd come back and snap a shot or two.

Movement and sound on her right. Franklin must have finally heard her. He popped up from his squat like a deranged jack-in-the-box, fumbling with his rifle until it pointed in her direction. Hopefully his finger wasn't on the trigger. She'd hate to get shot accidentally. Stepping out into the open, she ignored him as well as the other guns she could feel trained on her. They would all disappear in a few minutes.

"Adrik?" she called. "I know you're in there. Come out and talk to me."

She counted off a full minute before she saw movement inside the cabin doorway. But it wasn't Adrik who stepped through.

"About time you got here, bitch." Chet snapped the words out sharp, quick, and slightly slurred, as if he'd had too much to drink. When he stepped into the fading light she immediately noticed the busted lip and large bruise on the side of his face. Someone had clocked him a good one. Probably Adrik. No doubt he'd been pissed about losing Chambliss along with her.

Keeping her tone casual, she asked, "Where's Adrik?"

Instead of answering her, he pulled a knife out of his pocket and flicked it open. Amy forced herself not to move when he stepped behind Farrah and laid the edge of the blade against the woman's throat. Farrah let out a small sound, her frightened gaze locking on Amy.

Amy's muscles tightened in fury. Still, she didn't move or look away from Chet. She couldn't even glance at Farrah to try to reassure her. There was no telling what instructions Adrik had given Chet.

"That's right," Chet said softly. "I'm in control of the situation for a change. No more talking down to me or brushing me off like I'm nothing. You want her to live, then you do what I say. You step up here to the porch and let Frankie boy tie you up proper."

Confront her old ex-lover weaponless *and* bound? She didn't think so. "I want to see Adrik first."

His hand tightened on the knife. Slowly, he grabbed a handful of Farrah's hair, using the punishing grip to pull her head back. "You heard me. Now move before my knife slips."

She took a few steps forward, but when Franklin moved to intercept her, she held her palm out toward him. "Stay right there." Idiot actually obeyed her, though he cast a confused glance at his brother. Amy shook her head at Chet. "We both know you aren't going to hurt Farrah, Chet. You're a lot of things, but a murderer isn't one of them. Adrik, now, he's a stone cold killer." She paused at the foot of the porch steps, making sure he was looking straight at her when she said, "So am I."

Chet licked his lips, the first sign of nervousness she'd seen. "What are you saying?"

A chuckle came from inside the cabin. It was a deep, rich sound that used to send chill bumps down her arms. Still did, but for an entirely different reason now. Amy swallowed back a wave of disgust as Adrik moved enough for her to see him inside the cabin.

She acknowledged him with a stiff nod. "Adrik."

The smile he gave her was beautiful, but lacked warmth. The cold smile of a snake. "Amelia. How wonderful to see you again. Keep your knife ready, Mr. Wassile. My little *bopoh* will not want to endanger this woman, but she has a habit of striking when you least expect. Like a little viper. But for her soft heart and streak of nobility, she would be my perfect match. Don't you think so, Amelia dearest?"

"As always, you need to get your facts, straight, Adrik. One, I'm not your little raven anymore. Two, you and I are nothing alike. I have never, nor will I ever, betray my country or my friends. And three, my name's Amy now. Get used to it."

"But why should I? We both know that very soon it will not matter what I call you." He chuckled again, as if sharing a secret with her. She knew exactly what he meant. If he had his way, she'd be dead soon.

Amy walked up a couple of porch steps, stopping when she heard Chet fidget. Adrik remained where he was, half-hidden by shadows. A poor target. She had to get him to move into the doorway at least.

Sighing deeply, she leaned against a support post. "All right, Adrik, you know what I want. What's it going to cost me?"

"You know my price. But let's not get ahead of ourselves. Such an exchange should await all the players, don't you think? Why not invite the Harrier to join us?"

She feigned a frown. "The Harrier?"

Adrik tsked. "Come now, sweet Raven, I am not so out of touch as that. I know Colby was sent to protect you. I also know about your fake engagement. Poor Mr. Wassile was quite relieved when I informed him of your deception."

Deception. Such a nasty word. She was coming to hate it. "Who says it's a deception?"

He laughed outright. "You forget Colby's reputation, my dear. Or has he fooled even you? If so, let me disabuse you of your fantasy. You are merely a duty to him. A mission. A body he guards. He'll remember you when this is over only because he failed. Everyone knows the Harrier puts no one and nothing ahead of his job, least of all a woman."

True enough. And painful. One way or another, her time as plain Amy Sheridan was almost over. If she lived to return to her old life, she doubted Joshua would want to continue seeing her. Trying to maintain a relationship while fighting the evils of the world would be complicated. Joshua didn't like complicated. He'd said so.

She forced a shrug. "You may be right about his reputation, but people change all the time."

"Not the Harrier. Besides, you forget that I have been searching for you. If you had spent any time at all with Colby overseas, I would have heard about it. I also know Fagan and he are best of friends. Curious, considering they both share a love for the same woman."

At his words, Chet ran a hand through Farrah's hair. Farrah flinched, and then held steady. For a moment, the anger in her eyes outweighed the fear.

"The Harrier's loyalty is well known," Adrik continued. "He would do anything to save someone he cares about. The wife of his best friend, for instance. Perhaps he would even sacrifice a former operative suspected of treason. Your presence here is evidence that my assumptions were correct. How else would you have gotten my message? Though I'm convinced he would not have let you come alone."

Amy smiled a real smile. "You're right, except that Joshua didn't want me to come at all. I had to dive off a waterfall to get away from him."

"Really? Most impressive. But that just means Colby had to trail you up here. Enough time has passed for him to catch up. Call him in." He tipped his head in Farrah's direction. "Or do you want me to do it?"

Bastard. She couldn't wait to get her hands on him. She raised her voice. "Joshua!"

He stepped out of the woods without a pause, arms out, one hand empty, the other holding her sniper rifle. He stopped just shy of the fallen log.

"Very wise," Adrik said. "Now please, toss your weapons into the clearing."

The rifle hit the pine needles, followed by a pistol.

"All of them," Adrik snapped.

Again, Joshua obeyed without a word. The array of knives and guns that joined the pile was impressive.

"Klein," Adrik called.

Amy tensed. She hated this part of Joshua's plan, the necessary risk he'd accepted. Who was Adrik calling? Did he have more men hidden inside? The possibility made sweat pop out on her forehead. It would be too easy for someone to pick Joshua off from inside the cabin.

No one answered. Adrik shifted impatiently, the edge of one shoulder coming out of the shadows. Irritation laced his voice as he called louder. "Klein!"

The tight coil inside Amy eased a fraction. Good. He was calling for one of his outside guards.

Franklin snorted and spat. "I'll get him." He started directly across the clearing. As he came even with Joshua, Amy saw the Harrier pull another knife from a pocket. Franklin slowed and swung his rifle in Joshua's direction, eyeing him warily.

"Forgot one," Joshua said. He held the butterfly knife up and flicked it open. Franklin froze. Joshua flicked the knife closed, then open again, back and forth, faster and faster. Franklin just stood there, his gaze fastened on the shiny metal, his face growing darker by the minute with rage. The barrel of his gun drifted down, forgotten.

"What is it," Chet demanded.

"He's got Arney's knife, Chet. I thought you said Arney got away and was just hiding out until things cooled down. He wouldn't leave that knife behind."

Amy held her breath as a taunting smile curved Joshua's lips. "That's the problem with dying, Franklin. You can't take things with you."

Several things happened at once. Franklin roared in pain and dove at Joshua. Chet's hand moved as he took a step away from Farrah, screaming for his brother to stop. Adrik barked at him to stand still. Then Chet's head jerked back as a bullet drilled a hole in his left eye socket and took out the back of his skull. He was still standing as Amy dove for Farrah. She grabbed the woman and pulled her, chair and all, off the porch. They hit the ground hard enough that the chair broke into pieces. A second later, she and Farrah rolled under the porch, a spray of bullets tracking them all the way. Not until they were both positioned safely behind the steps did Amy reach for the knife in her boot. She sliced the ropes around Farrah's wrists and ankles with a few quick strokes, separating her from the remains of the chair. As soon as she was free, the woman grabbed a handful of Amy's shirt, eyes swimming with unshed tears.

"My children? Kyle?"

"All safe," Amy whispered.

Farrah buried her face in her arms, her body shaking with silent sobs.

Only then did Amy notice how quiet it was. So quiet, she easily identified the sound coming from deeper under the house. The quiet ratcheting of a gun being cocked.

Chapter Twenty-Eight

Joshua caught Franklin as he lunged, knocking the rifle aside as the younger man slammed into him. Even as they fell, he still registered every move on the porch. Chet's shift and jerk. Amy's dive. Both women falling off the porch. The spray of dirt and pine needles as bullets slammed into the ground, following them, gaining.

Where the hell are those bullets coming from? His men should have had all the guards neutralized by now. Someone was going to lose a head.

Even as he thought it, the lethal spatter cut off. Joshua turned his attention to Franklin. It took a couple of minutes to subdue the raging man. He fought like a wounded animal, fast, wild, and mean. He had a hefty bag of dirty tricks and just enough skill to make him dangerous. Joshua finally had to resort to an old-fashioned head-butt to slow him down long enough to get an arm around his throat. He squeezed. Franklin gagged and lost interest in the fight. He fell back on top of Joshua, arms flailing, hands clawing, trying to break free. Joshua squeezed harder. When Franklin started to sag, Joshua hauled back and slammed his fist into Franklin's temple to hurry things along. The man went totally limp, unconscious. *Should have killed him,* Joshua thought, wiping his bloody mouth on his sleeve. He shoved the slack body aside and rolled away, scooping up a pistol from the pile of weapons as he ducked behind the fallen log. Rio was at his side the next second.

"Report."

"Perimeter secure. Gage and Sam are entering the cabin through the back window." Rio grinned. "Guess we'll know soon if they flush any garbage out."

Joshua didn't answer. He tried keeping his gaze fixed on the open doorway, but it wasn't easy. His eyes kept dropping to the porch steps. He thought he could make out part of the chair through the narrow openings between steps, but wasn't sure. Nothing moved that he could see. Were the women okay? Had they been hit? He had to find out.

Just as he started to rise, a voice called from the cabin.

"Coming out. Don't shoot me." Gage's voice, not Velavich.

A second later, Gage appeared in the doorway. He held his gun at his side, ready, but relaxed. Joshua didn't like the implication. He rose and stalked to the cabin.

"Where is he?"

"Not here," Gage said. "We're not sure how, but the snake's slithered away. Has to be an escape hatch somewhere. Sam's trying to find the hidey hole now." He tapped his ear piece. "Rashid's done. He'll do some scouting as he comes in."

Joshua nodded sharply, noticing for the first time that his own ear piece had fallen out during his scuffle with Franklin and was dangling against his collar. He replaced it and barked, "Ty, report."

"If he left," came the sniper's calm voice, "he didn't go through the woods. I've got a good view and haven't seen anything move around the cabin for a hundred yards."

"Keep looking." Joshua knew the order wasn't necessary, but couldn't hold it back. He was starting to get a very bad feeling. For one thing, Amy hadn't crawled out from under the porch yet. With Velavich's whereabouts up-in-the-air, she'd make sure Farrah stayed hidden, but as soon as Gage said Velavich was gone, he'd expected her to pop up. Why wasn't she in his face giving him hell for letting the bastard get away?

"Amy?" He fought back panic when she didn't answer. "Farrah?" Too much damn silence. He dropped to his knees and peered under the porch. Nothing moved in the heavy shadows.

"Son of a bitch," Rio muttered from the other side of the steps. "They're gone, too."

****

Amy hated dark, cramped, closed-in places. Especially ones that seemed to go on forever. The Wassiles' escape tunnel easily qualified as one of those on all counts. After the first fifty feet, the three foot square tunnel angled down...and kept going down. Logic said the tunnel was simply following the lay of the land. Amy's inner child didn't care a thing about logic. All she knew was that it felt like they were crawling into the very heart of the earth. A feeling she didn't like one bit.

The musty, barely breathable air didn't help matters, nor did the fact that the only light came from the tiny pen light Velavich refused to give up. He brought up the rear of their little parade, with Farrah in the middle. Half the time the wiggling light was completely hidden. At least, Amy fumed, if she had even that much light she'd be able to see what she was crawling into.

Something slithered over her shoulders. "More roots," she said. At least she hoped it was indeed just another hanging mass of root fibers protruding from the dirt ceiling. The possibility of spider webs and worms was just too creepy to contemplate. In any case, she voiced the warning for Farrah's benefit, not Velavich's.

"Shut up and crawl faster, Amelia."

Velavich's sharp order sounded muted in the

small space, as if the very earth around them soaked up the sound. She started to comment about snakes being at home in tunnels and thought better of it. Reminding herself of that was bad enough—reminding Farrah wouldn't be good at all. The other woman had balked at climbing into the tunnel, big time. Apparently she had a lot more trouble with closed-in places than Amy did. Only Velavich's threat to shoot her and Amy's quiet urging got her into the small opening beneath the center of the cabin. Even now, Amy thought she caught the sound of a soft whimper once in a while, coupled with some fervently whispered words. Prayers or cuss words, she wasn't sure.

Amy crawled faster.

She estimated they'd gone about three hundred yards when Velavich called, "Stop here." She did and twisted around in the small space to see him shining his light up at the roof. Or rather, where the roof should have been. He stood, the top half of him disappearing from view. She heard him grunt several times. Then light, blessed, beautiful light, flooded the tunnel. Velavich squatted, his gaze skipping over Farrah and settling on Amy.

"Her first, then you. If you don't come out, I shoot her. If neither of you comes out, I know how to collapse the tunnel on top of you." He shrugged one shoulder. "Not my first choice of death for you, my dear, but I'll take it if you insist."

Farrah's hands trembled. Amy took one in hers and squeezed. "No need to get antsy," she said. "We'll cooperate." At least until they were out of this blasted tunnel. Ravens were never meant to be underground. She needed open air and trees and sweet, sweet wind.

She needed Joshua.

Velavich hoisted himself up. Farrah needed little encouragement to follow him. When Amy crawled out into the open, Velavich already had Farrah by the arm. The other woman's face and arms were streaked with dirt, her long blonde hair snarled beyond the redemption of a brush. Still, her eyes were clear, bright with anger, and hard with determination. The tunnel hadn't broken her.

"You need to let her go," Amy said. She didn't bother including herself. He'd shoot her before he let her go. "It won't take the NightHawks long to find the tunnel. They'll be here soon. We're going to have to run fast to get away. She's only going to slow us down."

His brows rose. "You expect me to believe you would go with me willingly?"

"I will. *If*, you let Farrah go unharmed." She held her arms out to her sides when he hesitated. "What's the matter, Adrik, afraid you can't handle one little woman? Come on, you know you won't be happy with quick and painless. Didn't you always say that revenge, whether served hot or cold, is always best when it's savored? You want it long, and slow, and painful, don't you? Isn't that what all this planning was for? Now the only way you're going to get that is if you steal me away from the Hawks. Better make a decision quick. Clock's ticking."

When he let go of Farrah's arm and stepped away from her, Amy breathed a silent prayer of relief...until he motioned toward the tunnel's dark mouth. "Very well, she can stay behind. In the tunnel." Farrah paled.

Amy took a step forward. "No—"

Velavich put the gun to Farrah's head. "The tunnel or a bullet, your choice. I will not have her staying here and screaming her head off, calling down your new friends."

"If you shoot her, they'll still come running."

"Sound echoes strangely in the mountains. One shot will be hard to pinpoint. Several screams, however, can be easily traced. Now decide quickly, both of you."

"Let me gag her. I'll tie her hands—"

He cocked the pistol.

Amy threw her hands out. "All right, all right!"

"I'll go in the tunnel," Farrah cried.

Velavich shoved her toward the opening. Amy caught her friend, noting how badly she was shaking. How badly both of them were shaking. "I'm sorry. I'm so sorry," Amy whispered. The little smile Farrah gave her almost broke her heart.

"It's okay. Really. My husband and children are waiting for me. You'd be amazed at what someone can get through with that kind of incentive."

No she wouldn't, thought Amy. Not anymore. "Joshua will find you," Amy said fiercely. "You know he will."

"I know." Farrah patted her hand and sat at the hole's edge. Amy bent to help her, watching helplessly as her friend slowly disappeared out of sight. She had to literally bite her tongue to keep from screaming when Velavich motioned her back and replaced the cover. He stomped on it several times to wedge it in place. All Amy could think about was Farrah alone in that tunnel without a speck of light. She glared at him.

"You're a bastard, you know that? I honestly have no idea what I ever saw in you."

"Perhaps I'll remind you before I kill you." He motioned her ahead of him. "Let's go. And do not forget your promise to behave. I wasn't kidding about knowing how to collapse the tunnel. The Wassiles were most informative."

"Yes, they were."

The breathless, husky words snapped Amy's head around. Joshua stood on an outcropping above them, bow drawn tight, arrow aiming straight at her. No, at Velavich. She was in the way.

Amy dove to the side, rolling, trying to reach cover. Adrik had only one choice if he wanted her dead before he was. The sting of the bullet when it bit into her shoulder told her it wasn't bad. A flesh wound. She'd take one of those any day. The impact still rolled her hard, knocking her into a tree. Breath whooshed from her lungs and the world around her dimmed.

****

As soon as his arrow skewered Velavich's head, Joshua tossed his bow aside and sprinted for Amy. He was already out of breath from the run down the mountain, but didn't care. He'd been an idiot. He'd expected Velavich to aim for him, to try to take him out before Joshua could shoot him. The bastard had gone for Amy instead.

He dropped to his knees beside her. "Amy?" She blinked up at him. Her mouth opened and closed, but she didn't speak. When she reached for him, trying to sit, he put an arm around her shoulders to help her. As soon as he did, she drew in a deep breath.

"Damn, blasted, son of a bitch that hurt. I'm going to kill him."

Relief had Joshua's lips twitching. "Too late." He smoothed several strands of hair from her face, noting how shaky his hands were. "I told you I'd kill him for you. I always keep my word." He shifted so she could see around him to where Velavich lay sprawled on the ground. The arrow protruding up from his skull was a gruesome sight, but he figured she could handle it. She was, after all, part of his violent world.

"Finally." She sagged in his arms, then stiffened. "Farrah! We have to get her out." When she tried to get up, he held her down.

"Easy, take it easy. Tell me where she is, I'll get her."

"There, she's down there. He made her go back into the tunnel."

Joshua's gaze tracked her pointing finger to a square patch of flattened grass. His blood ran cold. Farrah's claustrophobia wasn't just some mild fear of small places. He'd seen her go to pieces in an elevator. He scrambled over to the patch and dug his fingers into the soil, feeling for the edge. When he found it, he realized it was stuck and had to heave to get it to budge. Finally, the cover came loose. He sent it flying, noting absently that it landed on Velavich.

"Farrah, honey?"

"Farrah, are you all right?" Amy called, crawling up beside him. Stubborn woman wouldn't stay where he put her. They both peered inside the opening.

Farrah sat huddled at the bottom, legs drawn up, arms wrapped tight around them, head buried in her knees. Slowly, she raised her head, blinked several times, and smiled. "Hi, Joshua."

"Hi, baby. Ready to go home? Kyle misses you."

Tears filled her eyes. "God, yes."

He reached down and helped her climb out. Rio, Ty, and Rashid joined them a few seconds later. Ty quickly set about bandaging Amy's wound. The bullet had gone through the top of her shoulder, just missing the tendon.

Joshua held Amy in his arms while Ty worked. She protested at first, but finally gave in when she realized he wasn't going to budge. She might be a lethal sniper, but she was his sniper. The first time she hissed in pain he almost decked Ty. After that, he tried to focus on something else.

A few feet away, Farrah sat on the ground, a phone cradled to her ear, talking to Kyle. She was shaking, fighting back tears so her husband wouldn't realize how badly she'd been traumatized. Joshua wanted to tell her it was too late for that. Kyle would know.

"I like your shot better. This one hurts."

Joshua turned back to see Amy frowning at Ty as he cleaned her wound. The stoic sniper snorted softly, lips lifting in a slight smile. The sight wasn't one Joshua had seen often.

"Mine was only meant to slow you down. This one tried to stop you for good. Luckily, Ravens not only see far, but they fly fast." Ty frowned suddenly, leaned closer to the wound. Joshua did, too. The torn flesh looked puffy and was still bleeding freely. That was normal, right?

Ty grunted. His gaze jerked up to Amy's face. "How are you feeling? Any dizziness, blurred vision?"

"What is it," Joshua demanded. He watched Amy blink slowly, his heart rate accelerating to a worried beat.

"Yes, now that you mention it," she said, the words sliding into one another.

Ty nodded and produced a pen light, using it to check her pupils.

"Ty?" Joshua warned when all the sniper did was put the pen light away and start rummaging in his pack.

"Tissue around the wound is swelling faster than normal, and the blood isn't clotting. That, coupled with the blurred vision and slurred speech indicates she's been poisoned. Considering our target, my guess is the bullet was dirty."

Chapter Twenty-Nine

Joshua's arms tightened around Amy. A dirty bullet. Dirty, as in coated with cobra venom. Hearing Ty say the words had Joshua's world crashing down around his ears. *Ah, God, please, no.* He couldn't lose her now, not when everything was over. Not when Velavich was finally dead. She could come out of hiding, join the SO again. Join him.

She'd be putting her life in danger every damn day.

Could he live with that? Hell, yes. As long as she didn't die from this, he'd find a way to deal with anything else. "Rio, call Capella," he snapped. "We need a chopper."

Ty pulled a small, rectangular box from his pack with a flourish. "Chopper evac is good, but we don't have to wait on it."

Relief coursed through Joshua. "Antivenin?"

The sniper nodded. "After reading the Hell Hounds' report Gage and I thought it would be a good idea to come prepared." Ty opened the box.

The sight of the line of syringes and three small vials went a long way toward soothing Joshua's frayed nerves. Not just antivenin. Vial number two was a powerful pain med/antibiotic combo. Enough to knock Amy out for the next several hours and jump-start the healing process. The third vial was the icing on the cake. "I'm not even going to ask how you got your hands on that, but as of now you're forgiven for shooting her."

Ty held up the vial in question. "At the risk of you changing your mind about forgiving me, this wasn't my idea. We requested two standard antivenin kits. When the boxes arrived, this was included."

Joshua watched anxiously as Ty filled a syringe from each vial. Amy was starting to moan and toss her head, her eyes squeezed tightly shut. Knowing what was coming, he forced back a wall of panic when her body went limp as soon as Ty dumped the syringes into her vein. He swallowed hard. "How long will she be out?"

"A few hours. Time enough to get her to a hospital." He tapped the bottle holding the *Cure* before replacing the lid on the box. "Hell of a requisition error."

Requisition error? Not likely. The experimental drug unofficially dubbed the Cure was highly classified and strictly regulated. You had to be dying in a Special Ops hospital to rate the wonder drug. Even the Harrier couldn't requisition the stuff for a field op. Someone with a lot more power than a unit leader had a hand in this. Just like some powerful someone had authorized Amy's top-of-the-line home security.

The sound of a helicopter intruded on Joshua's musings. Something fast and nasty. A far cry from the steady thump of the standard model used by the cleanup crews. Velavich's ride? Unwilling to take the risk, Joshua gathered Amy into his arms.

"Take cover. Ty, you're with me." He made for a trio of trees edged in brush.

Rashid and Rio hustled Farrah into hiding just as a sleek, black Sikorsky glided into view. The chopper's speed took it over them within a few seconds. Unfortunately, it didn't stay gone. The black bastard circled back and hovered directly over them, maneuvering back and forth like a demented dragonfly, impatient to set down but not having the room.

A series of beeps echoed in Joshua's ear followed by a familiar gruff voice. "This is Aberashoff. Alpha unit, respond."

Joshua met Ty's shocked expression with one of his own. What was Aberashoff doing here? Joshua tapped his ear piece. "This is the Harrier. You lost, Commander?"

"Where the hell are you? What's your status? Is Sheridan okay?"

"Everything's fine. Velavich is dead. Sheridan is..." He glanced down at the woman in his arms. Unconscious, the lines of pain around her mouth and eyes were gone, leaving her looking like a sleeping wood nymph, her face smudged with dirt, leaves stuck in her hair. She appeared far too delicate for the kind of life he knew she'd led. Only when her eyes were open, if you looked hard enough and were lucky enough, could you see that hidden inner core of strength that made her who she was. "Sheridan is alive but unconscious at the moment."

"I heard something about cobra poison."

A wave of irritation swept over Joshua. He wasn't used to having his missions monitored so closely, not by anyone. "Velavich nicked her with a dirty bullet. Antivenin was administered as soon as symptoms presented. She's going to be fine." He refused to even consider anything else.

No answer. The chopper abruptly veered off to the south and disappeared behind the tree line. The shift in the thrumming rotor pitch indicated it was landing.

"Commander?" Again, no answer. Joshua tapped his ear piece. "Rio, see if you can get me a positive ID on that chopper." Abe hadn't actually said he was on the vehicle hovering above them. If they were going to have company, he wanted to know if he needed a welcome mat or his bow.

Rio's voice whispered right back in his ear.

"Already confirmed, Cap. Chopper belongs to the Commander, and I mean that literally. Man, I like his taste in toys."

A feminine chuckle slid over the airwaves, low and sultry. If Joshua wasn't so into the woman in his arms he might have been more interested. Ty certainly seemed to be. The man stilled, head snapping up and to the south, those sniper eyes of his boring holes in the trees.

Before anyone could comment, the female voice changed gears, becoming all crisp and business-like. "NightHawks, this is Swift One. Be advised the Commander is approaching your location from the south accompanied by a squad of five. Maintain your position until he arrives."

Her voice did another quick change, slipping down an octave and dropping almost to a whisper. "Step carefully, Hawks. I've never seen him this pissed off before."

Pissed wasn't the word, Joshua decided as the SO commander dropped to his knees in front of him a couple minutes later. Stern lines bracketed the man's mouth and his jaw was clenched so tight white spots danced under the ruddy skin. His eyes seemed glued to Amy's face. Twice he lifted a hand as if to touch her, but dropped it back to his side. Finally, he stood and wordlessly motioned his men forward with the stretcher they'd brought. "We'll take her back to headquarters and monitor her recovery." A hard gaze fastened on Ty. "I assume you gave her the Cure?"

"Yes, sir."

"Good. Good. That should cut down on the chance of necrosis, too. Well, Colby, what are you waiting for?"

Good question. The stretcher was in place on the ground in front of him, but Joshua was having trouble setting Amy down on it. This was happening too damn fast. He felt like he was losing her somehow. If she were awake, it might be different. At least then he could tell her...something, he didn't know what.

Witnessing Abe's reaction to her had set off so many internal alarms his head was ringing. Hard to miss the look of love on a man's face. Aberashoff was obviously smitten with the little sniper. Which explained a hell of a lot of things, the drug and the jacked-up security system included. It was eating Joshua alive that he had no clue whether she returned any of the older man's regard.

Yes, she'd slept with Joshua. And, yes, the sex had been phenomenal. But did it mean anything more to her than that?

"Colby, we're in a hurry here. I want her in a hospital in the next thirty minutes."

Hospital. Right. She was going to a hospital. It wasn't like he wouldn't be able to find her there when the mopping up was over. Velavich wasn't a complete idiot. He had to have planned his escape route well. The NightHawks needed to track that route and make sure there weren't more mercenaries stashed on the mountain. Gently, he placed the woman who held his heart on the stretcher.

"Go," Abcrashoff snapped, and she was gone. So was Velavich's body. So was Farrah, though she made her escort wait while she hugged and kissed Joshua before allowing herself to be led away. The brief contact did little to dispel Joshua's growing sense of loss. Abe was the last to leave. As he turned away, Joshua couldn't help snatching a handful of jacket.

"What is she to you?" He had to know. Couldn't wait until he saw her again to ask her. With Velavich dead and her name cleared, she could go back to being the Raven...or not. Her future was wide open, the possibilities endless. He had no reason to think one of those possibilities was him.

For a long moment, he thought Abe wasn't going to answer him. Then the man stood straighter, shoulders squaring, as if coming to a decision long in the making. "She's mine."

Somewhere in the distance thunder rolled, underscoring the two words spoken with total conviction and irrefutable claim. *She's mine.*

Joshua wanted to snarl those words himself, right into Aberashoff's face. Wanted to beat the man until he took them back. Only years of discipline held him in check. One did not deck one's commanding officer. Not unless he wanted to spend months in a cell. Damn if he didn't have more important things to do than twiddle his thumbs in a military prison.

"We'll see," he managed.

Aberashoff's brows lowered. "What's that supposed to mean?"

"It means maybe she doesn't want to be yours anymore." *Maybe she wants to be mine.*

Instead of getting angry, the Commander waved a dismissing hand as he turned and started walking away. "She tried denying our relationship once before. Didn't work then, won't work now."

The clipped words shocked Joshua. He'd never known Caleb Aberashoff to be this callous before. Hard, yes, the man had to be to do his job. But dismissing Amy's feelings as if they didn't count was pushing way beyond hard. A red haze clouded Joshua's vision. His protective instincts were still running high and that jail cell was starting to look more inviting. He spun the older man around and got right in his face.

"Nothing gives you the right to decide if a woman will have you or not. Nothing. If Amy wants to walk away, she walks." He'd make sure of it even if it cost him his career. He loved her. That meant her freedom and happiness came first.

Aberashoff's ruddy complexion darkened, hands tightening into fists, eyes snapping with an anger that was almost tangible. "You think I'll let her go just like that? Disappear out of her life after all the years I spent searching for her? Not happening, mister. She's my daughter and always will be."

The world tilted. Joshua took a deep breath and stepped back, not sure he'd heard right. "She's your…"

"Daughter, yeah, she's my daughter." Abe seemed to deflate, the anger leaking out of him as he took a deep breath of his own. He scrubbed a hand across his face. "Walk with me. I don't want to hold up the chopper."

Joshua nodded and signaled his men to sit tight. Then he fell into step beside the man who'd been his mentor and friend from the day he joined the SO, waiting for him to speak first.

"Her birth name is Amelia Leann Faraday. Faraday was her mother's name at the time we were together. We weren't married. Six months after Amy was born, she and her mother disappeared. I was in the middle of a bad mission and couldn't get home to search for them right away. By the time I made it back, the trail wasn't just cold, it was non-existent."

Joshua frowned. There was always a trail. Always. Unless… "Someone wiped it clean."

"As a nun's wimple. Definitely a professional job. For a long time I thought they were both dead. Thought some sadistic bastard from my dangerous world had reached out and taken what was dearest to me. The reason didn't matter. Retribution, vengeance, or just plain meanness, they were still gone." He paused at the edge of a clearing where the helicopter waited. Facing Joshua, he said, "Wasn't until two years later that I discovered Amy's mother,

Leanndra Faraday, was a spy for the other side."

Joshua chewed on that for a second. The fact it had taken Aberashoff two years to learn the truth gave the term deep cover a whole new level of meaning.

"Took me twelve years, but I finally found them." Abe's lips curled up slightly. "Amelia had just turned fourteen. Little spitfire gave me hell for not finding her sooner. Had a mouth on her. Still does, though I expect you've already discovered that for yourself."

Was there a hint of censure in those words? If so, Joshua chose to ignore it. "How'd Amy come to work for the SO?"

"Same as anyone else. She applied and was good enough to be accepted." The look in his eyes hardened. "No one knew she was my daughter. We both wanted it that way for different reasons."

Joshua could guess those reasons. Amy wanted to make sure she wasn't favored, that everyone knew she earned her position with the Predators. Abe wanted to make sure she wasn't favored, too...as a target. The daughter of the commander of Special Ops would be a prize worth taking.

Abe put a hand on his shoulder. "Listen, Joshua, I can see you care about her. Under different circumstances, I can't think of a better man to take care of my little girl. But you're the Harrier, and the Harrier has almost as many enemies as I do. Don't make the mistake of thinking you can keep her safe and happy at the same time. She'd have to be on her guard every second of every day. No quiet walks in the woods with her camera. No having lunch with a girlfriend. She might tell you all that doesn't matter, but we both know it isn't the truth. I've never seen her more at peace than the times I've visited her here. She loves her life as it is. Don't take it away from her."

295

Anger surged. Hell if he would back off. "I won't—"

"You will if you go to her, if you pursue her. Don't try to tell me that's not your plan. I saw it in your eyes when you held her. You want to drag her back into our crazy mixed up world. Joshua, she's had to choose between two people she loves for most of her life. Two different worlds. I've seen what that does to her. Don't force her to choose again."

Joshua swallowed. It didn't help. Memories swarmed up out of the past, creating a god-awful lump in his throat. He recalled too damn clearly what happened when he tried to make a woman choose between him and the peaceful, quiet existence she loved. He'd lose Amy just like he'd lost Farrah. He couldn't even claim to walk away with his heart intact this time. Stupid organ had already crawled out of his chest and onto that chopper. Maybe it was just as well he wouldn't be getting it back. He couldn't do this again.

He must have nodded, because Aberashoff held out his hand. Joshua shook it. Then he watched his commander, *Amy's father*, jog to the helicopter and climb in. The big door closed. The rotors hummed, picking up speed. He shielded his eyes from the wind, barely catching the little salute from the female pilot before she slid the heavily tinted window of the cockpit closed. The engine settled into a contented whine as the black craft rose, pivoted, and zoomed out of sight.

He was surprised the sense of loss didn't crush him.

Chapter Thirty

The sun beat down hot and bright, glinting off the warm water lapping at the sandy beach a few feet away. Palm trees swayed in the breeze. Amy watched their shadows dancing over the white sand until the dappled patterns reminded her of the camo paint on Joshua's face the last time she'd seen him. With a wrench that was almost a physical pain, she jerked her gaze to the brilliant water.

He hadn't come for her. Hadn't once called to check on her. She knew he was alive and well only because she'd hacked her father's computer.

Adrik Velavich, a.k.a the Cobra, neutralized. Mission accomplished with no casualties. Alpha unit granted two weeks leave per commander's orders.

No casualties. Guess her heart didn't count.

Amy didn't know whether to laugh or cry, but knew a curse was in there somewhere. Once again she'd been betrayed by a man she trusted. Talk about a lousy track record.

Muttering that curse, Amy snapped open the book she'd brought with her. At the rate she was going, she might have it finished by the end of summer. Or not. Almost two weeks of forced relaxation on her father's secluded stretch of Florida beach was definitely one week too many. If she didn't get back to work soon, she'd go crazy for sure.

Her ears caught the sound of sandy footsteps. Amy didn't have to look to know who it was. Her father made the trek from the house down to the beach every day about this time to check on her. She knew she was making things hard for him, but couldn't help it.

"Are you coming up for lunch?"

Same question, same unconcerned tone. As if he didn't really care about her answer. Man was a fantastic actor.

"In a while. I'm not really hungry yet."

The deep sigh was out of character. So was his move to sit on the foot of her lounger. Amy started to lift her feet to give him room, but he picked them up and put them in his lap. She kept her nose in her book, the words on the pages running together as she waited for him to speak. Better that way. Despite the whole thing with Velavich being put to rest, her mood hadn't been the best lately. She was like a wounded dog, snapping at anyone who came within reach.

The dog analogy reminded her of Bors. Her brave little black knight was recovering well. Missed her, according to Susan. The vet had offered to keep him until Amy returned. Problem was, Amy was still debating whether or not to go back for him at all. Giving Bors up would be hard. Keeping him would be harder. Not only because she traveled so much, but because of the memories the sweet dog represented. She kept putting the decision off, telling herself she really needed to wait until she knew what came next in her crappy little game of life.

"Have you decided what you're going to do?"

Had her father added mind reading to his skill set now? She let the book plop into her lap. "About what?"

"Your life." He nodded toward her shoulder. "The doctor reports you're completely well. Not even a single lingering effect from the poison."

She rotated her shoulder to prove the doctor wasn't lying. "That new drug works wonders."

"No pain at all?"

Only in my heart. "Nothing worth mentioning."

"Good." He stared out over the water, one hand rubbing absently over the top of her foot. "Your mother called."

Wonderful. Just what she needed. "Did you tell her what happened?"

He snorted, forehead scrunching in a scowl. "Didn't have to."

Amy grinned. "She already knew, didn't she?" And that pissed him off.

A smile flashed across his face, only to be replaced quickly by the scowl again. "Woman's like a damn crystal ball. Sees all, knows all. Wish to hell I had her contacts. You wouldn't happen to know—" He snapped his mouth closed, but Amy decided to remind him anyway.

"You know the rules, Abe." She didn't talk about her mother's business when she was with him, and didn't talk about his on those rare visits to her mother. Being caught in the middle of two such strong-willed people sucked, especially when they worked for different employers. Sometimes it was like walking a tightrope…over a mine field…during a hurricane. As hard as it was, Amy would gladly add juggling grenades while blindfolded before giving up either one of her parents.

Her father patted her foot. "I know, I know. Can't blame me for being curious. Anyway, your mother wants you to know she has a few days free if you need her. Even if you don't, she wants you to call her."

"I will." She'd been putting that off, too, knowing her mother would pressure her to ditch the states and return home. Now that Velavich was dead, Europe was once again safe. Well, as safe as anywhere else, she supposed.

"I guess you'll be going back to Clear Springs soon."

"For a little while, maybe, but I don't plan to stay."

His scowl returned. "Why not? I know you like the house. The location is perfect. Plenty of room to run with that dog of yours. You even said you like the people. Maybe you could set up a little shop and sell your pictures."

"Why are you suddenly acting like the president of the Clear Springs Chamber of Commerce?"

"I'm not. I just thought you liked the place."

"I do, but I'm not ready to spend the rest of my life hanging out there. I'd go crazy. Thanks, but no. I want to go back to work. *Real* work."

"Thought you didn't like guns anymore," he said sharply. "Pretty hard to be a sniper without one."

She shrugged. "I got over it." *By killing a man who was about to kill someone I...* No, best not to even think that.

Her father mumbled something and ran a hand over his face. Another deep sigh. He was going for a record today. She was about to ask him what was wrong when he said, "I've re-activated Delta unit."

Amy sat up, jerking her feet out of his lap. "You have? When? Why wasn't I told?"

"Ten days ago, and I'm telling you now."

"I want back in."

"They already have a sniper."

"The hell they do." She jumped up and started pacing a trench in the sand. "You know I'm the best, Abe, you *know* it. More importantly, the Predators know it. They still trust me. Ask them. Talk to the new leader. He'll have to listen to you."

"I have talked to him. Today, in fact. The new leader *is* the sniper, Amelia. And he's at least as good as you, if not better. He's also smart enough to know that as leader, he won't always be able to take sniper position. That's why he's requested you as a second sniper."

His words brought her to a stop. Working again. With her old team. Not her first choice a couple of weeks ago, but she'd take it today. "That's great—"

"I told him you weren't available."

Her body went cold. She couldn't have heard right. "You did...what?"

"I told him you weren't available. That you had a prior commitment."

She walked over to stand stiffly in front of him, anger building in her like a wave, making her body tremble from head to toe. "Why are you doing this? And if you say it's to protect me I swear I'll turn around and go straight to Europe and never look back."

He pulled a folded piece of paper from a pocket. "Your prior commitment, if you want it. If not, you can call Delta Unit's new leader and accept his offer. His new code name is Red Wolf, but I think you know him already as Ty."

Ty? As in Joshua's Ty? Had to be. Couldn't be two snipers named Ty in the whole world, much less the smaller world of Special Ops. Amy slipped the paper from his fingers. Heart racing, she unfolded it, scanned it quickly. God, the temptation. It made her want to cry.

She shoved Alpha Unit's request for a new sniper back at her father. She wasn't a masochist. Forcing herself on Joshua was just asking for more heartbreak. "I decline. Tell Delta Unit I'm ready when they are."

He took the paper, re-folding it slowly. "Why are you declining?"

She did not want to go there. Not with him. "None of your business." She reached for her book and suddenly found herself falling down onto the lounger. Strong arms caught her as she fell, twisting her around until she was sitting upright next to her father. His look of innocence didn't fool her for a

301

second. "Did you just trip me?"

"Don't look so surprised. I may spend most of my days sitting behind a desk, but I still have a few moves left in me. Now, I'll ask you again. Why don't you want to work with the NightHawks? And for the record, it's Commander Aberashoff asking, not your father."

"Son-of-a... Fine. You want to know, I'll tell you. He doesn't want me."

"He?"

Damn it, he wasn't going to make this easy for her. "Joshua. The Harrier. Take your pick. Send me to him and he'll just send me back. Consider my refusal a cost savings all around."

"You're wrong."

"About the cost savings? Maybe. I'm not an accountant."

"No. About him not wanting you."

She so did not need to hear this. Amy tried to get up, but her father caught her arm and held her in place. Or was he still the commander? She didn't know and didn't care. He could fire her right now and she wouldn't care.

"I ordered him to leave you alone."

The soft words hit her like a shout in the face. "You did what?"

"When we flew you out, I told him not to contact you. Didn't think he was going to listen to me at first. But when I explained how he would only hurt you, he finally backed down."

She was stunned. "Why? Why would you do that?" Relationships in the SO were discouraged, but there was no rule against them. Heck, Beta Unit had two married couples and they operated just fine. Why would her father step between her and Joshua?

His hand slid down her arm, strong, thick fingers twining with hers. "I did it because I know about all the nights you cried after I found you and your mother. You hated being caught in the middle. I know exactly how hard it was for you to choose between us. I'm a little late to the whole 'father' business, but I wanted to spare my daughter more of that kind of pain. Didn't realize I'd be serving it to you in a different dish by keeping you and Joshua apart." He squeezed her hand. "I'm sorry about that. Guess your mother's right about me still having a lot to learn about women."

Amy forced herself to breathe slowly. She'd been slipping into royally pissed off at his high-handed behavior. How dare he try to control her personal life? But his softly spoken confession had her backing up. No mistaking the love in his voice. It overshadowed the pain and regret she heard in his apology. He'd really thought he was protecting her by sending Joshua away.

She closed her eyes, trying to take it all in. Her father's interference she'd deal with later, she decided. The only thing that mattered now was that Joshua hadn't betrayed her. He hadn't wanted to walk away from her. Had only done so because he was told if he didn't, he'd hurt her. "That's why he hasn't called."

Her father grunted. "Oh, he's called." He fished his phone out of his pocket and held it out to her. "See for yourself."

Hands shaking, she took the phone, flipped it open, and found the call history. One incoming number kept repeating, two, three, sometimes four times a day.

"Only a man in love does something like that. Ask your mother if you don't believe me."

Amy's heart jumped in her chest at her father's words, its strong beat bringing a smile to her lips. She swore the sun was getting brighter, the day lighter. Or maybe it was her. She felt as if she could almost walk on water. "That's okay, I believe you."

He tapped the phone with a finger, getting her attention. "So, what's it going to be? Want me to call him and tell him he has his new sniper, or do you want to do the honors?"

Amy threw her arms around him. "Neither, Dad. I think I'd like to deliver the new personnel re-assignment in person."

Chapter Thirty-One

Joshua walked out of his house, hands in his pockets, bare feet slapping stone. Having soaked up the last sunbeams of the day, the balcony was still slightly warm against his soles. He stopped to stare at the colorful sky. The pinks and reds were vivid this evening, a fantastic contrast to the deepening blue of the sky. Clouds huddled to the north, dark, bulky thunderheads piling one on top of the other. Storm bringers, Ty called them. It was going to be a wet night.

He took the stairs down to the patio, not sure where he was headed. Anywhere was better than inside. The once relaxing sanctuary of his home had turned into a vault of memories he could hardly stand, but didn't want to give up. Missing Amy had become his favorite pastime. Favorite only in the sense that he could think of nothing else. She was on his mind every minute of every day.

Pausing at the foot of the stairs, Joshua scrubbed his face with both hands. Damn, he was such a sorry mess.

The sun sank lower, fleeing the coming storm. Joshua rambled around the fat end of the tear-shaped pool. The patio lights started to bloom. He'd have to remember to turn them off before—

Something landed in the center of the pool with a loud splash. Joshua spun around, dropping to a crouch and reaching for the knife in his pocket. He could see a form kicking up from the bottom, the pool lights illuminating bare arms and legs, a compact body...and a flowing halo of dark hair. His heart started pounding.

No way. Couldn't be.

Even when Amy's head broke the surface and Joshua saw her face clearly, he still thought he was dreaming. Or worse. Twilight was the perfect time for hallucinations.

"Hi," she said, sounding so much like his Amy that she had to be real.

"Hi. What are you...?" His words dried up as she swam closer. Her limbs weren't the only part of her bare. She was naked, completely and utterly naked. The soft lights in the water highlighted every inch of her skin. He swallowed, feeling the blood rushing to his groin. Lips curving into an appreciative grin, he hooked a chair closer to the pool's edge and sat down.

She swam over to face him. "Aren't you coming in?"

Oh, such a sweet invitation. "In a minute. I'd like to enjoy the show first, if you don't mind." He pointed a finger at the water and lazily twirled it in the air. "Go ahead, enjoy your swim."

The smile on her face gave him the punch in his gut he'd been craving for days. She started to swim with slow, measured strokes. Hands reached out, pulling deep, shoulders and back flexing, ass rolling slowly from side to side—talk about a wet dream. She lapped the pool once on her stomach then flipped and showed him her back stroke. Sweet mercy, but the woman was pure sensual grace. Her tight nipples waved at him, beckoning above the lapping water.

Joshua was up and naked before he knew he'd even made the decision to join her. Pushing off from the edge, he knifed into the pool and came up right beside her. When he reached for her, she flowed into his arms, his semi-hard erection trapped between them. Their mouths met. The kiss was hot, devouring, and a hundred times sweeter than he remembered. And her skin...God, she was so soft. Even her scars were perfect.

He placed a reverent kiss on the one on her shoulder. From the way she'd been swimming, the wound didn't bother her, but he was careful anyway. She dropped her head back as he licked his way to her neck. His hands slid down her strong back and squeezed the cheeks of her ass, pulling her tight up against his hips. She snuggled closer, brought her legs up, and wrapped them around his waist.

Joshua couldn't hold back a shudder as her new position all but shoved his cock where he needed it to be. With a groan he started one-arming it for shallow water. Had to get inside her soon. Except, when he could stand, a bit of sanity had him leaning back enough to see her face. Breathing hard, he said, "Why are you here?"

Her brows rose.

"Not that I'm not happy to see you," he said hurriedly. "Because I am. Happy, that is."

Her legs squeezed and she rubbed herself against him. "I'm glad you're happy. So am I." Some of her smile left. "My father told me what he said to you."

Joshua brushed a few strands of wet hair from her eyes, his fingers lingering against her skin. "I didn't want to listen to him. Wouldn't have, except he made a hell of a case. You have your life back, Amy. You can stay here in Clear Springs if that's what you want. You can visit with Farrah and spoil my godkids, tease Kyle, and run with Bors. I have no right to ask you to give any of that up."

"What if that's not what I want?"

His throat tightened. He fought the rising hope back, just in case he was reading too much into her words. It took him a moment to ask the most important question of his life to date. "What..." He cleared his throat and tried again. "What do you want?"

Soft fingers caressed his cheek. "You. Assuming you want me in return."

Joy lit Joshua up from the inside. His arms tightened around her just shy of crushing. "Want you?" he growled. "Sweetheart, you just try leaving me again and see how far you get." He caught her delighted laugh on his tongue, licking the happy sounds right out of her wicked little mouth.

How he got them both out of the water, he was never sure afterwards. All he knew was that Amy was bent over one of the padded loungers and he was behind her, inside her, the luscious heat of her surrounding his cock while her moans of encouragement warmed the air. His fantasy come to life. Leaning over, he pressed his chest to her back, wanting to feel every inch of skin. The slick move of their bodies sliding together had him on the edge in moments.

Reaching under her, he pressed his fingers to the hot, bare skin where they were joined, easily finding her clit. "Come for me." He pinched the nub between his fingers.

She climaxed, crying out his name as she bucked back into his hips. Joshua pounded into her harder, feeling her tight muscles pull his release up and out of him like a roll of thunder. He chanted her name as he came, wishing they could stay joined like this forever.

They came down together, breaths mingling, hearts slowing. He didn't move an inch until a stiff breeze smelling of rain blew over them. He felt her shiver.

"Come on. Let's move this little welcome home party inside."

She looked at him over her shoulder. No mistaking the happiness dancing in her blue eyes.

And he'd put it there. Damn if she didn't make him feel as tall as a hundred-year-old pine. "Welcome home," she said softly. "I like the sound of that. Not sure I can make it up, though, much less inside. I'm boneless."

Make that a two-hundred-year-old pine. Joshua laughed and scooped her into his arms as real thunder rolled over the valley. When they reached the balcony, she pointed to her pile of clothes.

"Later," he said. "You won't be needing those for a while." A good long while, if he had any say in the matter.

She chuckled. "All right, we can leave the clothes, but you're going to want to save the envelope under them from the rain."

"Really? What's in it?"

"Oh, just my re-assignment papers." She tried for nonchalant, but couldn't hide her cat-in-the-cream smile.

Holy hell. Forget about the pine tree, he was flying. Joshua grinned. "You're my new sniper."

She tapped him on the nose. "You betcha. I'd like to keep my old code name if possible. Think the NightHawks will welcome a Raven?"

He squatted, holding her in his lap as she scooped up a manila envelope along with her clothes. As he stood, he said, "If they don't, we'll both quit the SO and start our own black ops group."

She went still in his arms. "You'd do that for me?"

He paused at the door. "Sweetheart, you should know by now that I'll do anything for you short of giving you up. Hell, I'm even going to walk down the aisle for you. That should tell you something."

"No need to go that far," she said with a shaky laugh. "The engagement's fake, remember?"

He held her gaze. "Not this one. I love you, Amy. Doesn't matter what name you want on the license.

Amelia Faraday, Amy Sheridan, The Raven, hell, you can even put down Sniper Extraordinaire if you want. Just so you say *I do* at the proper time."

She stared at him a long moment, making him wonder if he'd rushed things. To hell with it if he had. No way was she getting away from him twice.

Then she leaned forward and kissed him sweetly. "Yes, Joshua Colby, I'll marry you. I love you, too. You've been in my sights since you shot that arrow between me and trouble. And I always get what I aim for."

Lightning flashed, thunder cracked, and the bottom fell out of the clouds. Joshua tightened his hold on his very own personal sniper and carried her inside, not at all bothered by the idea of being in her crosshairs. She was part of his world, now and always, and that was all that mattered.

A word about the author...

Kathy is a central Florida native who devours books on a regular basis. Fiction is her favorite because it allows her to exercise her ever active imagination.

She started writing short stories and poems in high school, continuing to dabble in science fiction and fantasy off and on until 2006 when her spunky niece, Darelle, dragged her to a writers convention. There her desire to write morphed into the dream to write well enough to be published. Four years, three manuscripts, and numerous edits and revisions later, the dream became reality with her Bloodsworn series.

Now Kathy writes for her fans, inviting them to return once again to the world of Avalyr and all its wonderful characters.

Visit Kathy at her website:
http://kyrlane.com/